The Godly Shepherd Chronicles

Ascending Mount Zion

The Shepherd of Kedar Book 2

DeLacy A. Andrews, Jr.

Psalm 24:3
Who shall ascend into the hill of the LORD?
Or who shall stand in His holy place?

WESTBOW®
PRESS
A DIVISION OF THOMAS NELSON
& ZONDERVAN

WestBow Press books may be ordered through booksellers or by contacting:

WestBow Press
A Division of Thomas Nelson & Zondervan
1663 Liberty Drive
Bloomington, IN 47403
www.westbowpress.com
1 (866) 928-1240

All Scriptures are taken from the King James Version of the Bible.

ISBN: 978-1-4908-3874-8 (sc)
ISBN: 978-1-4908-3875-5 (hc)
ISBN: 978-1-4908-3873-1 (e)

Library of Congress Control Number: 2014909655

Printed in the United States of America.

WestBow Press rev. date: 06/25/2014

To My Family

My Wife

Debbie Andrews

For all the love and sacrifice she made so
that this book could be published

My Daughter

Christine Parker

For her unceasing love and labors in making me a much
better writer and this book a much better book

**My Son, Josh and His Wife, Megan
My Son-in-law, Ben
My Grandchildren: Garrett, Brianna and Warren**

All of Whom I Love

In Loving Memory of My Mother

Wanda Andrews
June 8, 1928 – April 23, 2014

She taught me the Shepherd's Psalm when I was a boy.

Her children arise up and call her blessed; her
husband also, and he praiseth her.
Proverbs 31:28

Contents

Acknowledgments

In addition to my family, I want to express my heartfelt gratitude to many who helped me as I wrote this book.

To the members of the mission works of the Presbytery of the Southeast of the Orthodox Presbyterian Church, among whom I labor.

To the students of a course I taught at Graham Bible College on the Songs of Ascents, who read an earlier version of the book as part of their required reading for the course. Their insights were invaluable to me.

To Dr. Philip Blevins, president of Graham Bible College, for reading and critiquing the book, offering his expertise, especially regarding the passion narratives.

To the Board of Graham Bible College for their generous support in the publication of this book.

To the family of Jon and Emma Davis, members of Heritage Presbyterian Church in Hartwell, Georgia, for their special interest in the book.

To the family of Seth and Sheryl Long, members of Neon Reformed Presbyterian Church in Neon, Kentucky, and especially to Seth for his expertise in animal husbandry.

To my father, Buddy Andrews, for his unceasing encouragements.

To my mother-in-law, Lillian Allen, who read an early manuscript of the book.

To my sister, Lori Mosher, and her husband Marty, along with their son, Brett, for their encouragement.

Ultimately, I want to thank God for the Songs of Ascents and for creating in my soul the desire to ascend Mount Zion to worship and honor His name, through His Son, the Lord Jesus Christ.

For details regarding the Seder Service, I found the online version of *The Union Haggadah,* edited and published by the Central Conference of American Rabbis (1923) to be a great help. http://sacred-texts.com/jud/uh/uh02.htm.

About Historic Fiction

The writer of historic fiction faces a challenge. Actual events provide the context of the story, but many of the characters and the details of the story-line are the invention of the author. The goal is to provide an interesting and intimate depiction of the historical event to enable the reader to experience it vicariously through the characters. However, care must be taken to keep from embellishing that which is historical fact and altering what really happened.

This danger is compounded when the historical context comes from the infallible, inerrant Word of God, because the author's contribution certainly cannot share those attributes. The Bible is inspired of God, while the details of the story supplied by the author arise from his imagination.

In doing the research for this book, I found something unique about the Scriptures. God is amazingly concise in His revelation. His revelation is sufficient, but sometimes we are left wanting more details. This is especially true when we try to harmonize the events as depicted in the various Gospels. In our study of the Scriptures it is not necessary to find answers to all of our questions, however the writer of a story based in the events recorded in Scripture must make definitive decisions. I was surprised at how difficult this was to do at times.

The Approach I chose:

1. First, I sought to study the text for myself and come to a conclusion about what I believe the Bible is teaching. If I came to a decisive conclusion, that was the interpretation I used in the book.

2. If I was unsure, I considered those interpretations that seemed plausible and are held by noted commentators, and always made a decision from those options.

3. Finally, if I was still unsure, I picked the interpretation that best fit with the telling of the story. It was my deep desire to always be faithful to the text itself. If I erred, which is certainly possible, it was unintentional and in spite of these safeguards. I ask your forbearance as you read the story.

A Second Difficulty:

The details of Passover celebration in the first century prior to the destruction of the Temple in 70 AD are difficult to determine. In doing research for the book, I read both Christian and Jewish resources – often finding contradictory explanations in both. I simply could not find an authoritative description of some of the details I needed for the book. To tell the story, I utilized a measure of poetic license, but labored to be as accurate as possible. It must be remembered that this book is historical fiction and not a scholarly work of history.

Preface

It is hard to believe the pilgrimage of the Shepherd of Kedar and his family is almost over. Yet, that is the point of pilgrimage. There is a destination at the end of it. It was within sight when they were atop Mount Nebo. Now, all they have to do is cross the river Jordan. Jerusalem is on the other side – the Temple stands high against the eastern wall of the city. The respite Josiah has sought from persecution and isolation in Kedar is within reach. The worship of God at His House is before him.

However, there is more to this journey for the shepherd. He's been driven by questions – questions that have plagued him since his visit to Jerusalem as a boy. Who was the old man who prophesied over the baby of great things regarding both Jew and Gentile? He'd seen and heard him with his own eyes and ears. Who was the special baby? Now, He would be a man. Could He be the Messiah? All along the way the shepherd and his family have learned more and more about Messiah. They even heard of a teacher who heals the sick and speaks like no man ever spoke before. His name is Jesus. Can he possibly be the Messiah? Was He that baby at the Temple so long ago? Josiah has questions that need to be answered.

Come, with the Shepherd of Kedar. Cross over the river with him and his children. Come and see if they find the Messiah.

CHAPTER 1

Twelve Stones

Joshua 4:20

*And those twelve stones, which they took out of
Jordan, did Joshua pitch in Gilgal.*

The Shepherd of Kedar looked at the Jordan River in front of him. Once they crossed it, they would be in the Promised Land. The Lord had watched over them on their pilgrimage through the land of the Kedarites, the Nabataeans, the Edomites and now the Moabites. Along the way, they'd only had one real encounter with danger, and God had delivered their enemies into their hands. The weather had been extraordinarily mild, with very little rain, and nothing that really threatened them. Sandstorms were short-lived, but their tent had served them well.

On their journey they'd seen wonderful sights in Wadi Rum and the Gulf of Elath. They'd witnessed the blindness of pagan idolatry in Petra, but in Elath had tasted the sweet fellowship of the brethren. It was hard to believe the pilgrimage was almost over, yet that is the point of pilgrimage. There is a destination at the end of it. That final destination was within sight when they were atop Mount Nebo. Now, all they had to do was cross the river, even as the children of Israel had done long before them. Josiah felt tears forming in his eyes. By God's grace, he'd brought those he loved to the brink of the Promised Land.

He took a moment to look at each one of them. His dear wife, Deborah, was busy helping their youngest, Naomi, prepare to ford the river. Isaac, his oldest, gave special care to his wife, Haifa. Josiah still marveled at God's grace that brought his eldest to repentance and rescued his daughter-in-law from the idolatry of Kedar. He gazed at each of his other children in turn:

Michael, his second son, Dinah, his oldest daughter, then Martha, Simon, Benjamin, Ruth, Nathan, Jared, and Judah. He offered a silent prayer of thanksgiving to God. They were all, each and every one of them, a trophy of His grace.

He was interrupted from his thoughts by the voice of his wife.

"Don't forget our grandchild."

The shepherd looked at her, realizing she could practically read his mind and that she knew the content of his secret prayer.

"Don't forget to give thanks for our grandchild," she repeated, glancing toward Haifa.

He nodded his head, thanking God for the newest member of their family, not yet born. God had brought them to the threshold of the Holy Land.

Michael mounted his horse in anticipation when his father announced it was time to cross over the Jordan.

"Get off of your horse," Josiah instructed firmly but gently.

His son was confused. He thought it would be easier to control the animals from horseback but noted the determined look on his father's face and obeyed him immediately.

"Son, I want all of us to feel the cool waters of the Jordan, just like the Levites did when their feet touched the water."

"Do you think the waters will part for us?" Naomi asked innocently.

The shepherd smiled at his youngest. He knew it wouldn't surprise her in the least if they did. She had that kind of faith.

"No Sweetheart. I don't expect the waters to part, but I do want us to cross on foot, like our forefathers did."

In God's providence the river was well within its banks and the water was shallow at the ford. The boys moved into position to drive the sheep and goats across, while leading their horses and camels by hand. The girls knew how to handle their own horses, and followed the boys into the water. Naomi's legs were a wee bit too short, and about a third of the way across, Deborah picked her up in her arms and carried her the rest of the way.

Once they got to shore Naomi exclaimed, "Daddy, my feet are wet!"

Her giggle indicated she wasn't upset about it, and her father smiled at her before gathering his children around him.

"According to the Scriptures, Joshua placed twelve stones as a memorial to the Lord in the midst of the river at the place where the Levites stood with the Ark of the Covenant. Then he instructed each tribe to appoint one of its men to select a stone from the dry river bed to be placed at Gilgal. The last time I counted I had twelve children, the same number as the tribes of Israel."

"I want each of you to select a stone from the river bed, according to your ages. Make sure that Isaac's is the largest, and then Haifa's and Michael's. Naomi, you choose a small round stone to go on the top of the memorial."

All of his children obeyed their father, each searching out a stone. As he watched them he remembered his own experience long ago. He had stood at this same place with his father when he was ten. Now, after all of these years, he had returned with his family. When his father told him about the memorial stones left in the river and those placed at Gilgal, he'd asked him if he could place his own stone. His father agreed, and the young boy spent several minutes selecting a stone from the riverbed. He recalled vividly that it felt like his stone chose him. When he saw it, he knew it was the one. It was large, but rather thin, with a unique shape that reminded him of a lamb. His father feared it was too big for him, but little Josiah carried it on his shoulder all the way to Gilgal and placed it there as his own memorial to God's goodness. It had been so long ago, he doubted his stone would still be where he'd set it.

Deborah was thinking of her own childhood. It had been twenty years since she'd seen her family. Shortly after she and Josiah were married, her mother and father left Kedar for Israel. Her younger brother and sister had accompanied them.

In those first years she was able to correspond with them from time to time, because one or another of the families from their tribe would make pilgrimage to Israel. The tribe was called Bin-Micah after their famous ancestor who had become the shepherd of the royal flock in Babylon at the recommendation of Daniel. He was the same Daniel who was protected by God in the lion's den. Those families gladly delivered letters back and forth between loved ones. However, through the years, as one family after another gave up and departed Kedar in the face of persecution, opportunities for posting letters became less and less frequent.

She'd sent a letter to them with their kinsmen, Nathaniel and Elizabeth, who'd recently left Kedar for Israel, but had not heard from her parents in almost ten years.

She wondered whether they were still living. She did know that her brother had married several years before, but as of the last letter she'd received; her sister still lived with their parents. At that time they lived in Bethlehem, and with each passing day she longed all the more to see them again.

"Look Mommy, I found my stone!" Naomi exclaimed holding it high over her head.

"Yes, I see you have," she responded as her little girl's cry brought her back to the present. "It looks like it's perfectly round."

Josiah saw that the others had selected their stones as well and led the way toward Gilgal, which was located outside the eastern wall of Jericho. As they approached the ancient city, the shepherd was surprised by how different it looked. It wasn't so much that the city had changed, but that he had changed. The walls seemed shorter somehow, and Jericho appeared to have shrunk. He knew that was impossible and suddenly realized the difference between the perspective of a ten-year old boy and that of a man. In his memory the wall rose higher, because that's how it appeared when he was a boy.

He remembered setting his rock in a hollow at the base of an old sycamore tree. Jericho was known as the "City of Palms" which made the sycamore stand out to him. Searching with his older eyes, it didn't take him long to find the tree, even after all of these years. The shepherd hurried to the base of it and moved around behind it to look into the hollow. There were other stones near the base, but to his disappointment he didn't see his stone in the hollow of the tree. He realized it would have been almost miraculous for the rock to have remained hidden in the hollow for over thirty years.

"Father, what are you looking for?" Isaac asked on behalf of the rest of the children.

"Oh, nothing..." he responded, his voice trailing off betraying his disappointment.

As Josiah stepped back from the hollow of the tree, his oldest son got down on his knees and began digging in the sand that had blown into the hollow. It didn't take him long before he recovered a large, thin rock.

"Is this what you were looking for?" He asked his father, as he picked up a rock that was remarkably shaped like a lamb.

The utter joy in his father's eyes gave him his answer.

"That's my stone!" Josiah exclaimed. "It looked so much like a lamb to me at the river's edge I had to pick it up. My father let me place it here over thirty years ago."

He had an astonished look on his face when his wife said, "It must have been waiting for you to return."

A tear escaped his eye as he took his stone from Isaac's hands and placed it back in the hollow of the tree.

"Can we put our stones in the tree, too?" Naomi asked.

"Yes, you may," her father replied. "But let Isaac put his in first on top of mine, then Haifa, you place your stone, then Michael, and the rest of you."

It was a solemn moment of thanksgiving as Josiah's children put their stones in place, building a pyramid in the hollow of the sycamore. Naomi had a big smile on her face, when she could finally put her stone on top of the others.

"Just as our forefathers commemorated crossing the Jordan on dry land and established a memorial of stones, we do the same. We left the wicked land of Kedar, and passed through the regions of other peoples who reject the Lord to worship idols; but now we've finally arrived in the Land of Promise, a holy land, where God's chosen race dwells and worships our God, the Lord!"

Everyone could see the joy in his eyes. After thirty years, he'd returned to the Promised Land. He'd come to worship God, and his stone was waiting for him.

His heart was full of love for God as he lifted his eyes to heaven to pray:

"O Lord our God, You have been faithful to the covenant You made with our father, Abraham. You delivered Your people from bondage in Egypt and brought them to this place in the Promised Land. Now, You've demonstrated Your continuing faithfulness to this son of Abraham and to his children. You've delivered us from those who would oppress us in the land of Kedar and brought us to this place of memorial in the Promised Land. Lead us to Your Temple that we may worship You together with Your people. *Amen.*"

All of those gathered around the sycamore tree said, *"Amen!"*

When he finished his prayer, Josiah took them to the wall of Jericho. "Touch it," he instructed his children.

They reached out their hands to touch the wall in obedience to their father.

"Feel the solid stones of the wall. It seems to be an impenetrable fortress."

"But the walls came crashing down," Naomi said interrupting her father.

The shepherd smiled at his sometimes impatient daughter before replying, "Are you going to let me tell the story?"

Her face fell as she realized what she'd done until her father gently reached out his arms to her. The little girl reacted immediately and ran to him.

"I'm glad you know the story so well," he whispered in her ear, before looking up to speak to the others.

"Long ago, God promised all the land before you to His people; but in a time of famine, they had to flee to Egypt. Does anyone remember who was waiting for them in Egypt?"

"It was Joseph," Michael replied immediately.

Josiah nodded his head before continuing, "Yes, it was Joseph, but that's another story for another day. While God's people were in Egypt, they came under bondage to a Pharaoh who didn't remember him. During the time our people were in bondage, wicked people who worshiped idols came to dwell in this land. When the Children of Israel arrived they had to conquer those who'd settled here. Jericho was the first place they encountered the enemy after crossing the Jordan."

He paused for a moment and turned to look at the wall.

"Can anyone tell me how God delivered Jericho into the hands of His people?"

Michael again responded, "For six days the priests and other leaders marched around the city wall with the Ark of the Covenant and the blowing of the *shofars*. Then on the seventh day, they marched around seven times, and when they completed the seventh rotation, all of the people shouted on Joshua's command."

Michael stopped to give someone else an opportunity to speak.

When no one responded Josiah asked, "Then, what happened?"

"The walls came tumbling down!" Naomi shouted out, as if she was one of the children of Israel on that day so long ago.

"That's right, little one. The walls came tumbling down, and Jericho was delivered into the hands of God's people," her father declared.

He didn't intend to press it any further, but Simon had a question.

"Father, why did God command his people to kill everyone in Jericho, even the women and children, along with all of the animals?"

He knew it was a fair question and one that often troubled him. He'd always taught his children that God is a God of love and mercy. He saw an anxious look on Naomi's innocent face when she heard her brother ask about the children and the animals.

"Did God command them to kill everyone?" Josiah asked, seeing an opportunity to point to God's mercy.

Simon had a confused look on his face momentarily before he replied, "Everyone except for Rahab and her family."

"Yes, and why was Rahab spared?"

"Because she protected the spies when they hid in her house," Simon answered.

"There is an important lesson to be learned here, my son," Josiah responded in all earnestness. "Rahab was not only spared. She later was married and is in the lineage of King David, which means that she is our mother as well. So, you see, God did have mercy during the battle of Jericho."

His son's concern was not that easily satisfied.

"But why did God instruct them to kill everyone else, even the women and children?"

Josiah paused for a moment before responding, "Everyone, listen carefully. Remember when we were at *Shittim*? I told you that even though Balaam was helpless when he tried to curse the Children of Israel by divination, that he found another way to aid Balak. Do you remember what it was?"

Michael was the first to respond, "Balaam encouraged Balak to quietly introduce the daughters of Moab to the sons of Abraham."

"That's right, and what happened?" Josiah asked.

"The daughters of Moab led many of them into idolatry," his son replied.

"And on that day, God's wrath was kindled against His people and the Lord struck down twenty-four thousand of the sons of Abraham with a plague. When God's people crossed the Jordan River, it was time for a holy people to settle the land of promise and to worship the Lord. Lest the Canaanite people of Jericho prove to be a temptation to God's people, the Lord commanded that they all be destroyed," Josiah said solemnly.

Simon nodded his head in assent, but still had a perplexed look on his face.

"Son, do you have another question?" His father asked.

"Sir, it still seems cruel for God to tell them to kill the children. Weren't the children innocent? I understand that the daughters of Moab were wicked when they seduced the sons of Abraham at *Shittim*, but what about the children?"

Josiah took a deep breath before responding. These things were hard for him to understand as well.

"First, the children were not innocent," he said, perplexing everyone in his family, even Deborah. "None of us are innocent. We are sons of Adam and are all born with a nature that is bent toward evil and at enmity with God. My children, you are not spared from unbelief because of your nature. God has had pity on you and has chosen you to know the truth by grace. He didn't choose us because of our righteousness. He chose us in order to make us righteous by His grace."

Josiah's words awakened them all to their own sinfulness, but also to God's mercy to them.

"God chose Israel to demonstrate His grace. Now, look at the city of Jericho. Her walls are strong, but even that was at a cost. After the fall of Jericho, Joshua placed a curse on the city and on any man who would rebuild her walls. He said, *'Cursed be the man before the LORD, that riseth up and buildeth this city Jericho: he shall lay the foundation thereof in his firstborn, and in his youngest son shall he set up the gates of it.'* Jericho was to remain desolate as a reminder to God's people that He purged the land of wickedness when they entered it. It was also to be a warning to them against committing the idolatry of the Canaanites. Does anyone remember when the city was rebuilt?"

No one answered, not even Michael knew the answer.

"We read of it during the reign of King Ahab. Ahab was the wickedest of Israel's kings, marrying Jezebel, the worshiper of Baal. During his reign, a man name Hiel rebuilt the city of Jericho. The Scriptures tell us that *'He laid the foundation thereof in Abiram his firstborn, and set up the gates thereof in his youngest son Segub.'* As prophesied by Joshua, both the firstborn and the youngest of the man who rebuilt Jericho were killed during construction."

The children were amazed at the story, but wondered about the apparent blessing on the current Jericho that stood before them.

"What of the city now?" Michael asked.

Josiah smiled before answering, "With the Lord there is redemption, even for a city once cursed. Jericho now is inhabited by God's people. A day of redemption is coming not only to Israel but to the whole world. I believe that day is nigh."

CHAPTER 2

The Inn

John 11:25-26

*I am the resurrection, and the life: he that believeth in
Me, though he were dead, yet shall he live: And whosoever
liveth and believeth in Me shall never die.*

The children immediately saw the difference between the city of Jericho
and other cities they'd visited on their pilgrimage. People in the streets
of Jericho constantly greeted them with *shalom*. They'd not often heard
the conventional Jewish greeting since they departed Kedar. They were
accustomed to hearing Arabic as the primary language, though the dialect
changed along the route. In Jericho the most prominent language was
Aramaic. Because Josiah and his family dealt with traders from all over
the world, they were fluent in multiple languages.

Knowing the people of Jericho were sons and daughters of Abraham,
Isaac and Jacob gave them a sense of security and unity. For the first time
in their lives, they shared a common faith with most of those around them.

The visit to Jericho was brief. Josiah intended to get to an inn situated
at the crossroad to Bethany before nightfall. He hoped it was still there.
If not, his family could always pitch their tent along the side of the road.
Ever since he'd started thinking about the inn, he wondered about the
little girl who'd befriended him there when he was a boy and what might
have become of her. He even remembered her name, Sarah. The shepherd
hadn't thought of her in years.

The road between Jericho and Jerusalem was somewhat desolate and
dreary, but Josiah didn't seem to notice. The closer they got to the inn, the
more he wondered if it was still standing, and what of Sarah. His thoughts

about her troubled him momentarily until he looked over at Deborah. Sarah may have been a childhood friend for a couple of spring days in his youth, and perhaps even a boyhood crush; but Deborah was his life. He eased his horse close to that of his wife so he could reach out and grasp her hand, and he still felt the magic when their fingers touched.

He smiled when he saw the inn still standing and was surprised to find no other travelers; but then again, they were probably a day or two ahead of most of the pilgrims. Many on pilgrimage would press ahead to Jerusalem once they got as close as the inn.

Josiah was a bit anxious when he dismounted his horse and led his family inside. Once they entered the inn they found it strangely quiet. For a moment he wondered if it was still open for business, when suddenly the loud voice of a woman could be heard coming from a back room. The voice grew louder as she emerged, wiping flour off of her hands on her apron. As soon as he saw her, he knew it was his old friend. She had the same round face and broad smile.

"May I help you?" She asked when she saw she had guests.

Josiah didn't say a word for a moment, confusing everyone, especially Deborah. Sarah studied him as if she was trying to place him.

"Sarah…" he said, his voice trailing off.

"Yes," she replied, still sporting a bewildered look.

He finally came out of his temporary stupor and said, "When I was a boy, my family stayed at this inn. We played together."

Her smile immediately lit up the room, and she nearly knocked him down as she wrapped her arms around him and squeezed him tight.

"Josiah!" She cried.

Deborah was stunned that a strange woman would hug her husband, until the woman began to shout, "Nathan! Nathan! Hurry in here!"

A man rushed into the room with a puzzled look on his face.

"Nathan, you have to meet Josiah!" She said enthusiastically, pulling her long lost friend by the arm toward her husband.

Josiah was shocked at her reaction. He'd wondered if she would even remember him, but it was certainly apparent that she did.

"Nathan, when I was a little girl, a boy stayed at the inn with his family for two nights. Out here in the middle of nowhere I rarely had other children to play with, unless Mary and Martha came to visit from Bethany.

Most of the other children who lodged with us stayed close to their parents, but not Josiah. We became friends almost immediately."

Everyone was astonished as the words rolled off of her tongue. Josiah smiled because she was still as vivacious as she'd been as a child.

"Oh, excuse me," she interjected, almost blushing, "Josiah, this is my husband, Nathan."

The two men embraced and felt an immediate bond. Sarah took that moment to reach out to Deborah. She was different from any other woman Deborah had ever known, but she liked her immediately. It wasn't long before the two of them hurried off to the kitchen, leaving the men with the younger children. As usual, Dinah and Haifa followed them. This time Martha accompanied the women too. She'd grown up on this pilgrimage, especially since her relationship had blossomed with Joseph, the son of the rabbi from Elath.

Sarah was the most out-going woman Deborah had ever met, and all the while they worked in the kitchen she talked non-stop. Suddenly, the shepherd's wife realized Sarah's personality reminded her of one of her children. She thought for a moment about some of them. Isaac was the impulsive one. Michael was serious and reflective. Dinah was her tom-boy, and Martha her little lady; but without a doubt, Sarah reminded Deborah of little Naomi. She was the most outspoken and animated child she had by far. As she thought about it, she realized that Naomi could very well grow up to be like her husband's childhood friend. It made her enjoy Sarah all the more.

In no-time, Deborah had the full story about her husband's previous visit to the inn. One thing was clear; those two days were memorable to Sarah.

At one point, their hostess paused for a moment and shook her head before saying, "Just listen to me. I can't keep my mouth shut."

A sudden look of loneliness covered her face, but was quickly replaced by her big smile when she continued, "I suppose most children who visited the inn when I was a little girl were afraid of me because I talked so much, but not your Josiah. I'll admit that he didn't get to say much around me, but he didn't seem to mind and was friendly. It meant a lot to me. I never forgot him and often wondered what became of him after he returned to Kedar."

Deborah didn't say anything when Sarah took a moment to collect her thoughts.

She looked at Deborah, and a warm smile came to her face as she said, "He did very well. His wife is certainly a beautiful woman…and…and…all of those children…"

Her voice trailed off as she looked straight ahead, not focusing on anything in particular; but once again her smile faded and a tear appeared in the corner of her eye.

"I just had one child…"

Deborah knew something dreadful had happened and immediately took her into her arms.

Sarah shook her head before saying, "He only lived for a few minutes, but I got to hold him." A smile returned to her face when she declared joyfully, "He's with father Abraham now, and with Father and Mother."

Deborah suddenly admired her husband's childhood friend. The shepherd's wife rejoiced that God had blessed her with eleven children, now twelve with Haifa. Glancing at Haifa's belly she knew her first grandchild was growing there, though her daughter-in-law was not showing yet. What impressed her most about their hostess was her joy for life, even though she'd not been blessed with children. Deborah peeked at her daughters and rejoiced in God's blessings to her.

Even though Sarah never ceased talking, she knew her way around the kitchen, and in no time had a meal prepared fit for a king. Deborah was impressed with her culinary skills and couldn't wait to dine with the others. She knew her husband and sons would especially be happy.

While the women worked in the kitchen, the younger children were playing outside. Josiah, Isaac, Michael and Simon reclined with Nathan in the main room of the inn and told him about their lives in Kedar. He was enthralled as they spoke about their flock and how many sheep they raised. He'd often wondered what it would be like to be a shepherd.

The ladies brought out the food, and the aroma was welcomed by the men and the boys. Michael only had to tell the younger children to come in for dinner once. They were as hungry as the rest. The men reclined around the table and the women gladly served them. They fed the younger children in the kitchen. At one point Josiah asked about Sarah's parents. He remembered them with fondness.

"Father passed away about ten years ago, and Mother followed him the next year," she said. "Nathan and I have managed the inn ever since. What about your parents?"

Josiah's eyes betrayed a momentary sadness before he answered, "Both of them passed away about the same time yours did. I miss them."

"I understand, they were lovely people, but thanks be to God for the resurrection."

"Yes, thanks be to God," Josiah responded enthusiastically.

Near the end of the meal, they heard a knock on the door.

Sarah spoke out loud as she walked to the door, "Unless it's the Teacher, we are full for the night."

It didn't take her long to tell the other travelers that there were no more vacancies. Josiah was perplexed by her comment, but waited until she returned before saying anything.

"What teacher are you talking about?" He asked.

Her face literally beamed when she said, "Jesus, of course. He's stayed with us at our inn."

Josiah remembered Zacharias, the rabbi of Elath, speaking of Jesus and was immediately intrigued, even though he knew little about Him.

"Tell me about this teacher," he said excitedly.

Sarah began to speak, but then looked to her husband. He smiled and nodded his head, giving her permission to continue.

"I guess you wouldn't know about Him, since you've been in Kedar. Jesus of Nazareth began His ministry about three years ago, mostly in Galilee," she said. "No man ever spoke the way this man speaks."

When she paused, Josiah took the opportunity to say, "I've heard more about another teacher named John. I have a friend who was baptized by him in the Jordan, and another Gentile friend who came to believe in the Lord after hearing him preach."

Sarah and Nathan looked at each other and smiled before Nathan said, "Yes, John was a great prophet and teacher. We heard him preach many times ourselves."

"He baptized us too," Sarah interjected before looking to her husband and deferring to him again.

"John was a great prophet," he repeated, "But he wasn't the promised one."

"How do you know?" Josiah asked.

"We know one of John's former disciples. His name is Andrew and he told us what John said of Jesus. Now, Andrew is one of Jesus' closest disciples, along with his brother, Peter."

"What did he say?" Michael asked excitedly.

"Andrew told us that John pointed to Jesus and said, *'Behold the Lamb of God, which taketh away the sin of the world!'*" He replied.

When Michael looked perplexed he continued, "He then said, *'This is He of whom I said, After me cometh a man which is preferred before me: for He was before me. And I knew Him not: but that He should be made manifest to Israel, therefore am I come baptizing with water. I saw the Spirit descending from heaven like a dove, and it abode upon Him. And I knew Him not: but He that sent me to baptize with water, the same said unto me, Upon whom thou shalt see the Spirit descending, and remaining on Him, the same is He which baptizeth with the Holy Ghost. And I saw, and bare record that this is the Son of God.'"*

"The Son of God!?" Josiah asked, raising his eyebrows in disbelief.

"Yes, the Son of God," Nathan responded, "And when you meet Him, you will know that it's true."

"He heals the sick and raises the dead," Sarah added, her eyes full of wonder.

"Raises the dead!?" Again, Josiah was overwhelmed by what he was hearing.

Sarah looked directly at him and said, "Do you remember your last day at the inn when we were children?"

The shepherd nodded his head.

"I was so sad that you were leaving, and then my cousin came from Bethany. You met her, because the three of us played together right before you left."

"I seem to recall that," Josiah said, but was a little unsure.

"If you think about it, you will remember her," she continued. "Her name is Mary. Mary has a sister named Martha and an older brother named Lazarus."

Tears came to her eyes as she had to pause to collect herself. Nathan tried to help her, but she shook her head, indicating that she could continue.

"My cousin, Lazarus, died a while back. We were there for them. As soon as he got sick, a messenger was sent to Jesus in Galilee. We knew He could heal Lazarus, if He could get to Bethany in time. He didn't make it before Lazarus died, and my cousin had been in the grave for four days before He arrived."

She stopped momentarily to wipe the tears out of her eyes.

"Nathan and I were at Mary and Martha's house mourning his death, when Mary received a word from a messenger. When she got up we followed her, and then we saw Jesus. We stayed back to let the Teacher comfort her. All of us were thinking that He could have healed Lazarus had He arrived in time. After speaking with her, I saw Him weeping. It was clear to me that He loved my cousin. When He and Mary went to Lazarus' grave we followed them."

For a brief moment she became overwhelmed and tears were streaming out of her eyes. Deborah attempted to comfort her in her loss, but Sarah shook her head vigorously.

"No…no, you don't understand. I have wonderful news!"

Deborah was shocked and stepped back so she could continue.

"When we arrived at the grave Jesus told some of the men to take the stone away. I heard Martha tell Him that there would be a stench because Lazarus had been dead for so long."

Again, she had to pause to regain her composure.

"The men did as He said; and after praying, Jesus said in a loud voice, *'Lazarus, come forth!'*"

Sarah became so overcome with emotion she couldn't continue. She looked to her husband, beckoning him to finish telling them what happened. The children had all come into the room just before she began her tale, and all of Josiah's family waited with bated breath. They prepared themselves to hear the news they anticipated was coming, but couldn't believe it could possibly be true.

Nathan spoke slowly, his voice breaking with emotion, "Lazarus came out of the tomb, wrapped in his burial cloths. He was alive…he was alive again!"

Josiah was astonished.

"What did you do?" He asked.

"I hurried to him with a couple of the other men and began unwrapping the burial cloths that bound him. We threw them on the ground, and there he stood. Lazarus was alive…fully restored!"

Sarah was finally able to speak again.

"Later, Martha told me what the Teacher said to her when He first arrived outside of Bethany. He told her, *'I am the resurrection, and the life: he that believeth in Me, though he were dead, yet shall he live: And whosoever liveth and believeth in Me shall never die.'*"

"Lazarus was really raised from the dead! You saw it yourself!" Michael asked, overcome by what he'd just heard.

"Yes, I saw him with my own eyes," Nathan replied. "I unwrapped him. He was alive again and is still living to this day."

"Can we meet him?" Josiah asked.

Nathan looked at his wife before he responded, "That's not possible right now."

"Why not?" Josiah asked, clearly both perplexed and disappointed.

"The Teacher has many enemies in Jerusalem," Sarah added. "They want to kill Him, and my cousin has received word that they want him dead too, because Jesus raised him from the dead. They refuse to believe that He is the Messiah. Mary, Martha and Lazarus are in hiding. We know where they are, but they've asked us to tell no one except Jesus. We have to honor their request."

The shepherd nodded his head. He certainly understood about living in the midst of enemies; but when he thought about it, this news troubled him greatly.

"Why do they refuse to believe in the face of this evidence?" He asked.

"These are trying times," Nathan responded. "Many prefer to believe a lie instead of the truth."

"We hear the Teacher is coming to Jerusalem for the feast!" Sarah added excitedly. "Perhaps this is the time He will take his rightful place upon David's throne."

"Is Jesus a son of David?" Michael asked.

"He is," Nathan replied. "He was born to a Joseph and Mary in Bethlehem during a census when Caesar Augustus was the Roman Emperor."

Josiah started to get excited.

"That was right before I came to Jerusalem with my father! We heard about the birth of a special baby in Bethlehem and even talked to some shepherds who saw Him. They told us about hearing the news from an angel."

Sarah and Nathan were very excited by this news. For a moment Josiah wondered why he hadn't told her what he'd seen when they were children; but they were just children, playing at the time.

"Father, tell them about the old man and the baby," Simon said, his tone of voice almost insistent.

Josiah had been thinking the same thing and lowered his voice as he told them of his experience in the Temple when he was with his father.

"When I was a boy my father and I visited the Temple one day. I noticed a woman enter carrying her baby. After she placed five shekels in one of the tills and had offered her sacrifices, she sat down on a bench in the Court of the Women. She caught my eye and beckoned me to come near. I could immediately tell how much she loved her baby. His little hand was outstretched and I put my finger in it. He had a strong grip for a little baby, and then suddenly an old man came up to us and picked him up. He held him high over his head, and his eyes were full of light."

Josiah paused for a moment to collect himself. Telling the story always moved him.

"I'll never forget his words," he said as he re-lived that moment. "When he lifted the baby high over his head he said, *'Lord, now lettest Thou Thy servant depart in peace, according to Thy word: For mine eyes have seen Thy salvation, which Thou hast prepared before the face of all people; a light to lighten the Gentiles, and the glory of Thy people Israel.'*"

"He spoke those words about the child?" Nathan interjected to reassure himself that he understood correctly.

"Yes, but it was the rest of what he said that's always troubled me. After he put the baby back into His mother's arms he said to her, *'Behold, this child is set for the fall and rising again of many in Israel; and for a sign which shall be spoken against; Yea, a sword shall pierce through thy own soul also, that the thoughts of many hearts may be revealed.'*"

"Could it be that the baby was Jesus?" Sarah asked with an astonished look on her face.

Josiah thought for a moment before speaking, "It all makes sense, now. My father and I wondered if the baby we saw at the Temple was the same baby the angel told the shepherds about in Bethlehem. You told us that Jesus was born in Bethlehem during the census. That's precisely when the shepherds found the baby in the manger. It must have been the same baby. Now that I've learned about those who oppose Him in Jerusalem, the second part of the old man's prophecy is starting to make sense. He said that the baby would be *'For a sign which shall be spoken against.'* It sounds like Jesus is being spoken against even as we speak."

"Yes, but the Teacher is coming to Jerusalem for the feast. At least that's what we've been told," Sarah said again. "Could it be that He will fulfill the old man's prophesy at the feast?"

"Let's pray it is so," Josiah said. "I've sensed that something is about to happen. Perhaps we now know what to expect. If Jesus does come to the feast, surely things will come to a head. Let's pray that He puts down those who would oppose Him and establishes His rule in Israel."

The shepherd bowed his head and began to pray, "O Lord of Thy people, fulfill the words of Thy prophets. Send Thy Messiah...Thy King... Thy Son. *Amen.*"

All in the room shouted in unison, *"Amen!"*

CHAPTER 3

Bethlehem

Micah 5:2

*But thou, Bethlehem Ephratah, though thou be little among the thousands
of Judah, yet out of thee shall He come forth unto me that is to be ruler
in Israel; whose goings forth have been from of old, from everlasting.*

Michael was up before dawn the next morning. After all of the talk about
Jesus of Nazareth, he couldn't wait to get to Jerusalem. He had all of the
animals fed before the others arose from their beds inside the inn.

"I can't wait to see Jerusalem!" He exclaimed when his father stepped
outside.

"Well, you're going to have to wait a little longer," Josiah replied.

Michael was confused. The inn wasn't too far from Bethany on the
road to Jericho, and he knew Jerusalem was only three miles beyond
Bethany.

Josiah saw his son's troubled face and explained, "I understand why
you're excited, but today is Friday. Sabbath begins at dusk, and I want
to celebrate it in Bethlehem at the house of my father's cousin, Ephraim.
Nathaniel and Elizabeth should be there, and your mother is hopeful
that her family will be as well. She hasn't seen them since before you
were born."

Michael knew about his maternal grandparents, even though he'd
never met them. From time to time his mother told him stories about
them. He remembered his father's parents, but they died in Kedar when
he was a little boy.

However, his mind was on someone else who would be waiting in
Bethlehem. Miriam was Nathaniel and Elizabeth's oldest daughter,

and Michael secretly loved her. When they were in Kedar he'd decided to approach her and her father about courtship, but before he had the opportunity he stumbled upon her with Isaac at the oasis. He could see the affection they had for each other. Heartbroken, he backed away because he loved them both.

Isaac and Miriam's relationship came to a tragic end after her brother, Caleb, was killed by their enemies. After the funeral, Nathaniel was resolute that he and his family would not spend another day in Kedar. This news troubled Isaac and he immediately asked her father for her hand. Nathaniel agreed, but only on the condition that he accompany them to Israel. Josiah needed his oldest son and refused to let him go. In desperation he asked Miriam to run away with him. When she tearfully refused to disobey her father, the angry young man left his father's tent in rebellion. For a time he lived like the Kedarites and that's where he met Haifa.

Everything had changed, but Michael realized that Miriam would know nothing of what had happened. He longed to see her, though he feared the news of Isaac and Haifa would hurt her deeply. The young man felt helpless. He knew he'd want to comfort her, but how?

"All in good time, Michael," Josiah said, awakening him from his secret thoughts. "We will take our rams and goats to Jerusalem first thing Sunday morning."

Michael was still anxious and reminded his father that Jesus would be coming to Jerusalem for the feast.

"Sarah told us that she heard He was coming," his father replied to correct him. "We'll have to wait and see. Besides, the feast doesn't begin until next Thursday."

He had another reason for waiting until Sunday to go up to Jerusalem. The first day of the week would be the Day of Presentation. He and Isaac had carefully selected a year old lamb without spot or blemish to present at the Temple. The lamb would be examined by the priests for four days to insure its perfection. On the following Thursday, he would offer the lamb for Passover, and the family would eat it that evening during the meal with bitter herbs and unleavened bread. He was eager to tell the story of the Passover of God to his children, while fully celebrating the Seder Service. The shepherd couldn't perform the ceremony in Kedar, because they were too far from the Temple to offer the sacrifice. One of his most vivid memories was the night his father led them in the Seder while they were in Jerusalem.

Deborah was pleased with her husband's decision to delay their trip to Jerusalem. Though she longed to visit both the city and the Temple, she had a deep desire to see her parents. The closer they'd gotten to the Promised Land on their pilgrimage, the more excited and anxious she'd become. It had been so long since she last heard from them, and she couldn't be completely settled in her mind until she saw them. In her heart she knew she couldn't wait much longer.

Before Elizabeth left Kedar, Deborah made her promise that she would search for her mother and father and tell them when she expected to arrive in Bethlehem. She trusted her dear friend to do as she asked.

Martha was the most disappointed about the detour through Bethlehem. She was dying to see Joseph again, and even one day's delay was almost more than she could bear. Her one consolation was that she would get to see Abigail, Nathaniel's second daughter. They were the same age and like Dinah and Miriam they'd been best friends their whole lives. When she thought about Abigail it lifted her spirits, because she couldn't wait to tell her about Joseph.

Miriam was anxiously awaiting them in Bethlehem. She'd heard her parent's talking, and they anticipated Josiah's arrival on that day. Her parting with Isaac had been difficult. He didn't even say goodbye to her, but she still held him close in her heart. From the day they left Kedar, she hadn't mentioned his name to anyone; but she thought of him every day and secretly prayed that somehow they could be together after he came to Israel. Her love for him had not diminished in her heart.

After leaving the inn, Josiah decided to pass through Bethany without stopping and traveled southward on a far less trodden road than the westward road to Jerusalem. He hoped his memory would serve him well enough to find Ephraim's house. As they approached Bethlehem, he longed to find his father's cousin still living. He would be an old man, and Josiah had wonderful memories of him. One of the things that had impressed him about the man was his godliness. The shepherd wanted to learn what he thought about Jesus.

The streets of Bethlehem were crowded with those who were arriving for the feast. It wasn't just Jerusalem that was filled during the festival, because many sought lodging with family members in the surrounding villages. This was true especially of Bethany and Bethlehem. Josiah was surprised at how little the town had changed in the past thirty years, and he had no trouble finding his kinsman's house.

Michael jumped off of his horse and rushed to the door as soon as they arrived; but even before he could knock, it opened, and Nathaniel and Elizabeth hurried outside. Deborah couldn't wait to hug her best friend, but found her eyes searching the door behind her. When she saw her mother and father emerge from the house, she burst into tears. Elizabeth understood when she quickly moved to them. After all of these years, her parents had aged but appeared to be in good health. She didn't realize until she held them, just how much she'd missed them. Josiah was elated to see Nathaniel, but took special delight in watching the tears of joy running down his wife's face as she hugged her parents.

The other children dismounted and began to greet their cousins as they poured out of Ephraim's house. It was no surprise to him when he noticed them pairing off according to their ages. Martha immediately found Abigail, and Ruth was so excited to see Anna and Lydia she couldn't stop giggling. When Deborah saw their youngest, Naomi, hugging Elizabeth's little Joanna, she couldn't help but shed a tear. It was like they never thought they'd see each other again. The younger boys, Benjamin, Nathan, Jared and Judah warmly greeted their cousins, even though they were girls.

Isaac had just climbed down off of Midnight and had his back turned when Miriam finally came out of the house. At the last minute she'd become anxious, wondering how he would respond to her. Michael was standing at the door, and she warmly greeted him with a smile and a hug; but she was searching for Isaac over his shoulder with her eyes. What she saw stunned her, and Michael felt her grimace. Isaac was gently helping his wife off of her horse. The affection he had for her was clear for all to see.

Miriam suddenly broke away from Michael's grasp and ran back into the house with tears streaming down her face.

"Miriam!" He called out, but before he could follow her Dinah stopped him.

"Let me," she whispered.

He felt helpless, but trusted that his sister would do her best to comfort her.

Haifa knew immediately who Miriam was, and her heart broke for her. She understood her pain, because she felt it herself. Miriam was a beautiful woman. No wonder Isaac had been so taken with her. Haifa's own insecurities returned. If she lost Isaac it would destroy her. She understood exactly what Miriam was feeling.

Elizabeth saw what was happening too and uttered under her breath, "Dear me."

Though Miriam had not spoken openly of Isaac since they departed Kedar, she knew her daughter's heart. She'd watched how excited she was as the day of his arrival drew near. None of them were aware of Isaac's flight to Dumat al Jandal and had no idea that his journey to Jerusalem was ever in doubt. Much had happened since they left Kedar.

Deborah was standing nearby and heard Elizabeth's quiet response.

"We have a lot to talk about," she whispered to her friend.

"Evidently, we do," she replied. "Miriam never gave up hope that things would somehow work out between the two of them."

Deborah couldn't help but shed a tear for the girl. She loved her and would have been very happy to have her as a daughter-in-law, but she'd also grown to love Haifa.

She closed her eyes and whispered a prayer for her young cousin, "You were good to Isaac when You brought Haifa into his life. Now, bless Miriam with a godly man to love her."

After heartily greeting his cousin, Josiah asked, "Is Ephraim…"

Before he could finish his question a big smile came to Nathaniel's face.

"He can't wait to greet you."

Nathaniel escorted Josiah into the house and led him into a back bedroom. He was surprised when he saw his father's cousin, but not because he was showing his age. That was to be expected. What struck him was that his cousin was blind, but that didn't stop a smile from crossing the old man's face when he heard Josiah greet him.

"Come here, my son!" He said eagerly.

Josiah moved to his bed and embraced the patriarch of their family. As he hugged him, memories of his own father flooded his mind.

"It's been so long," Ephraim uttered, his voice trembling with age. "Nathaniel told me about your father and mother."

A sad look crossed his face before it was quickly replaced with a smile, "I'd hoped to see them again this side of heaven; but now they await me, along with my father and mother and especially my dear wife. If it be God's will, I will join them soon."

Josiah was amazed at the way this man spoke of his own death. He knew death to be an awful intrusion into the created order, the result of the first man's sin; but he also understood that it was a portal to heaven for those who put their trust in God. His frankness was a sign of the maturity of his faith.

By that time, Deborah, Isaac and Michael had entered the bedroom as well. Josiah took a moment to introduce them to his kinsman. Each in turn embraced him with respect and affection.

"I want to teach from the Scriptures tonight after supper," Ephraim said to them.

Then he pulled his blanket up over him, closed his blind eyes and whispered, "Children, let me rest."

All of them knew it was time to go, so they left the room.

Deborah hurried to the kitchen where she found Elizabeth working. Abigail and Martha were with her, along with Haifa; but neither Miriam nor Dinah were there. She immediately realized that her daughter must be with Miriam. Haifa was quietly working, instinctively knowing what to do to help, though there was little actual conversation between her and Elizabeth. Everyone understood what caused the awkwardness between them, but it was not the proper time to address it. With so many mouths to feed, Elizabeth knew she would have to wait until after dinner for Deborah's explanation.

Dinah found her cousin out behind the house sitting on a bench, weeping. Her heart broke for her as she took her into her arms.

"I've missed you," she whispered.

"I've missed you, too," Miriam managed, as she lifted her face, her eyes still filled with tears.

"Who...who is she?" She asked.

"She's Isaac's wife," Dinah replied softly, as Miriam began to sob again. For a long time, she held her without saying a word. She just let her cry.

Finally, Miriam looked up and said, "Tell me…"

"The day you left Kedar, Isaac ran away. He just got on Midnight and ιυde into the desert. He was angry and hurt, and Father couldn't find him. We didn't see him for a long time and were even afraid he might have died. Then one night he came back home. He'd learned of a plot to kill us and steal our sheep. The man who planned the attack was the very man who killed Caleb."

Miriam squinted her eyes in anger as she remembered her brother's brutal murder.

"God delivered our enemies into our hands, and Isaac killed the wicked man," Dinah declared.

"I'm glad for that," Miriam managed to say before tearing up again.

"Isaac had Haifa with him when he came home," Dinah said.

"Haifa…that's an Arabic name," Miriam replied with a surprised look on her face.

Dinah nodded her head as she said, "Yes, Haifa was a Kedarite."

An astonished look crossed Miriam face, "A Kedarite!"

"She's not anymore," Dinah replied earnestly. "Miriam, she believes in the Lord and was instrumental in Isaac's repentance."

"Why did Isaac need to repent?" She asked in disbelief.

"He wasn't just angry at our fathers the day he left. Isaac was angry at God. He even called himself Ishmael and for a season lived among the Kedarites. He met Haifa when he was reveling in sin and rebellion."

"How did…she," Miriam struggled to bring herself to speak Haifa's name. "How did…how did Haifa help him repent?"

"It's a long story, but the important thing to know is that Isaac did repent and she is becoming a godly wife to him."

Though Miriam was jealous of her, she was glad she'd become a believer in the Lord for Isaac's sake.

"Miriam, Isaac is a changed man in every way. He's not the same man you knew. He's a better man," his sister declared.

Dinah realized she needed to tell her the rest of it.

She took a deep breath before softly saying, "Haifa's going to have a baby."

"A baby!" Miriam exclaimed, though she immediately realized she shouldn't be surprised.

"Yes, I'm going to be an aunt," Dinah replied, unable to keep from smiling.

"Is Isaac happy?" Miriam asked, not really sure of what she was hoping to hear.

"He is. Like I told you. He's a different man – a godly man, and Haifa is a big reason why."

She put her arms around her cousin and said, "I'll always love you, Miriam. You've been my best friend my whole life, but it's good to have a big sister. When you get to know her, you'll love her too."

Miriam began to cry again, shaking her head.

"I'm not ready for this," she uttered as she sobbed.

"I know...I know," Dinah said, trying to soothe her.

Elizabeth didn't say anything when the two girls joined them in the kitchen. Deborah hugged Miriam, gently wiping a tear off of her cheek, but only communicated her love with her eyes. Haifa was sensitive to her pain and avoided making eye contact with her. Her heart went out to her; but she didn't know what to do, so she simply busied herself with the final preparations for the meal.

It was Elizabeth who broke the silence in the room.

"Abigail, you and Martha go round up the younger children and tell the men we're ready for supper. Miriam, you and Dinah go help Ephraim into the dining room."

Miriam smiled for the first time since Isaac's arrival. In the months since they'd come to Bethlehem she'd grown close to the old man. She found him to be gentle and caring, and felt like he was the grandfather she never had. Dinah was excited for the opportunity to meet him. She'd often heard her father speak of him.

By the time they had him settled in his place at the head of the table the others had gathered around. Ephraim always insisted that everyone sit at table together in his house – men, women and children. This made Josiah and his family feel right at home. The shepherd had long ago abandoned the custom of segregating the men from the women at meals. Both men loved the sound of children laughing around the table.

Isaac took his place beside his wife, while Dinah kept Miriam occupied. Michael was sensitive to what was going on and sat across from her so they could talk. Ironically, it was Isaac who was most unaware of her distress.

He did look in her direction once, but didn't catch her eye. She did a good job hiding her emotions, paying special attention to Dinah and Michael. Things were so different for Isaac, he assumed they were for her.

Deborah's parents, Seth and Judith, also joined them at the table. It was a special pleasure for her to sit beside her mother and hold her hand. She learned that her brother and his wife lived in Bethany. They'd passed right by his house on the way to Bethlehem without knowing it. Her sister had married also, and she lived in Jerusalem. Both of her siblings planned to be with the family the next week for Passover. Deborah was looking forward to seeing them.

Nathaniel caught them up on what was going on in their lives. Josiah was especially interested when he learned that Ephraim's only son, Samuel, had gone to Galilee to follow after Jesus. He remembered him from when he was a boy. Ephraim's son was a young man at the time of Josiah's first visit to Israel and was a shepherd. He had a wife and a son, who was only a few weeks old at the time. Thinking of Samuel's son reminded him of the baby he saw at the Temple. Momentarily, he wondered what had become of Samuel's wife and son, if he was in Galilee. He thought perhaps, he'd taken them with him. Then he realized his son would be over thirty years old. That was the strange thing about returning after so long, while many things seemed to be the same, much was different. When Nathaniel and Elizabeth arrived in Bethlehem, it provided an opportunity for Samuel to go to Galilee. They had gladly taken up the responsibility of caring for his father.

Deborah's parents lived only a few houses down the street and their home would be a suitable place for her and Josiah to stay. They would decide how to divide up all of the children after supper.

At the conclusion of the meal, Ephraim summoned Miriam and whispered something to her. She quietly left the dining room, only to return momentarily with a scroll. It looked very much like those that belonged to Josiah. Naomi wondered why he wanted the scroll when he was blind and couldn't see.

The old man asked Josiah to open the scroll to a certain place and to guide his finger to a particular sentence.

He traced his finger over the words from memory as he cited them, *"But thou, Bethlehem Ephratah, though thou be little among the thousands of*

*Judah, yet out of thee shall He come forth unto Me that is to be ruler in Israel;
whose goings forth have been from of old, from everlasting."*

"My beloved children, you have come to Bethlehem – a small village,
but one of great significance in the purposes of God. This little place has
been favored by our Lord. This is where our father, David, was born.
We are descendants of David through his son, Nathan. That's why I live
here and why you've come to this place for the festival. It is Micah who
prophesies of Bethlehem. The prophet lived two hundred and fifty years
after David. Also remember that our most significant forefather was a man
taken into captivity by Nebuchadnezzar. He was named after the prophet,
Micah, and that's why our tribe is called Bin-Micah. In this passage, the
prophet is not speaking of David, but another who would come forth from
Bethlehem, one *whose goings forth have been from of old, from everlasting.*
He is speaking of the Messiah."

Though the old man was blind, his countenance was shining from
his faith.

"Many years ago a small boy came to my house. Now, he is here again,
much to my joy. When Josiah was a boy he came running into my house after
visiting the Temple with his father one day. He struggled to catch his breath
before telling me about an old man and a baby. His father soon followed and
confirmed what he had seen and heard. That day, I told them about another
event that had occurred a few weeks earlier. It was about a baby, born in a
stable, wrapped in swaddling clothes. Some shepherds found that baby not
far from this house. He seemed like any other baby, though oddly placed in
a manger for his crib. What they learned was that He was not an ordinary
baby. They found Him because an angel had appeared to them while they
watched their flock by night. It was the angel who told them about Him."

He paused and lifted his blind eyes as if trying to remember something
important.

"If I recall correctly, the angel said to them, *'Fear not: for, behold, I
bring you good tidings of great joy, which shall be to all people. For unto you
is born this day in the city of David a Saviour, which is Christ the Lord. And
this shall be a sign unto you; ye shall find the babe wrapped in swaddling
clothes, lying in a manger.'"*

Ephraim was silent for a long time after quoting the words of the angel,
and no one else dared to speak.

Finally, he declared boldly, "I am convinced of the Scriptures that the baby the shepherds saw in the stable is the very one of whom Micah wrote. Micah spoke of Bethlehem and the ruler who would come forth from this city. That baby was born right here in Bethlehem. It was the angel who called Him *'Christ the Lord.'* And then the old man prophesied over the child at the Temple only a few weeks after the baby was born in Bethlehem. Josiah, you were there. You heard him. Tell us what the old man said?"

Josiah's voice was shaking as he uttered the words he'd repeated again and again through the years – the very words that had haunted him since that day in the Temple long ago. He'd relayed them so often his children had them memorized.

Once he finished speaking them again, Ephraim said with unwavering conviction, "It must have been the same child! Ever since I heard what Josiah told me when he was a boy, I wondered if I would live to see His day, the day of the one in the manger, the one at the Temple, the day of the one of whom the angel spoke and the old man prophesied, the day of the one whom Micah proclaimed. I declare to you this day that I believe His time has come. Samuel, my son, has gone to Galilee to follow Him. His name is Jesus, and I hear He's coming to the feast. Beloved, listen to me. He has enemies in Jerusalem in high places. They are seeking His life; but if He is the Promised One, He will prevail and establish His kingdom as prophesied."

Then a deep sadness came to the man's face and tears started to stream down his cheeks.

"What's wrong?" Josiah asked in alarm.

Miriam rushed to his side to comfort him. It took a few moments for the old man to compose himself.

"This is not the first time wicked men have sought His life."

He had to pause for a moment before he could continue.

"Josiah, do you remember that my son had a baby when you were a boy? He was my only grandson."

The shepherd nodded his head.

"Where is he?" He asked hoping to see his kinsman, now that he was a man.

"You could ask that question to hundreds of fathers and mothers in Bethlehem," he replied with a trace of ire in his voice. "Not too long after you and your father left to return to Kedar we had some unusual visitors in Bethlehem. I saw them riding down the street on their camels. They were clothed in purple, and I learned later they were bearing gifts. They were magi from the east."

"What were they doing in Bethlehem?" Josiah asked eagerly wanting to know.

"It seems they were wise men from afar who saw His star while in their homeland. They traveled many miles to pay homage to the newborn king. Not knowing where to find him, they stopped in Jerusalem and inquired of Herod."

The old man's face betrayed his bitterness toward the former king.

"Herod's sages looked to the Scriptures and read the passage I just cited from the prophet Micah. 'Bethlehem Ephratah,' they declared to the king. So, King Herod sent the men to Bethlehem to find the child and told them to return and tell him the location, so that he could go and worship Him as well. After the magi found the child they presented Him with gifts – gold, frankincense and myrrh, I'm told. Then they were warned in a dream to avoid King Herod because he intended to harm the child. They went back to their homeland a different way, steering clear of the evil king altogether."

"What happened?" Michael interjected when the old man paused momentarily.

"Herod was livid when he learned they'd gone back to their country without revealing the location of the child to him. So he issued a decree that all the little boys of Bethlehem be killed from the age of two and under."

Josiah and his family were shocked by the unmitigated wickedness of Herod and waited to hear the awful news.

"Roman soldiers broke down my door in the middle of the night. I was asleep on my bed and my grandson, Eleazar, was nursing at his mother's breast in another room. They were staying with me because Samuel was out in the fields watching over his sheep. The soldiers snatched my grandson out of his mother's arms..."

He couldn't say any more as he re-lived that horrific night. There was silence in the room for several minutes, before finally he was able to continue.

"His mother tried to protect him, so a Roman soldier stabbed her. I got to the door just as a sword pierced through my grandson's heart. Somehow, my daughter-in-law was able to pick him up in her arms before he died. She passed away three days later from both the wound and a broken heart."

He paused to collect himself before uttering, "That night, I could hear weeping and wailing in the streets of Bethlehem. In Egypt, it was the wicked who mourned and wept over their firstborn because of the hardness in Pharaoh's heart. In Bethlehem, it was the slaughter of the children of Israel."

The room was silent. Even in Kedar they'd never heard of such horrors.

Finally, Michael asked the question that was on everyone's mind, "What happened to the child the magi visited?"

Ephraim suddenly smiled. It was like a dark cloud lifted from his countenance as he thought of the child.

"I have it on good authority that an angel warned his father of Herod's intention in a dream. He took the baby and his mother during the night and fled to Egypt before the soldiers arrived."

"Why didn't God warn the others before the attack?" Josiah's youngest son, Judah, asked.

"I don't know why," the old man replied softly. "I don't know why. All I know is that God has His purposes; and that the baby He spared that night is now a man, and that His day is at hand."

After speaking those words, he closed his eyes and began to pray, "Hasten the day of His coming, O Lord. Give Him safe passage to Mount Zion. Subdue His enemies and seat Him upon the throne of His father, David. Vindicate the death of my grandson and all the other sons of Bethlehem that died on that tragic night. *Amen.*"

And everyone responded by saying, *"Amen!"*

The prayer being ended, Naomi, ever the brave one, had a question for Ephraim.

"Sir..." she asked, raising her hand as if to get the attention of the blind man.

"Yes, and who might you be?" He replied tenderly.

"My name is Naomi," she exclaimed.

"And how old are you?" The old man inquired.

"I just turned five years old."

"You have a pretty voice. Now, do you have a question to ask me?"

"Yes sir," she said confidently. "We learned that Jesus heals the sick and that He even raised Lazarus from the dead. If you believe in Him, then why didn't he heal your blind eyes?"

"Naomi!" Deborah scolded. "You shouldn't ask such things."

Ephraim smiled and said, "Let her be. That's a very good question. You see, I've never met Jesus face to face. Samuel has and so have others I know and trust. I believe in Him because of what they've told me. Besides, I don't need to be healed. I can see very well."

Naomi was confused because she knew he was blind.

His face lit up when he continued, "I can see all that matters through the eye of faith. I'm an old man now. I'm prepared to go to heaven. I can remember all the things I need to remember, things I saw with my eyes before I became blind. Did you see how I asked your father to open the scroll for me?"

"Yes," Naomi replied. "I wondered why you did that when you couldn't see it."

"Oh, I could see it. I could see the passage in my mind. I could feel it on the scroll with my finger. You thought I was quoting it, but I was reading it from memory. I wanted the scroll to be open before me so that all of you would know where the words came from. They didn't come from me. They came from God."

CHAPTER 4

An Unusual Proposal

Genesis 29:30

And he loved also Rachel more than Leah.

Haifa quietly made sure that she and Isaac would be sleeping at Seth and Judith's house instead of in Ephraim's home where Miriam was staying. Her motivation was mixed. As a caring person she wanted to spare Miriam from sorrow as much as possible, but as a woman who loved her husband, she was fearful of what might happen. She knew Isaac loved her, but was still unsettled, because she also knew he once loved Miriam. She would never forget the look on Miriam's face when she first saw them together.

All of the other children stayed at Ephraim's house with their cousins, including little Naomi. Dinah would watch over her. Seth's house was spacious, and Isaac and Haifa had a room to themselves. They'd had precious little privacy since departing Kedar, and he wanted to show affection to his wife. She started to give in to him in a desperate attempt to keep his heart, but she couldn't do it. She had to know for sure that he loved her above all others. When she didn't respond, he suddenly realized she was crying softly.

"What's wrong?" He asked in alarm.

Haifa shook her head, not wanting to answer him, even though she knew she must.

When he asked what was troubling her again, she began to sob before managing to say, "It's Miriam."

Her husband was surprised. It was apparent that everyone noticed Miriam's reaction to seeing him with Haifa except Isaac.

"What about Miriam?" He asked, clearly perplexed.

In frustration Haifa cried out, "Isaac, she loves you!"

"You can't be serious," he responded looking incredulously at his wife.

"You didn't even look at her, did you?" She replied. "How could you do that to her?"

Isaac was clearly mystified. He loved his wife so much that he didn't look at another woman and she was upset about it? The confused young man sat up in the bed and shook his head in utter bewilderment.

"What makes you think she still loves me?" He asked, shrugging his shoulders.

"I saw her when you were helping me off of my horse. When she saw us together, she burst into tears and ran back into the house."

"I didn't see her, so how could I have known?" He asked.

"What did you expect?" Haifa asked, not understanding how her husband could be so blind.

"Look, what Miriam and I had between us was a long time ago," he retorted.

"Maybe to you, but not to her," she replied, trying to help him understand. "It really wasn't that long ago. Things have changed in our lives quickly; but it's only been a few months. Miriam has been waiting for you."

"It just seems like it was so long ago," he responded. "I assumed when she refused to leave with me that she didn't love me anymore."

This was the first Haifa had heard of Isaac asking Miriam to run away with him. He'd been so set on putting it behind him; he didn't want to even think about it, much less talk about it. Suddenly, he realized he needed to tell his wife everything.

"It was lonely for us in the desert," he began. "By the time I became a teenager there were only three families left from Tribe Bin-Micah in Kedar. The last year, there were only two. Miriam and I grew up together. It was natural for us to fall in love when we got old enough, and the same thing happened between Caleb and Dinah."

Haifa knew about Caleb and that he was Dinah's soul mate. She also knew that he'd been murdered by a Nabataean named Asad. When Isaac and Haifa were still in Dumat God had used the wicked man to stir Isaac's heart to repentance. In God's providence he discovered Asad's plan to steal his father's sheep and kill his family. That knowledge prompted him to return to his father's tent.

"Miriam and I began our relationship before Caleb and Dinah discovered how they felt about one another, but once he professed his love to her he was resolute. He was determined to marry her. I knew I wanted to ask Nathaniel for Miriam's hand as well, but I was hesitant."

"What made you hesitate?" Haifa asked, hoping he had some reservations about how he felt about her.

"It was my father's expectations. Haifa, my heart was far from God already. I just didn't realize it. I wanted what I wanted, and I didn't want to wait for it. Father was planning this pilgrimage to Jerusalem, but I didn't want to go. All I wanted to do was start my own flock with my inheritance and marry Miriam. I was waiting for the right time to talk to my father about it. I knew how much he wanted me to go to Jerusalem with him."

He paused for a moment and looked into his wife's eyes. Though he'd gone through very hard times, he was grateful to God for everything. In the end, his rebellion had led him to her, and then she had led him back to God. He didn't regret anything that had happened, other than his disobedience.

"We had a Sabbath's feast at Nathaniel's tent one night, and both Miriam and I were shocked when Father announced that Caleb had visited him that day and asked for Dinah's hand. Caleb hadn't said anything to me about his plans. When I saw how happy they were, I was excited. I couldn't think of a better husband for my sister. He was a much godlier man than I was."

The young shepherd lowered his head in humility. He was truly a different man since God brought him to repentance.

"After the celebration, the four of us walked together from Nathaniel's tent to ours. We stopped at the oasis; and I told Miriam I wanted to marry her, and that I intended to ask her father for her hand the next day."

Haifa noticed a far-away look in her husband's eyes, knowing he was reliving the moment. It frightened her when she realized his feelings for Miriam were being reawakened; but deep-down she knew it would be fruitless to try to build a relationship with him, if he tried to hide his true heart. She felt very vulnerable.

"What happened?" She asked, fearful of his next thoughts.

"When we got to our tent, Dinah and I went inside and Caleb and Miriam started the hike back to Nathaniel's tent. They hadn't been gone very long when I heard her screaming my name. She was running and crying when I hurried out of the tent. I'd just taken her into my arms when I saw the light from a fire in the direction of Nathaniel's tent. I knew immediately what had happened. By that time, Father and Michael had emerged from the tent, and we quickly mounted our horses. She wanted to go with me, but I made her go with Mother and Dinah to the hiding place at the oasis. She didn't want to let me go."

All of the emotions Isaac had felt for Miriam came surging back as he remembered that night.

"We rode as fast as we could to Nathaniel's tent…" his voice broke as he remembered seeing Caleb, bleeding in his father's arms.

"Caleb…Caleb was dead," he whispered and then began to weep.

Haifa held him in her arms. He didn't realize that his anger had never let him fully grieve the loss of his best friend. He felt no anger that night in Haifa's arms, only sadness.

"The next day," Isaac finally said after regaining his composure. "Nathaniel told Father that he was leaving Kedar for good. When Miriam told me what her father had said, I went to see him and asked for her hand in marriage."

Once again he paused as he searched for words.

"What did he say?" Haifa asked gently.

"He told me that he would be honored to have me as his son-in-law, but only under one condition. I had to go with them to Israel the next day. He was determined that none of his family, including Miriam, would spend another day in Kedar."

"What did you do?" She asked, needing to know everything.

"I was shocked. My whole life I wanted nothing more than to have my own flock in Kedar. I couldn't imagine leaving my home, but I loved Miriam more than anything."

As soon as the words left his lips he looked at Haifa fearing he'd hurt her. She hid her emotions very well, knowing that he had to find his own way.

"I told my father what Nathaniel said and asked him if I could go with them to Israel. Haifa, he flatly refused. He told me he needed me more than ever. Father asked me to be patient, but I had no patience. That was my downfall. I wanted what I wanted, and I wanted it right then."

"So, what did you do next?"

"I pled with my father, but to no avail; so I decided I would go with Nathaniel without his permission."

"Why didn't you go?" She asked, now perplexed herself.

"Nathaniel asked me what Father said; and when I told him, he told me I couldn't have Miriam as my wife, if I disobeyed my father. He was adamant about it. He can be as hard-headed as Father."

Haifa realized that Isaac got his stubbornness naturally. It seemed to be a common character trait among the men of Tribe Bin-Micah.

"I didn't know what to do. Later that night I snuck into the girls' chamber and got Miriam to go outside with me. I took her to the oasis and told her what our fathers had said. Of course, she was as upset as I was. That's when I asked her to run away with me."

The pain of that night came back to him as he told it.

"She refused to go with me," he said lowering his head. "It made me think that she didn't love me the same way I loved her."

"So you ran away by yourself," Haifa declared.

"Yes…yes…I ran away. I was so angry, and you know what happened after that."

She nodded her head before saying, "Isaac, Miriam didn't refuse to go with you because of a lack of love for you. She was being true to everything she held dear. She had to obey her father in order to obey God. She knew that the two of you would never find true happiness by disobeying God."

She hesitated for a moment before uttering softly, "Isaac, she still loves you."

Both of them lay there for a long time in silence before Haifa got the strength to ask, "Do you still love her?"

"I don't know!" He blurted out, not in anger, but in frustration.

"I love you. You are my wife. You're carrying my baby."

She had no question about his love for her, but knew his feelings for Miriam were still there.

"You have to go to her," she said softly.

"I…I can't," he replied, almost in a whisper.

"You have to. You need to find out if you still love her. I need to know."

"But then what will I do? What if my feelings for her return? I don't know what to do," he responded shaking his head.

"You must go to her," Haifa said resolutely.

It broke her heart to tell him that, but she knew she had no other choice. If she tried to come between them, she could never have the relationship with her husband she longed for. She would rather lose him than have him live a lie.

"What if she still wants to be my wife?" He asked, seeking counsel from the woman he loved so deeply.

"You wouldn't be the first Jew with two wives," she replied.

In her heart, she didn't know whether she could share him, but she knew he had to find out the truth about his feelings for Miriam. It had ended badly before, but had it really ended?

Isaac slept fitfully that night – his dreams chaotic, moving from the horror of Caleb's death to the pain of Miriam's refusal to flee with him. Then, his dreams took him to the oasis and the first kiss he shared with her. Finally, his subconscious mind became serene as he watched himself, as if an outside observer, walking hand in hand with Haifa, her belly distended, as she neared the time of her delivery. His dreams were as conflicted as his emotions.

The next morning he was nervous as they made their way to Ephraim's house for breakfast. He couldn't concentrate when the patriarch of the family led them in the reading of the Scriptures and Psalm-singing on that Sabbath morn. All he could think about was what he would say to Miriam. Haifa sat dutifully beside him, but avoided any gestures of affection. She still was concerned to spare Miriam's feelings, but also to allow her husband to work his way through this dilemma. He once again avoided looking directly at Miriam. He just couldn't, not until he could talk to her.

Ephraim asked Josiah to close their Sabbath meeting with prayer, and as soon as he pronounced the *"Amen,"* the company responded with an enthusiastic corporate *"Amen!"* However, Isaac simply mouthed the words, his mind elsewhere. He wasted no time and made his way to Miriam as soon as they were dismissed. She was distracted by Dinah and didn't realize he was there, until she heard him speak her name.

"Miriam…"

Shocked to hear his voice, she was speechless. She looked to Dinah for support, but her friend couldn't come to her aid.

"Miriam," he said again.

"Y…yes," she stammered.

"Could I speak to you in private?"

Again, she looked to Dinah, not knowing what to do. Dinah nodded her head, indicating that she should go with him and then offered a quick prayer in her heart. She knew that Miriam was heart-broken but trusted her brother to be gentle with her. She then looked over at Haifa. Her sister-in-law tried to smile, but she knew her well and realized how frightened she was. The next prayer she whispered was for her.

Deborah watched what was happening. As soon as Isaac and Miriam went out the back door, she made her way to Haifa. Dinah met her there and both of them embraced her. When the tears started to flow, they took her into an empty room to console her.

"I'm frightened…" Haifa confessed as Deborah held her in her arms.

She gently lifted her daughter-in-law's face with her hands and looked into her eyes.

"My son loves you. The Lord will direct him. You have to trust in God and believe in your husband."

Haifa nodded her head. It was hard for her to let him go to Miriam, but she knew it was right.

Miriam instinctively led him to the bench behind Ephraim's house. It was the same place where Dinah found her the day before and had become her own personal refuge since arriving in Bethlehem. She frequently went there to get away from the crowd in the house, and yes, she'd often dreamed of Isaac when she escaped to that place.

Though he had rehearsed what he wanted to say, he suddenly drew a blank. He didn't know what to say; and when she began to cry, he took her into his arms as he had many times before at the oasis in Kedar. The months they'd been separated seemed to evaporate in that moment, and they were together once again. She felt safe with her head pressed against his chest. His lost memories suddenly resurfaced.

It was Miriam who spoke first, "You didn't even say goodbye."

"I know," he said in an apologetic voice. "I was so angry."

"Were you angry at me too?" She asked.

"I was angry at everyone – at Father, at Nathaniel, and yes, I was angry at you when you refused to run away with me. I thought it was because you didn't love me the way I loved you."

"How could you have ever thought that!?" She asked with a look of hurt in her eyes.

"I know…I know, I should have trusted in our love; but I was stubborn and wanted only what I wanted."

She could tell he was beating himself up all over again.

"Dinah told me about your repentance," she whispered, looking into his eyes.

When she saw the shadow depart from them she knew he was a different man.

"Yes, I suppose I was most angry at God when you left, but now I know His tender mercies. He softened my heart."

"That's great," she responded with all sincerity.

"Haifa…" Isaac hesitated as soon as he realized he'd mentioned her name.

Miriam was observant and could tell immediately how he loved his wife, just from the way he spoke her name. She remembered the way he touched Haifa when he helped her down from her horse.

"It's okay. You can say her name," she said. "She is your wife after all and is going to have your baby."

Isaac felt relieved. All of the love he felt for Haifa filled his heart. Miriam would have had to be blind not to see it.

"What about Haifa?" She asked.

"The Lord used her to bring me back to Him. Miriam, she's wonderful, truly she is." Isaac began to speak quickly as if he was trying to convince her that everything would be okay, or perhaps he was trying to convince himself. "She really is. You'll grow to love her too. Everyone loves her… Mother, Father, Dinah…everyone loves her. You'll be like sisters…sisters in the same tent."

Miriam suddenly realized what he was trying to say.

"Sisters in the same tent? What are you saying…or should I say…what are you asking me?"

A flustered Isaac took a moment to regain his composure.

"Miriam, I asked you once before." He took her hands into his hands before saying it again, "Miriam, would you become my wife?"

Those were the words she'd longed to hear again, ever since the day she departed Kedar with her family. Many times, she'd sat on that bench and imagined him saying them, but something didn't seem right to her. She knew she loved him, more than life, and she believed he still loved her. She could see it in his eyes, but when he spoke of Haifa there was something more.

She collected herself and looked directly into his eyes as she said, "You don't know how I've prayed to hear those words again. My heart was devastated when I thought I'd lost you."

Suddenly, she began to cry. Isaac pulled her to himself and held her tightly.

"It'll be alright," he whispered, letting his lips touch her hair. "It'll be alright."

She cried for a few moments before taking a deep breath. When she looked up again, he wiped the tears from her cheeks.

"Isaac, I do believe you love me, but I have an important question to ask?"

He stood there waiting for her to speak.

"I know you love Haifa too, and I understand. Dinah's told me how wonderful she is and so have you. I could be her sister and your wife, if…"

She paused, and he didn't know what she was going to say.

"Isaac, I know you love me, but can you honestly say that you love me as much as you love her?"

That question had not occurred to him when his feelings for Miriam were being rekindled.

"I…I…"

He was at a complete loss for words, but it wasn't necessary for him to say anything. She could tell by the look in his eyes that he could never love anyone the way he loved Haifa. It must have been the earnest prayers of Deborah, Dinah and her mother that suddenly made a difference. She was overwhelmed with a sense of calm and knew what she must do.

"Isaac," she said tenderly, "There's nothing more I'd rather be than to be your wife."

She paused again reflecting on how to say what she must say.

"But the answer is no."

He was confused. The young man knew he loved Miriam; and more than anything, he wanted her to be happy. He thought she would be happy if he took her as a wife.

"I...I don't understand," he said, the bewilderment evident in his eyes.

"Isaac, I can't be your Leah."

Still, he didn't understand until he thought for a moment and remembered the story in the Bible about Leah and Rachel. Jacob loved Rachel and contracted with her father, Laban, to marry her. On the wedding night, Laban slipped Leah, Rachel's older sister, into his tent under the cover of darkness. The next morning Jacob was incensed when he realized what Laban had done. When he approached his kinsman, Laban argued that it was improper for the younger daughter to marry before the older daughter. He then offered Rachel to Jacob as a second wife on condition that he work for him for another seven years.

Isaac remembered what the Scriptures said of Jacob, *"And he loved also Rachel more than Leah."*

"But I love you," Isaac tried to protest. "You could never be my Leah."

"I know you love me," she replied as tenderly as she could, "But you could never love anyone the way you love Haifa. I can't be your Leah."

Isaac couldn't deny what she was saying. Even though he loved Miriam, his heart was overwhelmed by his love for Haifa, his wife and the mother of his child.

"It's alright," she said. "Go...go to her. Go to your wife."

He hugged her one last time, and she could see the relief on his face as he turned to go find his wife.

Haifa had gone back over to Deborah's parents' house. She just couldn't stay at Ephraim's house knowing that Isaac was outside with Miriam. She had gone into their room and was lying on the bed, when she heard him come in the door.

"Haifa..." he said.

She jumped up off of the bed and ran into his arms, weeping. He held her and just let her cry.

Finally, she stepped back and looked at him before asking, "What happened?"

"I asked Miriam to marry me," he replied.

Suddenly, she burst into tears again fearing the worst.

"She said no," he whispered into his wife's ear.

"What…she said no?" Haifa asked in surprise. "Why…why did she say no?"

"She told me she could never be my Leah?"

Haifa was as confused as he had been at first, so he took a few moments to tell her the story of Jacob, Rachel and Leah.

When he finished, she asked, "Why did she think she would be your Leah?"

"Because when she asked me if I could love her the way I love you…"

She threw herself into her husband's arms. There was nothing more he needed to say. Joy filled her heart, because she knew he loved her like he could never love another woman.

She kissed him all over his lips and face, saying between kisses, "I love you! I love you! I love you!" And then took his hand and led him to their bed. It was time to give herself to her husband.

Though Miriam knew she'd done the right thing, her heart was still broken. She sat down on her bench and cried. Then she felt his presence beside her, his strong arms surrounding her as she leaned her head against his chest. He held her, speaking soothingly to her. When they were ready to go back into the house, Michael reached out his hand to help her stand to her feet. There was something special in his touch. She looked at him really for the first time since Josiah's family arrived in Bethlehem. Back in Kedar she'd been so infatuated with Isaac; she hadn't realized that Michael had also become a man, and a handsome young man at that.

CHAPTER 5

The Glorious City

Psalm 87:3

Glorious things are spoken of thee, O city of God. Selah.

The shepherd's family was excited when they woke up before dawn on the first day of the week. Finally, the time had come to go up to Jerusalem. Michael couldn't wait to see the city and especially the Temple. Isaac was more solemn, desiring to offer his sacrifices because of his fall into sin. He knew that God had already forgiven him, but his heart yearned to be faithful to the law and to offer a trespass offering as well as a whole burnt offering. Josiah was mindful of his son's desire.

Each of them seemed to have a different reason for their enthusiasm, including Martha. She knew her longing should be to go to the Temple, but she couldn't get a certain young man off of her mind. Josiah had told Joseph's father the day he expected to arrive in Jerusalem. His second daughter was hoping her young man would be waiting for her outside the Temple gate.

The distance was roughly six miles on a well-traveled road. As they emerged onto the road they noted something extraordinary. A spring rain had cooled the earth the night before as they slept in Bethlehem, and now a heavy fog covered the land. This was an unusual sight for the travelers, but didn't hinder their progress. It produced an eerie scene as daylight arrived, but nothing could dampen their spirits.

Nathaniel and his family would be going to Jerusalem later in the day, so it was just Josiah's family leaving in the early morning. The shepherd decided it would be best to walk to Jerusalem instead of riding their horses. Michael and the younger boys made sure the rams and goats stayed together along the road, and that none of them wandered off. Though they got an early start the road already had many wayfarers on it.

They heard some pilgrims up ahead singing the second Song of Ascents, a very fitting song while approaching the city.

I will lift up mine eyes unto the hills, from whence cometh my help. My help cometh from the LORD, which made heaven and earth. He will not suffer thy foot to be moved: He that keepeth thee will not slumber. Behold, He that keepeth Israel shall neither slumber nor sleep. The LORD is thy keeper: the LORD is thy shade upon thy right hand. The sun shall not smite thee by day, nor the moon by night. The LORD shall preserve thee from all evil: He shall preserve thy soul. The LORD shall preserve thy going out and thy coming in from this time forth, and even for evermore.

It was a psalm Josiah's family had sung often since leaving Kedar, and without even thinking about it they joined in the singing. The shepherd especially remembered hearing Zacharias and those with him singing this particular psalm when his family emerged from Petra onto the King's Highway. It had been a moment of great comfort on the trip after seeing the idolatry of the rock city first hand.

He lifted his eyes, looking northward in the direction of Jerusalem. Though Bethlehem was at a slightly higher elevation it was too far to see the city, especially in the fog. Yet in his imagination, he could make out the hills, the hills upon which Jerusalem was built. His heart was full of joy. The day had finally arrived.

As they approached the location of Rachel's tomb, he pointed it out to his family. Isaac and Haifa looked at each other and smiled as he squeezed her hand, remembering their conversation about Jacob and Rachel. She was now confident that her husband loved her the same way.

Josiah's mind was full of the Scriptures as he neared the tomb. He struggled within himself about what to do, wanting very much to discuss them with his sons, but believing he needed to press ahead to Jerusalem.

Michael made up his mind for him when he caught up with his father and asked him a question,

"Father, I remember Jeremiah the Prophet saying something about Rachel, but I never really understood what he meant. Can you help me?"

His father stopped alongside the road and said, "You are right. Let me see if I can remember his words. I believe he said, '*A voice was heard in Ramah, lamentation and bitter weeping, Rachel weeping for her children, refusing to be comforted for her children, because they are no more.'"*

"Yes, that's the passage I had in mind. What was Jeremiah talking about?" Michael asked.

By this time Isaac and Simon joined them, wanting to hear what their father had to say.

"The passage comes at the beginning of a promise of restoration to Ephraim, the northern kingdom, and just before a similar promise to Judah, the southern kingdom. Rachel was a suitable choice to represent the sorrow of the exiles of both kingdoms. Even though Jacob loved her the most, she'd struggled to get pregnant. Her sister, Leah, was jealous of her and ridiculed her because of her barrenness. It was only after much prayer that she finally gave birth to Joseph."

All three of the boys knew this story, but were anxious to learn why Jeremiah spoke of Rachel. Did he actually mean that Rachel's ghost cried out for her lost sons from the grave?

Their father sensed what was bothering them and continued, "When Jacob was old he gave Joseph a double portion of the land, which was divided between his two sons, Manasseh and Ephraim. Manasseh was the older, but when the nearly blind Jacob blessed his grandsons before his death, his right hand fell upon Ephraim, granting him the blessing of the firstborn instead of Manasseh. Joseph protested what his father had done, but Jacob would not change his blessing. Ephraim thus became the father of the foremost tribe of Israel."

Deborah saw Haifa touching her belly as she looked over at Rachel's tomb. She knew the passage her husband had quoted from Jeremiah must have troubled her. Sensing that she needed to be comforted, she took her hand and led her to the tomb. Dinah joined them there, and Deborah realized her oldest daughter had her own burden to bear.

Haifa looked at Deborah and began to cry. Not only did Rachel grieve for her sons from her grave, but Haifa remembered what Josiah heard the old man say to the baby's mother at the Temple. Then images of Roman soldiers killing all the little boys in Bethlehem tormented her.

"Am I going to give birth to my baby only to weep for him in sorrow?" She cried.

Deborah took her into her arms and said, "This world is full of sorrow, but also joy. Look at my children. Must I grieve at times? Yes, my heart ached for Dinah when Caleb was killed."

Dinah leaned into her mother for comfort, and she held her close as well.

"And I cried myself to sleep on many of the nights when Isaac was gone, but the pain is there only because the love is so deep. And the love – the love breeds joy, joy unspeakable. To be here with my husband and my children – and yes, with my grandchild, is my greatest delight."

She looked into her daughter-in-law's eyes and said, "Haifa, we must trust in our God. He has His purposes in our suffering, but He will make all things right. The day will come when Rachel will weep no more. We have to believe this."

Haifa nodded her head and smiled when she thought of her baby. She knew how much Deborah adored her family. Once again, her mother-in-law became her wise mentor.

Dinah's burden was unspoken, but her mother knew what she hid in her heart. Rachel may have struggled to conceive, but in the end she had children to grieve. Haifa had a glow about her as she carried Isaac's child in her womb. Dinah would never have children with Caleb to grieve or to enjoy. Asad's arrow not only killed her soul mate, it also killed her children, who would never be born. She, too, had to rest in God's goodness, which is at times hidden from us as if behind a veil; yet His goodness always remains.

Along the road near the tomb, Josiah continued to instruct his sons.

"Many years after the birth of Joseph, Rachel conceived again and gave birth to a second son. Her labor was hard and she named him 'Ben-Oni,' which means 'Son of My Sorrow.' Then she died from the complications of childbirth. Jacob was grieving and couldn't call his son Ben-Oni because it would always remind him of his wife's death, so he called him Benjamin instead, which means 'Son of the Right Hand,' or 'Son of the South' because he was born near Bethlehem, way to the south of Padan Aram where his other sons were born. This is the place where he buried his favored wife."

Josiah paused to give his sons time to assimilate what he was saying before he continued.

"As the mother of Joseph, Rachel was the matriarch of the northern kingdom, a kingdom that had already been in exile in Assyria for over 130 years by the time of Jeremiah's prophecy. Then as the mother of Benjamin, she was the matriarch of the southern kingdom, for Benjamin allied with Judah in the south. At the time of Jeremiah the southern kingdom was on the brink of suffering the same judgment from God that had befallen the northern kingdom. This time, God would use Nebuchadnezzar and the Babylonian army to chastise His people. When the prophet spoke of Rachel weeping, she was weeping for both those already in exile from the north, and those about to be taken away in the south."

"Did Rachel's ghost really weep from the grave? I didn't think we believe in ghosts." Simon asked, reflecting on what he'd been taught.

"You are right. We don't believe that the spirits of dead men roam the earth. It is hard to say what Jeremiah meant, my son," his father responded.

"Do you think Jeremiah was speaking figuratively of Rachel's weeping?" Michael asked, suggesting the answer he believed his father would give.

"I believe that's the most plausible explanation," Josiah declared. "Remember that Moses tells us that Rachel called her second son, Ben-Oni. I told you that the name means 'Son of My Sorrow.' Moses doesn't tell us the cause of her sorrow. Perhaps she was sad because she knew she wasn't going to live to see Benjamin grow up. It's also possible that she prophetically saw what would happen in the future to the descendants of her sons, Joseph and Benjamin. Maybe, naming her son Ben-Oni is the beginning of her weeping for us all."

Michael suddenly remembered what Ephraim told them about the slaughter of the sons of Bethlehem.

"Could Rachel have been weeping for the babies that died in Bethlehem too?" He asked. "The cries of their mothers could certainly be heard from the site of her grave."

Josiah hadn't thought of that, but understood what his son was suggesting.

"Think of the impact of the exile," he said, measuring his words as he thought through them.

"Though a remnant of God's people returned to rebuild the Temple and the city, the lingering result was that the Promised Land remained under occupation, and most of God's people were still scattered. King Herod sat on the throne when I was a boy; but when the rightful King of Israel was born, he tried to kill Him."

Josiah closed his eyes and began to pray, "Thank you Lord, for thwarting the evil plan of Herod, but we still grieve the sons of Bethlehem, who died instead of the child king on that horrible night. Hastily, reveal Your Messiah. May He come to Jerusalem to avenge their deaths, that Rachel will weep no more. *Amen!*"

To which his sons responded, *"Amen!"*

The three women returned to the rest of them, and they continued the journey toward the holy city. Emerging onto what appeared to be a broad plain, Josiah immediately recognized it to be the Valley of Rephaim. Most of the valleys around Jerusalem were deep and narrow, but not the Valley of Rephaim or as it was also called, the "Valley of Giants." It was at this place where David finally defeated the Philistines after he consolidated all of Israel in his kingdom.

He peered to the southwest along the Valley, realizing that it merged into the Valley of Elah as it headed toward the coast of the Mediterranean Sea. That was the location of David's first victory over the archenemy of Israel, the Philistines. At the time, he was little more than a boy, but from the Brook of Elah he gathered five smooth stones before heading out to face the Philistine champion, Goliath. Josiah smiled as he remembered how God gave his forefather the victory over the towering giant. From the Valley of Elah to the Valley of Rephaim, God fought for His people through His servant David to give him full authority and power over all of the Promised Land. Such stories of God's work encouraged the shepherd's soul as they continued the trek toward the city.

Michael was getting anxious to see Jerusalem and with every rise up ahead, he'd leave the animals with his brothers and run to the top to see if he could finally see the city. He was frustrated by the fog. Josiah noted the disappointment on his face the first few times he tried but suddenly realized what his son had seen when he made one last climb. His face betrayed his joy, for finally he'd seen the city.

"Father, Mother…hurry! I can see the holy city!" He exclaimed.

Everyone felt a surge of excitement and quickened their pace to get to the top of the rise. Almost miraculously the fog had lifted and the morning sun shone brightly. As each of them saw the city, still somewhat in the distance, Josiah heard their gasps. For a moment, they all stood there in awe.

"Look! The Temple!" Michael cried out pointing to a high building on the eastern end of the city.

All eyes focused on the Temple. It was a magnificent sight. Though Herod had been an evil king and rebuilt it for his own glory, he now lay dead in his grave; but the house of the Lord stood arrayed in God's glory. The white marble of the Temple shone brightly in the sunlight. The House of God dominated the entire scene of the city.

"Isn't she glorious!" Michael declared, seeming to be the only one able to speak.

Haifa looked on the holy city and the Temple, knowing immediately that the temple of Atarsamain in Dumat could never compare.

Instinctively, Josiah began to quote the prophet Haggai:

"For thus saith the LORD of hosts; Yet once, it is a little while, and I will shake the heavens, and the earth, and the sea, and the dry land; And I will shake all nations, and the Desire of all Nations shall come: and I will fill this house with glory, saith the LORD of hosts. The silver is Mine, and the gold is Mine, saith the LORD of hosts. The glory of this latter House shall be greater than of the former, saith the LORD of hosts: and in this place will I give peace, saith the LORD of hosts."

Josiah believed they were beholding the fulfillment of Haggai's prophecy.

Just before they'd left Kedar Josiah had an interesting conversation with the Idumean who purchased his flock. His name was Omar, and he was a God-fearer. Much of what he'd said and the questions he'd asked of Josiah excited the shepherd, but one thing troubled him. He'd told Josiah that things were not as they should be at the Temple – that there was great corruption among the priesthood. However, in the euphoria of this moment, he pushed aside what Omar had told him.

'That just can't be true,' the shepherd thought to himself. 'There must be some other explanation. If Omar is not mistaken, surely Jesus, the Messiah, will set all things in order once He arrives in the city.'

Josiah comforted himself with these thoughts. This visit was the consummation of the deepest desire of his life, and he was not going to let naysayers spoil it for him, not even those he loved and trusted.

The shepherd took his eyes off of the city long enough to notice the impressive image of the Mount of Olives on the far side. They'd seen it from the other side when they'd made the trip down the less-traveled road from Bethany to Bethlehem. Then he looked around him at the fields of the fertile valley they were following. The barely was ready for harvest. Later, the fields would be full of wheat. For a moment he considered extending his stay, but knew in his heart he needed to return with his family to Kedar after The Feast of Weeks.

Josiah let his gaze move northward to the juncture of the road to Joppa. So much history raced through his mind, he finally had to stop and sit down. Though he wanted to hurry into the city and go to the Temple, there were things he had to teach his children. He couldn't let the moment pass.

"Gather around me, children," he said, not at all afraid to call his older offspring "children" as well.

He had them sit, so they could look at the city before them.

"See the city as she stands on the other side of the Valley of Hinnom. Yes, she's glorious. Not because she looks that way to us in the sunlight, but because God declares her to be glorious."

As he often did before citing the Scriptures he paused to remember, so that he could quote the words accurately.

"Glorious things are spoken of thee, O city of God."

"These words were sung by the sons of Korah. God's Word tells us that Jerusalem is glorious. Look at the city carefully. She is protected on the east by the deep-cut Kidron Valley, and on the south by the Valley of Hinnom. Note, the wall all around the city. It is built for defense."

"Another psalmist says, *'For the Lord hath chosen Zion; He hath desired it for His habitation. This is My rest for ever: here will I dwell; for I have desired it.'"*

"But I thought God lives everywhere," Naomi exclaimed, eliciting a frown from her father for speaking without being addressed.

The frown quickly disappeared as Josiah realized why she must be confused.

"Yes, little one, God does live everywhere, but He has a peculiar presence in Zion. Next time, lift your hand for permission before you speak when I'm teaching," he instructed, but when he saw that she was about to cry from his reprimand, a little wink soothed her feelings.

Michael dutifully raised his hand with a look of confusion on his face. "Yes, Michael?" He asked.

"What do you mean by 'peculiar' presence?"

He realized that his son was confused by his word choice when addressing Naomi.

"His presence is special on Mount Zion," his father replied before continuing to explain. "Of course, God is everywhere. He is omnipresent, but in a special way, in a peculiar way, He lives in the midst of His people. In a most special way He is present when His people are gathered at the Temple to worship Him. You will see my son. Just wait and you will see."

The shepherd turned his attention back to the rest of them, "Now, see the houses…see how close they are together. The city is built to facilitate the fellowship of God's people within the protected confines of her walls."

"In the third of the Songs of Ascents, David says, *Jerusalem is builded as a city that is compact together.*"

"This is new to us, visiting such a place. We live in open space in Kedar. Since we dwell among heathens it is a good thing we do, but not here – not in Jerusalem. These are God's people, so the city is designed to demonstrate the unity of the people of God. It is built to elicit fellowship. There's no other city quite like it on the earth."

Next, the shepherd told his children to stand and pointed behind them.

"What do you see on the road coming this way?"

"People, people with sheep and goats," Simon replied.

"Now, look before you on this road. What do you see there?"

"The same thing, people, lots of people," Simon answered again.

"Now, look in the distance and see the road to Joppa. What do you see walking on that road toward the city?"

"More people, hundreds of people," Judah responded.

Josiah pointed to the Temple, "See the pinnacle of the Temple. If you could stand at the top of it…," he suddenly paused in mid-sentence, turned and pointed to a tower near the gate the people were entering from the road to Joppa and exclaimed, "That is the Tower of David. If you could stand on top of the tower…or on the pinnacle of the Temple either one, you would see the roads approaching Jerusalem…from Galilee in the North…from

Jericho and Bethany in the east. If you could see all the roads leading to Jerusalem, you would see the same thing – pilgrims, travelers, those who are going to the city to worship our God."

"The Psalmist continues to say in the Third of the Songs of Ascents, *'Whither the tribes go up, the tribes of the LORD, unto the testimony of Israel, to give thanks unto the name of the LORD.'*"

"David is describing in this marvelous psalm the very thing we are witnessing."

"It looks like rivers of people," Benjamin exclaimed in awe.

For the solitary nomads from Kedar, seeing such crowds of people was new and exciting.

"Yes, my son, another psalmist, one who sang after the exile says, *'Turn again our captivity, O LORD, as the streams in the south.'* We are a part of those streams flowing back to Jerusalem to worship our God. When we left the desert in Kedar to make this long journey we were alone. It was just our family, but lift up your eyes and look now. Hundreds are within your sight at this moment, like streams, flowing through the gates into the city. Others have already entered, and many more will follow us. It's time for us to worship our God!"

Josiah was overcome with emotion and tears of joy ran down his cheeks, but there was one more thing he needed to be certain his children understood.

"Children, hear me," he said almost in a whisper as he motioned for them to be seated. "We are pilgrims, but we are not strangers to the city."

Naomi in particular frowned in confusion. How could she not be a stranger to the city? This was the first time she'd ever seen it.

"The very psalm that pronounces the city glorious goes on to say, *'I will make mention of Rahab and Babylon to them that know me: behold Philistia, and Tyre, with Ethiopia; this man was born there. And of Zion it shall be said, This and that man was born in her: and The Highest Himself shall establish her. The LORD shall count, when He writeth up the people, that this man was born there.'*"

"But I wasn't born in Zion, or in any of those places. I was born in Kedar," little Naomi cried out in frustration.

Josiah smiled at his youngest daughter, "Don't you see Naomi. It doesn't matter where you were born if you are one of God's people. Even though you were born in the desert of Kedar within our black tent, it is the same as if you were born in Zion, right there in the midst of the holy city."

He then looked around at them all and declared, "Because we belong to God by His covenantal faithfulness to our father, Abraham, his God is our God, and this city is our city too. Look across the city at the place of the Temple. Does anyone know the name of that mountain upon which it is built?"

"It's Mount Moriah," Michael declared, always ready with an answer.

"You are right, my son. Now, where was it that God told Abraham to go and offer up his son, Isaac?"

At that moment, Josiah looked at his oldest son, who was named after the patriarch.

"God told him to go up into one of the mountains in the land of Moriah," Isaac responded.

Josiah nodded his head before continuing, "Do you remember how David sinned against God by numbering the people? God's hand of judgment was heavy upon him; but in the midst of it, God instructed him to purchase that place from Araunah, the Jebusite. It was there that David's son, Solomon, built the Temple, the very place where Abraham offered Isaac."

"Is that the Temple that Solomon built?" Judah asked pointing at the Temple, but with a bewildered look on his face.

"No Son, you remember what happened. God's people sinned against Him yet again and it grieved Him. Remember our forefather Micah? He was taken into captivity to Babylon by Nebuchadnezzar. Who were his friends?"

"Shadrach – I mean Hananiah, Mishael and Azariah," Naomi exclaimed, correcting herself by using their Hebrew names.

"And which one did Naomi forget?" Her father asked, leaving her with a little pout on her face.

"Daniel," Ruth answered with a smile.

"That's right, and that's how we ended up living in Kedar instead of in Israel."

Then a sober look crossed his face as he continued, "Twenty years later, the Babylonians destroyed this wonderful city, tearing down her walls and then demolishing the Temple itself. All the glory departed Israel."

A silence overcame them as they realized the extent of God's punishment of His people.

"But then, God sent a remnant back to rebuild the Temple and the city. Behold, my children, look at what God has done! She is glorious, because God says she is glorious."

He paused for a moment before declaring, "Let us go up and enter the city. Let us go worship our God!"

Again it was Naomi who spoke, "But we are already higher than the city. How can we go up?"

Josiah smiled before answering, "Remember, little one, Jerusalem is always *up* for the one who trusts in the Lord."

CHAPTER 6

The Temple

Psalm 122:1

I was glad when they said unto me, Let us go into the house of the LORD.

Josiah could hardly contain his excitement as he led his family down the slope of the hill. With each descending step it appeared to the children that the wall of Jerusalem rose higher. To their right was the lower pool of Gihon near the upper end of the Hinnom Valley. The way became more crowded as they moved closer to the gate as pilgrims where funneled into the city from the road to Bethlehem, Hebron and beyond, and also from the road to Joppa.

As they drew ever nearer the city, Michael and the younger boys brought the rams and goats in closer to them, and Isaac took special charge of the paschal lamb. Once the two roads merged, Michael noticed that the wall obscured the view of the Temple, which had dominated the sight of the city from above. He remembered how it looked like a snow-covered mountain peak when he first saw it in the morning sunlight from a distance, and he longed to see it up close.

Finally, they passed through the gate and entered the city. Instinctively, they stopped to take in the view, but they were not the only ones. It seemed everyone did the same thing. Josiah noted David's Tower nearby, but when he saw the house of Herod on Mount Zion he felt a fleeting sense of sadness. Everything was not as it should be in Jerusalem. Herod's palace stood at the traditional location of the house that David built, which was later destroyed by the Babylonians. Though the pagan king died shortly after he ordered the slaughter of the babies in Bethlehem, the presence of occupation was still all around them. Now Pilate, another unbeliever, was governor; and Roman soldiers rode their horses through the streets of Jerusalem in a show of power.

It's not surprising that it was Michael who brought his father out of his momentary stupor by quoting the Scriptures.

He moved up to him and whispered in his ear, *"Let us go into the house of the LORD!"*

To which the shepherd responded by completing the passage with a smile, *"I was glad when they said unto me, Let us go into the house of the LORD!"*

Both of them looked straight ahead and beheld the Temple. It was the most awe-inspiring sight Michael had ever seen, and Josiah's memories of it didn't do it justice. The walls surrounding the Court of the Gentiles were tall, but still the Temple proper towered proudly above them from within.

They followed the multitudes as they approached the Temple walking along David's Road. As Josiah thought about how David had traversed that very road while dancing mightily before the Ark of the Covenant, he suddenly remembered the refrain from the psalmist commemorating that event, *"Arise, O Lord, into Thy rest; Thou, and the ark of Thy strength."* The shepherd was mindful that every step within the city walls was a step on holy ground.

As they drew nearer to the Temple, they followed those who were leading their animals to offer as sacrifices. In order to check them, they needed to circle to the southern end of the Temple and enter the Huldah Gates. Many of the worshipers without animals proceeded to the western gates which were closer.

When they rounded the corner, Josiah could see the pinnacle of the Temple once again. It was also called "The Place of Trumpeting," because that was where the trumpeter would blow his horn to announce the morning and evening sacrifices, as well as the beginning and ending of each Sabbath. The shepherd intended for his family to experience the morning sacrifice one day soon; but on this particular morning, his first objective was to offer his personal sacrifices and present his paschal lamb. They'd left Bethlehem too late to observe the ceremony of the morning sacrifice. He remembered the experience from when he was a boy. It was thrilling to hear the blowing of the silver trumpet, and then the singing of the psalm of the day by the Levites. It was quite spectacular, and he especially wanted his older sons to experience it; but that would have to wait another day.

The line was long at the checking station, but Josiah patiently waited his turn. Isaac and Michael helped him keep charge over the animals, while the others waited for them at the foot of the stairs that led to the triple entrance of the eastern Huldah gate. On busy days, such as this one, the eastern gate was used as an entrance and the western gate as an exit. The rest of the family awaited his lead, having never visited the Temple.

He and Isaac had selected three of their finest rams and three goats from the herd. Josiah would offer one of the rams for himself as a whole burnt offering to the Lord and another for the entire family. The third would be offered as a trespass offering by Isaac. The men would then offer the three goats as peace offerings on behalf of the family. Deborah carried the unleavened cakes to accompany the sacrifices as grain offerings. Her mother helped her prepare them on the afternoon before the Sabbath.

Isaac was confident of the fitness of their animals. Not only did he give due diligence in selecting them, but he'd cared for them during the pilgrimage to insure they remained without spot or blemish. He'd examined them himself carefully the afternoon before. Each animal was perfect in every detail.

When it was their turn to check their animals, Josiah gave the inspector all the pertinent information he required. The paschal lamb was taken to a different location where it would be viewed over the next four days to insure its suitability. The others would be inspected for certification as fitting for sacrifice, while he and his family purified themselves in one of the many *mikvehs* near the gate.

As he showed his family how to wash themselves in the *mikveh*, he lifted his cleansed hands and declared from one of the psalms, *"Who shall ascend into the hill of the LORD? Or who shall stand in His holy place? He that hath clean hands, and a pure heart; who hath not lifted up his soul unto vanity, nor sworn deceitfully."*

The rest of them eagerly followed suit. After washing themselves, the three men got in a separate line to retrieve their animals. Isaac noticed that several of the worshipers in front of them had their sacrifices denied, but he had no doubt that his would pass inspection. To his utter astonishment the examiner curtly informed them that their animals did not meet the proper standards.

"What do you mean?" Isaac retorted, raising his voice. "I'll have you know these animals are perfect in every detail!"

The inspector was shocked at his reaction and got a little testy himself, "I say they're unfit, and what I say goes!"

Before Isaac could respond his father put his hand on his shoulder.

"Sir, what should we do about making our sacrifices today?" He asked in a soft voice.

He could feel his son trembling and knew how angry he was.

"You can make your purchase from those already approved," the man replied, thankful for the older man's calmer demeanor.

"Where can we find them?" Josiah asked looking around.

"Inside," the man replied, trying to hurry them along so he could attend to the next worshiper.

"Inside where?" Josiah asked, clearly perplexed.

"Inside the Temple...where else?" The man replied before quickly asking, "Who's next?"

The shepherd was dumbfounded by what the man said and curious to know where they'd moved the market place. When he was a boy, worshipers could purchase sacrificial animals across the Kidron on the western slope of the Mount of Olives, but certainly not in the Temple itself.

Suddenly, he remembered his conversation with Omar. His Idumean friend had warned him about the Bazaar of Annas, telling him that it had been set up in the Court of the Gentiles. The shepherd didn't want to believe it and had subconsciously put it out of his mind. His heart sank as he anticipated what he would see once they entered the court.

"Sir," Josiah said, momentarily interrupting the inspector's conversation with the next in line, "Where might I dispose of my animals?"

The man pointed across the road to a fenced-in area. The pen was full of livestock, many of which looked perfectly fine. A vendor stood outside the enclosure, and Josiah approached him with his rams and goats. Isaac was curious and accompanied his father.

"How much for my rams and goats?" He asked.

When the vendor declared his price, Isaac became infuriated again. He offered them less than half what they were worth. Josiah didn't think he heard the man correctly, so he repeated what he thought the man said.

"That's right. That's the price. You can take it or leave it, but that's the price set by the high priest."

"The high priest?" Josiah responded in astonishment.

"Yes...yes, the high priest, well the former high priest. This is the part of the Bazaar of Annas that's outside the Temple. These animals are not deemed fit to take into the holy Temple."

Isaac couldn't believe what he was hearing and was shocked when his father agreed to the deal.

"Father, they're worth at least twice that much," he protested.

"I know, Son, but we don't have use for them now."

He knew his eldest was exceedingly troubled and tried to calm his soul, "Isaac, let's not let others spoil our worship of God."

The young man was not satisfied, but obeyed his father. He was insulted by the way their animals were treated. Secretly, Josiah felt the same way, but he was determined to let nothing hinder his worship of God, not even being cheated by the former high priest.

Deborah had a puzzled look on her face when the three of them returned to the rest of the family.

"Where are the animals for sacrifice?" She asked.

"They were rejected," Isaac retorted bitterly.

"What?!" Deborah asked in astonishment, stunned by the news.

She knew her husband and son had painstakingly chosen the very best of their flock and that the flock of the Shepherd of Kedar was renowned for its prized animals. She realized they were being defrauded, but sensing her son's anger she understood it was best to say nothing else.

"Isaac, we need to put it behind us," his father said rather sternly, struggling to cover his own frustration.

His oldest son nodded his head and returned to his wife. Josiah led them up a magnificent stairway, three-stories high, to the triple doors of the eastern Huldah gate. Once they entered the gate they followed a long tunnel that sloped upward before finally arriving at another flight of stairs. After climbing the stairs they emerged into the Court of the Gentiles.

Michael looked behind him and marveled at the four rows of monolithic Corinthian pillars, made of marble, each towering in height. This was the Royal Portico and a magnificent sight. To the East he saw a portico called Solomon's Porch. Straight ahead, he could see the inner courts of the Temple rising high into the sky, made of carved white marble, ornamented with gold on the front and sides. Nothing could be more beautiful.

While he was taking in the sights, his father was disgusted by the spectacle in front of him. It looked nothing like it had when he was a boy. He now understood what Omar was talking about. In the Court of the Gentiles, intended by God to provide a place where even Gentiles could pray, he saw the Bazaar of Annas spread out, hindering access to the people entering the Temple. God's house had become an open marketplace.

Priests, dressed in white robes, walked about giving instructions to worshipers. When Josiah made inquiry with one of them about making an offering, the priest asked him what kind of coin he had. The shepherd told him it was Roman currency, which was used for buying and selling all over the world. The priest immediately directed him to go to one of the many tables near the wall to exchange his Roman coin for Tyrian coinage. The priests had declared Roman currency to be an abomination to the Lord; and since the Romans didn't permit the Jews to coin their own money, Tyrian money was the approved currency in all monetary transactions in the Temple. This was a strange concession, because the Tyrian shekel had the image of the pagan god Melqarth-Herakles engraved on it. Nevertheless, the Jews hated the Romans more than the Tyrians and ironically tolerated a pagan image in the Temple courts, while piously rejecting the image of Caesar. Josiah was about to learn that the true motive was greed.

The shepherd was fully knowledgeable of all kinds of currencies and their different denominations, having bartered with traders from all over the world. He intended to pay the Temple tax for himself according to the Law of Moses for every year since his twentieth birthday. In addition, he had decided on a substantial sum to present as a freewill offering to the Lord. Deborah also wanted to honor the Lord and had entrusted some coins to her husband that she wished to contribute from her earnings in Kedar.

Isaac accompanied his father to one of the moneychanger's tables. The man behind the table raised his eyebrow at the size of Josiah's offering, but both father and son immediately knew something was amiss when the transaction was made. The rate of exchange was grossly skewed against the worshiper.

Isaac started to protest, but again his father silenced him. He took what was offered and headed back to his wife. When he explained the rate of exchange to her, she was shocked as well and felt cheated.

"We must remember, we're giving it to the Lord," Josiah said, though the tone of his voice betrayed his uncertainty.

It was Isaac who reminded his father of words he'd often repeated to his sons while engaged in trading, *"Ye shall do no unrighteousness in judgment, in meteyard, in weight, or in measure. Just balances, just weights, a just ephah, and a just hin, shall ye have: I am the LORD your God, which brought you out of the land of Egypt."*

"I know, my son," he said in resignation. "They will have to answer to God, but my conscience is clear before Him."

"Not only do they cheat the worshipers with their moneychangers. They're also cheating God Himself out of the full value of the offerings," Isaac declared to his father.

"Your son is perceptive," Josiah heard a familiar voice say from behind him.

A big smile crossed his face when he looked to see it was Zacharias, his friend from Elath. The two men embraced in the middle of the court. It didn't take long for his wife, Zipporah, to find Deborah, and the reunion was sweet. Deborah looked over and saw Joseph embrace Martha. She couldn't blame them for being excited to see each other but was aware of proper decorum in public places. A little frown was all it took for them to put a more respectable distance between them. It would have been different had they met outside the Temple, but Deborah wanted them to show respect to God. Though they were in love, they were not yet husband and wife. Still, she could see the joy in her daughter's eyes, though her smile was hidden behind her veil.

It was the good rabbi who spoke first, "You were so excited about visiting the Temple when you were at my house in Elath that I didn't want to spoil it for you. I knew things would not be the same as they were when you were a boy. There is much corruption in Jerusalem and it extends to high places. Annas and Caiaphas have lined their pockets at the expense of God's people, but you and Isaac are right. They must answer to God for their indiscretions."

As they started to make their way in between the pens and cages toward the Beautiful Gate, Zacharias said, "Annas lives in a virtual palace on the Mount of Olives, and Caiaphas' extravagant house is across the valley in the wealthy Upper-City on Mount Zion. Things are not as they should be, but it is what it is."

Josiah was so thrilled to see his friend he almost forgot to purchase animals to sacrifice. It was Michael who reminded him. Fearing he would only become more frustrated over the price, Isaac decided not to accompany his father; so Michael and Simon assisted him. Josiah simply paid the price without comment, though he couldn't help but be troubled by it. The asking price for sacrificial animals was four times their market value.

Annas and Caiaphas had found ways to bilk the worshipers of God in every way. Their inspectors rejected perfectly good animals, which forced the people to sell them outside the gate at a price far below market. Again, they cheated the people by inflating the currency exchange, and then charged them overinflated prices for the animals they had to purchase to offer their sacrifices to God. The people had no choice but to comply. The law required them to make sacrifices.

Josiah hid his anger but felt it. What Annas had turned the Temple into was nothing short of an abomination. It was not the Babylonian pagans who desecrated the Temple, or Antiochus Epiphanies during the time of the Maccabees. This time, it was the high priest himself, the one standing in the heritage of Aaron, Moses' brother.

Putting these disturbing thoughts behind him, he followed Zacharias' lead to the Beautiful Gate. The gate was made of Corinthian brass and shined in the sun like gold. As they got closer to the gate, Michael noticed a beautiful ornate short rock balustrade between them and the wall to the Temple courts. This was called the *Soreg*. Set periodically along the *Soreg* were signs engraved with a message, some in Hebrew but most of them in Greek and Latin.

They paused long enough for Josiah to read one of the signs aloud that happened to be in Greek. When he finished Haifa was perplexed. She'd quickly picked up Hebrew since joining the family, but had never been exposed to Greek, so Isaac translated it for her into Arabic.

"No foreigner is to enter the barriers surrounding the sanctuary. He who is caught will have himself to blame for his death which will follow."

Josiah was mindful of what was going on and saw the trepidation in her eyes.

He gently took her arm and said, "Haifa, you are my daughter and a daughter of Zion. When you professed faith in the Lord as your God and married my son, you became one of us. You are most welcome by God in His House."

She smiled and glanced heavenward in a gesture of thanksgiving. Once again, she was overwhelmed by the grace of God that would snatch her in His mercy from paganism in Dumat and now bring her to His House in Jerusalem. Deborah put her arm around her daughter-in-law to lead her through the *Soreg* and the Beautiful Gate into the Court of the Women.

They climbed the stairs, ascending into the court. It was called the Court of the Women because this was as far as the women could advance in the Temple. Above the colonnades were galleries the women and children could use while the men went into the Court of Israel to make their sacrifices. Near the pillars of the colonnades were thirteen trumpet-shaped tills for the worshipers to deposit their offerings. Deborah had retrieved hers from her husband when he returned from the moneychangers. She immediately went to one of the tills to make her offering.

As she knelt she prayed, "Dear God, thank You for all of Your many blessings, for a godly husband who loves me and provides for our tent, for twelve wonderful children of Your covenant, and for the grandchild Haifa is carrying. Thank You for delivering us safely from Kedar to Your House. Now, receive this offering that I make joyfully to You. You've blessed my hands so that I can help provide for our tent. I gladly give this tithe of my earnings to You. *Amen.*"

She rose to her feet and cheerfully placed her offering in the till.

Josiah watched his wife and remembered that day when he saw the mother of the baby put her offering of five shekels in one of the tills to redeem her son. He looked across the Court of the Women and saw what appeared to be the very bench she was sitting on when he was a boy. Suddenly, that day was vivid in his memories; and he found himself looking for the old man, even though he was certain he'd died. The tender touch of the baby's hand, the mysterious words of the old man, and the look of fear in the woman's eyes – all of these things flooded his memory, as he re-lived that day.

"Josiah," he heard his wife say softly as she touched his arm. "It's time to present your offering."

Regaining his composure, the shepherd approached the first till, designated for the Temple tax. He placed eleven shekels into the till, one for every two years since he turned twenty-years old. The tax of a half-shekel per year was required by God's law. He then moved to the last of the tills, designated for free-will offerings, and looked around to see if anyone was watching. He didn't want to be seen making the offering. The size of the gift was large, a full ten percent of all of his assets from the sale of his flock. When the priest near him moved to assist someone else, he slipped the bag of coins into the till, insuring they made no noise, and then quickly rejoined his family before the priest returned. His wife watched him the whole time, admiring her husband's humility. Some worshipers made a great demonstration of their offerings for the eyes of men, but not the Shepherd of Kedar.

Zacharias introduced him to a particular priest.

"This is my dear friend, Nahor," he said to Josiah. "He's a priest who honors the Lord and will be glad to assist you. Serving the Lord and His people is his joy."

Nahor was very helpful, giving Josiah some hope that things weren't as bad as they seemed. It was clear he was a godly man and led Josiah, along with Isaac, Michael and Simon, up the staircase to the Nicanor Gate. As always, Michael took it all in, while his brothers took care of the animals.

The gate was magnificent, and even larger than the Beautiful Gate standing sixty feet wide and seventy-five feet tall. It was made of Corinthian bronze by a Jew named Nicanor who'd lived in Alexandria, Egypt. Josiah remembered the fanciful tale his father had told him about the great doors of the gate and the trip to Israel by sea. The ship wrecked in a storm. According to the legend, God miraculously saved both Nicanor and the mighty doors. It was believed by many that he presented them to Herod near the time the king began his massive renovations of the Temple.

Josiah presented Nahor with the grain offering and then listened carefully as he gave instructions to them about how to proceed with the sacrifice. First, they laid hands on the animals before killing each of them in turn before God just inside the gate. Isaac in particular was moved as he placed his hands between the horns of the ram he was sacrificing as a trespass offering. The imputation of his sin to the animal, and God's grace to him in forgiveness overwhelmed him. He began to weep.

Nahor put his hand upon his shoulder and said, "God is merciful to sinners."

Isaac looked heavenward in thanks to God, just as his wife had done while passing through the gate of the *Soreg*.

Making the sacrifices was a bloody ordeal, but commanded by God. Nahor captured the blood from each animal in order to apply it to the altar in the manner prescribed for each sacrifice. The four of them skinned and butchered the animals under the careful tutelage of the priest. The whole burnt offerings would be entirely consumed on the altar; the trespass offering made by Isaac would be consumed by the priests, and the peace offerings would be shared by the priests and Josiah's family according to the provisions of the law. They watched in awe as Nahor poured and sprinkled the blood on the altar. The four of them worshiped God in reverence, bowing before His holiness, basking in His grace.

After the sacrifices were made, Nahor brought them their portion of the peace offerings. Before the godly priest left to assist another worshiper, Josiah felt compelled to bless his new friend and God's servant.

He embraced him and whispered in his ear the opening words of the last of the Songs of Ascents, *"Behold, bless ye the LORD, all ye servants of the LORD, which by night stand in the house of the LORD. Lift up your hands in the sanctuary, and bless the LORD."*

As Josiah stepped away from his friend, Nahor, the priest, lifted his hands and cried out in benediction by finishing the recitation, *"The LORD that made heaven and earth bless thee out of Zion."*

Josiah received the blessing with gladness and exited the gate to return to his wife and the others. Deborah could see the awe on his face and secretly wished she could have gone with them, but it wasn't permitted in the law. They waited a few minutes until Zacharias and Joseph came out of the Court of Israel and then prepared to head back to Bethlehem. The law required them to eat all the remaining meat of the peace offerings that day.

The shepherd was struck by the contrast between what took place inside the Temple proper and what was going on in the outer court. Once again, his heart was troubled by what he saw. What Annas and Caiaphas were doing was terribly wrong. He watched other frustrated worshipers trying to deal with the injustice just so they could worship God. The Court of the Gentiles was crowded and people struggled to move about. A part of him wanted to do something about it, but what could he do? What could anyone do?

With mixed emotions they headed out of the Temple through the double-door Huldah Gate on the western side of the southern wall. As they began to descend the massive steps, they all suddenly stopped when they heard a great crowd singing. They couldn't see anyone yet, as the procession was coming down the road outside the western wall. The closer the singers came, the clearer they could be heard.

Josiah recognized their words. They were singing the last psalm of the *Hallel*, *"Blessed be He that cometh in the name of the LORD!"*

The shepherd looked at his dear friend, the rabbi. Their expressions communicated what both of them were thinking:

'Of whom are they singing? Could it be…? Could it possibly be…?'

Zacharias smiled and nodded his head at Josiah before saying, "It must be Him!"

CHAPTER 7

Cleansing His Father's House

Psalm 69:9

The zeal of Thine house hath eaten Me up!

The sound of singing grew nearer, interspersed with shouts of "Hosanna!" The shepherd and his family were standing on the staircase leading down from the double-doors of the Huldah gate. Josiah and Zacharias instinctively moved nearer to each other. Deborah put her arm around her husband in anticipation as the throng drew closer and closer.

Finally, they saw the first of the crowd round the corner. Some of them were running in the front, waving palm branches in the air. Josiah searched through the emerging multitude for Jesus, and then he saw Him. He was neither on foot nor riding upon a great horse. He had the appearance of a humble man, riding on the foal of a donkey, the jenny in tow.

It was Zacharias who spoke with a trembling voice as soon as he saw Him, reminding Josiah of Zechariah's prophecy, *"Rejoice greatly, O daughter of Zion; shout, O daughter of Jerusalem: behold, thy King cometh unto thee: He is just, and having salvation; lowly, and riding upon a donkey, and upon a colt the foal of a donkey.'* This Word is being fulfilled before our very eyes!"

The shepherd was in awe and unable to speak. All he could do was nod his head.

They expected the crowd to move past the foot of the staircase below and proceed to the triple-doors of the other Huldah gate, since the double-gate was being used as an exit on that day. Instead, Jesus stopped below them. He dismounted the colt, as the crowd grew quiet, except for some of the children who continued to sing. Everyone was waiting to see what He would do next.

To Josiah's surprise, He started climbing the steps toward him. Several men crowded around, seeking to shield Him, but He pressed ahead of them picking up the pace as He climbed toward the gate. Suddenly, two Levites came running down the steps past Josiah. It was clear they were agitated.

When they got to Jesus one of them said tersely, "This is the exit. You must enter at the other gate."

Jesus stopped and turned, looking at the throng behind him.

He took one more step forward causing the Levite to protest again, "I told you that you can't enter this gate!"

Jesus paused momentarily before responding, "Look at the people. There are so many, it is better for them to enter this gate because of the staircase."

Josiah glanced down below and noticed for the first time that the staircase to this gate was much wider than the one he'd climbed to enter the Temple that morning. In fact, the staircase in front of the triple-gate was only fifty feet wide, while the one leading to the double-gate was over two hundred feet wide. He realized that Jesus was thinking of the safety of the crowd. The Levite didn't know what to say and followed Jesus as He climbed the stairs.

When Jesus drew near Josiah, He looked into his eyes, though He didn't speak a word. Suddenly, Josiah felt overwhelmed. He knew that he was in the presence of the Holy One. It seemed like Jesus could see deeply into his soul. If the Teacher's eyes weren't so full of love, Josiah would have dropped his head in shame. It was as if Jesus knew everything about him, even his darkest secrets; and yet the shepherd felt fully accepted by Him. He knew instantly that Jesus was merciful.

A strange hush overcame the crowd, even the children, until little Naomi unexpectedly broke the silence. She loved to sing, especially the psalms, and in child-like faith began to sing and repeat the things she'd heard from the multitude.

"Hosanna!" She shouted, and then she sang a line from one of her favorite psalms, *"Blessed be He that cometh in the name of the LORD!"*

The Levite, who'd previously tried to get Jesus to use the other gate, quickly tried to hush her; but she wouldn't stop singing the psalm to Jesus, *"Save now, I beseech Thee, O LORD: O LORD, I beseech Thee, send now prosperity. Blessed be He that cometh in the name of the LORD!"*

"Teacher, silence the girl!" The Levite shouted at Him.

Instead, Jesus ignored him, reached down and picked her up. Both Josiah and Deborah felt secure with their youngest child in His arms. He looked at her, smiled and whispered something in her ear.

Neither Josiah nor Deborah could hear what He said, but His words caused Naomi's face to light up with a big smile. He kissed her forehead and placed her in her mother's arms, before quickly heading up the remaining steps.

"What did He say?" Deborah asked.

Naomi's eyes were shining when she replied, "He whispered to me, 'I've got a secret for you. If you don't sing, the stones will immediately cry out.' Mommy, I don't want the stones to sing for me."

Deborah responded as she hugged her child, "You can sing to Jesus as much as you like."

At that moment, Josiah and Zacharias realized that the crowd was moving past them. Desperately wanting to see what Jesus was going to do, they led their families back up the steps toward the gate.

Josiah had just entered the gate, when he heard a loud crashing sound. Tables were being hurled through the air and coins were bouncing off of the wall and rolling across the marble floor. Somehow, Josiah, Isaac and Michael were able to maneuver through the crowd so they could see Jesus. His tender countenance when He spoke to Naomi had now changed into one of unmitigated fury.

Rushing through the Court of the Gentiles, He knocked over cages and opened the doors of the pens holding the sacrificial animals. Doves and pigeons filled the air, while bulls, sheep and goats stampeded through the court. The vendors who sold them ran from the Temple in abject terror.

Suddenly, He cried out in a loud voice to those who were fleeing, "Is it not written, *'My house shall be called of all nations the house of prayer? But ye have made it a den of thieves!'"*

Zacharias hurried to Josiah's side in the midst of the chaos and whispered in his ear the words of a psalm of David, *"The zeal of Thine house hath eaten Me up!'* Josiah, David spoke of Him. David spoke of this moment!"

The shepherd nodded his head, realizing he'd just witnessed the fulfillment of prophecy and an act of righteousness. He felt a sense of shame at his own lack of zeal. He'd seen everything Jesus saw when he entered the Temple that morning. The sight of the moneychangers and vendors had sickened him. His son was justly angry at the injustice perpetrated by the High Priest against those gathered to worship, yet Josiah had done nothing about it. It made him admire Jesus all the more for what He'd done. He looked at Isaac and saw vindication in his eyes, while Michael's were wide open with wonder.

Priests and Levites came running at the commotion, but quickly became silent, for fear of the people who were following Jesus. Josiah was amazed, for as soon as the Temple was purged, Jesus calmly sat down. He was in control of God's House, not the priests. Then the people began to bring the blind and the lame to Him.

Josiah was desperate to see, remembering the stories he'd heard from both Nathan and Sarah about Jesus healing the sick. As he worked his way through the crowd his family followed him. He gasped when he saw Jesus heal a blind man with just the touch of His hand. Next, two men carried a boy to Him who was paralyzed from the waist down.

Jesus looked at the boy and simply said, "Rise up and walk."

Gingerly, the boy stood on his legs and began to walk around. Soon, he was skipping about and praising God. Josiah looked at Jesus and saw a big smile on His face. It was evident that He loved them all, all of those weak and infirmed. One by one, He healed each and every one of them, sending them to the priests for confirmation.

Zacharias had managed to move alongside of the shepherd. He'd heard tales of such things, but couldn't believe what he was seeing with his own eyes.

"Truly, He must be the Messiah," he whispered to his friend, and Josiah could only smile in return with tears of joy in his eyes.

Though Josiah and Zacharias were overwhelmed with awe, some in the crowd realized that the chief priests and scribes were among them. They knew of the power of the High Priest and still feared him. They'd watched Jesus heal those who came to Him, but they dared not sing His praises in the Temple, for fear of the priests.

Naomi was encouraged by her earlier encounter with Jesus and wasn't afraid. Her father had taught her many of the psalms by heart, and one of her favorites was a psalm about Messiah.

With great joy she started to sing once again, *"My heart is overflowing with a good matter: I speak of the things which I have made touching the King: my tongue is the pen of a ready writer."*

Knowing not the fear of their parents, many other children responded to her antiphonally, *"Thou art fairer than the children of men: grace is poured into Thy lips: therefore God hath blessed Thee forever."*

Then Naomi returned to the shout from the procession, *"Hosanna to the Son of David!"*

To which the other children responded, *"Blessed be He that cometh in the name of the LORD! Blessed be the kingdom of our father David, that cometh in the name of the Lord: Hosanna in the highest!"*

And then Naomi declared, *"Hosanna in the highest!"*

The chief priests couldn't take anymore, and even though they'd seen the miracles with their own eyes, they were incensed.

Along with some of the scribes they cried out to Jesus, "Do you hear what they are saying?"

Jesus looked up at them and said confidently, "Yes, I hear them, but have you never read, *'Out of the mouth of babes and sucklings Thou hast perfected praise?'"*

The chief priests were irate, but were afraid to say anything else. Jesus looked at Naomi and smiled, before nodding His head at her father. Then He got up and departed the Temple.

As soon as He was gone, the boldness of the priests reappeared. They started barking orders to the people, and the Levites began to clean up the clutter left in His wake.

Josiah and Zacharias were also about to leave when they heard someone say, "It's the High Priest."

They turned to see a stately man dressed in his "golden garments," as his daily attire was called. He wore a golden crown on his head. Though adorned for holiness, the look on his face was one of utter indignation. Another priest of stature accompanied him. Josiah thought it must surely be the Captain of the Temple, the chief priest who was second only to the High Priest in power and influence.

A hush fell over the crowd at the sight of them. Rather than instill a sense of God's grace and peace, the presence of both men incited fear in the hearts of the multitude. It seemed everyone was aware of the corruption that had befallen the priesthood.

They stopped nearby Josiah and Zacharias while looking over the rubble left by Jesus.

"He must die!" The Captain of the Temple whispered to Caiaphas, but loud enough for Josiah and Zacharias to hear.

The High Priest turned to him and said, "Make all the necessary arrangements."

After that the two men departed, neither Josiah nor Zacharias knew what arrangements he meant. They only knew that they intended harm to Jesus. A sense of foreboding momentarily overwhelmed the shepherd.

As soon as the High Priest left the Court of the Gentiles Zacharias whispered to Josiah, "The prophecy of the old man is certainly coming true. Jesus is a sign that is spoken against, and will cause the rise and fall of many in Israel."

The shepherd nodded his head, but suddenly felt confident that Jesus would be victorious over His enemies. He'd already demonstrated His authority over God's House, and God's favor surely rested upon Him, else He couldn't work such remarkable miracles. He may have enemies in high places, but Josiah knew beyond a shadow of a doubt that God was on His side.

"Jesus will prevail," he said to the rabbi. "He must prevail."

Zacharias agreed. Both men were caught up in the moment, and not even the dire words of the High Priest could squelch their enthusiasm.

"He's no longer here, so we might as well go," Zacharias said to his friend.

Realizing that he was right, Josiah called his family around him. We're going to go back to Bethlehem. Ephraim will want to hear about what happened today.

"I love Jesus," Naomi said giggling.

"I can tell He loves you too," her father responded.

Just as they started to leave, he heard someone call his name from across the court. He looked up and saw Nathaniel coming toward him with Elizabeth and their children. All of them were with him except for Miriam, who'd stayed in Bethlehem to care for Ephraim.

"What happened?" Nathaniel asked looking all around the court.

"Jesus was here," Josiah replied.

Nathaniel's eyes lit up as he exclaimed, "He was. Did you see him?"

Naomi interrupted in a way she probably shouldn't have, but she couldn't seem to help herself.

"He picked me up and told me a secret."

"What secret?" Her cousin, Joanna, asked.

She looked at her mother for permission to tell.

Deborah smiled and nodded her head before saying, "I don't think Jesus meant for you to keep it a secret."

Naomi, ever the bright-eyed little girl exclaimed, "He told me that if I stopped singing to Him, then the stones would immediately cry out."

"You sang to Jesus?" Joanna asked, her eyes opening really wide.

"Um Hum, I sang a psalm to Him on the steps and then another one in the Temple."

"You sang to Him twice?" Her cousin asked in disbelief.

"Mommy said I can sing to Him anytime I want."

"Could I sing to Him too?" Joanna asked with a hopeful look on her face.

Naomi hugged her cousin and said, "Jesus likes it when all the children sing to Him. I hope you get to soon."

Nathaniel was still perplexed as he looked around the Temple.

"Who did this?" He asked.

"Jesus did it all," Michael responded before his father could speak. "He knocked over the moneychangers tables, and let out all of the sacrificial animals, and then drove the vendors out of the Temple."

"Why?" Nathaniel asked, clearly still confounded.

It was Josiah who answered him this time.

"I'll never forget the look in His eyes nor the words that He said. He cried out with a loud voice, *'My house shall be called of all nations the house of prayer? But ye have made it a den of thieves!'*"

"He said that?!" Nathaniel responded with his eyes wide open.

"He said it, and He meant it," Michael replied. "And then after He drove them out of the Temple He healed the sick. We saw a man who was blind healed…"

"And a little boy was lame and He made him walk. He was jumping around the court, praising God," Simon interjected.

Nathaniel couldn't believe he missed it.

"I should have been here earlier," he said in a voice of disappointment.

"I'm sure He'll be back," Josiah said to his cousin. "He'll be back, and we will be here to see it. It's time for Him to restore the kingdom to Israel. Soon, He will take His rightful place on Mount Zion."

"Do you really believe He's the one?" Nathaniel asked.

"Yes, I have no doubt that He's the one we've been waiting for," Josiah said almost in a whisper.

Elizabeth and Deborah hugged each other. It was a glorious day.

During the conversation between Josiah and Nathaniel, Zacharias and Zipporah stood by silently. Josiah suddenly realized he'd been rude and quickly introduced them to his cousins. They greeted each other as brothers and sisters, and then Elizabeth looked over and saw Joseph standing close to Martha.

She smiled at him and said, "You must be Joseph."

He had a sheepish grin on his face and nodded his head, knowing that Martha must have been talking about him. She couldn't stop smiling either. Not only had she seen Jesus; her Joseph was with her, and she was determined never to let him go again. The young man felt the same way and asked her father if he could go to Bethlehem with them. When both Josiah and Zacharias gave their approval, Martha could not have been happier.

Haifa stayed close to Isaac. She'd said nothing, but had taken it all in. Her heart was full, knowing the grace of God. She couldn't believe that she was able to worship Him at His Temple. She was still overwhelmed by the demonstration of God's grace to her and longed to return to Dumat to tell her family the good news about Jesus.

Josiah couldn't wait to see the smile on Ephraim's face, when they told him about what had happened. So, they headed out the Huldah gate, down the long staircase and on to Bethlehem.

CHAPTER 8

Laughter

Genesis 21:6

God hath made me to laugh.

If a blind man's eyes could shine with laughter, Ephraim's did. He listened carefully to the stories of what Josiah and his family had witnessed at the Temple. Everyone was so excited. They each offered their own input, sometimes talking at the same time. He had to slow them down at times, but cherished each word.

Though usually content with his blindness, once in a while he wished he still had his sight. This was such an occasion. He would have loved to have seen Jesus; but more than anything, he longed to see the looks on the children's faces as they excitedly told him everything that happened.

Josiah was happy to let the younger children talk, though Michael and Simon both had their say. When Naomi told everybody about her little secret with Jesus, Ephraim leaned his head backward and literally chortled, tears from his laughter streaming down his face.

"I don't guess it's a secret anymore!" He cried out, roaring with glee.

He couldn't remember when he'd last laughed so heartily, but the emotion came from a place deep within him. This was a day for which he'd waited so long, a day when the Messiah would enter the city in fulfillment of Zechariah's prophecy. In his joy he couldn't contain his laughter.

Ephraim was amused by Naomi's tale of the frantic priests who tried to stop her from singing and felt a sense of satisfaction when he learned how Jesus cleansed the Temple with righteous indignation. How he would have loved to have seen that with his own eyes, eyes now darkened by age.

Instead, he closed them to imagine what it must have looked like as they described it. Only he knew it wasn't the first time.

Once they were exhausted from telling their tales, he motioned for them to be silent.

"It must have been wonderful to see Jesus cleansing the Temple, but there is something you should know," he said, awaking their curiosity.

"This wasn't the first time He did it," he said softly.

Everyone in the room had baffled looks on their faces.

"Did what?" Josiah asked.

"Cleansed the Temple," the old man replied. "Have you ever wondered what it was that convinced my son to become a disciple of Jesus?"

Josiah had, but never thought to ask.

"Three years ago, when Jesus was just beginning His ministry, He did the very same thing. It was Passover. When He saw the money changers tables and the sacrificial animals for sale, He made a whip of cords and drove them out of the Temple, shouting, *'Take these things hence; make not My Father's house an house of merchandise!*

"He used a whip?" Michael asked in astonishment.

"Samuel was there," he said, nodding his head. He saw it. From that day forward he has been a disciple of Jesus."

Everyone was amazed at what Ephraim told them.

Then he smiled broadly and called Miriam to him. He asked her to retrieve one of his scrolls and Michael to assist her.

The young man secretly enjoyed spending the moment alone with her, even though there was no way he could tell her how he really felt. He couldn't keep from looking at her as she searched through Ephraim's collection until she found the scroll of Genesis.

"Here it is," she said as she held it up.

Michael smiled, hoping she hadn't sensed him staring at her. His heart was conflicted. Seeing her again had reawakened all of his feelings for her, yet he was helpless to do anything but be her friend. He knew she must still be heartbroken over Isaac.

"Are you ready to go?" She asked.

"Y…yes," he stammered before following her back into the main room.

She placed the scroll in front of Ephraim, and Michael helped him find the place he designated. As was his habit, he let his fingers roam over the parchment as he remembered the words. In his mind he was reading them to refresh his memory before teaching.

Then he sat up straight and said, "In Genesis there was an old woman and an older man. You all know who they were. The man's name was Abraham. What was his wife's name?"

Simon, who was becoming more outspoken everyday answered, "Her name was Sarai until God told him to change her name to Sarah."

"Yes…yes," the old man responded.

Ephraim was silent for the few moments before he said resolutely, "Now, I want to tell you about the day 'Laughter' was born."

Had the old man been able to see, he would have noticed the confusion on the children's faces, as they tried to think about when laughter was born. He perceived their silence and figured he had them stumped.

"Isaac, you should know what I'm referring to," he said.

Josiah's eldest had a bewildered look on his face for a moment before his eyes widened in recognition.

"You must be speaking of the birth of Isaac," he declared.

"You are correct. You're named after that Isaac, and your name means 'laughter' or more precisely 'he laughs.' Now, there are different kinds of laughter. There is the laughter of amusement, often trite and shallow, sometimes the product of too much wine."

When he said that he lifted his cup; it was a night to celebrate after all.

"Then there is the laughter of derision, such as in the second psalm, when God looks down from heaven upon the vanity of men and scoffs at them in His laughter. In the story of God's dealing with Abraham and Sarah, there are two other kinds of laughter. The first is the laughter of unbelief, but the second is the laughter of true joy when God's faithfulness is displayed. Does anyone remember the first occasion of the laughter of unbelief?"

Naomi was quick to respond, but as often happened when she blurted out the first thing that came to her mind, she was not quite correct.

"It was when Sarah laughed from inside the tent," she declared confidently.

Not wanting her to feel too bad, he corrected her gently in an affirming manner, "Actually, that was the second occasion; but you are right, it is an example of the laughter of unbelief. Can anyone help Naomi out?"

Joanna was usually much quieter that her younger cousin but had a ready answer.

Speaking more circumspectly she said, "Sir, didn't Abraham laugh first?"

"Yes, Joanna, you are absolutely right, and I think Naomi would have come up with the right answer had we given her a moment to think about it."

The way he handled it made both girls smile.

"First, Abraham and then his wife sinned against God by doubting His promise. Even though both of them were old, God told them that she would conceive and bear a son."

"Didn't Sarah tell a lie and deny that she'd laughed?" Simon asked, becoming more and more the inquisitive one.

"Yes, she did and Abraham rebuked her for it. She shouldn't have laughed, but neither should she have lied when confronted about it."

He paused for a moment to let them think about what he'd said before proceeding, "A wonderful thing about our God is that He forgives our sins and keeps His promises. Now, can anyone give me an example of the laughter born of true joy when God manifests His faithfulness?"

It seemed that Michael always got to answer the more substantive questions; but then again, he was usually thinking more deeply.

"If I recall correctly, after Isaac was born, Sarah said, *'God hath made me to laugh.'*"

"Michael, you know the Scriptures well," their teacher said. "Not only did she say, *'God hath made me to laugh,'* but she added further, *'So that all that hear will laugh with me.'* Tonight, we laugh with Sarah."

The children were still confused. They remembered what they'd learned about Rachel and how she'd wept. They even understood weeping with her when they heard about how Herod killed the babies in Bethlehem, but they did not understand how their gaiety that night was connected to Sarah's laughter.

Ephraim was wise and recognized their silence as puzzlement.

"Do you want to know what all of this has to do with what happened today, and why I laugh tonight?"

"Yes! Tell us!" They answered enthusiastically in unison.

"The birth of 'Laughter' was miraculous. An old woman, barren her whole life, conceived and gave birth to a son. Remember that miracle, because I have another one to tell you about; but first, there is something important I have to say."

He paused to collect himself before continuing, "Isaac's birth was not the first birth to a promise. Another baby was promised long before Abraham, Sarah and Isaac. Does anyone know what baby I'm referring to?"

No one seemed to know. Even Josiah wasn't sure. Ephraim knew he had their undivided attention.

"In the first instance, the promise wasn't made to either a man or a woman, at least not directly."

Still, all of them were baffled and remained silent.

"The first promise that a woman would bear a special child was made in the Garden of Eden to the serpent."

He opened his eyes wide and raised his voice when he spoke the word, 'serpent,' causing the younger ones to shiver.

Josiah nodded his head and caught Michael's eye. Both of them remembered an occasion when Zacharias spoke of this passage at the Dead Sea.

Ephraim continued, "God said to the serpent, *'And I will put enmity between thee and the woman, and between thy seed and her seed; He shall bruise thy head, and thou shalt bruise His heel.'*"

He paused after quoting the passage to let the words resonate in their minds before continuing.

"Children hear me. Note the final clause: *'He shall bruise thy head, and thou shalt bruise His heel.'* Of whom was God speaking?"

No one tried to answer, instead preferring to let their teacher tell them.

"God promised that a particular son would be born, who would bruise the serpent's head. Do you understand the meaning? It's the most important promise in the Scriptures. The promised child would come to destroy the works of the devil."

Josiah was enthralled by the teaching and could already anticipate where he was going with it.

"Why do you think God instituted circumcision as the sign of the covenant?" He asked.

It seemed to those listening to be a question far afield from what he was discussing, because the promise was given to the serpent and indirectly to Adam and Eve in the garden, while circumcision wasn't introduced until the time of Abraham.

"Bear with me," Ephraim said, sensing their confusion. "I ask you again – why circumcision?"

The silence in the house was conspicuous. No one dared offer an answer.

"Listen, even you little ones. This is important. Remember, it was God who chose the sign. Circumcision is the cutting away of the flesh at the place of the issue of the seed of man. It is a cleansing to carry the promised seed through the line of Eve until such a time when that seed would become one seed, one child, one man, one Messiah. His work will destroy the work of the devil. Whenever a faithful Jewish woman is with child, deep in her heart she wonders if she might be carrying the one who would be that seed."

Realizing she was now a member of God's covenant people, Haifa instinctively touched her belly when she heard his words. Isaac saw the gesture and smiled pulling his wife close to him.

Michael looked at his father in amazement, but immediately returned his attention to the patriarch of their family.

"I'm going to tell you a story, a wonderful story. You already know some of it, but I'm going to tell you things you've never heard. Remember, I said earlier that I would tell you about another miracle? Actually, it's about another miraculous birth. I learned of this from my son, Samuel. As you know, he has been in Galilee with Jesus. The last time he visited, he told me something truly remarkable."

A big smile brightened his face as he remembered that day. He missed his son, but knew he was where he was supposed to be.

"Samuel heard some rumors about Jesus that were being circulated by those who oppose Him. It was said that He was not of legitimate birth, that his mother was pregnant before she married her husband. Being concerned about this, my son approached one of Jesus' closest disciples privately. His name is Andrew, and his brother's name is Peter."

Josiah and Deborah looked at one another. They remembered Sarah speaking of Andrew when they were at the inn.

"Andrew took him to meet a woman. Her name is Mary, and yes, she is Jesus' mother. She's the one who told him what happened. At this time, it is a closely guarded secret, but some of Jesus' closest disciples know about it. Can I trust you to keep the secret?"

The children nodded their heads, anxious to hear it. Though he couldn't see them, he knew they were all in agreement.

"Many years ago, Mary was betrothed to a carpenter from Nazareth named Joseph. One night, she was visited by the angel, Gabriel."

Michael's eyes widened in awe. He could hardly believe what he was hearing.

"The angel said to her, *'Fear not, Mary: for thou hast found favour with God. And, behold, thou shalt conceive in thy womb, and bring forth a son, and shalt call His name JESUS. He shall be great, and shall be called the Son of the Highest: and the Lord God shall give unto Him the throne of His father David: and He shall reign over the house of Jacob forever; and of His kingdom there shall be no end.'"*

No one uttered a sound as they listened, astonished by his words.

"Mary was uncertain how these things could be, since she was still unmarried and was a virgin, so she inquired of the angel, *'How shall this be, seeing I know not a man?'"*

"He said to her, *'The Holy Ghost shall come upon thee, and the power of the Highest shall overshadow thee: therefore also that holy thing which shall be born of thee shall be called the Son of God.'"*

"The Son of God!" Michael gasped, "That's what Nathan told us John called Jesus!"

Ephraim nodded his head before saying, "Yes, my son. John's mother was Mary's cousin. Immediately after God did this for Mary, she visited Elizabeth. It was during her sixth month of carrying John in her womb."

Josiah couldn't believe what he was hearing, and asked. "What did the man, did you say his name was Joseph?"

Martha couldn't help but look at her Joseph when she heard the name.

"Yes, it was Joseph," Ephraim replied.

"What did Joseph do when he learned of Mary's pregnancy?" The shepherd asked.

"From what Samuel told me, he was an honorable man, who is now with father Abraham. He sought to put Mary away secretly, because he didn't want her to bear public shame; but an angel appeared to him in a dream and explained to him what God was doing for Mary. He obeyed the voice of the angel and married her."

It was Joseph who spoke up for the first time. He'd sat with Martha quietly the whole time, not thinking it was his place to speak in the midst of Josiah's family, but a passage came to mind he wanted to ask about.

"Sir, my name is Joseph," he said tentatively. "My father is a rabbi in Elath."

"Yes Joseph, I believe I've heard of you from Martha," Ephraim responded with a smile, while Martha blushed.

"Yes sir, you probably have. I remember a passage from Isaiah…"

Before he could go further, Ephraim raised his blind eyes heavenward and declared, *"Behold, a virgin shall conceive, and bear a son, and shall call His name Immanuel."*

"That's the one I had in mind," he responded.

"That is an intriguing passage," Ephraim explained. "In the immediate context it is speaking of a sign to King Ahaz of God's promise to deliver Judah from the alliance between Ephraim and Syria. Of course, Ahaz was a wicked king who doubted God's promise. The prophecy was fulfilled with the birth of the prophet's son, Maher-Shalal-Hash-Baz, but it is clear that this doesn't exhaust the meaning of the prophecy. First, the prophet's wife was not a virgin; and second, Maher-Shalal-Hash-Baz doesn't fulfill the full meaning of the name Immanuel, which means, 'God with us.' Joseph, you are correct. This passage must be speaking of Jesus, the one the angel called the Son of God."

Josiah was beside himself, tears flowing down his cheeks as he considered everything he'd learned on the pilgrimage, and especially the things he'd seen that day. He realized that it must have been Mary and Joseph he saw that day at the Temple when he was a boy. Joy erupted within him as he laughed out loud.

"Praise God! Praise God!" He cried out as he laughed.

The joy was contagious and soon they were all shouting praises to God as the laughter of men, women and children filled the air. It was a day to rejoice. The Messiah had come to Jerusalem, riding on the foal of a donkey. He'd entered in triumph, driving out those who would turn God's House into "a den of thieves," and ignoring the hypocrites who tried to silence those who would worship Him.

When he realized that Jesus actually received the worship of men, even that of his own daughter, the staggering impact of the title given to Him by the angel and then confirmed by John began to set in.

"Jesus is truly the Son of the Living God!" Josiah declared.

"Yes, Jesus is the Son of God!" They all responded.

"Pass the wineskin!" Ephraim directed.

Miriam picked it up and handed it to Dinah who was seated beside her. Dinah poured some into her cup and then passed it on. The wineskin made its way around the table, and when everyone's cup was full, Ephraim stood and lifted his cup high in the air. Everyone followed suit and lifted their cups as well.

"Unto Jesus be praise!" He declared. "Today, Messiah made His way to the top of Moriah to set right the worship of His Father. May the day come soon, when He will rise to the summit of Zion and sit in the King's palace, assuming David's throne, and may His kingdom never end!"

"*Amen…Amen…Amen!*" They all shouted in response.

Laugher suddenly filled the room, nothing could subdue it. Everyone began to hug each other as they contemplated the events of the day. They talked of all the things they were learning. Joy abounded among them. Spontaneously, they began to sing psalms and dance. Merriment born of true joy created celebration.

Michael hugged his father and mother and then sought out his older brother. The smile that wouldn't leave Haifa's face was beautiful. Then, he thought of Miriam and looked around the room for her. He was surprised when she wasn't with Dinah or with her mother. Quietly, he slipped out the back door of the house and found her sitting on her bench.

"The party's inside," Michael said trying to break the ice.

"I know," she responded with a weak smile. "It is an exciting day."

Somehow, her voice didn't have much conviction as she spoke.

Michael was concerned for her and simply said, "Miriam, what's wrong?"

"Nothing," she whispered but she wouldn't meet his eyes.

"Something's bothering you," He prodded gently.

The young woman began to cry. She wasn't sobbing, but he still put his arms around her and pulled her head to his chest.

"Please tell me what's troubling you," he whispered.

Miriam was silent for a few moments, letting him hold her.

"It's just…" she started to say before hesitating.

"Go on…" he said encouraging her, while putting his fingers under her chin to lift her face so he could look into her eyes.

"I shouldn't feel this way…" she said shaking her head.

"What way?" He asked, giving her permission to confide in him.

"I guess I feel a little left out," she replied. "First, well you know what happened with Isaac."

Michael's face fell when she mentioned his brother's name, but he quickly recovered. As her friend it was his duty to comfort her, not add to her confusion.

"Really Michael, I don't resent Haifa at all. She's everything everyone says about her and more. She's lovely and a wonderful woman. I'm truly happy for them."

She spoke quickly for some reason, desperately wanting him to know she had put her relationship with Isaac behind her. Of course, he couldn't know what she was thinking.

"Then, today, everyone got to go to the Temple but me. I wish I could have seen Jesus like you did. I'm not complaining. I love Ephraim. I've never met a man like him before. He's like the grandfather I never had. I just feel left out. I shouldn't feel this way…"

Michael shushed her by saying, "Miriam, there is nothing wrong with what you're feeling. I wish you could have been with us too, but there will be other times to see Jesus. He's only just begun to establish His kingdom."

Once again, he took her into his arms and then started to pray, "Dear God, thank You for Your mercy to us. Thank You for letting us live to see this day. Now, cheer Miriam's heart. She is precious, a wonderful woman and Your servant. Give her laughter, Oh Lord. Fill her heart with joy and give her laughter."

She was touched by his prayer, feeling a bond growing between them.

"I feel so foolish," she confessed. "This is a great day. Ephraim didn't get to go to the Temple either, yet his soul is full of laughter."

She looked into Michael's eyes and was glad he was the one with her. He saw her eyes in the moonlight, shining with joy. A smile appeared at the corners of her mouth as she looked at him. She thought of all of the things she'd heard that night: of Jesus riding into the city, of Him cleansing the Temple, of the moneychangers fleeing in fear, of Naomi leading the children in singing God's praises. She giggled when she thought of her littlest cousin. The giggle deepened, and Michael laughed in response to her. Before they knew it both were laughing hysterically, but it wasn't trite or shallow. It was laughter that arose from joy deeply within.

CHAPTER 9

Authority

Matthew 7:29

For He taught them as one having authority, and not as the scribes.

Early the next morning, long before the break of dawn, Michael and Joseph slipped quietly into the girls' quarters so that Joseph could tell Martha goodbye. The night before the two boys managed to get permission from Josiah to go into Jerusalem for the morning sacrifice. He knew they were hoping to see Jesus again. Michael was so excited he'd gotten very little sleep. Every time he closed his eyes, he saw Jesus, either riding upon the colt or cleansing the Temple. Never in his wildest imagination would he have ever dreamed of the things he saw that day.

Martha awakened with a smile when Joseph gently nudged her, but the smile soon disappeared when she remembered that he was leaving and would be gone all day. It seemed to her that she'd just found him again, and she longed to spend every waking moment with him.

Michael couldn't keep from looking for Miriam among the sleeping girls and expected to find her asleep, but when he saw her in the candlelight she was looking at him. She smiled and waved, which caused his heart to beat a little faster. The young man waved back, resisting the temptation to go to her. When the boys finally left the room, Miriam felt a strange sense of loneliness.

"What does that mean?" She whispered softly to herself.

She closed her eyes and remembered strong, comforting arms surrounding her – not Isaac's, but Michael's. She realized how much he'd grown up since she left Kedar; but then again, he couldn't have grown that much, it had only been a few months. She hadn't really looked at him for a long time. He'd always been the friend she could depend on, but she'd been so wrapped up in Isaac she'd never noticed that his brother had also become a man.

'And a very handsome young man as well,' she thought before suddenly realizing that something special was happening to her.

She recognized the feelings she was developing for Michael, but did he feel the same way? Insecurities troubled her heart. If Isaac didn't want her, what made her think that his brother would? She realized that such thoughts were premature at best and tried to put them out of her mind.

Michael knew how he felt, but realized he needed to give her time to get over what had happened with his brother. Even then, she might not develop the same feelings for him that he had for her. They'd always been close friends, and he was afraid that was how it would remain. He decided that he would be the best friend he could be to her, but deep down he hoped for more.

As he and Joseph left for Jerusalem, he realized he couldn't dwell on Miriam, not now. This was a special time in the lives of God's people. Messiah had come to the Temple, and Michael couldn't wait to see what He was going to do next.

Dinah was also awakened by the boys and watched the silent exchange between Michael and Miriam. Secretly, she smiled, hoping and praying that God would lead them to each other. She closed her eyes and could see Caleb's face. The months that had passed since his death had not erased him from her memory. Her thoughts of him were vivid, though she mourned less than before. She knew that he was better off in heaven, though she would miss him until she could join him there.

The women in both houses woke up shortly after the boys departed. There was much to do to get ready for the feast. By law, they had to partake of the Passover within the walls of Jerusalem. Josiah remembered what it was like when he was a boy. Nothing could compare to the fellowship of over a million people gathered within the city, eating the paschal lambs and singing the *Hallel* from house to house.

Arrangements had already been made for Josiah's family to eat the Passover at Deborah's sister's house in Jerusalem. They would be crowded, but that was the case in every home. Families were not permitted to celebrate the meal alone, but were encouraged to invite the Levites and the needy to participate with them. Each company was required to seat at least ten worshippers, but not more than twenty.

Deborah was busy counting heads. With both of her parents still living, and having twelve children herself, the number was already at sixteen. She'd learned that neither her sister nor her brother had children, which saddened her. With them included that brought the total to twenty. Martha could count as well and was disappointed that Joseph couldn't partake with them. She hinted to her father about eating the meal with Joseph and his family, but the shepherd wouldn't hear of it. He wanted all of his children to celebrate the feast with him.

Josiah was a bit saddened that he couldn't partake with either Nathaniel's family or with Ephraim, but he wasn't too troubled by it. Deborah's sister was able to make provisions for the use of a house next door to hers. Nathaniel and Elizabeth, along with their five daughters, would celebrate there with Ephraim and Samuel. Zacharias, Zipporah and Joseph had decided to eat with them, and the host family added three more, bringing the total to fifteen.

Josiah, Ephraim, and Nathaniel spent the day talking about everything that was happening and pouring over the Scriptures. Josiah wanted Passover to be a night to remember for his family, so he carefully sought insights from Ephraim that he could use when telling the story of the Exodus. All three men searched the Scriptures together for application from the Exodus to the events unfolding before them. They were aware that there were still many things they simply didn't understand, but believed the Messiah would reveal all things as He fulfilled His prophetic office.

Ephraim smiled with joy when Josiah demonstrated from the Scriptures that Messiah would fulfill the threefold office of Prophet, Priest and King. He'd often reflected on the passages the shepherd cited, though this teaching was new to Nathaniel. By that time, Seth had joined them as well, but said little. Deborah's father had always been a man of few words.

As they talked about it, all four men realized Jesus was fulfilling His priestly role when He cleansed the Temple. He'd taken charge and purified the House of God from the abuses of the High Priest. They yearned for Him to ascend to the top of Zion and assume his rightful place as King and longed to hear His words as God's final Prophet. A sense of excitement could be heard in the men's voices as they conversed.

The women were hard at work in the kitchen, and Dinah was becoming more and more perceptive of those around her. Martha's gloomy expression was readily understood by everyone, but the sense of loneliness that Miriam felt was more subtle. She was able to hide her feelings from everyone else, but couldn't conceal them from her cousin.

Every day, Dinah became more like her mother. Not only did she have Deborah's physical features, she also shared her personality. Her mother was usually rather quiet, but strong when she had to be. She'd defended her children against the robber outside of Elath using her trusty *khanjar*. Dinah was always the tomboy growing up, exhibiting that same strength. Now, she was growing in sensitivity like her mother. Though no one else could see the effect Michael was having on Miriam, she could see it. Even Elizabeth and Deborah failed to take notice.

Before Caleb's death she might have teased Miriam under similar circumstances, but she knew better in this case. She realized that her cousin must have conflicting emotions. Only days before Miriam's hope had been that she and Isaac would be married; but now, she'd learned he was already married and expecting a child. Her hopes dashed, Miriam found herself in Michael's arms. He did nothing untoward when he comforted her. He was the perfect gentleman, acting as any older brother should. She found it was those very qualities that now attracted her to him. Dinah knew not to press the issue and to give her time to think it through.

She'd also noticed the way her brother looked at their cousin. A smile came to her face as she remembered the look. There was no doubt in her mind that he was smitten. The thought that God may intend for them to be together made her happy.

The women busied themselves in the kitchen with meals to cook for the extended family. The ingredients for the Passover meal had to be prepared. They would be baking unleavened bread and cutting up bitter herbs over the next couple of days, sufficient for forty people. The paschal lambs would be roasted in Jerusalem on Thursday. Thousands of ovens were readied all over the city for the pilgrims to cook their lambs. It was work, but joyous work, in order to celebrate the deliverance of God's people from bondage in Egypt.

They'd already begun serving dinner when Michael and Joseph came bursting through the door. They couldn't contain their excitement and everyone knew immediately that they must have seen Jesus. Deborah got up to prepare a plate for them, but neither of them wanted to eat. They felt compelled to tell everyone the things they'd seen and heard.

It was Ephraim who settled them down, "Eat your food. You'll have plenty of time to tell us after supper."

Both boys knew to obey and offered no protest, but they hardly tasted their food as they gulped it down. Josiah smiled at their impatience, but knew better than to rush Ephraim. After what seemed like an eternity to the boys, the patriarch of the family finally signaled the end to the meal. Deborah, sensing her son's urgency, hurried up the girls as they cleared the table.

Ephraim waited patiently while everyone found their seat before saying, "Michael, it is apparent you have something to tell us."

Suddenly, he didn't know where to start. He and Joseph had heard so much that day at the Temple.

When he hesitated for a moment Josiah finally asked, "Well, did you see Jesus?"

"Yes…yes, He was at the Temple," Michael stammered.

Miriam found his stumbling over his words a bit amusing, but she couldn't help admiring him. From his countenance anyone would know that he was full of the love of God.

He composed himself and then said as calmly as he could, "I've never seen anything like it before. We got there in plenty of time for the morning sacrifice. Maybe later, I can tell you about that. Jesus didn't come until after the sacrifice; or if He was there, we didn't see Him until later. A crowd gathered around Him in the Court of the Women, and we were somehow able to get close to Him."

He paused, while everyone waited anxiously for his next words.

"The people were flocking around Him to listen to His every word, but the chief priests and other religious leaders were not pleased. They didn't oppose Him openly. I think they were afraid to because of all the people, but they tested Him one by one. Jesus boldly took them on. First, they asked Him by what authority He did the things He did. I suppose they were still upset about how He drove the moneychangers out of the Temple yesterday."

"Was the market place set back up in the Temple today?" Josiah asked, briefly interrupting him.

"No...not yet, and after today, I wonder if it will ever be set up again," Michael responded to his father.

"Thanks be to God for that!" Ephraim declared emphatically.

"Like I said, I think that's what was foremost on their minds when they asked Jesus about authority," Michael replied.

"What did Jesus say?" Nathaniel asked.

"It was great! He answered the question with a question. He asked them, *John's baptism – is it from heaven or from men?'*"

Ephraim smiled when he heard Jesus' question. He knew immediately that He had put his questioners in a hard place. If they answered "from heaven," He could chastise them for not believing John, but if they said, "from men," they would incur the wrath of the people, who believed John to be a prophet.

"What did they say?" Ephraim asked.

"They didn't say anything at all. They just stood there dumbfounded," Michael replied.

"So, how did Jesus answer?" A thoroughly intrigued Simon asked.

Michael's face lit up as he answered his younger brother, "He said, *'Then neither will I tell you by what authority I do these things.'*"

"Good for Him!" Ephraim exclaimed. "Anyone with two eyes can see where Jesus gets His authority."

He was startled momentarily when everyone started laughing at his comment, but didn't mind laughing at himself once he figured it out. Still, all of them knew the blind man could see that Jesus' authority came from God. He knew it from the testimony of those he trusted, of Josiah and now Michael, and of course, the testimony of his son. He longed to see Samuel again and couldn't wait until Passover, for he had sent word that he would eat the Passover with his father.

After the laughter died down Michael turned to Joseph and said, "Tell them about the parables He told."

Joseph was happy for the opportunity to speak.

"Jesus' method of teaching was remarkable. He didn't speak directly about the scribes and Pharisees at first, but spoke of them using stories. First, He told a parable about two sons. Their father asked one of his sons to go into the vineyard to work. At first he refused to go, but later he regretted his action and did go after all. Then the man asked his second son to go into the vineyard, and he said that he would go, but then he didn't. Jesus asked them, '*Which of the two sons did the will of his father?*' They rightly answered, 'The first.'

Joseph glanced over at Michael and said with a smile, "Do you want to tell them what Jesus said after that?"

Everyone turned their attention back to Michael who said, "Jesus said firmly, '*Verily I say unto you, That the publicans and the harlots go into the kingdom of God before you.*'"

"Whoa!" Josiah said in surprise. "Was He that blunt?"

"That was nothing," Michael responded. "Remember how you taught us about oracles of weal and oracles of woe in the Scriptures?"

"Yes," Josiah replied, and to remind everyone he said, "An oracle of weal is a pronouncement of blessing, such as in the first psalm, '*Blessed is the man that walketh not in the counsel of the ungodly.*' And then the oracle of woe is a pronouncement of a curse, such as in Isaiah, the prophet, '*Woe unto them that call evil good, and good evil.*'"

Michael nodded his head in agreement before continuing, "Jesus moved from parables to pronouncing a litany of woes upon the scribes and Pharisees. Joseph, can you remember some of them?"

The young man thought for a moment before saying, "In one of them He said, '*Woe unto you, scribes and Pharisees, hypocrites! For ye devour widows' houses, and for a pretense make long prayer: therefore ye shall receive the greater damnation.*'"

Michael then chimed in, "In another one He declared, '*Woe unto you, scribes and Pharisees, hypocrites! For ye are like unto whited sepulchres, which indeed appear beautiful outward, but are within full of dead men's bones, and of all uncleanness. Even so ye also outwardly appear righteous unto men, but within ye are full of hypocrisy and iniquity.*'"

Even Ephraim was astonished at Jesus' frankness with the religious leaders.

"How did they respond to that?" He asked.

"They didn't say anything. You could see the hatred and the anger in their eyes, but they were afraid to say anything at all. I've never seen a man speak with such authority, and the masses adore Him. Surely, He is the Messiah and is about to establish His kingdom."

Michael then got a troubled look on his face, and his father noticed it.

"What's wrong?" He asked.

"He told another parable, one that unsettled me," he said lowering his voice.

"Tell us," His father responded.

"He spoke of another man who had a vineyard that he rented out to vinedressers before going away into a far country. When it came time to harvest, he sent his servants for the grapes; but rather than giving them the harvest the vinedressers attacked them, beating one, killing another and stoning a third. After that he sent even more servants, and the vinedressers treated them the same. Finally, he decided to send his son to them, thinking surely they would respect his son; but when the vinedressers saw it was the landowner's son, and the heir to the vineyard, they conspired together to kill him and take his inheritance for themselves. Jesus then told us that they cast the son out of the vineyard and killed him."

A solemnity fell over them all as they realized the possible implications of the parable.

"What did Jesus say after that?" Josiah asked.

"He asked them, *'What will the owner of the vineyard do to the vinedressers?'* Of course they replied that he would destroy them, and lease his land to other vinedressers."

Michael looked at Joseph to make sure he got the next part right before saying carefully, "Jesus then said, *'Did ye never read in the scriptures, the stone which the builders rejected, the same is become the head of the corner: this is the Lord's doing, and it is marvellous in our eyes?'*"

Michael paused again before finishing what Jesus said.

"He concluded by saying, *'Therefore say I unto you, The kingdom of God shall be taken from you, and given to a nation bringing forth the fruits thereof. And whosoever shall fall on this stone shall be broken: but on whomsoever it shall fall, it will grind him to powder.'* Father, what did Jesus mean by the parable? Is He the son that will be killed? I can't bring myself to believe it. Also, what is this other nation that will be given the kingdom? Will He take the kingdom from Israel? When He spoke this parable His expression was dead serious. He meant it, Father. Whatever, He intended to say. He meant it!"

Josiah was stumped, and for once, so was Ephraim. When Ephraim did not respond to Michael, Josiah knew he had to say something.

"Michael, there are some things we still don't understand. Surely, the chief priests and Pharisees intend to kill Him, but I don't see how they can in light of all the prophecies about His ascendance to the throne and the support He has from the people."

Everyone was silent. Ephraim was troubled in his soul. He knew of all of the Messianic prophecies of the triumph of the Anointed One, but other passages had always bothered him. The passage that Jesus quoted about the stone rejected by the builders came from the *Hallel*, the very psalm the children were singing to Jesus during His triumphal entry into the city. He also wondered what was meant by the Suffering Servant passages in Isaiah, and the psalm that began with the words, *"My God, My God, why hast Thou forsaken me?"* Could these Scriptures be speaking of Messiah? He didn't know for sure, so he said nothing.

Josiah was remembering similar words he'd heard on the road that sometimes haunted him in quiet moments. The words were spoken by Zacharias the night Josiah first told him about the old man's prophecy over the baby at the Temple. It was also the evening of the morning when the rabbi had first blown the *shofar*.

He'd gathered the troupe around him that night and said, "I must admit that there is much I don't know. I do believe the Day of the Lord is drawing near, but there are many things I simply do not understand. Tonight, I'm going to read a passage of Scripture without comment. I want to ask you to think about the answer to a simple question. Don't come to me for the answer, because I don't have it. Think and pray. After some things God has done today, I know this question is important. I trust we shall find the answer in Jerusalem."

Josiah thought about the question Zacharias posed: "Of whom is Isaiah speaking in the passage? Is it Israel, the people of God, or is he speaking of Messiah?"

Then he simply read this passage:

"Surely He hath borne our griefs, and carried our sorrows: yet we did esteem Him stricken, smitten of God, and afflicted. But He was wounded for

our transgressions, He was bruised for our iniquities: the chastisement of our peace was upon Him; and with His stripes we are healed. All we like sheep have gone astray; we have turned every one to his own way; and the LORD hath laid on Him the iniquity of us all."

Josiah had tried to put these thoughts out of his mind and for the most part had succeeded. Now, they returned when Michael related the parable Jesus told. Could it be that the Messiah must die? He couldn't bear the thought. It simply didn't add up. He sighed and decided to rest in God's sovereign plan. He knew that all things would be made clear.

Finally, he spoke, "I know there are many things we do not know about God's mysterious plan, but I cannot believe that the Messiah will fall. May He be victorious over those who seek to destroy Him. May He quickly conquer and inaugurate His kingdom, restoring the kingdom to Israel with times of refreshing!"

CHAPTER 10

Kiss the Son

Psalm 2:12

*Kiss the Son, lest He be angry, and ye perish from the
way, when His wrath is kindled but a little.*

Michael and Joseph wanted to go back to Jerusalem the next morning,
but this time Josiah didn't permit it. He'd wrestled with going himself
and talked it over with Ephraim and Nathaniel. Things were exciting, yet
volatile in Jerusalem. The crowds were practically fanatical in their support
of Jesus, but the leaders of Israel clearly opposed Him. From what Michael
and Joseph described, Jesus' confrontation with the leaders only made
matters worse; but Josiah believed that the Teacher must have a reason for
what He was doing.

After much thought and prayer, he was convinced that if Jesus did
decide to make a move to establish His kingdom, He would do it at the
feast and not before. So Josiah decided to go about his preparations for
Passover in an ordinary fashion and simply wait for God to do His bidding.
The boys were disappointed with his decision but understood.

The shepherd was troubled by what seemed to be conflicting testimony,
both from Jesus and the Scriptures. Then again, he'd always been haunted
by the apparent contradiction inherent in the old man's prophecy. He
remembered his countenance and how it suddenly changed from euphoria,
while describing the future work of the Messiah to that of utter sadness,
even despair, when he spoke directly to the baby's mother. Bringing these
two things together proved difficult for him.

He wrestled long into the night, mulling over the Scriptures in his
head, and couldn't find sleep until at last he came to contemplate the

second psalm. In particular, he remembered the words, *'Yet have I set my King upon My holy hill of Zion. Thou art my Son; this day have I begotten Thee. Ask of Me, and I shall give Thee the heathen for Thine inheritance, and the uttermost parts of the earth for Thy possession. Thou shalt break them with a rod of iron; Thou shalt dash them in pieces like a potter's vessel.'* It was like he experienced a sudden moment of clarity, and he determined to talk it over with Ephraim and Nathaniel the next morning.

After breakfast the men gathered to discuss everything that was happening. Isaac, Michael, Joseph and Simon joined them. Josiah was very eager to ask Ephraim about the second psalm.

"Ephraim, I've been trying to bring together various passages of Scripture that seem at odds regarding the Messiah," he said.

The old man nodded his head, indicating he had been doing the very same thing.

Josiah started to explain, "There are so many passages that speak of the Messiah's conquest and the restoration of Israel that I cannot believe we've seen the fulfillment of those prophecies in the estate we find Israel in today, especially when we consider the occupation of Rome, and the apparent apostasy of the leaders of God's people. It even extends to the highest places of the priesthood. I believe Messiah is coming to rectify these things, but I can never escape the words of the old man that I heard so long ago. They contain the same seeming contradiction. First, they promise glory to Israel and light to the Gentiles, but his words of warning to the baby's mother are unsettling to me. I couldn't see how these two things could be reconciled, until I thought of the second psalm last night and everything seemed to make sense."

Ephraim nodded his head vigorously and exclaimed, "Michael, hurry and get the scroll of the psalms!"

The young man practically sprinted into Ephraim's room and quickly recovered the scroll. He brought it to his father who hurriedly opened it and laid it out on the table. They all gathered around so they could see. Even Ephraim leaned over the table as if he could see the words.

"First, the psalmist asks a question," Josiah said. "It's clear that his question is rhetorical as he seems to shrug his shoulders, baffled by the actions of men. Listen to his words, *'Why do the heathen rage, and the people imagine a vain thing? The kings of the earth set themselves, and the rulers take counsel together, against the LORD, and against His Anointed.'* The psalmist is dumbfounded at the folly of men who would plot against God and His Messiah. Look at what they say, *'Let us break Their bands asunder, and cast away Their cords from us.'*

Josiah paused so they could consider the folly of the nations and that the kings of the earth would actually try to rebel against God and overthrow His rule.

"The absurdity of their plotting is demonstrated in the next words, *'He that sitteth in the heavens shall laugh: the LORD shall have them in derision. Then shall He speak unto them in His wrath, and vex them in His sore displeasure.'* All of the opposition to Jesus we have seen is being described by the psalmist. This even explains why at the conclusion of His parable He spoke of taking the kingdom from apostate Israel and giving it to another nation. The leaders, even the High Priest and the chief priests, are acting like heathens by rejecting God's Messiah. Then I remembered what Ephraim told us about Herod. He was not a believer, and he opposed the newborn king to such a degree that he slaughtered the innocent children of Bethlehem in his rage in a vain attempt to destroy the Lord's Anointed. I'm certain that the psalmist was speaking of the very things we are seeing. Will the Romans conspire with the leaders of Israel against Him? It would not surprise me."

Everyone paid careful attention to Josiah's words.

Then he smiled when he said, "But we have our answer in this psalm. Look at what God says, *'Yet have I set my King upon My holy hill of Zion.'* We might think He is speaking of David, but no. Look at what He says to this King, *'Thou art my Son; this day have I begotten Thee. Ask of Me, and I shall give Thee the heathen for Thine inheritance, and the uttermost parts of the earth for Thy possession. Thou shalt break them with a rod of iron; Thou shalt dash them in pieces like a potter's vessel.'* These words could not have been spoken of David, but rather of David's greater Son, the Son of God, and God's Messiah."

"It's clear to me, now," he said with confidence. "All of the passages that seem to speak of His suffering are fulfilled in the opposition that has risen against Him. When I was a boy I heard the old man say to His mother, *'Behold, this child is set for the fall and rising again of many in Israel; and for a sign which shall be spoken against.'* Have we not heard the voices of them that are speaking against Him? But they speak in vain. The message of the second psalm is clear. Jesus will triumph over His enemies. He will rule the nations with a rod of iron!"

A sense of excitement and expectation swept through the men, as each of them longed to see His day.

Josiah continued what had now become a sermon, "God gives to the rulers of the earth an opportunity to repent. Listen to His call, it is an offer of mercy to them, *'Be wise now therefore, O ye kings: be instructed, ye judges of the earth. Serve the LORD with fear, and rejoice with trembling.'* My brothers and my sons, this call extends to the ends of the earth. From Arabia to Egypt, from Mesopotamia to India, from Greece to Rome, the call goes out to all the earth. It is an offer of peace from God to the princes of Arabia, and even to Tiberius Caesar in Rome."

The universality of the call was staggering to the men as they contemplated it, and then Josiah finished the reading.

"Yet, God's Anointed has not come merely to take His place among the kings of the earth. No, He has come to reign supreme. Hear the next words of the psalm, *'Kiss the Son, lest He be angry, and ye perish from the way, when His wrath is kindled but a little.'* Beloved, this is not the kiss of greeting or affection that one ruler would give to another in order to make peace, but this is the kiss of surrender. God is calling upon all the kings of the earth to bow the knee to His Anointed. The Son extends the signet ring of His finger for them to kiss, thus putting themselves in subjection to Him as the King of kings and Lord of lords. Every king who refuses will perish in His wrath."

All of them knew the psalm, but had never contemplated it like this and were strangely fearful in their hearts from its teaching. If even the mighty ones on the earth must bow the knee and kiss His ring lest they face His wrath, what hope could there be for the common man?

Then Josiah's expression softened and turned into a smile as he whispered, "But there is hope. Hear the last words of the psalm, *'Blessed are all they that put their trust in Him.'*"

"It's an oracle of weal," Michael said intuitively.

"Yes, my son. Will you put your trust in Him?"

His son nodded his head as a tear ran down his cheek. Josiah looked at the rest of them, and each in turn nodded their heads, even Ephraim.

It was a solemn moment as they recognized the authority and power of Jesus, the Messiah. Their hearts were suddenly full of hope, their doubts vanquished.

The women were hard at work while the men were studying the Scriptures, but labored to keep an open ear to listen to the conversation going on in the next room through the door. Deborah heard much of her husband's exposition of the passage, and it thrilled her heart. She remembered how restless he was the night before and knew it was best not to bother him. In fact, she could recall the moment when he must have thought of the second psalm. He'd quietly whispered thanks to God, rolled over, and fallen asleep.

It was a busy day, with much to do in preparation for the feast. However, in the early afternoon Deborah started to grow weary. Thankfully, they had just finished their work for both the evening meal and for Passover.

"I guess this trip has taken its toll on me," she whispered to Elizabeth. "I feel like I'm about to pass out; I'm so tired."

Elizabeth laughed before saying, "Me too, and I've not been on the road. Do you think we might be getting older?"

"Not me," Deborah declared, but her smile betrayed her. "Do you mind if I go lay down for a few minutes?"

"Why would I mind? I'm headed for my bed, myself," her friend replied.

After shutting down the kitchen, the women scattered in different directions. Of course, Martha immediately found Joseph with the men. They had ended their more formal discussions and were conversing among themselves throughout the room. She took his hand and led him toward the door. It was a beautiful day to take a walk in Bethlehem.

At first, Haifa was surprised when she didn't see Isaac with the men, but then she knew where she would find him. She slipped through the back door and headed for the stable. Sure enough he was sitting on the ground petting Little Micah. Isaac had rescued the young ram from a cave in Kedar and bought him back from the Idumean after his father sold the flock. He was determined to have the blood of his father's flock in the herd when they returned to their home in Kedar. Little Micah was named after a prized ram the Kedarites had killed during one of their raids. Isaac had raised Old Micah from birth after his mother died giving birth to him.

"I see who you love the most," she said teasing him. "As soon as you get a free moment you run out to see Little Micah rather than seek out your devoted wife."

He realized his wife knew him all too well and didn't try to defend himself.

"I feel sorry for him. Since the other animals were sold when they were rejected at the Temple, he must feel lonely," the tough, yet tender-hearted shepherd replied.

Haifa couldn't help herself and soon was petting him too.

Both of them laughed when she quipped, "He may miss them, but I'm sure he'd rather be here with us than with the Pascal Lamb."

After a few minutes, Micah grew weary of their attention and wandered off, leaving Haifa alone with her husband. He was quieter than his younger brother, but she had no doubt that he was just as earnest in his faith as Michael. Things were changing rapidly in Israel, and she couldn't help but wonder about their future.

"Do you believe Jesus is about to establish His kingdom?" She asked.

"I do," he replied. "Everything points to it."

"What will we do?" She questioned, letting him know her concerns.

"I'm not sure," he answered as Micah came back to him and rubbed against his leg, like a big old lapdog.

Haifa watched the two of them and knew her husband would always be a shepherd.

"Will we stay here or go back to Kedar?" She asked.

He was startled by her question. There was much he hadn't thought through. They didn't know for sure just what Jesus was about to do, but Kedar was never far from his heart. Then he thought of her parents and realized that she must miss them.

"I can't imagine not going back to Kedar," he responded looking toward the east. "Your mother and father are still there."

The young shepherd's mind was suddenly flooded with memories of the beauty of the place where he grew up. For most people, all they saw was a barren desert, but not Isaac. He'd inherited his love for beauty from his mother, and he saw things other people didn't see – the contrast in the color of the sands, the green of the date palms, tiny flowers near the oasis, the stunning starry nights, the crystal-clear reflection of a full moon on the waters of the oasis, sheep scattered about grazing in the fields. He remembered what he loved and how much he loved it.

"Father says that the blessings of Abraham will come upon the nations and has always believed that would include Kedar," he said still looking far away to the east.

A tear came to Haifa's eye. She knew it to be the truth. God's grace had come to her and to her parents. They were marvelously touched by God when she told them about Jehovah, the Creator of all things. There was so much she'd learned and so much they needed to know. She believed that somehow God's grace would come to Kedar. Looking at her shepherd-husband, she wondered if God may use him to deliver the good news to her kinsmen according to the flesh. Though she now belonged to Isaac's people, she longed for the people of her birthplace to forsake their idolatry and come to know the one true God.

Joseph and Martha hadn't gone too far when Michael caught up with them on the street.

"Would you like to try to find the stable where Jesus was born?" He asked excitedly. "Ephraim told me about where it is."

Joseph's eyes lit up.

"That would be great!"

Martha squinted her eyes at her brother to show her displeasure. He hadn't seen that look since they were children, but quickly realized she wanted to be alone with Joseph.

"On second thought, we can find it another day," Michael said, acquiescing to his sister's wishes. Why don't you two go for a walk together? I'll go back to the house. There's something I wanted to ask Ephraim anyway."

A satisfied smirk crossed Martha's face until Joseph responded to Michael, "No, let's go find it. I'd really like to see it!"

Michael glanced at his sister and saw that look again.

"No, we can do it another time. I really need to get back to the house."

Joseph shrugged his shoulders, while Martha took his arm possessively. She gripped his arm as the two of them walked down the road. Though she was happy to be alone with him she was a little bit angry. Things had been so hectic since the day they visited the Temple. He'd gone off with Michael the next day, spending the whole day in Jerusalem. Now that they finally had a few moments to spend together, he was all excited about going off with Michael again. She knew she was invited to go with them this time; but she didn't want to share Joseph with anyone, not with her brother, not even with Jesus.

She was glad that Jesus was about to establish His kingdom, but she had other things on her mind. She wanted to think about a wedding, a house, having Joseph's babies. For a moment she wondered if he felt the same way about her that she did about him. She squeezed his arm tighter, pulling him close. He looked at her and his smile melted her heart once again. She couldn't stay angry with him for long.

Michael did have a question for Ephraim but had forgotten it by the time he got back to the house. Instead of going inside he circled around back, hoping to find Miriam. Sure enough, she was seated on her bench. For a moment he just stood there and admired her. Her beauty took his breath away.

"I thought I might find you here," he said as he approached her.

Her smile immediately warmed his heart.

"I suppose this has become my special place," she responded, almost in a whisper.

"Do you mind if I join you?" He inquired in a gentlemanly fashion.

"I would be delighted," she replied, patting the seat beside her.

For a few minutes they sat there in silence, both a bit surprised by the awkwardness of the moment.

Michael didn't know what to do, so he finally launched into a discussion about Jesus and everything he'd heard Him say at the Temple. Miriam found it all a bit amusing. She'd already heard what he was saying and could tell he was nervous. Secretly, it pleased her, giving her hope that he might have the same kinds of feelings toward her that she had for him.

Finally, she interrupted him, changing the subject, "Michael, what do you think about me?"

His eyes grew wide, and the ever-loquacious young man was suddenly speechless.

"Do you think I'm pretty?" She asked demurely, lowering her eyes.

Immediately, she was afraid she'd said too much, but then he reached over and took her hand.

"I think you are the most beautiful woman I've ever seen," he said, somehow finding his voice.

His heart was pounding, as he wondered if he'd revealed more than he should have; but he couldn't lie to her.

"Do you really?" She asked.

"Yes, but not just on the outside. I think you have a beautiful heart that is full of the love of God."

Though flattered by his praise, she was still somewhat insecure. She longed for him to desire her as a woman, not just as a godly sister. Moment by moment her thoughts changed from believing he must love her to wondering how he ever could.

"I'm not so sure," she responded dropping her eyes again, fearful of rejection.

"Look at me," he insisted. "You are the most loving, caring person I know. You sacrifice every day to care for Ephraim. Everybody else got to go to the Temple on Sunday except for you."

"It's no sacrifice caring for such a wonderful man," she replied, still not seeing anything special in what she was doing for him.

"I mean it, Miriam," he declared. "I've always admired you, for as long as I can remember."

The young woman was glad he thought so well of her, but desperately wanted him to feel more.

"It's just that I'm still so confused over what happened with Isaac," she whispered.

Michael was fearful that she still hadn't gotten over his brother and didn't know how to respond. His heart was bursting within him to tell her how he really felt, but he couldn't do it.

"What if nobody ever wants me?" She asked, looking into his eyes, hopeful he would tell her what she longed to hear.

"Of course someone will want you. Lots of men will line up outside your father's door to court you," he responded.

That was not what Miriam hoped he would say, and she wondered if she may have been projecting her own feelings on him. She wanted him to be the only one to pursue her. Maybe he didn't see her as a woman after all, only as a sister.

"Thank you, Michael," she replied putting her arms around him. "Thank you for believing in me."

The two of them hugged on the bench, both yearning to say more; but neither of them dared to do it. When he left her to go inside to speak to Ephraim, she didn't know what to think. A tear ran down her cheek, even as she whispered a prayer. "Lord, if it be Thy will, help Michael love me."

Deborah enjoyed having her husband beside her for an afternoon nap. Neither of them said very much. It took her a few minutes to drift to sleep. There was so much to think about. Earth-shattering events were on the horizon. She knew that very well. Things could change for her and her family. Would they return to their home in Kedar, or would they stay in Israel? She thought of her children, of Martha in particular. Her daughter was anxious to start a new life with Joseph. She knew her second daughter could be impatient. As always before going to sleep, she prayed for each of them beginning with Isaac, and in the end she prayed for her beloved husband, that God would grant him wisdom. Secure in the rest that God provides, she finally fell asleep.

After supper, Ephraim gathered them all around him.

"In two days it will be Passover," the old man declared. "It is a time of celebration, rejoicing in God's mighty saving act when He delivered our people from bondage in Egypt. It is a time for feasting."

He paused for a moment to collect his thoughts before proceeding.

"This is no ordinary Passover," He said in all earnestness. "When Jesus revealed Himself at the Holy Temple on the Day of Presentation, I believe He set in place an order of events that will change not only Israel but the whole world. If I understand the Scriptures properly, He will next ascend Mount Zion and take His rightful place upon the throne of His father, David. I believe that will take place sometime during the feast. Whether it will be on the day of Passover, or on the first day of the Feast of Unleavened Bread is a mystery yet to be revealed. In due course, He will fulfill His destiny as our Messiah."

Everyone was thrilled with his words and believed them to be true. The Scriptures were coming together in the person and work of Jesus.

"Elizabeth, how far along are you and Deborah in the preparations for Passover?" He asked.

"We've completed all we intend to do here in Bethlehem. We will finish what remains once we get to Deborah's sister's house in Jerusalem on Thursday," she responded.

"Excellent!" He exclaimed.

Then he surprised them all when he said intently, "I declare that tomorrow will be a solemn day of prayer and fasting for our family. This is unusual as we approach the feast, but I believe that we need to pray for Jesus as He institutes His kingdom reign. The enemy will oppose Him, but He will be victorious. Let's summon the power of God to aid Him. Will you pray with me – all day tomorrow?"

"We will!" They all said in unison.

Josiah immediately saw the wisdom of the decree, and began to think about how to organize them to pray. He approached Ephraim along with Nathaniel. It was decided that everyone would begin praying upon their beds when they awakened, and that the entire group would gather for corporate prayer at times ordinarily reserved for meals. Mid-morning and mid-afternoon, they would divide into groups to pray. Once they decided on the details, Josiah explained them to everyone.

The next day was unusually quiet around Ephraim's house, other than the whispers of prayer. Even the youngest children participated, praying with each other. It was a holy day of preparation. Now, all that remained was to eat the Passover and to wait for God to fulfill all of His promises in His Son, Jesus, the Messiah.

CHAPTER 11

The Lamb

Exodus 12:13

*And the blood shall be to you for a token upon the houses where ye are:
and when I see the blood, I will pass over you, and the plague shall
not be upon you to destroy you, when I smite the land of Egypt.*

Everyone in both households was up long before daylight on the morning
of Passover. Ephraim insisted, not only of going with them, but also
walking the six miles from Bethlehem to Jerusalem. Josiah offered to
make a gurney for him, and the boys were more than willing to take turns
carrying him, but he wouldn't hear of it.

"God will give strength to my legs," The old man declared. "I want to
feel the holy ground under my feet, because this will be my last pilgrimage
to Jerusalem."

"Sir, you'll have many more Passovers to observe," Miriam objected,
but he just smiled at her with a knowing expression on his face.

The blind man understood that his days upon the earth were coming
to an end. He'd secretly prayed that he would live to see the day of the
Messiah, even if he must see with his ears through the testimony of others.
He was confident that the Day of the Lord was at hand. God would grant
strength to his weary legs.

"I'll do fine with my trusty cane and with help from you and Michael,"
he said, putting the matter to rest.

Josiah knew the road would be crowded, so he wanted to start out
early. If the children thought there were lots of people making the trek
to Jerusalem on the Day of Presentation, they would be shocked by the
numbers on Passover. Hundreds of thousands would be ascending Mount

Zion that morning from the north, south, east and west to join the throng that had already arrived in the city. Though the inhabitants of Jerusalem spent weeks preparing for the feast, efficiently hosting the vast number of pilgrims was nothing short of miraculous.

Isaac brought two of the camels around to the front of Ephraim's house, so that all of the food that Deborah and Elizabeth had prepared, and other things they'd need for their stay in Jerusalem could be loaded on them. This way, they didn't have to carry anything on their backs. When Deborah saw Little Micah with the camels she raised her eyebrow at her son.

"I'm not leaving him here," Isaac said. "Jared and Judah will help me take care of him."

His little brothers quickly agreed, and she knew better than to say anything else. Besides, she had too many other things on her mind.

By the time they departed, Bethlehem was already awake; and the light of a multitude of lamps could be seen exiting the town.

"Look at all the lights!" Naomi squealed with glee.

"Yes, they're beautiful, but listen to the singing," Ruth replied.

The sound of the singing of the Songs of Ascents filled the air. Josiah and his family took their place among the masses going up to worship God on this most holy day. The single-mindedness of the pilgrims created an atmosphere of genuine fellowship. Other travelers from distant places merged with them, and those who dwelt between Bethlehem and Jerusalem joined the ever-growing caravan along the way. There was no pushing or shoving, no hurrying past one another. Patience and kindness marked the paths of the worshipers. Even those who did pass them greeted them warmly, especially the old man who slowed the pace.

Josiah thought of the great hymn of unity and began to sing it:

"Behold, how good and how pleasant it is for brethren to dwell together in unity! It is like the precious ointment upon the head, that ran down upon the beard, even Aaron's beard: that went down to the skirts of his garments; as the dew of Hermon, and as the dew that descended upon the mountains of Zion: for there the LORD commanded the blessing, even life for evermore."

Not only did the shepherd's family sing with him, but all of those within hearing distance did the same. Those singing ahead and behind were joined by even more, so the sound of it spread up and down the road for a long distance. His family was utterly amazed by the experience. It was so far removed from the isolation they'd felt in Kedar. They were surrounded by thousands who shared a common purpose – to worship the one true God and give Him thanks for His salvation. Josiah wondered how many of the other travelers sensed that great things were about to happen in Jerusalem.

It was just breaking daylight as they entered the city, once more using the western gate that led to the road to Joppa. The pace slowed as the line narrowed while going through the gate, and Michael and Miriam steadied Ephraim, lest he fall from being inadvertently bumped by the people surrounding them. Shortly after entering the city, Deborah and the younger children bid farewell to Josiah. They would go to her sister's house, while the men headed for the Temple. She was excited about seeing her sister for the first time in years. Her mother and father knew the way and had given directions to her husband. He would meet them there after offering the paschal lamb.

The men expected to meet Zacharias in front of the Huldah Gate. From there they would retrieve their lambs and then head into the Temple. With over a million worshippers in the city, between fifty and seventy-five thousand lambs must be slain and prepared during the prescribed time in the early afternoon. Josiah couldn't wait to see the wonderment on his sons' faces in that solemn moment.

Sure enough, Zacharias was waiting for them outside the Temple gate. Each of the men ceremonially washed in a mikveh nearby, and then made their way to where the lambs were being held. Once again, the precision of the process was remarkable. The line was long but moved rather rapidly until at last it was their turn to get their lambs. Josiah presented his paperwork, and Isaac immediately recognized their lamb when it was brought to them. At least, this time the lamb wasn't rejected. He believed it was due more to the overwhelming task placed on the inspectors rather than actual care to insure the lambs were without spot or blemish. Of course, he never doubted the perfection of the lamb he'd helped his father select.

Once they had their lambs, they ascended the stairs to the triple Huldah gate and entered into the Court of the Gentiles. Immediately, Josiah looked to see if the moneychangers' tables and the animal cages were back in the court. To his joy, the floor was filled with worshippers not traders.

He looked in the direction of Mount Zion across the Central Valley and thought to himself, 'Jesus took Moriah on Sunday, Mount Zion, you're next.'

The shepherd led the others through the *Soreg*, and then passing through the Beautiful Gate, they emerged once again inside of the Court of the Women. He knew the sacrifices would be made in three separate divisions and intended to be among the first. Without pausing, they made their way to the entrance of the Nicanor Gate where a line was already being formed. The gate was closed so that the priests and Levites could make all the necessary preparations to process so many sacrifices. Once the gate opened, worshippers would spill through bringing their lambs with them. Josiah wanted to be as near the front as possible. He'd been too young to accompany his father for the sacrifice when he was a boy and had longed to see it all of his life. Besides that, he wanted this to be an experience his sons would never forget.

Deborah's heart was full when her sister came running out of the house to greet her. It had been over twenty years since she'd last seen her. She smiled when she saw that Hannah was pregnant. One glance at her mother revealed a mischievous look.

"She wanted to surprise you," their mother said.

"And a pleasant surprise it is," Deborah replied, but she had a slightly confused look on her face.

Though Hannah was still within childbearing age, she must have been married for a long time. Deborah knew she didn't have any other children.

"I prayed like Hannah of old," her sister explained, before breaking out into a big grin. "God heard me, just like He heard the wife of Elkanah."

Deborah knew the story well – of how God answered Hannah's cries and gave her Samuel, a son she promised to give back to the Lord. Hannah could not have known the plans God had for her son. He would grow up to be the most significant man in Israel, the one chosen by God to anoint David as king.

Deborah's thoughts were interrupted when her brother came out of the house with his wife. She ran into his arms and held him tightly. They'd been close when they were growing up in Kedar. James was a strong man, but still had the same boyish smile she always remembered. After meeting Hannah's husband, Joel, and James' wife, Esther, they all went inside Hannah's house.

"Look at all of these precious children," Hannah declared.

"I have two more sons with their father at the Temple," Deborah exclaimed proudly.

Hearing this caused Simon to frown just a little. He really wanted to go with his father and brothers to the Temple, but realized that each band could only be represented by two or at most three men when offering the paschal lamb. It was a concession that had to be made in order to accommodate so many worshipers.

All the women hurried into the kitchen in Hannah's house to finish the preparations for the meal. It was spacious, and though Elizabeth and her family would be partaking of the Passover next door, the women decided to work together at Hannah's house. It would be a day of fellowship for them. There was much Deborah wanted to learn from her sister and Esther, and she had many things to tell them.

Even though it was Hannah's kitchen, Deborah instinctively took charge. Her sister smiled and winked at their mother. Some things never change, but she didn't mind at all. She was overjoyed having her sister back. Elizabeth and Deborah worked in tandem as they had for many years, and preparations for the meal came together quickly.

It was Dinah who brought up the subject of Jesus. The men talked openly about Him, especially while the women were hard at work; but the women were just as intrigued about what was taking place as the men. Deborah was also a student of the Scriptures, and Dinah admired her mother's wisdom.

"Mother, do you believe that now's the time when Jesus is going to establish His kingdom?"

"Yes, I do. Your father has studied the Scriptures, and I've been listening to him and to Ephraim. I'm certain of it," she responded.

"It's exciting!" Dinah exclaimed.

"It sure is," Hannah interjected. "I'll never forget the first time I saw Him."

"You've seen Him too?" Deborah asked with a look of astonishment on her face.

"Oh yes, more than once," she replied.

"Tell us," Dinah said enthusiastically.

"The first time was in Jerusalem during one of the feasts. Joel and I were walking by a pool that's called Bethesda near the Sheep Market. It is believed that periodically an angel comes down from heaven and troubles the waters of the pool. When that happens, the first to enter the pool will be immediately healed. As we walked by we saw a lot of infirmed people lying in five porches that surround the pool waiting for the waters to stir. It was at that time, that Jesus walked up to the pool."

"Did you recognize Him?" Dinah asked.

"We hadn't even heard of Him, but we never forgot Him after what we saw that day," she replied.

"What happened?" Deborah interjected.

"He walked up to an infirmed man who'd been waiting for many years and asked him, *'Wilt thou be made whole?'*"

"What did the man say?" Dinah asked, excited to hear the story.

"He said, *'Sir, I have no man, when the water is troubled, to put me into the pool: but while I am coming, another steppeth down before me.'* It was clear to us that the man was desperate." Hannah explained.

"Tell us what Jesus did," Elizabeth said, speaking for the first time.

"He told him, *'Rise, take up thy bed, and walk.'*" Hannah responded.

When she hesitated again, a slightly frustrated Dinah asked, "Well, what happened?"

She smiled before replying, "What do you think? The man stood up, took up his bed and walked. He was instantaneously healed by Jesus. I was amazed and looked at Joel. His mouth was as wide open as mine. We couldn't believe what we'd just seen. After that Jesus departed, and we didn't see Him again that day."

"We saw Him heal a lame boy at the Temple," Martha exclaimed.

Even Martha, who found herself so consumed with thoughts of Joseph, couldn't help but be fascinated by her aunt's tale.

"That's what I heard," Hannah replied.

"You said there were other times," Dinah said, turning everyone's attention back to Hannah.

She reflected for a moment and then said, "Actually, I saw Him two more times, but they were on consecutive days."

"Was it at the Temple?" Deborah asked.

"No, it was in Galilee, not too long after the first time. Joel and I went to Galilee to visit his brother. Thomas is a fisherman who lives in Tiberias. When we got to his house, he was very excited, because Jesus was in that region. We told him what we'd witnessed at the pool of Bethesda in Jerusalem and were anxious to hear Him too."

Hannah couldn't help but get excited as she remembered what happened, and all the women could see it in her eyes.

"When we tried to find Him, we learned that He had gone across the lake to a deserted place in a boat along with His disciples; but the crowds continued to seek Him out by going around the lake by land. We got in Thomas' boat and headed in that direction. When we got to the other side thousands had gathered to hear His words. As it got late in the day, people lingered, and most of us were not prepared for the evening meal. I'll never forget it as long as I live. Ephraim's son, Samuel, was there too, and he'd befriended one of Jesus' disciples named Andrew. He helped us move close enough to Jesus to see what He did." She said almost in a whisper.

All of the women waited with bated breath to hear what happened next.

"Jesus was concerned that everyone needed to eat and asked His disciples what provisions they had. Of course, they didn't have nearly enough. It was Andrew who said to Him, *'There is a lad here, which hath five barley loaves, and two small fishes: but what are they among so many?'* Jesus didn't respond directly to him, but instructed His disciples to have everyone sit down."

"How many were there?" Dinah asked.

"Later, we heard the number was about five thousand men, but that count didn't include all the women and the children."

"Five-thousand!" Martha said in disbelief.

"Yes, five-thousand," she responded before continuing. "Jesus took the five loaves and two fishes, looked heavenward, and prayed. Then He began breaking them, first the loaves and then the fishes and gave them to His disciples to distribute."

"That's hardly enough to feed the little boy," Martha declared.

"That's what I thought too," Hannah replied, "But the more bread He broke, the more He had to break. The same thing happened with the fish.

At the end of the day, everyone had eaten their fill, and Joel helped them pick up what was left. He couldn't believe it. Not only had thousands been fed by Jesus, but there were twelve baskets full of food left over."

The women couldn't even imagine what they were hearing. They'd seen Him heal the sick, but to perform a miracle sufficient to feed thousands was unbelievable.

"What happened the next day?" Deborah asked.

"After everyone had eaten that first day, Jesus disappeared. Samuel told us that He'd slipped off into the mountain by Himself to pray. At dusk, His disciples went down to the beach, got in a boat, and started to sail across the lake. We left at the same time and sailed back to Joel's brother's house in Tiberias. During the night there was a terrible storm, but the skies were clear when we got up early the next morning. We decided to go by boat to the place where Jesus was the day before; but when we arrived, He wasn't there and neither were His disciples. When we saw several boats headed north across the lake we followed them, until we came to Capernaum. After docking the boat, it didn't take us long to find Him. We just had to follow all of the people."

"Did Samuel go with you?" Miriam asked, finally getting involved in the conversation.

"No, he was on one of the other boats, but we saw him in the crowd. He was excited when he came up to us and told us something remarkable. Andrew had told him that morning, that during the storm, Jesus came walking on the water to the boat."

"He did what?" Dinah asked, thinking she must have misheard what she'd said.

"He was walking on top of the water, as if it was dry ground," Hannah said, inflecting her voice for emphasis.

"That's unbelievable!" Miriam responded.

"Yes, it is, but it's true." Hannah replied.

"We shouldn't be surprised," Deborah said softly. "After all, He is the Son of God."

"*Amen!*" The women responded.

"What happened in Capernaum?" Martha asked. "Did Jesus feed the crowds again?"

"Not with bread and fish," Hannah replied, "But He did feed us with His words."

"Tell us what He said," Dinah said pleadingly, longing to know.

"I'll never forget His words. He said, *'I am the bread of life: he that cometh to Me shall never hunger; and he that believeth on Me shall never thirst.'*"

"He said that?" Deborah asked.

"Yes He did, and at the end of His teaching something strange happened." Hannah said with a perplexed look on her face.

"What?" Miriam asked.

"Most of the crowd started shaking their heads and walked away. Finally, there were just a few of us left. Jesus took His twelve disciples away to talk to them. Joel and I didn't know what to do, and neither did Samuel or Thomas; so we got back in the boat and returned to Tiberias."

"Why did they forsake Him?" Dinah asked.

"We didn't know; but I think it was because they wanted Him to feed them again, something He refused to do. Instead, He taught us about Himself, profound things, and they didn't want to hear them. He said to us, *'Whoso eateth My flesh, and drinketh My blood, hath eternal life; and I will raise him up at the last day. For My flesh is meat indeed, and My blood is drink indeed. He that eateth My flesh, and drinketh My blood, dwelleth in Me, and I in him.'*"

"What did He mean by that?" Dinah asked, clearly perplexed.

"We weren't sure. We've talked about it often among ourselves. Ultimately, we concluded that Jesus was calling upon all of His disciples to depend completely upon Him. He was declaring Himself to be our Savior."

Deborah quietly reflected on what she'd just learned from her sister. If the crowds abandoned Him so quickly after He'd fed them the day before, she wondered how committed the people would be to Him now, especially with the opposition from the leaders of Israel. The thought troubled her, and she pondered what the next few days might bring.

There was still work to be done, so Deborah started giving directions again. Hannah looked at her mother and smiled. It was so good to have her older sister back.

At the Temple, both Josiah and Nathaniel were able to maneuver to a place near the front of the line. While they waited for the gate to open,

Josiah looked around the crowd for Jesus. He wondered if Jesus would make His entrance into the Temple first and then cross the Zion Bridge, which spanned the Central Valley between Moriah and Zion. If He made His move, the shepherd was intent on following close behind. However, as he looked around he didn't see any sign of Him, or of the men who seemed to always be with Him. Remembering his discussions with Ephraim, he wondered if Jesus might wait until the next day to take His rightful place on Mount Zion. He doubted that He would disrupt the holy festival. Surely, He would want to eat Passover with His disciples first.

A sound at the gate turned his attention back to the task at hand. It took dozens of Levites to push open the massive doors of the beautifully ornate Nicanor Gate. Josiah felt a sense of excitement and the swell of the crowd behind him as they instinctively pressed forward toward the opening gate.

Then the crowd seemed to pause spontaneously and stand at attention, until a priest blew the silver trumpet from high atop the pinnacle of the Temple. At the signal, the worshippers poured into the Court of Israel, bringing their lambs to be sacrificed. Josiah was glad when he was able to move to the very front of the line with his boys. Nathaniel also managed to do the same with Zacharias and Joseph. The priests beckoned them to move forward even beyond the wall of division between the Court of Israel and the Court of the Priests. On every other day, common Jews were forbidden to enter into the Court of the Priests, but not on Passover. There were so many worshippers to accommodate; they crowded as many in as possible.

Once again they heard the trumpet sound, and the heavy doors were closed. Josiah couldn't believe how close they were to the holy altar. He glanced at Isaac and Michael. Both of them were speechless as they took in the sight before them.

The High Priest stood above the altar, dressed in his regal priestly robes and called the assembly to worship with the *Shema:*
"Shema, Yisrael Adonai Elohenu Adonai echad."
"Hear, O Israel! The Lord our God, the Lord is one."
For a moment Josiah was distracted, knowing what he'd learned about the woeful apostasy of Caiaphas. With his own eyes he'd witnessed the greed of the High Priest, and how common worshipers

were cheated; but beyond that he'd heard him plotting the death of Jesus with his own ears. The shepherd had to remind himself that the priesthood was bigger than the man holding the office. As the rightful office-bearer Josiah heeded his call to worship and turned his attention to honor his God.

Priests were lined up in two rows extending from the worshipers all the way to the altar itself. In the hands of the priests on one side were silver bowls, while the priests on the other side held golden bowls. These bowls were rounded on the bottom so that they could not be set upon the floor of the Temple, lest the blood coagulate. When each lamb was slain, the priest closest to the worshiper would catch the blood in his bowl and then pass it to the next priest. Each would give the bowl to the next in line, being very careful not to spill a drop, until the last priest would pour the blood at the base of the altar.

Other priests were prepared to assist the worshippers as they made their sacrifices. According to the law, each worshiper would slay his own paschal lamb or kid. The priests provided the sacrificial knifes. They were made of metal, sharp as razors, rounded rather than pointed on the end. Instructions would be given to novices, but Josiah needed no coaching. The shepherd knew how to humanly slay a lamb.

Three more blasts from the trumpet signaled the start of sacrifices, and the Levitical choir began chanting the first line of the *Hallel*:

"Praise ye the LORD. Praise, O ye servants of the LORD, praise the name of the LORD!"

To which all the worshipers responded by repeating the line:

"Praise ye the LORD. Praise, O ye servants of the LORD, praise the name of the LORD!"

Then the Levites continued to chant line by line, with the worshippers responding with a robust *"Hallelujah!"* after each line:

"Blessed be the name of the LORD from this time forth and for evermore. From the rising of the sun unto the going down of the same the LORD's name is to be praised. The LORD is high above all nations, and His glory above the heavens. Who is like unto the LORD our God, who dwelleth on high, who humbleth Himself to behold the things that are in heaven, and in the earth! He raiseth up the poor out of the dust, and lifteth the needy out of the dunghill; that He may set Him with princes, even with the princes of His people. He

maketh the barren woman to keep house, and to be a joyful mother of children. Praise ye the LORD!"

Being first in line, Isaac and Michael steadied their lamb while Josiah made a clean cut, severing in one swift motion, the trachea and esophagus, as well as the carotid arteries and jugular veins. Death was instantaneous, and the accompanying priest caught the blood in the bowl, before quickly handing it to the next priest in line.

As the knife blade sliced through the skin of the lamb and the blood began to flow, Josiah felt a deep sadness. He was a shepherd who loved each of his sheep, even the one he'd just slain. Killing his sheep always caused him sadness, but it was sometimes the responsibility of a shepherd, and now the duty of a worshipper. He knew that the paschal lamb was not an atoning sacrifice, but rather a commemoration of God's great deliverance of His people from the destroyer on Passover night. Still, the very need for animal sacrifice was due to sin. The shepherd realized that apart from God's electing mercy Israel would have suffered the same fate as Egypt. The people of God belonged to Him according to His mercy and not because of their own righteousness. How often had they demonstrated their proneness to sin? He remembered that the sojourn in Egypt was preceded by a willfully sinful act, when Joseph's brothers sold him into slavery out of jealous wrath.

Even after the deliverance of the Children of Israel from bondage in Egypt, they repeatedly murmured against both Moses and God. Time and again in the wilderness they'd demonstrated their faithlessness, but God was faithful to them. Apart from the paschal blood, there was no difference between an Egyptian house and one of a Jew.

Josiah knew his own heart. Though he longed to please God and obey His commandments, he often fell short. His sin grieved him. As the blood flowed from the neck of his lamb, he recalled looking into Jesus' eyes. He'd felt unworthy, yet saw mercy in them. As he killed the lamb, he was fully aware of his need for grace. The blood was a covering for his house.

As soon as the lamb breathed its last, they were ushered to the side where the Levites took the carcass and hung it on special hooks, while the next lamb was being slain. Isaac was amazed at their skill as they gutted the lamb, skinned it, washed the edible entrails and burned the rest upon the altar. They moved so rapidly the task was accomplished in minutes. Before the boys knew it, the prepared lamb was tied on a stave and placed upon their shoulders. Another Levite led them from the Court of the Priests. A line quickly formed behind them of worshippers bearing their sacrificed lambs upon their shoulders.

The Levites continued to chant through the *Hallel* accompanied by harps and brass instruments, with the worshippers responding accordingly. Josiah and the boys observed the sacrifices and were amazed at the speed with which they were performed. It was as if the tempo quickened, as the Levites sang through the six psalms of the *Hallel*. Michael was astonished with the precision of the priests, as the lines moved non-stop and thousands of lambs were sacrificed in the time it took to recite the *Hallel* three times. The numbers of lambs to be sacrificed dwindled to the final few as the Levites drew to the end of last psalm.

Suddenly, Josiah was struck by the amount of blood flowing like a river in the floor of the Temple before the altar. He'd read about Passover and dreamt of it all of his life, but his imagination could not prepare him for what he saw. Their religion was a bloody religion, because God is a holy God, and His people a sinful people.

He paid careful attention to those last lines of the psalm as the final lambs were slain. He remembered them vividly. His own little Naomi had sung them to Jesus upon the Temple steps.

"Blessed be He that cometh in the name of the LORD: we have blessed You out of the house of the LORD!"

The shepherd joined in with the masses and sang:

"Blessed be He that cometh in the name of the LORD: we have blessed You out of the house of the LORD!"

He would not have been surprised had Jesus manifested Himself at that precise moment, while the singing continued.

"God is the LORD, which hath shewed us light: bind the sacrifice with cords, even unto the horns of the altar. Thou art my God, and I will praise Thee: Thou art my God, I will exalt Thee. O give thanks unto the LORD; for He is good: for His mercy endureth forever."

Josiah and his sons shouted with the congregation, *"Hallelujah!"* And in that moment the final sacrifice was completed. Standing now shoulder to shoulder before the Nicanor Gate were thousands of God's people, bearing their slain paschal lambs.

The trumpet sounded again, and the Levites reopened the massive doors. Josiah and his sons exited and made their way through those gathered as the second division to offer their lambs. Josiah was gripped with the repetition of the number three. Three notes of the trumpet began the sacrifices as three divisions offered their lambs, and with each division the Levitical choir chanted through the *Hallel* three times.

As they headed out of the Temple gate and climbed down the stairs Michael turned to his father and asked with astonishment, "How father? How could so many lambs be offered in such a short time?"

"It's a miracle my son," was his soft reply. "It's a miracle."

At that time they heard the trumpet sound again, three sustained notes to signal the beginning of sacrifices. As they departed from the Temple and headed into the city, they could clearly hear the Levites singing the *Hallel* again. The process was being repeated. Blood was flowing. Lambs were being slain.

Deborah was waiting for them at an oven located directly in front of Hannah's house. She had a pomegranate spit ready to impale the lamb. Josiah took it from her and inserted it through the lamb before putting the spit in place in the oven with Isaac and Michael's help. He was careful that the lamb not touch the sides of the oven, nor the coals beneath it. Just about the time he had his lamb in place, Nathaniel arrived with his sacrifice. As Josiah had done, he assisted his wife by inserting the spit. Soon, both lambs were roasting side by side. The coals were hot, and the meat would cook quickly. That was important because others would need to use the oven when they were finished.

Josiah left the roasting in the hands of his sons and followed his wife into the house. A smile lit up his face when he saw Hannah's extended belly.

He greeted her as a sister he'd not seen since she was a little girl and whispered, "What a wonderful surprise, congratulations."

Hannah hugged him, unable to hide her joy over answered prayer.

When he saw James, he warmly embraced his wife's brother. He'd been about Simon's age when Deborah's parents migrated to Israel and it was good to see him again as a man. The shepherd was introduced to their spouses and then admired the preparations accomplished by his precious wife and her sister. The main room was ready for them with plenty of space for the twenty souls who'd be worshipping together. He picked out his place and envisioned leading his extended family through the Seder Service. For a moment, he thought back to that Passover, so long ago, when he was but a boy, and his father led them in the service.

God's covenant blessings were evident. The younger children were excited, knowing there would be prizes for those who asked the right questions, already wondering just where their father might hide the *Afikomen.*

Josiah had often told his children about the Seder, even though they couldn't observe it in Kedar. The children in particular liked to hear about how the leader would break off a piece of the lamb and hide it. Then, at the conclusion of the meal, they were permitted to hunt for it. The one who found the treasure would take it to the leader and he would redeem it with a prize. The *Afikomen* would be blessed and become the dessert at the end of the meal.

All day long the children had been teasing one another, each predicting that they would be the one to find the treasure.

The day had finally arrived. Thirty long years had passed since the Shepherd of Kedar last celebrated the Passover. He considered it all: the years in Kedar away from God's people and His Temple, the long pilgrimage to finally come to this place, and the sacrifice of the lamb earlier in the afternoon at the Temple. Now at last, the time to celebrate was at hand.

CHAPTER 12

Bread from Heaven

John 6:58

This is that bread which came down from heaven: not as your fathers did eat manna, and are dead: he that eateth of this bread shall live forever.

Deborah watched her husband as he walked around the room where they would be celebrating Passover. He could immediately see his dear wife's touch. Evidence of her handiwork was everywhere.

"My lord, would you assist me in the arrangement of the table?" She asked, as she bowed before him.

Josiah responded immediately, "You know I don't like for you to call me lord."

"I just thought I'd follow the tradition of our people while we're here in Jerusalem," she replied, but the look in her eyes betrayed the fact that she was teasing him.

Realizing that they were alone in the room, which was remarkable with so many people around; the shepherd picked up his wife, kissed her gently on the lips and whispered, "You will never sit at my feet. You will always, always be by my side."

"It would be my joy to serve you for the rest of my days, my lord," she responded, before both of them started laughing.

"What can I do to help?" He asked.

She picked up three of the loaves of unleavened bread and said, "Hannah told me that the tradition has changed regarding the *Afikomen*. Instead of using a piece of the lamb as you've taught the children, the leader now breaks off a piece of *matzo* instead.

"I wonder why that has changed," Josiah replied in confusion.

"I don't know, but this afternoon Hannah told us something very intriguing."

"What did she say?" He responded as his interest was piqued.

"She said that she's seen Jesus three times. The first time was in Jerusalem, and that time, she and Joel witnessed Him healing a lame man at the pool called Bethesda."

He remembered the pool from when he was a boy, even though they had not passed by it on the Day of Presentation, nor had he seen it earlier that day.

"But it was the other two times that really made me wonder about things," she continued.

"Tell me," her husband responded.

First, she told him about how Jesus fed the multitude with just a few loaves and fishes. Josiah was just as stunned by the tale as she'd been when she first heard it.

"That's unbelievable!" He exclaimed. "He fed over five thousand men, plus the women and children with just five barley loaves and two fishes?"

"Yes, that's incredible," she responded, "But it was what happened the following day that troubles me most."

"What happened?" He asked.

"The next morning they sailed across the lake to the place where Jesus had fed the multitude; but He wasn't there, nor were any of His disciples. Then they saw other boats sailing to the north toward Capernaum. They followed in Joel's brother's boat and found Him soon after they landed."

"Did He work other miracles that day?" He asked.

"I don't know," She replied before pausing to collect her thoughts. "What perplexes me is what Jesus said to them and then what the crowd did."

Josiah didn't say anything as he waited for her to tell him.

"He said, *'I am the bread of life: he that cometh to Me shall never hunger; and he that believeth on Me shall never thirst.'*"

Josiah nodded his head before saying, "That seems in keeping with the miracle He performed the day before."

Deborah agreed with him, but then added, "After that, Hannah said that the crowds began to murmur against Him and deserted Him after He finished His teaching."

"Why would they do that?" A confused Josiah asked.

"Hannah said it was for two reasons. First, He refused to feed them again, but then it was what He said."

Deborah hesitated to make sure she got it right. "During His teaching He said something rather strange, *'Whoso eateth My flesh, and drinketh My blood, hath eternal life; and I will raise him up at the last day. For My flesh is meat indeed, and My blood is drink indeed. He that eateth My flesh, and drinketh My blood, dwelleth in Me, and I in him.'*"

Josiah was as baffled by the statement as the crowd must have been that day in Capernaum.

"Did Hannah know what He meant by that?" He asked.

"She didn't know and neither Joel nor Samuel understood either. All they know is that the crowds left Him that day."

Suddenly, Josiah's face lit up, "Do you think Jesus' teaching that He is the bread of life has anything to do with the change in the tradition regarding the *Afikomen*?"

"I don't know. That's what I was wondering."

He looked around the table and saw his favorite pillow resting at the very place he'd chosen for himself. Next to the place, he saw four pieces of linen cloth neatly folded on the table. Immediately, he realized they were there to cover the bread.

Deborah moved to the table and carefully put the first cloth in place. She then stacked the three loaves on top of each other, separating each of them with a piece of cloth, before covering the whole with the largest linen.

Josiah watched her do her work and then suddenly realized that her pillow was not beside his. Quickly checking the room he found it on the far end of the table. He didn't speak a word as he walked around the table, picked up her pillow, and placed it right beside his on the floor. She didn't say anything either, but the gleam in her eye revealed her mischief. She knew what he would do. Once again, they burst out laughing as soon as he realized she'd set him up.

"It would be my privilege to recline at your right hand in the place of honor, my lord," she whispered.

She knew there was never any doubt about where she would sit.

"I think I need to talk about all of this with Ephraim," Josiah said.

"That would be good," she replied. "You have plenty of time before the feast."

Realizing that he had better take advantage of a precious moment alone with his wife, he kissed her again, only to be interrupted by giggles from the door. When the two of them looked up, Naomi and Joanna were standing there staring at them.

"Daddy, why are you kissing Mommy?" Naomi asked, giggling again.

Josiah hurried across the room, picked up his little girl and said, "Because I love her."

Then he started kissing her cheeks, first one and then the other, causing the little one to burst out laughing.

"Why...why are you kissing me?" She cackled, trying to catch her breath.

"Because I love you too," he responded teasingly.

He put Naomi down and started out the door, when she suddenly said, "What about Joanna?"

The shepherd smiled, leaned over and kissed Nathaniel's youngest on the top of her head and replied, "Yes, I love Joanna too."

He heard both girls giggling as he left the house and headed next door. When he arrived, Miriam greeted him.

"Where's Ephraim?" He asked.

"He's resting in the back room, but he told me he would like to see you."

Josiah followed her and saw the old man sitting up in the bed, his face aglow with joy. At first, he didn't see the other man who was standing in the corner of the room.

"You must be Josiah," the man exclaimed.

Josiah looked at him and recognized him immediately. Other than his hair and beard being gray, and a few wrinkles on his face, Samuel looked just like he had thirty years earlier.

The two men quickly embraced, before Samuel leaned back and looked at him.

"The last time I saw you, you were a boy," he said, gesturing with his hand the height of a ten-year old.

"You've hardly changed at all," Josiah exclaimed.

After embracing him again, he turned to Ephraim and spoke to him.

"Deborah said that Hannah told her about seeing Jesus in Galilee, and of some of the things He said. His words are baffling to us, and I wondered what you might think of them."

It was Samuel who spoke up first, "I think I probably know what Hannah was referring to, because I was there with her and Joel."

By that time, several of the men had joined them in the bedroom.

Once everyone was settled, Samuel continued, "Was it Jesus' teaching on the bread of life?"

"Yes, it was," Josiah replied, "but specifically He said, *'Whoso eateth My flesh, and drinketh My blood, hath eternal life; and I will raise him up at the last day. For My flesh is meat indeed, and My blood is drink indeed. He that eateth My flesh, and drinketh My blood, dwelleth in Me, and I in him.'"*

Samuel looked at Joel, and it was clear that both men remembered the statement.

"Yes, He said that," Samuel responded before continuing, "Joel and I talked about it, and we had no idea what Jesus meant when He said that. Later, I was able to ask His disciple, Andrew, and he didn't know what to say either. Sometimes, Jesus can be so baffling. Many deserted Him that day, and those of us who remained were confused. It seemed like He offended the masses on purpose."

"When we were at the Temple on Monday, Jesus said all kinds of things to offend the Pharisees and the scribes," Michael added.

"The difference is that the Pharisees and the scribes already hate Him. They are His enemies. What I don't understand is why He must offend those who truly want to believe in Him. Sometimes the crowds come to hear His teaching, only to hear Him tell mystifying parables," Samuel replied with a slight note of frustration in his voice.

"I think I know why He's been doing that," Michael interjected, ever reflecting on things.

Everyone immediately turned their attention to the young man who was wise well beyond his years.

"He's weaning out those who are not serious about being His disciples. Surely, many followed Him to see the signs and wonders, like pagans seek after sorcerers and the workers of magic. Jesus wants His disciples to believe in Him with their whole hearts."

"I'm convinced this young man is right," Samuel answered. "What's your name?"

"That's Michael. He's my second son," Josiah responded.

"I can already tell he's a fine young man," he replied.

"Both of my older sons are godly men, by God's grace," Josiah declared with joy as he put his hands on their shoulders.

"I've come to believe, just as Michael said, that Jesus expects us to believe in Him with our whole hearts. That's got to be what he meant by *'eating His flesh'* and *'drinking His blood.'* Surely, He was speaking symbolically and not literally," Samuel explained.

All of the men nodded their heads in agreement.

Josiah suddenly remembered the lesson he'd learned from Zacharias.

"My brother, Zacharias, taught me a truth that has transformed the way I read the Scriptures. Do you remember what I'm referring to?" He asked the rabbi from Elath.

Zacharias smiled knowingly and said, "All the Scriptures speak of Him."

"Yes, that's right. I believe that now with all of my heart. All of the Scriptures point us to the Messiah. Samuel, do you know whether Jesus will be eating Passover in Jerusalem tonight?"

"He will, but the location is a closely guarded secret. I asked Andrew about it yesterday and he had no idea," he replied.

"Today, my wife asked me to help her prepare the table. I was surprised to learn that the tradition has changed regarding the *Afikomen* – that now a piece of *matzo* has replaced a piece of the paschal lamb." Josiah said.

"Yes, that tradition changed gradually over time since you were here as a boy," Ephraim interjected. "No one really knows why."

Josiah continued his thought, "After hearing her tell me about Jesus saying that He is the bread of life, I began to wonder if even the bread of Passover speaks of Him. Surely, it must, and this must be a special Passover. Could Jesus' coming be the reason for the change in the *Afikomen*? How will He transform the meal? If it speaks of Him, what will it say? If only we could hear what He will teach His disciples tonight about the bread, especially the *Afikomen*." Josiah said.

Samuel knew exactly what he was saying and added, "After Jesus spoke those perplexing words that day in Capernaum, He then said, *'This is that bread which came down from heaven: not as your fathers did eat manna, and are dead: he that eateth of this bread shall live forever.'"*

"Jesus is bread, greater than the manna," Michael exclaimed. "Just like Jesus is a prophet greater than Moses, and a priest greater than Aaron, and a king greater than David. He is bread greater than manna!"

"Yes Son, that's how we must read the Scriptures, if all the Scriptures speak of Him!" Josiah cried out with excitement.

All the men said *"Amen,"* and Ephraim began to pray, "Great God in Heaven, feed us with this Bread from Heaven. Glorify Your Son, Jesus, the Messiah. May He be victorious over His enemies. May He take up His rightful place as Prophet, Priest and King of His people. Do not let us go, O Lord. Do not let us forsake Him, but rather cause us to believe in Him with our whole hearts."

Again, all the men said, *"Amen!"*

The time for the feast was drawing nigh. Martha was waiting at the door for Joseph, and the two of them hurried outside to spend a few minutes together. As soon as they rounded the corner, she threw her arms around him and began to cry.

"What's wrong?" He asked.

"I want to be with you tonight, but my father won't let me," she cried, holding on to him like she never wanted to let go.

"It's okay," he replied. "We can be together tomorrow."

His words couldn't console her. She was frightened that everything was about to change because of Jesus. She didn't know what would happen to her and Joseph.

At that moment, Miriam stepped outside and heard what she said. She didn't mean to eavesdrop, but couldn't help but hear. Her heart broke for her cousin, so she decided to try to help. She went back into the house and asked Michael if she could speak to him privately. He nodded his head, and the two of them went outside the house.

"Martha is distraught because she can't be with Joseph tonight," Miriam said to him.

"I know, but Father is adamant that we all be together for Passover," he replied.

"Do you think he would let me switch places with her tonight? She really wants to be with Joseph. I could be your guest, and she could be Joseph's guest."

Michael liked the idea of being Miriam's escort to the feast; and besides that, he couldn't say no to her pleading brown eyes.

"I'll speak to Father about it, but you're coming with me."

She was taken aback a little about facing Josiah with such a request, but knew it would be better if she did. He would have a harder time saying no if she was standing there with Michael.

"Okay, let's do it," she said.

He took her by the hand and led her back into the house. His father was talking to Samuel.

"Father, can I speak to you for a moment?" He asked.

Josiah bid farewell to Samuel and turned to listen to his son.

"Sir, I know how much you want all of our family to be together tonight, but Martha would really like to celebrate the feast with Joseph."

"I've already addressed that," his father said tersely.

"Sir, I would be glad to change places with Martha. I could be Michael's guest," Miriam said sweetly.

Josiah was set to flatly deny the request when Michael spoke up again, "Father, you've taught us to look toward the future. I know that at Passover we remember the past, but haven't we learned that we look at the past to anticipate the future? Martha's future is with Joseph. Her desire to worship with him is a wonderful thing."

While he was speaking, Miriam realized that he was still holding her hand. She looked at him and admired him all the more. Could it be that her future would be with him after all? She could only hope.

Josiah hadn't thought about it that way before. Just at that moment he looked up, as Martha and Joseph walked in the door. His daughter looked at him and tears immediately welled up in her eyes. He suddenly realized he'd only been thinking of himself and not about her.

He took a deep breath before saying to Michael, "Son, you're right. It's okay with me, as long as Nathaniel doesn't mind."

Miriam smiled and hugged her older cousin.

"I'm sure he won't mind," she replied.

The shepherd decided to say goodnight to Ephraim, as Michael and Miriam sought out her father.

Nathaniel quickly agreed, because he couldn't deny his daughter anything she asked either. Of course, she rarely asked anything of him.

So, Michael and Miriam immediately started searching for Martha and Joseph. They found them outside where she had gone to compose herself.

"Martha," Michael called out.

She and Joseph turned around as her brother and Miriam approached them.

"You tell them the news," Michael said to Miriam.

"Michael and I just asked your father, if you and I could trade places tonight for the feast."

Martha's eyes got really big as she suddenly had a glimmer of hope.

"What did he say?" She asked, her eyes pleading to know.

"He said it would be okay with him, if Father said we could do it."

Miriam paused for a moment, and the suspense was getting to Martha.

"Well, what did he say?"

"I guess you're going to be Joseph's guest for the feast," she responded.

Martha squealed with glee and hugged Miriam first, and then her brother, before finally embracing Joseph. This time her tears were tears of joy.

Josiah walked back into Hannah's house where Deborah, Hannah and the children were busy setting the table.

He moved close to his wife and said, "I'm going to go into the back room to pray in preparation for the feast."

Joel knew how much Josiah wanted to lead the worship and had gladly relinquished the position of host for the meal to him. Hannah had also insisted that Deborah serve as hostess. It was an honor that both of them cherished.

Deborah nodded her head and said, "That would be good. We'll finish up everything out here.

The shepherd closed the door behind him and dropped to his knees in prayer. His mind was filled with so many things. This was the moment he'd been waiting for all of these years – to eat the Passover with his family. He cried out to God, asking for wisdom and insight to teach them on this special night. Many of the things he'd taught them through the years would be recalled vividly during the meal. As he prayed he felt inadequate to the task. He knew the Scriptures through and through. He could recite the *Torah* by heart, but he felt that there were so many things hidden, yet to be revealed by the Messiah. He longed to teach them to believe in Jesus, and to do it during the meal, but how?

"God, give me the words," he prayed. "Give me insight into your Word to see Jesus and to proclaim Him. I know all of the Scriptures speak of Him. Show Him to me in the story of the Exodus."

He rose to his feet and was surprised by the stillness in the house. In the distance, he could already hear others singing. The time had finally arrived. It was time to teach those He loved the most about their God.

When he stepped into the living room, it was aglow with candlelight. The table was fully prepared and beautiful. His extended family was gathered, all sitting in their places awaiting his arrival in silence. Deborah smiled, knowing the significance of this moment to him. As he approached his place, the family stood out of respect for him. Suddenly, he felt overwhelmed with emotion, with humility, with love. He looked at each of them gathered around his table and gave thanks to God for His covenantal faithfulness. All of them, each and every one of them were covenant keepers by God's grace.

There on the table were the plates, the cups, the wineskins. He saw the unleavened bread, and thought of Jesus' saying, *"I am the bread of life."*

He saw the bitter herbs and remembered the groaning of God's people under bondage in Egypt, but of God's great deliverance, as evidenced in this night of celebration.

In the midst of the table was the lamb. He remembered the feel of the knife cutting the flesh of the animal, its blood poured upon the altar, a substitute, a covering. Now, it's perfectly cooked, expertly prepared by his wife. John's words flooded his mind when he'd testified of Jesus, *"Behold the Lamb of God, which taketh away the sin of the world."* Surely, Jesus was about to provide a salvation that would exceed that of Moses, a salvation to which the Exodus was but a shadow.

Once again, the shepherd felt overwhelmed, almost lost. He closed his eyes and whispered, "O Lord give me the words to say to shepherd this, my flock, that my children might know You, through Your Son, Jesus, the Messiah."

CHAPTER 13

The Passover of God

Numbers 9:2

Let the children of Israel also keep the Passover at His appointed season.

With the setting of the sun the feast began. Suddenly the shepherd's family heard the sound of a *shofar*. The children looked in the direction of the sound, and Josiah immediately recognized its tone. It was the *shofar* he'd given to Zacharias on the pilgrimage. He knew that his teacher and friend was about to call the band next door to worship with the *Shema*.

The liturgy of the Seder had developed through the centuries to an almost fixed form. However, the shepherd knew that the *Torah* did not reveal the details of a liturgy, just the date of Passover, its symbols, and the things to be celebrated. Zacharias' blowing of the *shofar* was a departure from ordinary protocol, but in keeping with the spirit of the feast. Josiah intended to take some liberties himself in order to demonstrate how the feast points to Messiah. This task overwhelmed him because he knew there were many things still hidden, things Jesus had yet to reveal. He wanted desperately to get everything right.

Taking his cue from Zacharias, he called his own to worship by chanting the *Shema*.

"*Shema!*" He cried with a loud voice.

His children knew what to do and instantly responded, "*Yisrael!*"

"*Shema!*" Josiah repeated.

"*Yisrael!*" The band cried.

"*Shema!*" The Shepherd heralded.

"*Yisrael!*" The company proclaimed and then in unison sang, "*Adonai Elohenu Adonai echad.*"

As soon as they finished the *Shema*, Deborah, as hostess, removed the veil from her face. Until that moment all of the women and girls had their faces covered. By removing the veil, she was signifying that the celebration of liberty had begun.

Josiah took the wineskin and filled his cup, before passing it around the table. The older children assisted the younger ones pouring the wine. Once everyone was served, he explained the significance of the wine.

"The psalmist declares that God has given us wine to *make glad the heart of man.*"

He put the cup to his nose before continuing, "Smell the sweet fragrance, but don't taste – not yet. Because Passover commemorates God's mighty deliverance of His people from bondage in Egypt, wine is fitting for this feast. It is a time to celebrate. During the meal we will partake of four cups. Can you tell me the promise that each signifies?" Josiah asked, involving the children from the beginning.

Michael immediately answered, "The first is *V'hotzesi*"

"You are correct," Josiah replied. "Now, what does *V'hotzesi* signify?"

"It signifies God bringing His people out of bondage," Michael responded.

"Very good! Now, what promise is signified by the second cup?"

Michael raised his hand, but Josiah called on Simon who was also prepared to answer.

"*V'hitzalti,* which means deliverance from servitude." Simon answered confidently.

"Yes, my son. Now, who will tell us the name and meaning of the third cup?" The shepherd asked.

Miriam glanced at Michael, wondering if she should raise her hand. It was customary for only boys to speak, but neither Josiah nor her father had ever felt compelled to follow such customs. When he nodded his approval, she slowly lifted her hand for Josiah to see.

Josiah was pleased and called on her.

Miriam answered, "*V'goalti,* which means redemption – redemption from slavery to the Egyptians."

"Yes, Miriam, you are correct. Your father has taught you well."

It pleased her for Josiah to praise her father. In that moment, she silently thanked God for all of the men in her life. Each of them was a man of God. First, of course was her father, Nathaniel, and then Josiah. She'd always admired him. Then she thought of Ephraim and everything he'd taught her since her family had arrived in Bethlehem. Lastly, she considered Michael. She looked at him and admired how handsome he was, but more than anything, she respected him for his zeal for God. The Lord had blessed her with the men in her life. She glanced across the table and saw Isaac reclining next to his wife. It amazed her how much things had changed. Her love for Isaac was now a distant memory, almost like a dream. When she looked at Michael again, she prayed that he would be the man of her future.

Her thoughts were interrupted when Josiah asked, "And what is the name and the meaning of the fourth cup?"

Naomi was anxiously waving her hand, emitting little sounds in a vain attempt to get her father's attention; but he had something else in mind for his littlest one. Instead, he called on his youngest son, Judah.

Judah responded, "*V'lokahti*, which means that God will be our God and we will forever be His people."

"Very well said, my son," Josiah replied proudly.

Naomi had a look of frustration on her face until her father winked at her. She knew he was giving the others a chance to answer because it would be her responsibility as the youngest to ask the four questions a little later. Still, she wished she could answer all of her father's questions.

Haifa was a bit surprised that her husband didn't involve himself more. When she looked at him, he realized what she must be thinking.

He whispered into her ear, "I'd rather let the younger ones answer. It will help them concentrate on the teaching better."

She nodded her head and smiled. Everything her husband did made her love and respect him all the more. He had truly become a humble and godly man. Dinah sat in silence as well, content to let the younger children have their say, always assisting them when needed.

Josiah lifted his cup and pronounced the blessing:

"Boruch atto Adonai Elohenu melech ho'olom bore p'ri haggofen."

"Praised art Thou, O Lord our God, King of the universe, who hast created the fruit of the vine."

"Taste, but don't drink – not yet." He said.

Each of them lifted their cups and took a sip of the wine.

"The wine tastes sweet, but it also has a little bite of bitterness. The bitter taste reminds us that our forefathers toiled in hardship under their taskmasters in Egypt. Our people have always relished liberty and living in bondage was a contradiction to their constitutions. The sweetness of the wine brings to mind the wonderful exhilaration of redemption by God's mighty hand. He heard the cries of their toil and sent them a deliverer. Moses led them from bondage to freedom. Finally, they came to this land of promise."

He paused momentarily to make sure he had everyone's undivided attention.

"Now, who can cite the passage in the law where we find the promises from God represented by the cups?"

Josiah was surprised when none of his children raised their hands, especially Michael and Naomi.

Finally, it was Michael who spoke for the rest of the children, "We think Isaac should answer this question."

The oldest son was both surprised and moved by this gesture from his siblings.

He looked at his father and said, "This passage is precious to me, because it speaks of our birthright as God's people from His own promises. This is a birthright I foolishly abandoned for a season."

His voice cracked with emotion and a tear came to his eye. Then he felt the comforting touch of his wife. Miriam saw the tenderness between them and rejoiced secretly in her heart. This was right, of that she had no doubt.

Isaac was finally able to compose himself and continued, "But God was gracious to me and brought the prodigal home. Now, I claim these promises for myself, having been liberated from my own bondage, bondage to my sin. The passage is from Exodus and in it God says, *'Wherefore say unto the children of Israel, I am the LORD, and I will bring you out from under the burdens of the Egyptians, and I will rid you out of their bondage, and I will redeem you with a stretched out arm, and with great judgments: And I will take you to me for a people, and I will be to you a God: and ye shall know that I am the LORD your God, which bringeth you out from under the burdens of the Egyptians.'"*

There wasn't a dry eye in the house as Isaac spoke those words from his heart. Haifa couldn't have been prouder of her husband. His grandparents were also pleased, just now fully realizing, that had not God brought him to repentance, they would not have been able to see their grandson.

"Let's drink the first cup," Josiah declared.

All in the company drank the first cup with thanksgiving to God.

Josiah sat down and reclined at his place before continuing. He picked up a piece of watercress off of the plate in front of him, and thereby instructed the others to do the same before pronouncing the blessing:

"Boruch atto Adonoi Elohenu melech ho'olom bore p'ri ho'adomo.

"Praised art Thou, O Lord our God, King of the universe, Creator of the fruit of the earth."

The shepherd led them by example and dipped the watercress into a bowl of salt water before eating it. Each of those gathered around the table knew to do the same. The watercress reminded them of God's provision from the earth, especially after they entered the land of promise, a land flowing with milk and honey.

Once they'd all partaken, a big smile came to Josiah's face.

"Okay, everyone under the age of twelve close your eyes and cover them with your hands. No peeking!"

Jared, Judah and Naomi excitedly obeyed their father. Nathan was almost twelve, but didn't mind playing the game and covered his eyes with the younger ones. Benjamin and Ruth had recently turned thirteen and were proud to be included among the adults.

Josiah took the middle loaf of unleavened bread and broke it. He returned half of it to its place, but took the other half and stood, looking for a place to hide it. He knew he better keep an eye on Naomi, and when he saw her peeking through her fingers, he hurried over and started to tickle her.

"I told you to hide your eyes," he said playfully.

The little girl couldn't stop giggling, and Dinah knew they could never trust her; so she helped Naomi by putting her hands over her eyes.

"Hey, I can't see anything!" Naomi complained.

"That's the point," Dinah replied, laughing at her little sister's antics.

Josiah made quite a deliberate show of hiding the *Afikomen* to the adults.

"Should I put it here?" He asked himself out loud, before hurrying around the table and saying, "Maybe here?"

He repeated that several times, having hidden the bread in Haifa's lap under a piece of cloth.

"Or maybe here?" He finally said once he was seated.

He reclined on his elbow, picked up another piece of watercress and waited until one by one the younger children opened their eyes.

"What are you looking for?" He asked as if he didn't know.

"Daddy, we're looking for the piece of lamb!" Naomi cried out with glee.

"No, it's not a piece of lamb anymore," her father replied.

The younger children all had surprised looks on their faces.

"The tradition has changed, and now you will be searching for a piece of bread instead," he continued.

"Why the change?" Nathan asked.

"I'll explain that later," his father replied.

Naomi rose up and started looking all over the place with her little eyes – clearly searching for the *Afikomen*.

Not yet," her father said firmly. "After the meal, you children will be able to hunt for the bread, and I'll redeem it from the one who finds it with a prize."

She still had a look of amusement on her face, until her father's expression became more solemn.

He looked at her and said, "My youngest child, do you have any questions for me?"

Immediately, she knew it was time for her to ask the four questions, so that her father could tell them the story of the exodus by answering them.

"Father, why is this night different from all other nights? On all other nights, we eat either leavened or unleavened bread. Why, on this night, do we eat only unleavened bread?"

She looked to her father for direction, and he nodded his head indicating she should continue.

"On all other nights, we eat all kinds of herbs. Why, on this night, do we eat especially bitter herbs? On all other nights, we do not dip herbs in any condiment. Why, on this night, do we dip them in salt water and *haroses?* On all other nights, we eat without special festivities. Why, on this night, do we hold this Seder service?"

When she finished the questions, she had a look of satisfaction on her face and sighed audibly which made everyone chuckle, that is, until they saw the stern look on their father's face. He had to concentrate to keep from smiling himself, but knew this was a sacred moment. It was time to tell the story of God's mighty salvation of His people. So, beginning with Joseph, the shepherd told the entire story of how God's people came to be in Egypt in the first place, of how they became slaves in the midst of that country, and of how God delivered them mightily through His servant, Moses.

The whole time he told the story, he searched his mind for how it pointed to the coming of Messiah, but didn't think it wise to interject those thoughts into the narrative. To be truthful, much of it still escaped him. He knew that during the meal, his children would prompt him for answers, especially Michael, and prayed that God would reveal the answers to him.

The children all knew what was coming next.

Without having to be prompted Nathan asked, "What is the meaning of *Pesah?*"

His father replied, "*Pesah* means the 'Paschal Lamb.' It is the sacrifice of the Lord's Passover, because He passed over the houses of the children of Israel in Egypt – wherever the blood was applied – when He smote the firstborn of the Egyptians."

Jared spoke next, "What is the meaning of *Matzo?*"

His father responded, "*Matzo*, called 'The Bread of Affliction,' was the hasty provision that our fathers made for their journey, as it is said: *'And they baked unleavened cakes of the dough which they brought out of Egypt. There was not sufficient time to leaven it, for they were driven out of Egypt and could not tarry, neither had they prepared for themselves any provisions.'*"

Next, it was Judah's turn.

"What is the meaning of *Moror?*"

Josiah picked up one of the bitter herbs and said, "*Moror* means 'bitter herb.' We eat it in order to recall that the lives of our ancestors were embittered by the Egyptians, as we read: *'And they made their lives bitter with hard labor in mortar and bricks and in all manner of field labor. Whatever task was imposed upon them, was executed with the utmost rigor.'*"

Then Josiah lifted his voice and started to sing the first part of the *Hallel*, which included the first two psalms. The children knew them by heart and repeated each line after him.

"Praise ye the LORD. Praise, O ye servants of the LORD, praise the name of the LORD. Blessed be the name of the LORD from this time forth and forevermore. From the rising of the sun unto the going down of the same the LORD's name is to be praised."

Both Isaac and Michael immediately thought about hearing those words repeated in the Temple while the lambs were being slain. They would never forget the bass voices of the Levites as the massive choir sang. That night in the house, Josiah's extended family did everything they could to match the sound heard earlier that day. What they lacked in volume they made up in enthusiasm.

After singing the first *Hallel*, they immediately began the second as it describes the deliverance of God:

"When Israel went out of Egypt, the house of Jacob from a people of strange language; Judah was His sanctuary, and Israel His dominion. The sea saw it and fled: Jordan was driven back. The mountains skipped like rams, and the little hills like lambs. What ailed thee, O thou sea, that thou fleddest? thou Jordan, that thou wast driven back? Ye mountains, that ye skipped like rams; and ye little hills like lambs? Tremble, thou earth, at the presence of the Lord, at the presence of the God of Jacob; which turned the rock into a standing water, the flint into a fountain of waters.

Naomi giggled when they sang of the mountains and hills skipping like rams and lambs. She closed her eyes and imagined seeing them in the desert back home in Kedar and wondered how mountains and hills could skip, but knew better than to ask her father.

Once they finished singing the psalms, Josiah put his finger to his lips to silence them, and then his hand to his ear to encourage them to listen. Sure enough, Zacharias was leading the band next door in the singing of the psalms, and in the distance they could hear others, at various stages in the *Hallel*.

"Listen, my children and rejoice in the unity of God's people. Remember the wonder of the next to the last psalm of the Songs of Ascents as it extols the beauty of that unity. *'Behold, how good and how pleasant it is for brethren to dwell together in unity!'*"

"Beloved, let us sing to the Lord the psalm that is called the Great *Hallel*," he declared, closing his eyes as he began to chant:

"O give thanks unto the LORD; for He is good:"

The children needed no instruction in their refrain:

"For His mercy endureth forever."

As he continued through the psalm line by line, the worshipers repeated the refrain after each line.

"O give thanks unto the God of gods. O give thanks to the Lord of lords. To Him who alone doeth great wonders. To Him that by wisdom made the heavens. To Him that stretched out the earth above the waters. To Him that made great lights: The sun to rule by day, The moon and stars to rule by night. To Him that smote Egypt in their firstborn, And brought out Israel from among them, With a strong hand, and with a stretched out arm. To Him which divided the Red sea into parts, And made Israel to pass through the midst of it, But overthrew Pharaoh and his host in the Red Sea. To Him which led His people through the wilderness. To Him which smote great kings: Sihon king of the Amorites, And Og the king of Bashan. And gave their land for an heritage, Even an heritage unto Israel His servant. Who remembered us in our low estate, And hath redeemed us from our enemies. Who giveth food to all flesh. O give thanks unto the God of heaven!"

And all the company declared in unison, *"For His mercy endureth for ever."*

It was now time for the second cup, and Josiah began by offering this blessing:

"Praised art Thou, O Lord our God, King of the universe, who hast redeemed us and our ancestors from Egypt, and hast enabled us to observe this night of the Passover, the Feast of Unleavened Bread. O Lord our God and God of our fathers, may we, with Thy help, live to celebrate other feasts and holy seasons. May we rejoice in Thy salvation and be gladdened by Thy righteousness. Grant deliverance to mankind through Israel, Thy people. May Thy will be done through Jacob, Thy chosen servant, so that Thy name shall be sanctified in the midst of all the earth, and that all peoples be moved to worship Thee with one accord. And we shall sing new songs of praise unto Thee, for our redemption and for the deliverance of our souls. Praised art Thou, O God, Redeemer of Israel."

This was the traditional blessing before the meal, and Josiah was struck with the universal character of the prayer. Surely, God was about to answer this prayer powerfully through His servant, Jesus.

He lifted the wineskin once more, filled his cup and passed it around the table. Once all the cups were filled to the brim, he pronounced the blessing:

"Praised art Thou, O Lord our God, King of the universe, who hast created the fruit of the vine."

They drank the second cup together with gladness.

When everyone had finished their drink, he picked up the upper *matzo*, broke it and distributed it around the table.

Lifting it up, he said:

"Boruch atto Adonoi Elohenu melech ho'olom hamotzi lehem min ho'oretz."

"Praised art Thou, O Lord our God, King of the universe, who bringest forth bread from the earth."

He spoke an additional blessing:

"Boruch atto Adonoi Elohenu melech ho'olom asher kidd'shonu b'mitzvosov v'tzivonu al achilas matzo."

"Praised art Thou, O Lord our God, King of the universe, who hast sanctified us through Thy commandments, and ordained that we should eat unleavened bread."

Following his lead the company took a bite of the *matzo*.

He picked up a bitter herb, and placed it between two pieces of *matzo* along with *haroses*. The *haroses* is a sweet jam which makes the herb more palatable. It is also made in such a way that it has the appearance of the mortar the slaves used when building with bricks in Egypt. As with the wine, the combination of bitterness and sweetness reminded them of the toil of slavery and the pleasantness of liberty. Each of them followed his lead carefully. When Naomi struggled to get the *haroses* on the bread, Dinah was glad to help her.

The shepherd declared, *"With unleavened bread and with bitter herbs, they shall eat it."*

"Boruch atto Adonoi Elohenu melech ho'olom asher kidd'shonu b'mitzvosov v'tzivomu al achilas moror."

"Praised art Thou, O Lord our God, King of the universe, who hast sanctified us by Thy commandments, and ordained that we should eat bitter herbs."

They ate it together, and Josiah couldn't help but notice the look on the younger children's faces as they tasted the strange dish. Naomi, in particular made a face, but didn't say anything. She knew it was time to be quiet.

Now that the liturgy had ended thus far, Josiah smiled and said, "Let's eat!"

He didn't have to say it again as the boys began to dig in. The lamb was cooked to perfection, and for a while all that could be heard around the table was the sound of feasting. They were all thinking of different things. Of course, Naomi had her mind on the *Afikomen*, and even more particularly on the prize. She was determined to win the game. Michael's mind was full of questions, questions he could hardly wait to ask his father. Josiah was thinking about Jesus. Surely, He was nearby, somewhere in the city with His disciples, eating this same meal with them. Had he altered the liturgy and taught them how the feast pointed to Himself? The shepherd was certain of it and for a moment wished he could have been there with Him, but then he looked around the table and saw those he loved most. No, he was right where he wanted to be. He'd dreamt of this night for many years, and now it had finally arrived. There would be plenty of time later to learn what Jesus was about to reveal.

CHAPTER 14

The Afikomen

Exodus 12:14

*And this day shall be unto you for a memorial; and ye shall
keep it a feast to the LORD throughout your generations;
ye shall keep it a feast by an ordinance forever.*

The meal was delicious, but that was no surprise to Josiah's family.
Deborah's culinary skills were legendary. Even the bitter herbs were made
palatable by the sweet *haroses*. It didn't take the boys long to finish eating,
and Josiah could already see Michael's mind working by the expression
on his face.

Finally, his second son took a sip of wine and said, "Father, today has
been incredible, first at the Temple and now here in this house. So many
of God's people came to celebrate Passover together. What troubles me is
what's unspoken. God delivered our people from bondage in Egypt and
gave them this land, yet the land doesn't belong to us."

"What makes you say that?" His father asked.

"David's son is not seated upon the throne on Zion, at least not yet,"
he responded, with a slight smile in anticipation of what he believed Jesus
was about to do.

"Yes, but the land is ours. God gave us this land and no occupier can
take it from us."

"Do you really believe this is what God intended?" His son responded,
stretching out his arms to indicate everything they'd observed since
arriving in Israel.

"No my son, I understand what you mean. Judea is now ruled by Pontius Pilate, Caesar's emissary, and I cannot believe it is what God intended when He promised this land to Abraham."

"Father, I expected to see more Roman soldiers in the streets," Simon offered.

He'd looked for the soldiers when they passed through the city and saw them stationed in back alleys out of the way, instead of on the main thoroughfares. Josiah was pleased by how observant his son was.

"My father explained that to me many years ago," the shepherd replied. "The Romans are interlopers, and have no business occupying our land; but at times they exercise prudence in the way they rule. There is more of a visible Roman presence when it's not one of our holy days. If you will recall, we saw more soldiers on our first visit to the city on Sunday. Caesar knows that it's best to accommodate the various peoples he's conquered, by letting them observe their religious traditions without intrusion, unless of course, they openly rebel. The Romans learned long ago that a happy people is easier to rule than a resentful one."

"I resent their presence," Simon responded with the tone of a zealot.

"Yes, we all do," his father replied. "It's not how it should be, and alliances with the world can make the people forget who we are."

"Is that what's happened to the priests and the leaders of God's people?" Michael asked.

"I'm certain of it," Josiah replied. "They're afraid Jesus is going to shake things up, and they're satisfied with things just the way they are. They want to hold onto the power they have."

"They've sold out!" Simon exclaimed.

Josiah couldn't help but notice that Simon was a lot like Isaac had been before his repentance, yet he knew that his anger was justified. He hoped that his son would be able to control it better than his brother had. As he looked at his oldest, he couldn't help but wonder at the transformation that had taken place in him. The only time he'd seen him even remotely angry since his return was when they were cheated at the Temple on the Day of Presentation. That day, Josiah had understood his indignation. It was warranted and he shared it.

Turning his attention back to his younger son, he replied, "Yes, they've sold out; and but for the grace of God, we could as well. Guard your hearts that you not be tempted to compromise."

The shepherd was confident in his sons and their commitment to God, but realized the dangers of the world's temptations. Isaac knew this first hand and was determined by God's grace to remain faithful.

Still, the tenor of the conversation was about the occupation by Rome and the acquiescence in it of the Jewish leadership, in particular the High Priest. Josiah would never forget the hatred he saw on Caiaphas' face after Jesus cleansed the Temple. It was clear that both the High Priest and the Captain of the Temple intended to see to it that He was destroyed. With the shepherd's family so committed to Him as the Messiah, they couldn't help but be angry with those who opposed Him.

"Father, do you believe Jesus will ascend Mount Zion and take His seat upon the throne tomorrow on the first day of the Feast of Unleavened Bread?" Michael asked, voicing the question on everyone's heart.

Josiah had a gleam in his eye when he responded, "All indications are pointing in that direction. We must prepare ourselves."

"Should we take our *khanjars* with us in the streets tomorrow?" Simon asked with a growing excitement in his voice.

"We must pray that they won't be needed," his father replied.

"But shouldn't we be prepared to fight to defend Jesus, if necessary?" His son responded with a note of defiance.

Josiah didn't know what to say. The last thing he wanted to inspire in his sons was a militant spirit. Yet, on the other hand, Jesus' enemies meant Him harm. Would it not be the responsibility of His disciples to defend Him?

"Pray for peace," Josiah said softly.

"Remember the first of the Songs of Ascents," Simon exclaimed. *"I am for peace: but when I speak, they are for war!"*

"I know the psalm," his father replied, "But those words were uttered by the psalmist in Meshech and Kedar, not in the holy land."

"Yet, it's here in the holy land, where the leaders seek the life of Jesus; and are the Romans not here as a result of warfare, a war our forefathers lost?" Simon replied, his voice rising in volume until he saw his father's look of displeasure.

"Simon's right," Michael interjected. "We have to be prepared to fight if necessary."

Josiah knew that his sons were speaking the truth. He realized the stakes were high and that this was a significant moment in history. In his heart he was willing to take up arms if necessary to defend Jesus, but his soul was also weary from battle with the Kedarites. Caleb's death was never far from him, nor was the planned slaughter of his family by Asad. Like the psalmist, his heart longed for peace.

Finally, Isaac entered the conversation, and his father immediately tuned his ear to hear the wisdom of his eldest son.

"Remember the second psalm. It is God who declared to the nations, who plot vain things against Him and against His Messiah, *'Yet have I set My King upon My holy hill of Zion.'* We must be prepared to do whatever God requires of us, but God Himself has said that He will accomplish this. He is able to do so without sword or bow. He is Almighty God and is able to do all His holy will."

"Yes, my son," Josiah said with enthusiasm. "We must be prepared to do what the Lord asks us to do, but He will place His Son on Zion. He will crown Him King. Remember what God says to the King, *'Thou art My Son, this day have I begotten Thee. Ask of Me, and I shall give Thee the heathen for Thine inheritance, and the uttermost parts of the earth for Thy possession. Thou shalt break them with a rod of iron; Thou shalt dash them in pieces like a potter's vessel.'*"

Josiah raised his cup again and declared, "When you go to your bed tonight, sleep, rest in peace, for tomorrow our God will crown His Son King on Zion!"

"Amen!" They all shouted in unison, as they spoke of these things around the table.

Isaac had been listening carefully during the discussion, and something about it troubled his soul. Before he fled his father's tent, he would have been the first to take up arms. He still would if necessary, as he did when he fought with Asad; but his heart had been changed. He understood the problem of Roman occupation and the apostasy of the priesthood, but he also knew that God had delivered him from an even deeper bondage. Neither his father nor his brothers had ever known what it means to forsake the Lord and then to be forgiven such grievous sin. In his heart, he believed that the salvation that Jesus would bring would be more spiritual than political. Not knowing what to say, he didn't speak; lest he bring confusion to the table.

Sensing the discussion had ended, Josiah gathered the younger children around him.

"Okay, it's time to seek for the *Afikomen,* and I have a prize to redeem it for whoever finds it. Hurry, it will be the dessert of the meal!"

Naomi was quick as a cat as she scampered around the room. Nathan realized that she was so frantic that she'd never find it without help, so he quickly ceded his own opportunity for the prize to assist his little sister. Round and round the room the children moved, looking in every nook and corner. Of the boys, Judah took it most seriously. He'd already determined what he would do if he found it.

Naomi began to get frustrated, even with Nathan's help; and Deborah had to remind her that it was just a game. Finally, Judah stopped searching and decided to look at the faces of those reclined around the table to see if they would inadvertently give him a hint. When he looked at Haifa, who was sitting up, she wouldn't return his gaze. Smiling, he walked up to her and began to look carefully all around her. Sure enough, he found the bread under a linen cloth in her lap.

"I found it!" He cried out hurrying to his father with the loaf.

Naomi had to compose herself to keep from crying. She knew she should be happy for her brother, but she'd wanted so desperately to find it.

Josiah reached into the pocket of his robe and pulled out a small pouch. He gave it to Judah, and when he opened it he found five shekels inside.

"This is the price paid by the woman I saw at the Temple when she redeemed her baby boy," the shepherd said, as he exchanged the pouch of coin for the *Afikomen.*

He then looked at his oldest son and his daughter-in-law before saying, "And if my grandchild in Haifa's womb is a boy..." Josiah suddenly hesitated as he remembered Hannah's tender condition, "And if Joel and Hannah's baby is a boy, this will be the price they will pay to redeem their sons; for according to the *Torah,* the firstborn will belong to God."

Haifa smiled and instinctively touched her tummy, realizing once again the beauty of God's grace that had embraced her and her unborn baby. The infant would be a child of the covenant.

The talk of babies quickly eased Naomi's troubled heart.

"Do you believe Jesus was that baby in the Temple when you were a little boy?" She asked.

"I do," her father said almost in a whisper.

Judah held up the pouch and took out the coins one by one.

"One for God," he said holding up the first coin, "One for Nathan, one for Jared, one for Naomi, and one for me."

Naomi's smile at her brother's generosity would warm anyone's heart, and Josiah and Deborah couldn't have been more proud of their son.

After everyone was seated again, the shepherd took the *Afikomen* and blessed it:

"Boruch atto Adonoi Elohenu melech ho'olom hamotzi lehem min ho'oretz."

Before they ate the bread Nathan asked, "Father, you told us you would explain why the tradition has changed to substitute bread for the lamb."

Josiah paused, thinking it through. He wanted to make sure of his answer and not speculate too much.

"No one knows for sure, my son. The tradition changed between my first visit to Jerusalem and now. All I can tell you is that we've learned that Jesus said of Himself, *"I am the bread of life."*

Nathan seemed satisfied and nodded his head.

The shepherd broke the bread and passed it around the table. Once everyone was served, they ate it together.

It was now time to drink the third cup. Josiah lifted up the wineskin again, filled his cup and passed it around the table.

"Boruch atto Adonoi Elohenu melech ho'olom bore p'ri haggofen."

Just before he lifted his cup, he thought it best to remind them of its meaning. It had been a while since the cups were first explained.

"Does anyone recall the name and meaning of the third cup?"

Everyone remembered that Miriam had provided the answer earlier and looked to her again.

"It symbolizes *V'goalti*, which means redemption, redemption from slavery to the Egyptians," she replied.

"Yes," Josiah said, thinking as he was speaking, "This is the cup of redemption. God redeemed those from slavery to the Egyptians – all of those who had the blood of the lamb applied to their doors."

As he lifted his cup, he imagined Jesus with His disciples once again. What must He be telling them about the cup? He remembered he'd just used the word "blood" in describing the redemption God provided in Egypt. Then Jesus' words came suddenly to him, *"Whoso eateth My flesh, and drinketh My blood, hath eternal life; and I will raise him up at the last day."* Was He speaking of this cup of redemption? It was too much for him to bear, and thoughts of Jesus' shed blood troubled his soul deeply. The shepherd banished such notions immediately, yet he couldn't help but wonder what Jesus was teaching His disciples.

They drank the third cup together.

Josiah gathered himself, pushing thoughts of Jesus' blood from his consciousness. In the midst of the table was a large wine goblet. It was empty. He picked up the goblet and the wineskin, as if he was going to fill it.

Instead, he stopped and said, "At this point in the celebration, a cup is usually filled for Elijah. Once the cup is full to the brim, the youngest child goes to the door to open it."

Naomi was already fidgeting in her seat in anticipation of opening the door.

Josiah saw her and said, "Not tonight, Naomi."

Everyone sat there in silence as their father put the empty goblet back on the table.

"Why didn't you fill the goblet?" Simon asked with a perplexed look on his face.

"I said it is Elijah's cup; and according to tradition, the door is to be opened to see if Elijah might have arrived during the meal," he replied.

Those reclined around the table still looked confused.

He smiled, knowing they were puzzled.

"Elijah was to come to prepare the way of the Lord, to announce the coming of Messiah."

The light suddenly dawned on Michael, and he could not wait to tell everyone.

"Elijah's already come!" He exclaimed. "John came to prepare the way for Jesus. John is the fulfillment of that prophecy."

"Yes, my son. We don't have to wait any longer. Tomorrow is the day, or perhaps the next. Surely, sometime during the feast Jesus will ascend the holy hill of Zion! Come quickly Son of God. Come and restore the kingdom to Israel!"

"Amen!" They all shouted with joy.

Without hesitation Josiah began to chant the second half of the *Hallel*:

"Not unto us, O Lord, not unto us, but unto Thy name give glory, for Thy mercy, and for Thy truth's sake."

The family repeated every line with enthusiasm. Without pause, they sang through the remainder of those great psalms; and then they all stood as they came to the end of the last one. They remembered the crowd singing this psalm to Jesus as He approached the steps of the double Huldah gate at the Temple. In their hearts they sang the words to Jesus. It became their prayer.

"Save now, I beseech Thee, O Lord: O Lord, I beseech Thee, send now prosperity. Blessed be He that cometh in the name of the Lord: we have blessed You out of the house of the Lord!"

While they remained standing, Josiah filled his cup for the fourth time and passed the wineskin around the table for the final cup.

He then offered this blessing, "The feast is completed. With songs of praise, we have lifted up the cups symbolizing the divine promises of salvation, and have called upon the name of God. As we offer the benediction over the fourth cup, let us again lift our souls to God in faith and in hope. May He who broke Pharaoh's yoke forever shatter all fetters of oppression, and hasten the day when swords shall, at last, be broken and wars ended. Soon may He cause the glad tidings of redemption to be heard in all lands, so that mankind – freed from violence and from wrong, and united in an eternal covenant of brotherhood – may celebrate the universal Passover in the name of our God of freedom."

The shepherd knew that these words could only be fulfilled by Messiah. As he uttered them, they revealed the longing of his heart, his heart for his homeland, Kedar.

He lifted his hands and pronounced the benediction:

"The Lord bless thee, and keep thee: The Lord make His face shine upon thee, and be gracious unto thee: The Lord lift up His countenance upon thee, and give thee peace."

The whole company responded, *"Amen!"*

Once more the shepherd held up the cup and declared:

"Boruch atto Adonoi Elohenu melech ho'olom bore p'ri haggofen."

With joy, they drank the fourth cup together, concluding the Seder service. In their hearts, they were all anticipating the coronation of the Lord's King on Mount Zion. The shepherd looked around the room at his precious sheep, yes far more precious than a flock of ten-thousand. All his life he'd longed to bring them to Jerusalem and to eat Passover with them. Seeing their faces made it all worthwhile: leaving their home behind, the long and arduous journey, even the disappointment of the apostasy of the priesthood. He'd worshiped with those he loved most, including Deborah's family. Now, it was time to wait and see what the morrow would bring – a new day, a new King? God would reveal His holy will.

CHAPTER 15

Triumphant Dreams

Psalm 2:10-11

Be wise now therefore, O ye kings: be instructed, ye judges of the earth. Serve the LORD with fear, and rejoice with trembling.

"Wonderful job," Deborah's father said to Josiah as soon as the feast concluded. "I don't know that I've ever attended a more moving Seder Service."

Joel and James quickly agreed and embraced their kinsman from Kedar. The three men had enjoyed watching the interplay between Josiah and his children during the meal. Across the room, Michael and Simon were animatedly talking about what the next day might bring. Miriam stood by Michael's side admiring him for his godly zeal. After a few minutes, she put her hand on his arm to get his attention.

"Michael, would you take me back to my family?" She asked gently.

Feeling her hand touching his arm put a smile on his face.

"I'd be delighted," he replied.

When Josiah saw them heading for the door he hurried to catch them before they left.

"Michael, would you see to it that Martha comes back with you?"

"Yes sir," he answered before opening the front door.

"Don't tarry too long," his father said. "It's getting late."

He nodded his response before leading Miriam out into the darkness. The city, that had been filled with singing only a short time before, was now eerily silent. The streets were abandoned as everyone remained inside the houses. As they walked the short distance, Michael couldn't help but think of that first Passover night, when the destroyer moved through

— slaying the firstborn of Egypt. He wondered if another young man had been in a similar circumstance to his on that fateful night, finding himself momentarily outside, but somehow able to enter another house just before the Lord passed by. He shivered at the thought, and Miriam sensed his discomfort.

"What is it?" She asked.

"I was just thinking what it must have been like on that first Passover night, out in the streets of Egypt. I can imagine hearing weeping and wailing from the houses where the blood was not applied."

She paused, having never really thought about it.

"It was a night of judgment as well as a night of salvation, wasn't it?" She whispered, feeling that same eerie sensation.

Then he smiled before responding, "But we're not in Egypt. We're in Jerusalem, the city of peace, and tomorrow will be a special day."

"Do you really think it will be tomorrow?" She asked.

"I hope so," he replied, longing for God's promises made to Abraham and Moses to finally come to fruition. "I certainly hope so."

"I suppose tomorrow will be a day of judgment as well as a day of salvation," Miriam added.

Michael had to stop for a minute to think but realized she was right.

'The priests would have to be judged, if they didn't repent; and the Romans would be vanquished, unless….' His thoughts trailed off as he remembered the call at the end of the second psalm.

He turned to Miriam and said in all earnestness, "It will be unless they repent. Remember the ending of the second psalm, *'Be wise now therefore, O ye kings: be instructed, ye judges of the earth. Serve the LORD with fear, and rejoice with trembling.'*"

"And what if they don't? What if both the leaders of the people and the Romans resist Him?" She asked in alarm.

Michael continued to quote from the psalm, *"'Kiss the Son, lest He be angry, and ye perish from the way, when His wrath is kindled but a little.'* If they refuse to pay homage to Jesus, then it will most certainly be a day of judgment."

They entered the house where Nathaniel and Zacharias had celebrated the feast and found everyone gathered in groups discussing the very same things being talked about next door. When Joseph saw Michael he quickly waved him over. Miriam greeted Martha who was clutching Joseph's arm, but his attention was focused entirely on his conversation with Samuel. Michael immediately knew they were talking about Jesus.

"Did Andrew say anything about when Jesus would take His rightful place as king?" Joseph asked Samuel.

"Jesus won't say. When they ask Him His answers are often confusing. I'm convinced Andrew believes it will be tomorrow. It seems fitting that He do so after celebrating Passover tonight."

"Do you think the Romans and the religious leaders will try to oppose him?" Michael asked, interjecting himself into the conversation, and remembering what he and Miriam had just discussed.

"We talked about that tonight during the meal," Joseph responded.

"So did we," Michael interrupted. "Father, instructed us to pray for peace."

"We prayed for peace too, but I'm ready to fight if necessary," Joseph retorted.

"Do you have a sword?" Michael asked as an amused Samuel looked on.

Joseph was a rabbi's son, and Michael knew he didn't even own a weapon. A sheepish look came to his face, but Michael quickly let him off of the hook.

"I've got a *khanjar* and a short sword you can use," he said to his friend.

Even though Joseph was inexperienced in the use of weaponry, his heart was in the right place. He would willingly die defending Jesus if necessary.

Miriam realized it was getting late and touched Michael's arm again to get his attention.

When he turned to her she whispered, "Remember that your father told you not to tarry."

Realizing he needed to get Martha back to the house, he bid them good night and told his sister what their father had said. She wasn't pleased and only gripped Joseph's arm tighter. She was a little bit annoyed with him anyway. Ever since the meal concluded he'd been talking with Samuel and now with Michael. She'd hoped for at least a few moments alone with him.

Sensing her dismay, Miriam took Michael's hand and led him toward the door.

"Let's give them a few minutes," she said to him.

He nodded his head and didn't realize that he was still holding her hand. It was so natural for the both of them. She noticed that he'd not let go, and it pleased her.

"Thank you for inviting me to eat the Passover with you," she said.

"No, thank you for letting me escort you," he responded with a smile.

At that moment, they were looking into each other's eyes, wondering who was going to speak next, when they were interrupted by Joseph.

"I'll walk with you to Joel's house," he said.

As the four teenagers slipped out of the door, Samuel followed them.

"Where are you going?" Michael asked.

"I think I know where Jesus and His disciples will be spending the night. I'm going to go see what I can find out about His plans," he replied.

"Let us know what you learn," Michael said earnestly.

"You'll be the first to know, little brother," he said before bidding them all good night.

As soon as Samuel left they headed for Hannah's house. In those few moments Miriam remembered another occasion when she was a part of a foursome, walking in the night. On that night all of her thoughts were of Isaac. That seemed so long ago, a very distant memory. Michael still held her hand as they walked. Deep inside, she believed she'd finally found her true soul-mate, but did he feel the same way? The way he held her hand gave her hope.

It was only after they got to Joel's house that Miriam realized how silly it must seem that she was standing there with Michael. Only a few moments before, he'd walked her home; now here they stood outside of where he was staying.

When she giggled, he asked, "What's so funny?"

"It seems like you just walked me home and now I've walked you home," she said blushing ever so slightly.

The young man laughed himself before saying, "Do you want me to walk you home again?"

"No, no, that won't be necessary. I'm sure that Joseph can get me there safely," she said, as she released his hand and put her arm under Joseph's.

For a brief moment Martha frowned when she saw what she did, but then quickly realized it was innocent. The two couples hugged, and then

Michael and Martha entered the house. Both of them would have liked to have spent a little more time outside.

Martha immediately started to help her mother and the others finish the clean-up after the feast. They were almost done but welcomed the help because it was getting late. Michael found his father still talking with Joel and James and noticed that his grandparents had already retired for the evening.

Josiah was concerned that his family get some sleep. His heart was both exhilarated and anxious for what the next day would bring. He wanted them all to be well-rested.

Deborah and Hannah had already worked out the sleeping arrangements. It would be crowded, but they were confident it would work. They'd managed to find places where all five married couples would have at least some privacy. The remainder would all sleep in the big room where they had dined, the boys on one side and the girls on the other. With everyone working together, they all settled in for the night in short-order.

Haifa noticed that Isaac was restless soon after they lay down.

"What's wrong, my husband?" She asked. "Aren't you excited about tomorrow?"

"Yes, I am," he responded before pausing to reflect. "But there's something that has troubled me all evening."

She didn't speak, preferring to let him tell her when he was ready.

"It bothers me that there's so much emphasis on the Roman occupation and the prospect of having to fight to defend Jesus."

"Do you want to stay here tomorrow?"

"No, no, I'm willing to fight, even to die if necessary," he responded.

Haifa started to weep at the prospects of losing her husband, especially as she considered her baby.

He embraced his wife and comforted her, "Don't worry about me. God will be with me if we must fight. If it comes to that, God has already promised victory to His Messiah."

She settled comfortably in her husband's arms, before saying, "Then what is troubling you?"

"I know what God has done for me. I should be cut-off from our people and condemned for what I did, but God has been gracious to me. I don't ever want to forget that grace. It just seems to me that Messiah's reign would have more of a spiritual significance than a political one. Everyone keeps talking about the Romans, and a political kingdom. I do believe that Jesus will reign on the throne of David, but His reign must have a profound spiritual impact. Too many of God's people are simply going through the motions, that's clear at the Temple."

"Do you think anyone in our family is doing that?" She asked.

"Oh no. I'm certain that everyone in our family is faithful, especially my father. He is the godliest man I've ever known. I just know that they can't know the power of God's grace the way we can. They've always been faithful, and I'm thankful for that; but we haven't been."

"Thank God for His grace," she whispered into her husband's ear.

"Yes, thank God," he responded, as his eyelids suddenly became heavy.

Haifa smiled when she heard that first soft snore.

"Keep him safe tomorrow, dear Lord," she whispered before closing her eyes.

Josiah was also awake as he lay next to his wife. The house was quiet, the children having fallen asleep quickly. Deborah was aware that something was on her husband's heart.

When he didn't speak up, she finally said, "Tell me about the Temple today. Was it everything you expected?"

"Yes, and so much more," he exclaimed.

"I've never seen anything like it before. It was beyond my wildest dreams. There were so many there to offer their paschal lambs. We were not only in the first division, but were somehow first in line. Our paschal lamb was the first slain. The Levites were chanting the *Hallel*, and instinctively the congregation responded with *Hallelujah*. It was amazing to watch the Levites and priests working in tandem. I'm good with a knife, but have never seen such speed and efficiency. In what seemed to be only a matter of moments thousands of lambs had been sacrificed, and I was standing with our boys just inside the Nicanor Gate. The boys had our lamb on their shoulders. Then I just watched the procession. If anything, the Levites and priests picked up the pace, so that the last lamb was slain as they finished singing through the *Hallel* for the third time."

Josiah paused, but Deborah could tell there was more he needed to say. She snuggled up next to him and waited.

"Then it dawned on me…" his said, his voice trailing off into the night.

"What, my husband?" She asked.

"I'd imagined it all of my life. What it would be like to witness the Passover sacrifice, but I never expected what I saw."

When he stopped again, she felt the need to prompt him.

"What did you see?"

"Blood," he said. "I've never seen so much blood. It was running like a river before the altar. You know I'm not queasy. I've castrated rams and butchered lambs my whole life. It's part of being a shepherd, but our religion is a bloody religion."

"We are a sinful people," she reminded him.

"Yes, we are. I remember a conversation that I had with Omar. I'd asked him why he wasn't circumcised, and he told me that he had unanswered questions."

"What questions?" She asked, realizing her husband had never told her the details of that conversation.

"He asked about God's righteousness and how a holy God can forgive sinful people and remain righteous."

"Because God is merciful," she quickly added.

"That's what I told him, but he pressed me. 'How can God be merciful to sinners and just at the same time?' I told him about the animal sacrifices, but he knew all about them. He asked me how the blood of animals can be a sufficient substitute for sinful men made in God's image."

"What did you say?" She asked.

"I didn't know what to say. All I know is that God commanded us to present animal sacrifices to Him, but does that answer Omar's question? I'm not sure it does."

"My lord, you can't know everything," she said, trying to lighten the conversation with her little appellation; but his mind would not be eased.

"Deborah, there was so much blood today. Could a thousand lambs actually atone for a sinful man? I know the paschal lambs are not expiatory like other sacrifices. They're not the same as the Sin Offering and the Trespass Offering, or even the Scape Goat on the Day of Atonement; but they are a covering. We think of God seeing the blood applied to the doorposts of the houses in Egypt and passing over them, and of the destroyer entering every house where there was no blood; but did the blood indicate to God that those within were righteous? It doesn't make sense to me. Left to ourselves we're no better than the Egyptians. Our people were saved on that dreadful night by God's mercy."

Deborah tried to take in everything her husband was saying before asking, "What do you think Jesus is going to do tomorrow?"

"I believe He's going to assume His rightful throne, and pray it will be accomplished peaceably. Everything will change for our people, and I believe for the whole world. I'm wondering if somehow He will in His priestly office end these bloody sacrifices forever. Still, I don't know. How can a just God forgive sinners and remain righteous? We will have to wait for the answer, my dear wife."

With that he kissed her good night, and the two of them fell into a restful sleep.

It was early the next morning, just after dawn, when Josiah was awakened by a commotion in the front room. He rose quickly to his feet and hurried to see what was happening. Deborah was right behind him, and they were surprised to see Samuel with a terrified look on his face.

"What's wrong?" Josiah asked his troubled cousin.

"It's Jesus!" He cried, trying to regain his composure. "He's…He's been arrested!"

CHAPTER 16

A Mother's Face

John 19:26

Woman, behold thy Son!

Josiah's three oldest sons quickly dressed and armed themselves before heading out into the street. Nathaniel, Zacharias, Joseph and Samuel were waiting for them there, while the shepherd gave careful instructions to his wife and bid her an emotional farewell.

"May God be with you," she whispered just before he stepped out into the street.

The men decided it would be best for Joel and James to stay with Deborah's parents and the women and children until they heard from Josiah.

"Tell us what happened," the shepherd said to Samuel as soon as they were outside.

"Let's head to the *Praetorium*, and I'll tell you on the way," he insisted.

Josiah looked at Simon and saw his *khanjar* proudly displayed on the outside of his robe.

"Hide your weapon under your robe," he instructed. "There's no reason to invite trouble. We will resort to violence only if necessary."

Simon immediately obeyed his father, and the band headed up the street toward the *Praetorium*.

Josiah turned again to Samuel who told them what had happened.

"I left the house at the same time Michael and Martha did last night; and after leaving the city through the Eastern Gate, I headed across the winter-brook Kidron toward a garden at the foot of the Mount of Olives called Gethsemane. Jesus often takes His disciples there to pray.

As I headed up from the Kidron Valley, I heard shouts and saw men with torches, swords and clubs. Alarmed by what might be happening I put out my lantern and tried to hide. Suddenly, some of the men scattered and began fleeing in every direction. One of them ran directly towards me, and I was unable to get out of his way before he ran into me knocking us both to the ground. I jumped up to defend myself when I realized it was Andrew. When he saw me, he said, 'Samuel, run and hide! Judas betrayed the Lord, and He's been arrested by the chief priests and the captains of the Temple."

"Who is Judas?" Nathaniel asked as they hurried up the road.

"He's called Iscariot, and he's one of Jesus' twelve disciples," Samuel replied, still overcome with emotion over what he'd witnessed.

It distressed Josiah to hear of collusion between the High Priest and one of Jesus' closest disciples.

"Why are we going to the *Praetorium*?" Josiah asked.

"After Andrew told me to run, he took off toward the city; but I felt like I needed to stay to see what they were going to do to Jesus. So, I hid behind a rock near the trail and waited for them to bring Him down into the valley. His hands were bound behind His back, and He offered no resistance. I followed from a distance, and watched as they took Him first to Annas' house and then later to the palace of Caiaphas. I stayed in the street outside the gate of the courtyard for a long time; and then just before dawn, I saw Peter, Andrew's brother, running from the courtyard. He was weeping bitterly. I started to follow him, when suddenly, they brought Jesus out. It was still early, but it looked like He'd been beaten. It was then that I heard someone say that the Jews were taking Him to Pontius Pilate. I knew I needed to get help, and that's when I came to get you."

Josiah nodded his head, having most of his immediate questions answered. He believed that surely they must be seeing the fulfillment of the second psalm before their very eyes. The nations, as exemplified in the Jewish leaders and now the Roman governor, were conspiring together against Jesus. They'd made their move when they arrested Him, now it was time for God to do what He'd ordained. The shepherd was confident that God was about to set His King on His holy hill of Zion as prophesied in the psalm.

He said out loud to all of them, "What the psalmist prophesied is happening. Remember, God has promised victory to His Son."

With sudden anticipation of witnessing a coronation, he and the others climbed the mountain of Zion to Herod's palace, where Pilate resided when he was in the city. According to tradition, the spatial palace built by Herod the Great was on the site where David's palace once stood. Josiah realized the significance of the climb and had the expectant hope that Jesus was about to unseat Pilate and take His rightful place upon David's throne. His only question was whether God would fulfill His plan by direct intervention, or would He summon a multitude of Jesus' disciples to come to His aid, even as they were called to defend Him.

Renewed by their faith in God's promises, they eagerly climbed Zion; but what they saw when they arrived at the palace was shocking. Rather than finding the masses gathered to demand Jesus' release, they found the chief priests circulating through the crowd urging the people to ask for the release of Barabbas instead.

"What's happening?" Josiah asked Samuel.

"It's customary for Pilate to release a prisoner for the feast," Samuel responded before adding, "But why Barabbas? He's a murderer."

Baffled by the demeanor of the crowd, the band with Josiah circled around him.

"What should we do?" Isaac whispered.

"Let's wait and see," his father replied. "Keep your weapons hidden."

"I don't see any of Jesus' disciples," Samuel said as he perused the faces in the crowd.

Josiah and the others were confused and didn't know what to do, when Pilate suddenly emerged from the palace. He had a concerned look on his face and was arguing with the chief priests and leaders of the people. Josiah was too far away to hear what was being said. The governor did not appear happy when he went back inside the palace.

"What's going on?" Simon asked his father in bewilderment.

"Son, I don't know."

Shortly after that, the crowd ahead of them began murmuring as Pilate reappeared. He stood in front of the multitude, and some soldiers brought two men out. Josiah gasped when he saw Jesus. He'd clearly been beaten, and His face was downcast. The other man stood tall with a scowl on his face.

Pilate spoke to the crowd in a loud voice, *"Whom will ye that I release unto you? Barabbas, or Jesus which is called the Christ?"*

Josiah was utterly amazed when those near the front shouted out, *"Barabbas,* give us Barabbas!"

Sensing the danger, neither Josiah nor the others uttered a word to their shame.

"What shall I do then with Jesus which is called the Christ?!" Pilate cried out to them.

"Crucify Him! Crucify Him!" The crowd began to shout, with the chief priests leading the way.

Josiah couldn't believe how the vitriol against Him grew. The crowd was now an angry mob, and all the people thrust their fists in the air as they continued to chant, *"Crucify Him! Let Him be crucified!"*

Pilate was clearly disturbed and spoke out once again, *"Why, what evil hath He done?"*

The crowd would not be silenced and took up the chant, *"Crucify Him! Crucify Him!"*

Josiah staggered under the weight of what was happening. Only days before he'd heard the crowd singing, *"Blessed be He that cometh in the name of the Lord!"* Could it possibly be that some of those same people were now calling for Jesus' death? How quickly the tide had turned. The shepherd realized that their weapons would be useless in the midst of this angry mob. Still, he believed that God would vindicate His Son, and at any moment would send His angels to come to His aid.

"We must wait and see what God will do," he whispered to those gathered around him.

Pilate then did something striking. He sat down in the presence of the chief priests and all of the people and washed his hands in a basin of water.

Then he said for all to hear, *"I am innocent of the blood of this just person: see ye to it!"*

The anger of the crowd was utterly demonic, their faces filled with hate. Josiah was shocked when he heard a cry that caused him to cringe and surely would bring a curse from God upon the heads of the people.

"His blood be on us, and on our children!"

Having washed his hands of this, Pilate stood up and went back into the palace. The guards followed him, pushing Jesus in front of them, but releasing Barabbas into the crowd. Josiah watched as Jesus was taken from his sight, and didn't see how affectionately the insurrectionist was received by the people.

Through all of this, the shepherd still had faith that God would intervene on behalf of His Son. He wouldn't give up hope. He couldn't. The sound of a whip could be heard by the crowd, which brought forth cheers as if they were in an arena. Josiah winced with every blow, first hearing Jesus cry out after the fifth lash.

'Oh God, come and rescue Your Son,' he breathed in silent prayer. 'Fulfill Your promise to Him. Set Him on this Your Holy Hill.'

Each time he heard the crack of the whip, his faith began to fade, until finally Pilate brought Him out one last time.

Josiah had expected God to crown Him with a golden crown and for Jesus to sit down upon His rightful throne on Mount Zion. Instead, He stood before the crowd, a purple robe on His back and a twisted crown of thorns upon His head. His eyes were swollen shut from the beating, and the blood from His back oozed through the fabric of the robe. He never lifted His eyes, as He stood humiliated before wicked men in seeming defeat.

Josiah lost it. It took everything he had in him to keep from bursting into tears.

He turned to his sons and said, "Go back to the house and get your mother and the children. Take them to Bethlehem. Hurry!"

"But father, shouldn't we stay and fight?!" Simon said a little too loud.

Some of those standing nearby began to eye them suspiciously.

"Do as I say," his father said, almost hissing at his young son.

It was all the boy could do to obey his father, but somehow he managed to control his emotions. Isaac and Michael obeyed their father without complaint, though both of them wanted to stay with him.

Samuel whispered to him that he was going to search for Andrew and the other disciples to see what plans they might be making. Joseph was able to get leave from his father to go with Samuel. Both Zacharias and Nathaniel realized they needed to take care of their families as well. Nathaniel had no son to help him with his daughters and with Ephraim.

"I'll meet you in Bethlehem when this is over," Josiah said in dejection.

Hugging his sons, they departed, as he turned to see what would transpire next. Suddenly, feeling all alone, his faith began to crumble as he watched what was unfolding before him. The guards ripped the robe off of Jesus' back; and in His nakedness, Josiah was able to see the extent of His wounds. The *flagellum* had cut deeply during the scourging. It was a wonder He'd survived thus far. They put his tattered clothes back on Him and shoved Him forcefully off of the platform, laughing at Him and mocking Him as He struggled to get back to His feet. Josiah couldn't bear to see it, but something forced him to watch everything they did to Jesus.

They tied a crossbeam across the back of his shoulders and made Him carry it until He fell under the weight. One of the Roman soldiers tapped a dark-skinned man with his spear, ordering him to carry the cross for Jesus. The man looked sickened by the spectacle, and for a moment Josiah had hope that others were as offended by what was happening as he was. Reluctantly, the man bore the cross behind Jesus as the Roman soldiers led Him toward *Golgotha*. It was then, that Josiah noticed two other prisoners carrying their crossbeams behind Jesus. They were robbers destined for the same fate on that terrible day.

Through the streets they led Him in a ghastly parade, and Josiah felt compelled to follow. He got as close as he dared, seeing the hatred among those gathered along the streets, mocking Him, cursing Him. On one occasion Jesus fell to the pavement. He was weary in body. Josiah had never seen such exhaustion. He wondered about the burdens He was bearing, the beatings, the scourging, the ridicule. Had Jesus given up as well? Where was God!

Jesus fell a second time, and some women came to Him weeping and mourning. Josiah was astonished when he saw Him speaking to them. He listened carefully to His words.

"Daughters of Jerusalem, weep not for Me, but weep for yourselves, and for your children. For, behold, the days are coming, in the which they shall say, 'Blessed are the barren, and the wombs that never bare, and the paps which never gave suck.' Then shall they begin to say to the mountains, 'Fall on us;' and to the hills, 'Cover us.' For if they do these things in a green tree, what shall be done in the dry?"

Josiah found His words baffling. He was speaking of days of tribulation, not golden days of a Messianic Kingdom. Was everything coming to an end? Had God finally lost patience with an unbelieving, faithless people? Why, if God had decided to vacate His promises to Israel, was He letting them do this to His Son? None of it made sense, but he felt compelled to follow.

With every step, his faith faltered a little more. He'd been so certain that Jesus was the Messiah. Perhaps He was an imposter, or even worse, a deluded fool. Josiah wondered what that made him, because he'd so readily believed that Jesus was the One.

Instead of ascending Mount Zion to assume the throne, He was driven down the mountain and up another one. At least it was considered a mountain, though it was little more than a hill. The place was called *Golgotha*, which means, *"The place of the skull."* It was a wretched hill, used by the Romans for executions. Josiah dreaded drawing near, but couldn't help himself.

Even then, he held out hope that God would deliver Jesus from this travesty. He couldn't bring himself to believe that He was evil and deserved this treatment from the people, this treatment from God. He remembered the tenderness when Jesus held Naomi, and how He'd healed the sick at the Temple. Josiah fully agreed with Him regarding Annas' Bazaar. It was most certainly a desecration of God's House. Jesus was righteous when cleansing the Temple, and for His good deeds was He now being persecuted? None of it made sense to the shepherd.

He still had a glimmer of hope that God would come to rescue Jesus until they got to the top of *Golgotha*. The Roman soldiers crudely stripped off His clothes and threw Him down upon the crossbeam before driving the nails into His hands. Lifting Him up, they secured the crossbeam to the post that always remained in place as a token of the evil perpetrated on that hill. They hammered a nail through His feet, and there He was suspended above the earth, blood pouring from His wounds. Still, God did not lift a finger to save Him. Josiah's hopes were vanquished, but he still believed he must stay to the end of this horrific ordeal.

Amazingly, Jesus suddenly cried out from the cross, *"Father, forgive them; for they know not what they do."*

Josiah wondered about the character of this man. Was He deluding Himself? How could He pray for the forgiveness of those who crucified Him unjustly? Jesus remained an enigma to the shepherd.

The Romans made sport of Him, and many of the people near the cross spit out their hatred.

It was the leaders of the people who were most vocal, perhaps demonstrating the depth of the apostasy into which Israel had fallen.

"He saved others," they laughed. *"Let Him save Himself, if He be Christ, the chosen of God!"*

Above Him on the cross, Pilate had commanded an inscription, *"The King of the Jews,"* written in Greek, Latin and Hebrew, another indication of the conspiracy of the nations. The Roman soldiers used the title to mock Him.

"If Thou be the king of the Jews, save Thyself!" They cried, as they cast lots for His garments.

Josiah couldn't believe the cruelty of men on display. Even Pilate called Jesus a "just" man. In what had to be political timidity, he'd delivered Him over to be crucified, washing his hands of it. The shepherd was certain that the governor remained guilty of His blood, but he was not alone. The High Priest, the chief priests, the leaders of the people, even the people themselves shared it. Momentarily, he wondered if he was guilty too. He'd not drawn his sword to defend Him.

Even one of those being crucified beside Him joined in the mockery. The man jeered, *"If Thou be Christ, save Thyself and us."*

However, the second thief defended Jesus saying to the first, *"Dost thou not fear God, see thou art in the same condemnation? And we justly; for we receive the due rewards of our deeds: but this man hath done nothing amiss."*

Josiah was astonished by the interchange that followed, as the man looked over at Jesus and said, *"Lord, remember me when Thou comest into Thy kingdom."*

'What kingdom?' Josiah thought to himself. 'A man on a cross, naked of all royal garb and wearing only a crown of thorns can't be a king – can He?'

Again, the shepherd was perplexed by Jesus' answer to the condemned man, *"Verily I say unto thee, today shalt thou be with Me in paradise."*

He wondered what He was talking about. Paradise, isn't that the abode of the dead? What good would it do for the man to be with Jesus in paradise? The shepherd was becoming more and more convinced that all of them had misplaced their faith by believing in Jesus. Though not persuaded He was a wicked man, he had about come to the conclusion that all of them had been deluded, even Jesus Himself.

"How could this man, hanging on the cross before me, be as the old man prophesied, *'A light to lighten the Gentiles, and the glory of Thy people Israel'*?" He whispered to himself in dismay.

In that moment, the Shepherd of Kedar lost all hope. He'd wanted to return to Jerusalem to find the answers to his questions after his encounter with the woman and the baby at the Temple. He'd longed to learn the meaning of the old man's prophecy. Since hearing of Jesus he'd hoped that He was that baby, but now he knew for certain He couldn't be. The one of whom the old man prophesied couldn't die on a cross like a common criminal. Whoever Jesus might be; He was not the baby who'd closed His little hand around Josiah's finger when he was a boy.

Despondent, his hopes dashed, the shepherd finally gave up and turned to depart, when suddenly he heard Jesus gather Himself to speak. This time His eyes were set on a woman who was there at the foot of the cross, weeping. It was the first time Josiah noticed her. There were other women with her and also a man. The man looked vaguely familiar to the shepherd. Could he be one of those who'd been with Jesus that day in the Temple?

Jesus' suffering was taking a toll on Him. It was hard for Him to speak, but He was determined.

"Woman, behold thy son!" He cried.

Josiah looked at the foot of the cross, his eyes fixed upon the woman He'd addressed. A shawl covered her head and a veil her face. When she lifted her eyes to look at Jesus, her veil slipped to the side revealing her face.

The shepherd gasped at what he saw. He looked at her again to make sure it wasn't his imagination. There was no doubt about it. She was older, but it was the very same woman who'd brought her baby to the Temple that day so many years ago.

"It's her," he whispered out loud.

Josiah remembered the tender touch of the baby's hand, and let his eyes move to the hand of the man hanging on the cross. A nail had pierced it. His blood was oozing from the wound. It was that same hand, the hand he'd touched as a little boy, now battered and bruised.

Then the old man's last words, words he'd spoken directly to the baby's mother, came surging into Josiah's consciousness, *"Behold, this child is set for the fall and rising of many in Israel; and for a sign which shall be spoken against; yea, a sword shall pierce through thy own soul also, that the thoughts of many hearts may be revealed."*

Suddenly, the shepherd realized that he was witnessing the fulfillment of the second part of the old man's prophecy. Surely, a sword was piercing through His mother's soul as she watched her son die.

Even in the midst of the agony, Josiah wanted to shout. 'This is the baby! He is the one! What we are witnessing is God's doing! Jesus will somehow, through this cross become *a light to lighten the Gentiles, and the glory of Thy people Israel!'*

Josiah didn't know how God would accomplish this, only that He would. His faith renewed, he knew he must stay, stay to the bitter end. He must listen and learn, so that he could tell the others that what happened this day is God's will and will end in the salvation of not only Israel, but the whole world.

CHAPTER 17

The Cry of Agony

Psalm 22:1

My God, My God, why hast Thou forsaken Me!?

A sense of foreboding hovered over Deborah like a cloud. Even though the men were confident that Jesus was about to take His rightful seat upon the throne, something just didn't seem right. She found herself unable to concentrate or even focus her prayers. To compensate, she busied herself packing up for what could be a hasty retreat to Bethlehem. Dinah saw what her mother was doing, and took it upon herself to gather the younger children for prayer. Hannah also realized that Jerusalem could become a dangerous place if things didn't go as the men hoped and began making preparations for her and Joel to leave their home if necessary. She couldn't help thinking about the little one she carried in her womb.

When the boys arrived Isaac was the first through the door, followed by Michael and Simon. Deborah was happy to see them, but couldn't keep from looking for Josiah.

"Where's your father?" She asked with a bit of trepidation in her voice.

She remembered a particular night; it wasn't so long ago, when she and Elizabeth waited in the darkness at the oasis for Josiah and Nathaniel to appear. Instead, it was Isaac and Michael who came. That night, her first impulse was to ask about their father. She loved him with her whole heart and knew she'd be lost without him. That was the night her daughter's dreams were shattered by the news of Caleb's death.

Isaac spoke for the others, his voice breaking with emotion, "He stayed to watch them crucify Jesus."

"Crucify Jesus?!" Deborah gasped. "What happened?!"

Michael helped his brother tell them everything that had transpired, and also Josiah's direction for all of them to leave Jerusalem immediately.

"I'll not leave without your father!" Deborah objected vehemently.

"Mother," Isaac said firmly. "I understand how you feel. None of us want to leave, but we must obey Father."

She dropped her head and started to weep.

"But what if they kill him too?" She cried.

Isaac put his arm around his mother to comfort her.

"We must trust the Lord," he whispered into her ear. "You have to be strong for the others."

She gathered herself, knowing her eldest son was right and paused for a moment before looking up.

Everyone knew the old Deborah was back when she began barking orders, "Isaac, you go get the camels we brought with us, and Little Micah. Michael, you and Simon take these things I've already packed up and put them on the camels. Hannah, you and Joel are coming with us."

"You too," she said nodding her head towards James, Esther and her parents.

They all looked at her and immediately obeyed without questioning. In that moment, she relied upon the strength that everyone could see in her. She was the only one who ever doubted whether it was there. Frightened or not, she had a job to do.

"Martha, you go next door and help Miriam get Ephraim ready to travel," she directed her daughter.

Martha was relieved by her mother's instruction, assuming that she would get to see Joseph. When she entered the house, she saw both Nathaniel and Zacharias but didn't see him. She hurried to his father and asked him where he was.

Zacharias turned to the girl and replied, "He's with Samuel looking for Jesus' disciples."

Martha didn't know whether to be frightened or angry. Most certainly, she feared for his safety, but she couldn't understand why he would go with Samuel when he could have come to her. His actions hurt her feelings, and she began to cry. Miriam saw what was happening and comforted her.

"He'll be alright," she said. "The Lord will take care of him."

Martha nodded her head in agreement. Still, she was angry with him, for putting himself in danger and jeopardizing their future together. Isaac had come back to take care of Haifa. Why hadn't Joseph returned to care for her? Surely, they could flee this madness together and go to either Elath or Kedar.

Everyone moved quickly, and in short order they were ready to depart. Deborah desperately watched for her husband, hoping he would arrive in time, but he never came. While they made their way toward the Western Gate, Michael looked to the north and could see a crowd in the distance.

"I wonder what's going on over there," he said, though he was pretty certain of the answer.

"That's *Golgotha*," Joel replied with a distraught look on his face.

"What's *Golgotha?*" Michael asked.

"It's called *'the Place of the Skull,'*" he responded, causing Michael to look at him in bewilderment. "Tradition says that Adam's skull is buried there; but more than likely, it gets its name from the many executions that have taken place on that hill at the hands of the Romans."

They were overcome with a deep sadness as they saw three men atop the hill hanging on crosses. Instinctively, they knew that Jesus was on the center cross. Deborah wanted to run into the crowd and search for her husband, but knew she must obey him. Tears ran down her face, as the lonely caravan silently moved past the crowd and toward the city gate before taking the road to Bethlehem.

Josiah was trying to understand what was happening. He had no doubt that he was witnessing the fulfillment of prophecy. Though the wickedness of men and the maliciousness of Satan was on full display, somehow he knew that this was the Lord's doing. God had a deeper purpose that was yet to be revealed.

Suddenly, the wind began to blow and ominous clouds appeared in the sky. In a matter of minutes a deep darkness descended upon the land. Josiah had never seen such darkness, not even in the midst of the terrible sandstorm the day Isaac ran away. The shepherd knew it was a sign from God. The darkness exemplified the evil being perpetrated against Jesus by men, and the lighting and thunder was certainly a demonstration of God's wrath.

On the road to Bethlehem, even Ephraim sensed the darkness and knew that God's anger had been kindled.

"Woe to those who have rejected the Son of God!" He cried out in a voice of lament.

Deborah was once again stricken with fear that Josiah would suffer the fallout of God's judgment. She knew that even the righteous sometimes suffer when God chastises His people. There was a remnant of those faithful who were taken into captivity when God judged Judah through Nebuchadnezzar. Their forefather, Micah, was such a man. Would the walls of Jerusalem fall again, this time directly by God's hand? She prayed that her husband would be spared in the midst of such destruction.

The crowd on *Golgotha* grew eerily silent through the duration of the darkness. Some of them fled, others huddled together in fear, wondering what was about to happen. Still, the hearts of the multitude were not changed, but rather hardened against Jesus. Some even blamed Him for the storm. The depravity of mankind was on full display.

The darkness hovered over the land from the sixth hour until the ninth; and then the clouds began to break, and the sun started to shine.

Josiah looked once again at Jesus. He was still alive.

Suddenly, a look of abject sorrow came to His battered face, and He cried out in a loud voice, *"Eloi, Eloi, lama sabachthani?!"*

Josiah understood the Aramaic immediately. Jesus was crying out in agony, *"My God, My God, why hast Thou forsaken Me?!"*

In that moment Jesus looked utterly lost, a desperate man, despised not only by wicked men but by a holy God. It was the first time He'd spoken in hours, and His voice stirred the crowd.

One of them mocked Him and said, *"Behold, He calleth Elijah...Let us see whether Elijah will come and take Him down."*

The shepherd was full of the Scriptures. He'd studied them all of his life and committed many of them to memory, including the entirety of the Book of Psalms. At first, he thought Jesus was quoting Scripture. Then he wondered why, if He was simply citing the scriptures, it was in His native tongue instead of in Hebrew. Suddenly, the reason dawned on him. Jesus wasn't quoting the psalm. These were His words!

The whole of the psalm came to the shepherd:

My God, My God, why hast Thou forsaken Me? Why art Thou so far from helping Me, and from the words of my roaring? O my God, I cry in the daytime, but Thou hearest not; and in the night season, and am not silent… But I am a worm, and no man; a reproach of men, and despised of the people. All they that see me laugh me to scorn: they shoot out the lip, they shake the head, saying, 'He trusted on the Lord that He would deliver Him: let Him deliver Him, seeing He delighted in Him…For dogs have compassed me: the assembly of the wicked have inclosed me: they pierced my hands and my feet.

Josiah looked in astonishment at the nails, driven through his hands and feet into the wood of the cross. He gasped as he realized what was happening. Jesus wasn't quoting David; no – David was quoting Jesus! David, who lived a thousand years before Him, by the Holy Spirit, saw his Son and saw this day. David wrote Jesus' inner groanings on the cross. It was almost too much for Josiah to bear.

Shortly after uttering His agonizing prayer, Jesus opened His mouth to speak again.

His words were faltering because of His weakness but clear as He said, *"I thirst."*

Josiah was staggered as the words of the psalm came back to him, *"My strength is dried up like a potsherd; and my tongue cleaveth to my jaws."*

The inward agony expressed in the psalm had escaped the lips of Jesus with the simple words, *"I thirst."*

Josiah wondered why He would make such a statement. He understood why He was thirsty. Yet earlier, He had refused the offer of a drink to numb the pain. Why did He accept the drink now? Then the shepherd realized that Jesus had something to say. He needed the refreshment to be sure He was heard. A soldier extended a sponge to His lips that was filled with vinegar and attached to a hyssop branch.

After momentarily quenching His thirst, Jesus summoned all of the strength He had left, and cried out in a loud voice, *"It is finished!"*

Then, looking up into heaven to behold the face of God, He prayed, *"Father, into Thy hands I commend My spirit."*

Josiah couldn't turn away as Jesus closed His eyes and lowered His battered face. The shepherd watched in astonishment as the Messiah died.

For a brief moment everything was silent. Then suddenly, a soft roaring began from deep in the middle of the earth. It grew louder and louder as the ground started to shake all around them. Shrieks could be heard in the crowd as they trembled in fear, the crosses shook, and for a moment Josiah was afraid they would fall.

As the shaking grew stronger, he fought to keep his footing. Many who were standing nearby fell to the ground, and he feared for his life. Was this the end? Had God given up on mankind in the face of what evil men did to His Son? Would the ground open up and swallow them all? He knew that God would be just to exercise that sentence.

Then he saw Jesus' mother struggling. The man with her lost his balance and fell. Josiah instinctively ran to her, catching her before she collapsed. In that moment, the grieving woman looked into his eyes, and he thought he saw a fleeting note of recognition.

In her grief, it soon passed, but she did manage to whisper a thank you. He felt the presence of the man nearby.

"Thank you, sir," the man said firmly, making it clear to Josiah that his help was no longer needed.

The shepherd knew it was not the time to speak to her about that day in the Temple, a day so long ago. He silently prayed that God would grant them an opportunity to talk, when the time was right. Surely then, that memory would be a comfort to her. Seeing that she was in good hands, he backed away and returned to his place. Then it dawned on him that the earth had stopped shaking. Jesus' body hung lifeless on the cross.

A centurion was nearby, and Josiah heard him say in awe, *"Truly this man was the Son of God."*

Josiah nodded his head in agreement. 'Yes, truly this man was the Son of God.'

The shepherd's family was drawing near to Bethlehem when the darkness lifted. A short distance away was Rachel's tomb. It was Ephraim who first felt the vibration beneath his sandaled feet, and then everyone felt the earth begin to tremble. Michael and Miriam held Ephraim to keep him from falling, and Dinah put her protective arms around Naomi. Little Micah spooked from the earthquake, broke and ran, with Isaac right behind him – calling his name. Haifa sat down, lest she fall and injure the little one she was carrying. All of them were terrified.

When the shaking finally ended, it was Ephraim who spoke.

"Jesus is dead. Whatever God has done, it is finished!"

Everyone in the caravan began weeping in agony. Deborah looked back toward Jerusalem but they were too far away to see the city. Without thinking she turned and started running back toward the city, frightened for her husband's life. Isaac had just returned to his wife with Little Micah. Seeing his mother's desperate action, he turned the young ram over to Simon and ran after her. When he caught up to her he held her in his strong arms. At first, she fought him, trying frantically to get to Josiah, but he wouldn't let go.

"Mother, we must obey Father. He told us to go to Bethlehem. We're going to Bethlehem!"

She surrendered to her son, and he led her back to the caravan. Her children surrounded her, all of them weeping.

Relying upon God's strength, she rallied them, "Your father is wise. Let's go to Bethlehem and wait for him there."

The journey had been hard, and the ominous signs of darkness and the earthquake only made the final stretch all the more difficult.

Haifa glanced over at Rachel's grave and whispered to her husband, "If Rachel wept before, surely she weeps today."

He nodded his head. Overcome with sadness, tears streamed down his cheeks. His wife tenderly brushed them away.

"God has His purposes," she whispered in his ear.

After the earthquake, the soldiers let those who mourned have their moment on *Golgotha*. The man continued to comfort Jesus' mother, while the other women with her cried out in their grief.

Josiah looked at Jesus' body on the cross, wondering what God had just done. He thought of the things he'd witnessed that terrible day. The words of the psalm still invaded his mind. He'd never fully understood them until now. What David uttered had been so strikingly fulfilled before his eyes. David had described a crucifixion, even though he wrote long before the Romans introduced the brutal form of execution. He couldn't have known the method that was vividly depicted in his words.

"I am poured out like water, and all my bones are out of joint: My heart is like wax; it is melted in the midst of My bowels…they pierced My hands and My feet."

The shepherd remembered how they mocked Jesus. David, through the eye of faith, had seen that long ago.

David quoted their words exactly, *"He trusted on the Lord that He would deliver Him: let Him deliver Him, seeing He delighted in Him."*

Josiah even remembered a detail that seemed insignificant at the time. After lifting Jesus up on the cross, the soldiers cast lots for His garment.

David said long before, *"They part my garments among them, and cast lots upon my vesture.*

That never happened to David. Josiah knew it was Jesus speaking through David. David saw this day.

His mind was spinning. The words he'd heard Jesus utter from the cross echoed in his head, as many passages of Scripture came to him, words he'd never fully understood until now. Still, there was much that escaped him, and he realized he needed to search the Scriptures with his sons and his friends in order to grasp the meaning of what God was doing.

A commotion at the cross abruptly grabbed his attention. Three soldiers approached the thief on the right side of Jesus, and viciously broke the lower bones of his legs. The man cried out in agony, as they moved to Jesus. Seeing that he was already dead, they hurried to the man on his left. Josiah heard a loud crack when they broke the first leg, but the horrible sound was muffled by the man's screams when they fractured the second.

Sensing a sympathetic ear with the centurion, he asked him what the soldiers were doing.

"This happens every time we have a crucifixion on a Friday," the centurion declared, shaking his head.

"Why?" Josiah asked, daring to press him a little further.

"It's the Jewish priests," he responded, while pointing at Jesus' body. "First, they delivered the one in the middle to Pilate, asking that He be crucified, even though Pilate couldn't find any fault in Him deserving of death; but they wouldn't have it. They were determined to have that man's head."

Josiah still didn't understand, and thankfully the centurion continued to explain.

"The Jews are insistent that all dead bodies be disposed of before Sabbath begins at nightfall. They say that leaving them on the crosses would desecrate the land. How much more could the land be desecrated than to manipulate the *Prefect* to crucify an innocent man? But are they ever satisfied? No, no, they've got to strictly follow their religious rites. It smacks of hypocrisy if you ask me," the Roman soldier said in disgust.

Josiah couldn't agree more, and found it strange that a foreigner understood justice better than the religious leaders of God's people.

"Why did they break their legs?" He asked, still not understanding.

"To speed up their deaths," the centurion replied. "With their legs broken they can't push up to breathe. Pretty soon, they'll give up and die. God was merciful to the one in the middle. He's already dead.

"Sir, this one is dead. Should we break his legs anyway?" One of the soldiers asked the centurion.

"No, leave Him be," he replied.

The shepherd turned again to look at Jesus, as the soldiers pierced His side with a spear. He saw water, mixed with blood, run out of the wound.

The brutality of crucifixion was overwhelming. In his sorrow and grief as Jesus was being crucified, he'd not paid as much attention to this hideous form of execution. He immediately saw the effect of the broken legs on the thieves. In order to breathe they had to push up with their legs, but the pain was excruciating and both of them gave up quickly, causing them to suffocate while suspended on their crosses. In a short time, they too died, to the relief of the chief priests who'd stayed to the end. Now, they could honor their precious Sabbath with a clear conscience. Josiah couldn't imagine such blindness. No wonder, God turned the sky black and shook the earth when Jesus was dying.

Shortly after that, two men of means approached the centurion with papers from Pilate. He quickly read the papers and nodded his head, indicating to the other soldiers that these men could take the body of Jesus. Josiah watched as they tenderly took His body off of the cross, assisted by the soldiers. His mother wept bitterly and reached out her arms for her son. No one prohibited her from taking Him in her arms at the foot of the cross. The man Jesus had commissioned to care for her comforted her as she held her son.

Josiah couldn't keep from weeping, as his mind drifted back to that day in the Temple when he was a boy. He'd noticed her right off, the joy on her face as she held her baby. He remembered thinking about just how much the young woman loved her son. It was that love that caused her such despair at the old man's perplexing words. Now, as she tenderly touched the bruised face of her dead son, he could see how much she still loved Him.

Then the two men wrapped His body and carried Him away. Josiah followed, as did several women who were mourning. The location of the tomb wasn't far from *Golgotha*. The sepulcher was in a garden, a place of seeming serenity, after having left a site of such bitter violence.

The women assisted the two men with burial preparations, but they had to work quickly for Sabbath was approaching rapidly. Sensing there was nothing more he could do, Josiah turned to depart. He thought of Deborah and knew she must be worried sick about him. Picking up his pace he hurried toward Bethlehem. He needed to be with his family, and had much to tell them.

CHAPTER 18

Good Tidings

Isaiah 52:7

*How beautiful upon the mountains are the feet
of him that bringeth good tidings.*

Josiah turned and looked at Jerusalem one last time. Somehow, it seemed to be an entirely different place, certainly not the city of peace. He'd been so full of hope and joy two days earlier when they made the journey for the Passover feast. The shepherd could have never imagined what would transpire. If it were not for recognizing Jesus' mother at the cross, he felt certain all of his hopes would be dashed. Because of that one moment and what it revealed, he was confident that God had His purpose in the evil that happened that day.

Jesus' crucifixion was clearly the fulfillment of David's psalm in the most vivid way imaginable; but why? Josiah still didn't understand why Jesus had to die.

As he walked along the road to Bethlehem he thought carefully over everything he'd witnessed and especially paid attention to the words he'd heard Jesus say from the cross.

"It is finished," he whispered out loud. "That's what He said, but what is finished?"

Josiah didn't know. Surely the crucifixion was finished, but what else did He mean? He knew it was important, because he saw Jesus wet His lips to make sure He could be heard before He spoke.

He thought of everything he'd seen, beginning at the *Praetorium* that morning. Why didn't Jesus defend Himself? Why was He silent? It reminded him of something he'd seen a thousand times before. He was like a lamb being led to the slaughter.

The Suffering Servant passages of Isaiah immediately came to his mind.

"He was oppressed, and He was afflicted, yet He opened not His mouth: He is brought as a lamb to the slaughter, and as a sheep before her shearers is dumb, so He opened not His mouth."

Isaiah's description was precisely what Josiah witnessed in Jesus. He had surrendered to the hatred of men and allowed them to crucify Him.

The shepherd thought of a conversation he'd had with Sarah and Nathan at the inn. 'Nathan quoted John, *"Behold the Lamb of God, which taketh away the sin of the world."* He was talking about Jesus. Why didn't I think of this before? It was the third hour when the soldiers began pounding the nails into Jesus' hands and feet – the very hour the morning sacrifices began at the Temple.'

He gasped and staggered at the implication. It was now clear to him what he'd witnessed that day. He remembered his conversation with Omar when he questioned how the blood of an animal could be a sufficient substitute for that of a man. Just the night before he'd talked to Deborah about it, and now he finally had an answer to his Idumean friend's baffling question. Jesus, it was Jesus who died for the sin of the world. That's what John was talking about. Jesus was the perfect substitute for sinful men.

He realized that if Jesus was the Lamb of God, then all of the lambs that were sacrificed before found their fulfillment in Him. The shepherd had witnessed the sacrifice of all sacrifices. Could it be the sacrifice to end all sacrifices?

Suddenly, he stopped in his tracks and fell to his knees. Tears burst from his eyes as the awful truth overwhelmed him.

"Jesus died for me!" He cried out, as he tore his robe and beat his breast. "It was my sin that put Him on the cross!"

He wondered if Jesus was praying for him when He said from the cross, *"Father, forgive them..."*

Everyone believed the shepherd was a faithful man, but he knew himself to be a sinner. He remembered how he felt when Jesus looked into his eyes on the steps leading to the Temple. His sins came to him in a torrent – his selfishness, his doubts, his lack of commitment to God, and above all, how he had been a coward that day, failing to defend Jesus, because he knew it would have put his life and the lives of his sons in peril.

He looked up into the sky, as the sun began to set in the west. His sorrow suddenly turned to joy as he realized why Jesus didn't do anything to defend Himself. Jesus surrendered to the cross for him, for his family, for all who would believe in Him. He didn't just take away the sin of the world that day on the cross in some general way; He took away his sins! Josiah began to praise God and His Son for this glorious good news. Hastening to his feet, he quickened his pace toward Bethlehem. When he saw the town up ahead, he began to run.

He thought of what Isaiah said just before the Suffering Servant passages, *"How beautiful upon the mountains are the feet of him that bringeth good tidings."*

The shepherd approached Bethlehem as the bearer of good news.

Samuel and Joseph entered Ephraim's house without knocking. The forlorn looks on their faces spoke volumes. Joseph searched frantically through the sea of faces until he found Martha. His eyes beckoned her, and she quickly ran into his arms. It pleased her that he sought her out in his time of need, but also convicted her of how selfish she'd been. She let him cry as she held him.

Samuel looked at his father and said in a low voice, "Jesus is dead."

Ephraim already knew it to be true, but hearing the words of confirmation shook him. The voice bearing the dreadful news was that of the same man who'd excitedly told him story after story of the wonderful things Jesus had said and done. Now, he knew his son's hopes and dreams were shattered.

"Did you see the crucifixion?" Zacharias asked, feeling a bit ashamed he'd not stayed himself.

"No, we looked everywhere for Andrew and the other disciples. We even went as far as Bethany, but it's like they've vanished into thin air. No one seems to know where any of them are. There are rumors that some of them may have been arrested. By the time we made it back to Jerusalem, they were taking Jesus' body down from the cross."

"Did you see Josiah?" Deborah asked with a note of desperation in her voice.

"No, we didn't see him, but I'm sure he's okay," Samuel replied, knowing Deborah must be fearful for her husband's safety. "There were so many people there; it would have been hard to find him. We decided it was best to come to Bethlehem and tell you what's happened. I'm sure he will be back soon."

Deborah nodded her head in resignation. She would depend upon God's grace and her husband's resiliency to bring him back to her.

It didn't take long for the sad news of Jesus' death to sink in, and everyone in the house began to mourn. They'd put their faith in Him and believed He was the "Coming One," but now they were confused and overcome with grief. Even if He wasn't the one they were expecting, His crucifixion was still a demonstration of how far Israel had fallen. They remembered the dark skies and the earthquake and knew it must be a demonstration of God's wrath, but just what made Him angry? Was it the apostasy of the Priesthood? Was it the brutality of the crucifixion? Or – and none of them could bring themselves to even consider the possibility – was God angry with Jesus?

Tears flowed freely in Ephraim's house, and no one noticed when Josiah entered. Deborah happened to look up and saw him standing at the door. In a flash, she ran across the room and into his arms, thanking God that he was safe. She looked up into his face expecting to see the same sorrow that had enveloped the rest of them, but instead saw something quite different. The sorrow was there, for he'd watched them violently kill Jesus; but she saw something more – she saw hope in his eyes.

Bewildered, she waited for him to speak. When a smile came to his face, everyone was stunned.

Samuel grew angry and couldn't hold back his contempt, "What reason is there to smile!"

Josiah understood his confusion, but before he could say anything Ephraim addressed his son.

"Samuel, let him speak. Surely, he has something important to tell us."

Josiah had them all gather around him, each of them desperately waiting for some morsel of good news.

"Beloved, I have good news for you," he said. "Yes, Jesus is dead, and watching Him die was the most agonizing experience of my life; but I have good news to declare to you. In the midst of the evil today, God has a wonderful purpose."

"Surely, you mean the devil! Have you gone mad?!" Samuel cried, taking a defiant step toward Josiah.

"My son, let him speak!" Ephraim spoke sharply.

"Samuel, I understand your confusion and your anger. I felt those same things myself while Jesus was being crucified, but I made myself watch, listen and think about what I was witnessing today. Yes, the devil was mightily at work and used the hands of wicked men to slay Jesus, but behind the devil's labors God was working out His marvelous plan."

"Did God speak to you?" Michael asked.

"Yes, He did, but not in the darkened sky or in the earthquake, nor did He speak to me in a voice audible. He spoke to me from His Word hidden in my heart."

They all sat in silence, even Samuel, longing to hear what God had said to the shepherd.

"I heard Him speak to me through Jesus as He hung on the cross," he continued.

"Did Jesus preach from the cross?" Zacharias asked.

"No, His words were few, but profound. Yet, the words He spoke that opened my eyes were intensely personal, words addressed to a particular individual."

"Did He speak directly to you?" A confused Michael asked.

"No, my son. He spoke to a woman," Josiah said almost in a whisper.

When he hesitated, they all leaned forward to hear what he would say next.

"There was a woman weeping at the foot of the cross. A man, who I believe to be one of Jesus' disciples, was comforting her."

Samuel glanced at Joseph at the mention of one of the disciples, wondering which one it might be.

"Jesus said, *'Woman, behold thy son.'* When the woman raised her eyes to look at Him on the cross, the veil that covered her face fell away. At that moment, I knew the truth."

Those gathered around didn't understand what he was talking about, until Ephraim spoke, his blind eyes shining with hope.

"It was the woman from the Temple," the patriarch declared.

Josiah nodded his head, "Yes, I'm certain of it. It was the same woman I saw in the Temple with her baby when I was a boy."

"That's when you knew the old man's prophecy to be true," Ephraim added.

"Yes, I'd lost all hope until that moment. Then I realized the words that had confused me all of my life were being fulfilled before my very eyes."

Samuel was still bewildered and asked, "What woman? What baby?"

It was his father who answered him, "Surely, you remember what Josiah and his father saw at the Temple when he was a boy."

He tried to search his memory, but simply couldn't recall the details. It had happened so long ago.

"When I was a boy, my father and I visited the Temple one day. A woman came in carrying her baby. She presented her offering and when she sat down, she saw me looking at the baby. She waved at me and motioned for me to join them. I remember how cute the baby was, and how much His mother loved Him. He was holding my finger and cooing at me, when an old man came through the crowd and lifted Him out of His mother's arms. The old man looked up into heaven and began to prophesy."

As Josiah described what had happened, Samuel's memory was stirred. With each word, he recalled the details he'd heard long ago.

Josiah saw him nodding his head as he continued, "The old man's prophecy always baffled me, especially the second part when he said to the woman, *"Behold, this child is set for the fall and rising again of many in Israel; and for a sign which shall be spoken against; Yea, a sword shall pierce through thy own soul also, that the thoughts of many hearts may be revealed.'* This day, I saw the fulfillment of that prophecy. Surely, the sword that cut through my soul as I watched Jesus die must have pierced through that of His mother."

"I understand that you saw that prophecy fulfilled today, but how is that good news? It sounds to me like a prophecy of judgment not salvation," Samuel replied, still confused but no longer angry with the shepherd.

Josiah's smile returned, as he responded, "My brother, remember, there was a first part to the old man's prophecy."

Samuel was trying to remember, but just couldn't find it.

"The old man lifted his eyes toward heaven and prayed, *'Lord, now lettest Thou Thy servant depart in peace, according to Thy word: For mine eyes have seen Thy salvation, which Thou hast prepared before the face of all people; a light to lighten the Gentiles, and the glory of Thy people Israel.'*"

Samuel still seemed confused.

"It suddenly dawned on me that in order for Jesus to be the Savior, a light to the Gentiles and the glory of Israel, He had to go through the cross," Josiah said excitedly.

"But how does His death accomplish anything?" Michael asked.

"Son, you're a shepherd. Do you remember what Nathan and Sarah told us that John said about Jesus?"

Before he could answer Samuel spoke for him, "He said, *'Behold the Lamb of God, which taketh away the sin of the world.'*"

He looked up at Josiah and tears came to his eyes as he began to realize the significance of what had happened that day.

"John said that to Andrew. He told me about it himself. That was when he left John to follow Jesus."

Michael's eyes widened as everything started to become clear to him.

"Father, do you remember the question Omar asked you when he came to get the sheep?" He asked.

Josiah's eyes met Deborah's as both of them remembered their conversation from the night before.

"I do. Why don't you tell everyone else," his father responded.

"Who is Omar?" Samuel interjected.

"Omar is the Idumean who bought my sheep before we left Kedar," Josiah answered. "He's a God-fearer, who came to believe in the Lord through the ministry of John. Michael, tell them what Omar asked us that day."

"When Father asked him why he hadn't been circumcised, he told us that he had certain unanswered questions. If I recall correctly, he asked us how God could remain just and forgive sinful men at the same time."

"Because God is merciful," Samuel replied almost without thinking.

"That's what we told him, but he already believed in God's mercy. When we talked to him about animal sacrifices, he was still unconvinced. He asked us how an animal could be a sufficient substitute for a man, made in God's image," Michael responded, looking to his father to insure he'd gotten it right.

Samuel had never thought about it before and had offered sacrifices simply because God required it in the *Torah*. The question of God's justice when forgiving sinners had never crossed his mind.

"He said that he thought only a righteous man could be a substitute for a sinful man," Michael added.

Suddenly, Samuel's face lit up as he came to see the significance of Omar's question. Jesus was that fitting substitute.

"So Jesus died for sinners," he uttered.

"Jesus died for us," Isaac said almost in a whisper, his voice breaking.

Haifa remembered her conversation with her husband the night before and his concerns about everyone focusing on a political salvation rather than one with spiritual significance. Isaac was resting in God's mercy, but never forgot the depth of his sin. He knew he needed Jesus to die for him. Haifa took her husband's hand and squeezed it. She, too, realized that Jesus had died for her, even though she was a Kedarite, a former idol-worshipper and prostitute. Now, by God's grace, she was a member of God's covenant people.

"Surely He hath borne our griefs and carried our sorrows: yet we did esteem Him stricken, smitten of God, and afflicted. But He was wounded for our transgressions, He was bruised for our iniquities: the chastisement of our peace was upon Him; and with His stripes we are healed."

Ephraim uttered those precious words from Isaiah, the prophet.

Suddenly, the whole company joined in, for the first time understanding the true meaning of the prophecy.

"All we like sheep have gone astray; we have turned every one to his own way; and the Lord hath laid on Him the iniquity of us all."

Ephraim continued, chanting the words as if they were a psalm.

"He shall see of the travail of His soul, and shall be satisfied: by His knowledge shall My righteous servant justify many; for He shall bear their iniquities."

Everyone began to whisper to each other as they realized the sacrifice Jesus had made for them. He was crucified that they might be justified.

It was Joseph who finally summoned the courage to ask the one question the others were afraid to ask.

"I understand that Jesus is the Lamb of God and that He was sacrificed for us today; but how can He be our Savior, if He's in the grave?"

Josiah had no answer. In fact, an eerie hush came over the room with the realization that Jesus was in the tomb, until Ephraim's voice broke through the silence once again.

"Remember the psalm that just precedes the Shepherd's psalm," the old man said in a strong voice.

Josiah snapped back to attention and responded, "Yes, Jesus spoke words from that psalm when He was on the cross."

Everyone looked at him as he continued, "Just after the darkness, He cried out in a loud voice, *My God, My God, why hast Thou forsaken Me!?*"

"He was quoting the psalm," Zacharias declared.

"No, He wasn't," Josiah said to the surprise of everyone. "I thought so too at first, but He spoke those words in Aramaic, not in Hebrew."

"Aramaic is Jesus' mother tongue," Samuel said.

"Yes, I know, but David wrote the psalm in Hebrew," the shepherd replied.

Samuel was still bewildered by what he was saying.

"I heard Him speak those words. I heard the agony in His voice. Then I realized the truth. Jesus wasn't quoting David on the cross. No, David was quoting Jesus."

"When you think of the details of the psalm, it is descriptive of a crucifixion," Zacharias interjected.

Josiah took the next few moments to tell them all the things he'd seen and heard that were direct fulfillments of the psalm. Everyone was utterly amazed and could see it clearly.

When he finished, Ephraim spoke up again, "All that you say is true, but that's not what I was referring to when I first mentioned the psalm."

Josiah looked at him, not understanding what he intended.

"Remember the lad's question. It's a good one?" Ephraim replied. "Joseph, ask your question again."

Joseph was confused for a moment before he remembered what he'd asked.

He repeated it for all to hear, "How can Jesus be our Savior, if He's in the grave?"

Everyone looked to the old man for the answer.

Instead he said, "Michael, go get my scroll of the psalms."

Michael hurried into Ephraim's room and retrieved the scroll.

"Give it to your father," Ephraim instructed.

Josiah took the scroll and opened it to the psalm.

"Everything that Josiah has said about the psalm is true. I'd never understood it before tonight. The words He's cited for us are clearly the words of Jesus, but that's not all we find in the psalm. Josiah, find the line, *'I will declare Thy name unto My brethren: in the midst of the congregation will I praise Thee.'"* The blind man said.

"Here it is," Josiah responded.

"Now, look carefully at the lines leading up to it. Is there a change in person?"

He took a few moments to look over the passage, before shaking his head and saying, "No, there is no change of person. It is the same speaker throughout the psalm."

"Yes, you are correct," Ephraim said, his eyes widening as if he could see. "Listen carefully children. The first part of the psalm is a vivid description of the crucifixion of Jesus. It records His words, even His inner groanings. Sadly, we know that Jesus died on the cross today."

When he paused, everyone was perplexed, desperate for him to help them understand.

"Even though Jesus' death is recorded in the first section of the psalm leading up to the line Josiah just read, we find Him speaking in the midst of the congregation in the very next line. Josiah, read the line carefully that's just prior to the one you've just read."

"Save Me from the lion's mouth: for Thou hast heard Me from the horns of the unicorns."

Josiah still had a bewildered look on his face until Ephraim clarified the passage, "We all agree that these are Jesus' words. Now, Josiah, let me ask you a question. Did you see a lion or any unicorns at the cross?"

"No," he replied, clearly perplexed.

Ephraim smiled, knowing they were all thoroughly confused.

"The language is figurative. The word 'unicorns' is better understood as 'wild oxen,' and of course, there were no lions or oxen at the cross. I believe the lion and oxen are symbolic of Satan and His minions. Remember the promise made to the serpent in the Garden of Eden, *'He shall bruise thy head, and thou shalt bruise His heel.'* Jesus came under the power of Satan during the crucifixion, but God would not leave Him there. Jesus declared, *'For Thou hast heard Me from the horns of the unicorns.'* Beloved, Satan cannot hold Him!" Ephraim declared in a loud voice.

"I don't understand," Joseph said sheepishly. "Isn't Jesus still dead?"

"Yes, my son," Ephraim replied, "But the psalm goes on to say, *'I will declare Thy name unto My brethren: in the midst of the congregation I will praise Thee.'*"

"How can that be?" Joseph asked.

"I don't know," Ephraim admitted. "There are some things that remain a mystery. We'll just have to wait and see what God will reveal."

"Little children have faith," he declared, addressing the whole company. "Somehow, God will exalt His Son."

CHAPTER 19

Vindication of the Son

Isaiah 53:10

He shall prolong His days, and the pleasure of the Lord shall prosper His hand.

The men decided it would be best for the family to spend the Sabbath in prayer and fasting, even as they had the day before Passover. Certainly, Jesus had fulfilled His calling to be the sacrificial lamb, but there were many things yet to be revealed. The first half of David's psalm had come to pass, but how would God bring about the fulfillment of the remainder of the psalm? They all realized they needed to seek God's face.

Josiah found himself best able to sort through his thoughts when alone with his wife. Through the years that frequently occurred in their bed chamber. This night proved to be one of those nights. The shepherd tried to sleep, but every time he closed his eyes he had vivid memories of Jesus on the cross. Deborah could feel him stirring fitfully in the bed.

"What's wrong, Josiah?" She whispered to her husband.

He couldn't contain his emotions any longer and burst into tears. She put her arms around him and held him close as he sobbed.

"When I close my eyes, all I can see is Jesus on the cross. It was horrifying!" He cried.

She could only imagine what her husband had witnessed. Seeing Jesus on the cross from a distance as they left the city was more than she could bear. Secretly, she was grateful her children had been spared what their father had seen.

"There's so much I don't understand…" he gasped, unable to control his grief. "Last night I told you about all of the blood at the altar when we sacrificed the paschal lamb, but this was so much worse. Thousands of lambs were slain at the Temple, but each one died instantly. The knives were sharp and performed their duty. The animals didn't suffer."

She held him close and listened, knowing he had to say these things.

"But with Jesus…" his voice trailed off momentarily until he could compose himself enough to continue. "But Jesus suffered terribly on the cross. The lambs died quickly. He hung on the cross all day long. Moses said, *'For he that is hanged is accursed of God,'* and nothing could be truer."

Deborah remained silent, waiting on her husband.

"Crucifixion is the most vile and hideous invention of wicked men," he uttered in disgust. "But Jesus' suffering was more than physical. It was even more than emotional, as those around the foot of the cross mocked Him. It was profoundly spiritual. When the darkness that enveloped the land from the sixth until the ninth hour suddenly lifted, I looked up and saw His face. At first, I wondered if He was still alive, but then He raised His head heavenward and opened His swollen eyes. Deborah, they beat Him mercilessly before they crucified Him. His face was so marred, He was hardly recognizable. Somehow, He was able to open His eyes, and I'd never seen such agony before. He searched heaven for God, but God hid His face from His Son; and then Jesus cried out, *'My God, My God, why hast Thou forsaken Me?!'*"

Again, he paused as he relived that horrendous moment.

"Never was a man so lost, so forsaken, so cursed of God."

Deborah remained completely still as her husband sought answers to the questions that plagued him.

"Why? Why did Jesus have to suffer like that? The animals don't suffer. They're slain humanely."

"Because as Omar said, they could never truly be a sufficient sacrifice for men," Deborah replied softly. "Jesus didn't just die in our place. He suffered for us."

Josiah sat up in the bed, suddenly understanding something very profound.

"My wife, you are right. Jesus was truly cursed of God in our place. Somehow on the cross, He must have suffered an eternity of hell for us all."

"That's how much He loves us," she replied, remembering how tenderly Jesus held her youngest child on the steps of the Temple.

The shepherd looked at his wife pondering what she'd said, before uttering, "You said, 'He loves us,' not 'He loved us.' Do you think that somehow He still lives?"

"I don't know, but it seems to me that He must. Did He say anything on the cross that would help us understand?"

Josiah thought for a moment, trying to remember everything he'd heard Him say.

"Yes, there were two things," he responded as he searched his memory. "Two men were crucified with him. One of them mocked Him along with the crowd, but the other didn't. He asked Jesus to remember him when He came into His kingdom."

"What did Jesus say?" She asked.

He said, "*'Verily I say unto thee, today shalt thou be with Me in paradise.'* And then, just before He died He prayed, *'Father, into Thy hands I commend My spirit.'* He must somehow be with God. I don't understand it all, but yes, I believe He is still alive."

They lay there in silence for a few moments before he added, "When Jesus says in David's psalm, *'I will declare Thy name unto My brethren: in the midst of the congregation will I praise Thee,'* He must be speaking of the congregation of those gathered around God's throne in heaven."

Deborah pondered what her husband said and asked, "But how will the people on earth know that God has answered His prayer?"

He shook his head in confusion, "I guess we'll just have to wait and see what God will do."

She snuggled up next to her husband. As she closed her eyes, she remembered those anxious moments when he was away from her. It had been a traumatic day, but now she felt safe in his arms.

Early the next morning, everyone gathered together at Ephraim's house. The day would follow a similar pattern to the one they used on the eve of Passover.

Ephraim said, "I want you to spend the day in prayer and meditation upon God's Word. You've hidden the Scriptures in your hearts, and now it's time to call upon the Lord to bring them to your remembrance. Seek God's Word for how we should spend the coming days. Michael, you and your brothers get all of my scrolls and place them here in front of where I'm sitting. Then go to your grandfather's house and get the scrolls that belong to your father and set them on the other side of the room. As God stirs your spirits to recall His Word, get the scrolls and search them. See if there is something we've missed. At the end of the day, we will discuss what we've learned and then trust in the Lord."

Michael and his younger brothers brought out all of the scrolls and arranged them in the proper order. Between the two men, the whole canon of Scripture was represented.

Joseph and Martha approached Michael. It was natural for the two young men to study together. However, he was thinking of asking someone else to join them. Miriam was helping her younger sisters get situated when she heard his voice.

"Would you like to study and pray with us?" He asked.

She smiled broadly and gladly accepted his invitation. It delighted her that he wanted to include her.

The two young couples found a comfortable place, before Michael hurried over to his father's scrolls and chose the prophet, Isaiah. Ever since Ephraim brought the end of David's psalm to their attention, he'd been thinking of the conclusion of the Suffering Servant passages in Isaiah.

He opened the scroll and spread it out on the floor in front of them. Miriam and Martha joined the young men looking at the scroll. Contrary to custom, both of their fathers had insisted that they learn to read, so they could read the Scriptures.

Michael's fingers quickly moved over the words, searching for what his mind was trying to recall.

"Yes," he exclaimed, more to himself than to the others. "Here it is."

He paused to read it over carefully in his mind before he read the words aloud.

"*Yet it pleased the Lord to bruise Him; He hath put Him to grief: when Thou shalt make His soul an offering for sin, He shall see His seed...*' That's describing Jesus death, now listen, *He shall prolong His days, and the pleasure of the Lord shall prosper His hand.*'"

Michael slowed his reading as he continued, "*He shall see of the travail of His soul, and shall be satisfied: by His knowledge shall my righteous servant justify many; for He shall bear their iniquities.*"

"See, it was prophesied that Jesus would die for our sins; but now listen," he said as his voice picked up volume in his excitement, *Therefore*

will I divide Him a portion with the great, and He shall divide the spoil with
the strong; because He hath poured out His soul unto death: and He was
numbered with the transgressors; and He bare the sin of many, and made
intercession for the transgressors.'"

Michael paused, his eyes jumping with excitement, "God is going to reward Jesus for His work to redeem us. Somehow, the grave is not the end of Jesus!"

Joseph couldn't sit still either, and their enthusiasm caught Josiah's attention.

When Michael saw his father looking at them, he motioned him to come over. Deborah followed her husband and listened as their son quickly pointed out the things he'd discovered in the prophet, Isaiah.

"Yes, my son. I've come to the same conclusion. Somehow, Jesus will be rewarded by His Father for what He's done; but how? Where will God *'prolong His days'* and *'prosper His hand'*?"

Michael didn't know the answer to his father's question. He looked again at the text, but it didn't give him a clue.

"I don't know – heaven? Do you think God will reward Him in heaven?" He asked.

"That's the only conclusion I can come to," Josiah responded to his inquisitive son. "Your mother and I thought about this last night, but what matters is that the Scriptures are clear, both in the psalm and here in Isaiah. God has rewarded Him with life. How He will accomplish this remains a mystery."

Michael nodded his head, and Josiah and Deborah left to pray.

Instinctively, Michael led the others in prayer, "O Lord, thank You for giving us Your Word to explain all that Your hand has done. You've sent Your Son to die in our place, as a lamb to the slaughter. Reward Your Son for His obedience to Your will. Now, grant to us patience to await Your revelation. *Amen.*"

Joseph, Martha and Miriam all responded with the *"Amen."* Miriam looked at Josiah's second son and saw a man she knew she would admire for the rest of her days. He had a zeal for the Lord that was unshakable. She realized the days ahead would be uncertain, but in the end she was hopeful that God would bring the two of them together. He loved God, of that she was certain. She was starting to believe that maybe he loved her as well.

The four of them bowed their heads again, and they knelt together as they joined hands and continued to pray. Their hearts were searching but also surrendered to God's will, trusting He would fulfill His holy will and the end of it would be salvation.

Ephraim paused from his prayers to listen. Since losing his eyesight, his hearing had been heightened. He noticed things he'd never heard before. Silently, he thanked God as he listened to the sounds of God's covenantal faithfulness. Some were praying earnestly, even the little children. Others were discussing the Scriptures. All of them were kept by God's power to have faith, even at this time when the wickedness of the devil and of men had been on full display. He knew that God was greater than the wicked and that somehow He would vindicate the work of His Son.

Around mid-afternoon, he summoned Deborah and Hannah and instructed them to prepare a light supper to break the fast at sundown.

"I don't want you spending much time on the meal, so that you can devote yourselves to prayer as the Sabbath comes to a close," he said.

Both women did as he said without hesitation and hurried to the kitchen to make the necessary preparations. Hannah was almost as talented in the kitchen as Deborah, and in no time they had sufficient loaves of unleavened bread, along with dates and olives for the meal. As Deborah baked the bread, she remembered how God's people in Egypt prepared it on the night of Passover without yeast, because God was about to deliver them quickly before it would have time to rise. She couldn't help but wonder what God was about to do in Jerusalem. Both women returned to their husbands, and the four of them prayed together as the Sabbath came to an end.

After they broke their fast and finished supper, Ephraim called them all to come near him. They discussed the things they'd studied in their groups that day. Josiah let Michael demonstrate the parallel structure of David's psalm and the passage in Isaiah. The shepherd wasn't surprised to learn that both Zacharias and Ephraim had come to the same conclusion. All of them believed that God had somehow vindicated His Son in heaven, but Ephraim had another thought.

"There is a debate among the learned in Jerusalem regarding the resurrection," he said for all to hear. "The party of the High Priest, the Sadducees, denies that there will be a resurrection at the last day. The

Pharisees were no better when they conspired with the Sadducees to crucify Jesus, but they are correct regarding the resurrection. Surely, Jesus' soul is now with God in heaven, but the day will come at the end of this age when the dead will be raised. I believe that on that day God will vindicate His Son, Jesus the Messiah, and all eyes will behold Him. Those who believe in Him will find rest, but those who have rejected Him will find perdition."

They were all satisfied with Ephraim's answer to the nagging question of Jesus' whereabouts, but still didn't know what to do. If He was now in heaven, who would instruct them? All they knew to do was wait, but Samuel couldn't sit still and wait in Bethlehem. First, he spoke privately with his father; and once he'd gained permission, he told the rest of them that he was going out again to search for the disciples. Surely, they would know what to do. They all bid him farewell, before he slipped out into the night.

"Michael, you and Miriam, help me get to my room," the weary Ephraim said.

They quickly moved to either side of him and helped him to his feet, before assisting him as he walked to his bedroom. When he got to the door, he turned and asked Josiah to join them. Once he was comfortable in his bed, he asked Michael and Miriam to leave him alone with Josiah. The shepherd had no idea what the old man wanted to say to him.

"Look over there in the corner," he said pointing him in the right direction. "You'll find something there wrapped in linen."

Josiah moved to the corner and picked up the linen only to find a sheaf of barley inside of it.

"What's this?" He asked.

"Tomorrow is *Reishit Katzir*, the Feast of Firstfruits," Ephraim said. "I want you to represent our company and take the sheaf to the Temple tomorrow and present it to the priest, so that he might offer it as a wave offering before the Lord."

Josiah nodded his head. He remembered the instructions in Leviticus regarding the Feast of Firstfruits to dedicate the barley harvest. The feast was to be celebrated on the day following the Sabbath after Passover. Firstfruits marked the beginning of seven weeks leading up to the Feast of Weeks to give thanks for the wheat harvest

"Miriam has prepared a cake of bread for the grain offering, and there is a fourth part of a *hin* of wine for the drink offering. I've also purchased a young ram of the first year for you to offer as a whole burnt offering. I want you to do this for our family. Arise early in the morning and present these offerings to the Lord in obedience to the *Torah*."

Josiah agreed to do it and asked if he could take Isaac and Michael with him.

"By all means take your sons. They have become men who fear the Lord."

His eyes were getting heavy, and Josiah could tell he was about to go to sleep.

The shepherd turned to depart when he heard the old man speak once more, "Josiah, God has been faithful to our family."

Tears from his blind eyes ran down his wrinkled face, as he said, "Why has God been gracious to us, but allowed so many others to rebel against Him?"

"I don't know," Josiah replied. "I'm thankful He has been merciful to us."

A smile came to the old man's face.

"He's kept every single one of them," he exclaimed. "Praise be to God. He's kept them all."

His eyes closed and Josiah heard a soft snore. Quietly, he left the room to tell his sons about their duty for the next day. Even if all of Israel turned away from the Lord, Josiah prayed that God would keep his family faithful.

When he saw the excitement in Isaac's eyes upon hearing the news regarding the offerings, he couldn't keep from embracing his eldest son. He held him close, realizing that this was the one lamb of his flock that he'd almost lost. Silently, he gave thanks to God for bringing his lost sheep home.

"Why did you do that?" Isaac asked.

"Because I love you, and I'm thankful to God," his father replied.

CHAPTER 20

Come Back to Me

Matthew 28:6

He is not here, for He is risen, as He said.

Josiah was up long before dawn, but not as early as his wife. Deborah was determined to serve a good breakfast to her husband and sons before they departed for Jerusalem. The shepherd woke Isaac and asked him to go to Ephraim's home to get Michael, and then sat down at the table, admiring his wife as she finished cooking their breakfast.

"Did Samuel return last night?" He asked Michael, as soon as the young men entered the house.

"No. I'm sure I would have heard him had he come in. I slept near the front door, so I wouldn't disturb the others when I left this morning."

Josiah wondered if perhaps Samuel had found Andrew and the other disciples and stayed the night with them. He was anxious to hear from him and hoped they would see him in Jerusalem. Ephraim had told his son that Josiah would be presenting the wave offering, but they knew it would be hard for them to find each other in the crowd.

After a hardy breakfast, Isaac went out back of Ephraim's house to get the young ram for the whole burnt offering, and Michael headed over to fetch the loaf for the grain offering from Miriam. The beautiful young woman met him at the door with a smile, having anticipated that he would be back for the loaf of bread.

"Be careful." She spoke softly lest she awaken the others.

"I will be," he replied.

Only days before neither of them would have considered a visit to the city to be remotely dangerous, but things had changed drastically in the last couple of days.

The three men made their way to Jerusalem in relative silence, each pondering how different it was than before. Only a week earlier they'd made their first journey on this very same road. Their hearts had been full of joy and expectancy, but on this day they didn't know what to expect.

Finally, Michael broke the silence, "Father, should we be presenting the wave offering after what the priests did to Jesus?"

Josiah had to admit to himself that he'd wondered the same thing.

"I know what you mean," he responded, "But Ephraim was insistent, and I believe he is right. God commanded us to celebrate the Feast of Firstfruits and we must be obedient to Him regardless of what's happened. I intend to perform the duties required by the law until our God reveals otherwise."

Still, his determination to obey God's law didn't help him prepare his heart for worship. When they presented their offerings, he found himself going through the motions. It seemed more like a ritual of duty. How could he participate in worship through a priesthood that had conspired to crucify their own Messiah?

Suddenly, he looked across the Court of Israel and saw a face he recognized. It was Nahor, the priest who had assisted them when they first visited the Temple. He was a long-time friend of Zacharias, and Josiah knew him to be an honorable man. Their eyes met, and instantly the shepherd realized the priest felt the same way he did about what had transpired. There was sadness in his eyes. He looked heavenward and placed his hands together in a gesture calling on Josiah to pray. The shepherd nodded his head and returned the gesture. That moment gave him hope that there were others in Israel who had not apostasized.

He looked around the Temple court at the worshipers and wondered how many others God had kept holy for Himself. Suddenly, he remembered the plea of the prophet Elijah, and it made him feel foolish.

Elijah had said in dejection, *"I have been jealous for the Lord God of hosts: because the children of Israel have forsaken Thy covenant, thrown down Thine altars, and slain Thy prophets with the sword; and I, even I only, am left; and they seek my life to take it away."*

It was God Himself who responded to His weary prophet, *"Yet I have left me seven thousand in Israel, all the knees which have not bowed unto Baal."*

Josiah was ashamed he'd let himself believe that God had only kept his family from falling away. Surely, there were others at the Temple that grieved what the priests had done to Jesus. He wondered if any of those gathered for the Feast of Firstfruits were among the procession that ushered Jesus into the city and to the Temple the week before. Yet, he couldn't escape the cries from the crowd that He be crucified on Friday. The city that was built for fellowship was now deeply divided.

Once again, he recalled the old man's words, words he'd pondered his whole life, *"Behold, this child is set for the fall and rising again of many in Israel."*

The shepherd couldn't help but wonder which of those gathered at the Temple would fall and which would rise. He knew in his heart that somehow Jesus would accomplish this.

Josiah and his sons found it remarkable that those at the House of God were performing their duties, business as usual. They didn't hear a single word uttered about Jesus until they were leaving the Temple.

"The tomb is empty," Josiah heard one man whisper to another.

"What tomb?" The shepherd blurted out anxiously.

A look of fear could be seen in the eyes of the two men, and they hurried away without responding to him.

Josiah realized immediately that they had to be talking about Jesus' tomb and quickly led his sons through the double Huldah Gate and down the very staircase where they'd met Jesus the week before. Hurrying, they crossed the Central Valley and made their way toward the garden where he had watched them bury Him.

His sons wanted to skirt *Golgotha*, but Josiah was determined that they see where Jesus had been crucified. The three vertical masts still stood in place atop the hill as a reminder of the cruelty of Roman domination. As they approached the awful place, they could smell the stench of death. The rocks beneath the beams were splattered with blood, and they knew that Jesus' blood was co-mingled with the blood of criminals who'd died there. They didn't linger and tears ran down their faces as they passed by.

It didn't take long to arrive at the garden, but Josiah knew to be cautious as they made their approach. Sure enough, the stone had been removed from the entrance to the tomb. Just as they were about to look inside, they heard voices coming and quickly hid behind some rocks.

"Now remember," they heard the officer of the guard say in Latin. "Remember to tell anyone who comes seeking the body, that the followers of the King of the Jews came and stole it away during the night."

They watched as the other guards meekly nodded their assent, while looking like they'd seen a ghost.

"You've been well paid, so you best do what you're told!" The officer barked at the beleaguered men.

As soon as he departed, the soldiers set up their regiment to guard the empty tomb. Josiah had seen all he needed to see and led his sons away quietly.

When they got out of earshot Michael asked, "What was that all about?"

His father stopped along the path, looked at his sons and responded, "I don't know, but it's clear the guards have been paid to lie. Whatever happened to Jesus' body, it was not stolen by His disciples."

"Why would they post a guard to secure an empty tomb?" Michael asked, thinking out loud.

Neither Josiah nor Isaac ventured a response. They recognized the folly of the chief priests' attempt to hide what had happened at the tomb. As the three men headed for Bethlehem each of them harbored a ray of hope. They knew the body had not been stolen away by His disciples, but what did happen that morning? Dare they think the unthinkable? Could they bring themselves to believe He'd actually been raised from the dead?

They hurried back to Bethlehem with lingering questions. As they entered Ephraim's house they were happy to find that Samuel was there. He and his father were talking in Ephraim's bedroom. The three of them approach the door and were quickly invited inside. Samuel couldn't contain his enthusiasm.

"There are reports that Jesus has been raised from the dead," he announced.

"I'm not surprised," Josiah replied to the shock of his cousin. "We visited the grave, and the tomb is empty. Then we overheard the soldiers being told to tell anyone who asked the whereabouts of His body that His disciples had stolen it away."

"Who would believe such a report?" Samuel asked in amazement.

"Those who are determined not to believe in Jesus," Michael retorted.

"Tell us what you've learned," Josiah said anxiously. "Did you see the disciples?"

"No, they're still in hiding, but I found someone who knows where they are. He couldn't tell me, but he did say that some of the women reported seeing angels at the grave and that the tomb was empty early this morning. They told the disciples that one of the angels said to them, *'He is not here: for He is risen, as He said.'* Then the angel said that Jesus would go before the disciples into Galilee and they would see Him there. One of the women was very close to Jesus. Her name is Mary. She testified that she's seen the Lord Himself and that He told her to tell the disciples, *'I am ascending to My Father and your Father, and to My God and to Your God.'* My friend didn't know whether the disciples believed the women; but if you saw the empty tomb, maybe they were telling the truth."

"What are you going to do?" Michael asked Samuel as Zacharias, Joseph and Nathaniel entered the room.

"I'm going to go to Galilee. I have too. I can't just wait around here, and I know some of the places that Jesus would surely visit," he replied animatedly, as he paced around his father's room.

Josiah could already see the look in his second son's eyes.

"Father, can I go with Samuel?" He asked, his voice practically pleading.

The shepherd was at a loss. Part of him wanted to keep his sons near him during these trying days, but he realized his son had become a man in his own right.

"Let me speak with your mother," he replied.

Unlike many Jews in his day, Josiah treasured his wife's counsel above that of any man, including the godly men that were gathered together in Ephraim's room.

Joseph looked at his father, but was afraid to voice his request.

Zacharias knew his son and answered his non-verbal question, "If Josiah decides that Michael can go, it will be alright for you to go with them."

Joseph's eyes lit up with excitement.

"Men, this could be dangerous," Samuel warned. "Joseph, do you have a horse you can ride?"

A blank looked crossed his face because he didn't even own a horse.

"Joseph can ride Midnight," Isaac offered without being asked.

Michael nodded his head at his older brother to thank him. He really wanted Joseph to go with them.

"When are you leaving?" Josiah asked Samuel.

"As soon as I can get everything together, hopefully within the hour," he replied.

The shepherd immediately left to consult with Deborah in the kitchen. Michael wanted to go with him to plead his case, but knew it was best to stay behind. Assuming their fathers were going to grant permission to the boys, Isaac took Joseph outside to prepare Midnight for the ride. He was a splendid steed, but he belonged to Isaac and wouldn't let anyone ride him unless instructed to do so by his master.

Michael was a bit antsy waiting for his father's return.

Josiah was smiling when he came out of the kitchen and said, "We've decided to let you go."

His son was overjoyed and ran into the kitchen to thank his mother. Joseph was right behind him.

"I'll put together some provisions for you to make sure you have what you need on the trail," she said as he hugged her.

Things were happening so fast, Joseph forgot to talk to Martha about it. She was not pleased when she overheard her mother talking to Michael about the trip.

"Where are you going?" She asked Joseph in an incredulous tone.

The young man suddenly realized his error and quickly took her aside.

"Samuel heard that Jesus was raised from the dead, and it's rumored He's going to Galilee. Michael and I have decided to go with him to see if we can find Him," he said holding both of her hands and hoping she would understand.

Tears welled up in her eyes as she asked, "How long will you be gone?"

He had no idea what to tell her, and just at that moment Samuel stuck his head in the kitchen and said, "Let's get going, we've got a long ride ahead of us."

Martha held onto Joseph's hands and asked again as she fought back her tears, "How long, Joseph?"

When he didn't respond, Samuel realized he better say something.

"Martha, we really don't know. We'll stay as long as it takes."

"Are you talking about days?" She asked turning to look at Samuel.

Not wanting to deceive her he said, "Maybe longer, but I promise you, I'll bring him back safe and sound."

She threw her arms around Joseph's neck and started to sob. The boy didn't know what to do. He didn't know how to comfort her or what to say, so he just held her and let her cry. The others in the kitchen realized they needed to give them a moment and slipped into the big room where everyone else was waiting.

"Why do you have to go?" She asked, her voice pleading with him to stay.

"I'll come back," he whispered as he continued to hold her.

She finally leaned back so she could look at him.

"You didn't answer my question. Why do you have to go?"

"I don't know," he said, not really having a clear answer. "I just feel like God wants me to go."

She had no reply for that. How could she question what he believed God was leading him to do?

"I don't want you to go," she cried. "I don't want you to go."

"I know," he said in as comforting a voice as he could manage. "I understand, but I feel like it's something I have to do."

For several moments she held onto him, doing everything in her power to regain her composure. Deep down, she knew he must follow his heart, though it broke her heart that he was willing to leave her.

"You better come back," she finally said firmly.

When a tiny smile appeared in the corner of her mouth, the young man breathed a sigh of relief.

"Martha, listen to me. I love you with my whole heart. The day will come when you will be my wife. I promise you that, but today is not that day. What's happening today is bigger than you and me. If Jesus has actually come back from the dead, it is the most significant event in all of history. I have to find out, and Samuel and Michael do too. Please tell me you'll pray for me and wait for me."

"Kiss me, Joseph, and then I'll let you go. And yes, I'll pray for you every day, and I'll wait right here until you come back to me."

Their lips met in a tender kiss, and then he whispered in her ear, "I promise you, I'll come back to you, and then we'll get married."

It was hard to let him go, but she knew he had to leave quickly. The two of them walked hand in hand into the other room and then out the door. Isaac had all three of their horses ready, and Deborah gave each of them enough rations to get to Galilee. Joseph gave Martha one last hug and then mounted Midnight, as Isaac held the horse and spoke softly to him. Midnight willingly accepted him in the saddle.

Michael prepared to mount his horse, when Miriam suddenly rushed to him. Feeling the gentle touch of her hand on his back, he turned around to face her.

She hugged him closely and whispered in his ear, "And you better come back to me."

His face lit up when he heard her words. He pulled back enough to look into her eyes and knew beyond a shadow of a doubt that she loved him.

Pulling her close, he whispered in her ear, "I will come back to you. Will you wait for me?"

"Yes," she whispered as the tears ran down her cheeks.

Once Michael mounted his horse, Josiah led them all in prayer, asking God to protect them. As the three of them goaded their horses forward, Deborah and Elizabeth's eyes met. Both of them were smiling from ear to ear.

As they all turned to go back into Ephraim's house Deborah whispered to her best friend, "It looks like we'll have two weddings to plan pretty soon."

"Thanks be to God," Elizabeth exclaimed looking heavenward.

"Yes, thanks be to God," Deborah prayed.

CHAPTER 21

Wandering Sheep

Isaiah 53:6

All we like sheep have gone astray; we have turned every one to his own way; and the LORD hath laid on Him the iniquity of us all.

They could hardly contain their enthusiasm as they entered the house. Dare they believe that Jesus had actually risen bodily from the dead? Deep in his heart, Josiah prayed that it was so. Later that night, the men met in Ephraim's bedroom.

"Zacharias has thought of some things and wanted to get your input," Nathaniel said to the other men.

The two men had become close since meeting the week before at the Temple, and celebrating Passover together.

As soon as they were all seated the rabbi said pointedly, "I'm convinced that Jesus is the Messiah of God and has actually risen bodily from the dead."

"Tell us what's brought you to that conclusion," Josiah responded.

"It's not because of the witness of the women who went to the tomb. Though I'm certain they are sincere, they could be deluded because of their grief. Neither am I convinced because the tomb is empty. Regardless of how improbable the guards' explanation may be, it is still possible for it to be true. My conviction is due to my understanding of the Scriptures."

The other men sat in rapt attention as he continued, "We've seen a pattern in Jesus' activities the past few days. First, He made His entry into Jerusalem and cleansed the Temple last Sunday. We now understand what John meant when he declared that Jesus is *the Lamb of God which taketh away the sin of the world.* That day when He cleansed the Temple it was not only the fulfillment of prophecy, but also the Day of Presentation. He was presenting Himself as the Lamb of God without spot or blemish. You see, Jesus is the fulfillment of the paschal lamb."

Josiah couldn't help but remember all of the things the good rabbi had taught him since they first met at the synagogue in Elath. In particular, he remembered the statement, "All the Scriptures speak of Him." That principle was pervasive in the rabbi's thinking every time he opened the scrolls and had been for years. Now, in the light of everything that was happening, so much was becoming clear to him. The shepherd was suddenly grateful that his kinsmen finally had the opportunity to hear this man of God.

"Then when we ate Passover," the rabbi continued. "I remembered Josiah telling me about how Samuel, Joel and Hannah heard Jesus' teaching about the 'Bread of Life' in Capernaum. I thought to myself, what a hard saying it was, when Jesus said, *'Whoso eateth My flesh, and drinketh My blood, hath eternal life.'* I must admit, at first I found His words to be repugnant, for the law forbids all Jews from eating any blood; but then I realized He was speaking spiritually. When Ephraim was leading us in the Seder Service I couldn't help but think of that discourse, especially when he presented the *Afikomen* and then when we drank the third cup. Don't you see, the Seder Service itself finds its fulfillment in Jesus' death. Jesus is the *Afikomen*! He is the Bread of Life, and His shed blood is the true cup of redemption."

The other men were astonished at his insight, but Josiah was not surprised.

Becoming even more excited, Zacharias declared, "Jesus was crucified on the first day of the Feast of Unleavened Bread after eating Passover with His disciples the night before. Now, remember what today is. Josiah, you represented all of us at the Temple this morning when you presented the sheaf of barley for the wave offering. Today was the Feast of Firstfruits. It's no coincidence that the tomb was empty this morning, or that the women testified that they'd seen the Lord. It is fitting, for Jesus is the firstfruits of those raised from the dead. His resurrection guarantees our resurrection at the end of the age. He is fulfilling all of the feasts and festivals of Israel in His life, His death and now His resurrection."

Ephraim had tears running down his face. Zacharias' teaching confirmed what he'd already been thinking.

"Yes, I believe God has raised Him from the dead!" The old man exclaimed.

He was so excited he said, "Josiah, help me out of my bed. Nathaniel, summon everyone to come into the main room. I want the whole family to hear what our teacher has taught us."

The rabbi was humbled by being called a teacher from the mouth of such an esteemed elder, but was also excited about the things God had revealed to Him from the Scriptures. The anointing of the Spirit that had come upon him on the road was never far from him. It began the morning he blew the *shofar*. Since that moment while on pilgrimage, he'd sensed that God was about to reveal His Messiah at the feast. He'd never dreamed it would unfold the way it did, but now saw the beauty of God's plan. As the men headed into the main room, he believed he had a message from God.

After everyone was assembled and Zacharias stood to teach, Josiah wondered why the rabbi had been so quiet over the past few days. Then he realized that his friend only spoke what he'd come to know with certainty. Finally, it had all come together, and now it was time to teach.

He had a way about him that was striking when he spoke. This gentle man's eyes were aflame with the zeal of the Lord. An ordinarily quiet man, he was full of passion. He spoke of things now settled in his spirit and the entire company was overjoyed with his words. Momentarily, Josiah wished Michael had been there to hear these teachings, but he believed his son was about to witness things even more glorious in Galilee. He prayed that God would permit his son to see the face of the risen Jesus.

When the shepherd retired for the evening with his wife, they spent time praying for Michael's safety. They also prayed that God would keep their family faithful. Though they believed that God had raised Jesus from the dead, they still knew there would be trying days ahead of them. Josiah recalled Jesus' words to the women when the soldiers were leading him up the road to *Golgotha*. He spoke of dreadful days ahead. There was still much the shepherd didn't know, but he did trust that God was in control of these events.

He lay quietly with his wife by his side, settled in the things he was learning, expecting that God was about to reveal much more. Then his thoughts drifted to Kedar, to his home, to all of the people who lived there and those they'd passed by while on pilgrimage. Though the apostasy of his own people grieved him, at least they had the Word of God and the covenants. The pagans who dwelt in Kedar were utterly blind, devoid of the knowledge of God, having chosen to worship idols instead.

He found himself burdened for his neighbors, though they were his enemies. God had made promises long ago to Abraham that included the nations. He prayed for them, prayed that God would open their blind eyes so they could see His beauty and the glory of His salvation. He remembered the old man's prophecy, words that had plagued him and driven him to search out their meaning since he was a little boy. Now he finally understood. The old man had said that the child would be *a light to lighten the Gentiles.* Josiah knew with certainty that God's promise to Abraham would be fulfilled by Jesus.

"Use me. Use my family to bring this good news to my homeland," he whispered before closing his eyes.

He thought Deborah was already asleep, but she was listening. *'Amen,'* she prayed silently, realizing that when the time was right they would be returning to the place she called home. What a home it would be if God did open the eyes of the Kedarites to His truth.

The days turned into weeks, and there were anxious moments for the shepherd and his wife. Michael had never been away from their tent. Miriam faithfully prayed for him every day, remembering the way he looked at her just before he left. Memories of her love for Isaac were far from her, swept away in her newfound affection for his brother, her true soul mate.

On the other hand, Martha's heart became more desperate with each passing day, and she began to resent God. In particular, she became bitter toward Jesus. He's the one her beloved felt compelled to seek.

The name of Jesus was often mentioned around Ephraim's table. Everyone was waiting to see what God would have them do. However, whenever His name was uttered around Martha, her eyes would darken. She tried to hide her emotions and only cried in her bed at night. At first, she prayed that Joseph would return the next day, but when he failed to do so day after day, she stopped believing and ceased praying altogether.

Deborah realized what was happening to her daughter, but she didn't know what to do for her. She discussed it with Josiah and they committed it to prayer. Both were confident of the spiritual condition of the rest of their flock, but were concerned for Martha's soul. She seemed to be a wandering sheep.

One night, as they lay upon their beds, they cried out to the Lord for her, "Oh Lord take heed of our little wandering sheep. Martha seems so lost without Joseph. Show her the glory of the things happening before our very eyes. Cause her to become lost in her love for You, and bring Joseph back to her arms."

Isaac also noticed what was happening to his sister. He could see what was going on in her, because he'd been there himself. Long before he made his flight to Dumat in open rebellion and rejected his covenant name for the name of the son of bondage, Isaac's heart was cold toward God. He had no idea at the time. He thought himself to be a believer; but deep inside his heart was set on temporal things – good things, but temporal things. He wanted a flock of sheep, a wife, children and land to raise them. That was his passion. Whenever his father spoke of Jerusalem and pilgrimage he'd felt the same things Martha was trying to hide in her heart.

The very next night, words of Jesus, His death and resurrection, punctuated the sentences of nearly everyone around the table. Isaac saw his sister sigh and her face darken. When she quickly exited after the meal, he followed her. She'd found a lonely place to go to grieve and fret.

He surprised her when he walked up.

"Do you want to talk?" He asked his little sister.

"About what?" She asked while raising her head and putting on a straight face, trying to hide her troubles.

"About why you become sullen every time Jesus' name is mentioned," he replied, perhaps a bit too bluntly.

At first she tried to deny it, but he was persistent.

"Martha, I know what you're going through. Why don't you just tell me?"

It was like his question opened the floodgate.

"I'm angry!" She said raising her voice. "All my life it's been about you and Dinah and Michael, even about Naomi. You're the oldest. Dinah's the oldest girl and Michael is the holy one. Of course, Naomi's the baby. I've always felt left out in this family; and then finally, something good happens to me. I meet a boy and he likes me for me. I fall in love with him and think he feels the same way. He told me he does; but then Jesus died, and everyone thinks He rose from the dead. All that's good I guess; but then Joseph runs off to find Him, and he stays and stays and stays and stays…"

"Have you prayed for him?" Isaac asked.

"I did at first," she answered honestly, "But after a while I just stopped. God doesn't hear my prayers!"

Suddenly, she began to weep. Her big brother took her into his arms like he did when she was little, if she fell and scraped her knee, or got her feelings hurt by one of her siblings. There had always been a special bond between them.

She cried and cried, truly breaking down for the first time; and Isaac let her plumb the depths of her despair.

Finally, she was able to compose herself, and he tenderly wiped the tears from his sister's cheeks.

She looked at him and asked, "What did you mean when you said that you know what I'm going through?"

"Martha, I'm going to be straight with you," he said. "Long before I ran away, my heart was far from God. I just didn't realize it. Father kept talking about this pilgrimage, but I didn't want to go. I wanted Miriam, my own flock of sheep and land to graze them. That's all I wanted."

She was nodding her head.

"What do you want?" He asked.

"I want to marry Joseph and have lots of kids. I want my own tent or house, our own place, just like Mother and Father have."

"Those are good things," he replied. "Joseph is a wonderful man, and I'm pleased he loves you."

"Do you really think he does?" She asked.

"I do, and what's not to love? You are my beautiful sister."

For the first time a smile came to her face, but then he got serious with her.

"You said you want to have what Mother and Father have."

She nodded her head.

"What do they have now?" He asked.

She had a perplexed look on her face and hesitated before answering, "They have each other, and they have us."

"Yes, they do," he replied, "But Father is a shepherd at heart. In fact, he's renowned as the Shepherd of Kedar even among those who hate him. Martha, he loves his sheep and the land where we graze them. Where are they now?"

"He...he sold them," she said almost in a whisper.

"Why would he sell them, if he loved them, if he loves being a shepherd?"

"To bring us to Jerusalem to worship God," she said as a light began to dawn in her soul.

"That's right — because as much as Father loved his sheep, he loves something more. Do you know who father loves most?" He asked, looking directly into her eyes by the moonlight.

"I guess he loves God the most," she answered quietly.

"Before I ran away, I just thought I loved God; but I didn't. I loved the good things God gives us. When He brought me to repentance in His mercy, I realized the true meaning of the first commandment. Do you remember that commandment?

Thou shalt have no other gods before Me..." she answered instinctively, her voice trailing off.

"Do you want to know why I'm so thankful that Joseph loves you?" He asked softly.

"Why?" She replied, her eyes widening.

"Because like Father, Joseph loves God most too; and because he loves God most, he can love you the way a man should love his wife."

"Is that why you love Haifa so much?" She asked.

"Yes. Haifa loved God before I did. Now that I love Him most, I can love her in ways I never could before."

"What about Miriam?" She asked, never having it all explained to her.

"Miriam is a wonderful woman and will make Michael an extraordinary wife..."

"You saw them too when Michael left with Joseph and Samuel," she interjected.

"Yes, I think we all did. God has always meant for them to be together, and it pleases me; but when I loved Miriam, and I truly did, I was incapable of loving her the way she deserved to be loved. She'd become an idol in my heart, which meant I couldn't love anyone or anything the way I should. You may not know this, but I asked her to marry me after we arrived in Bethlehem."

"You did? What did Haifa think about that?" She asked in astonishment.

"Haifa made me go to her," he replied.

"Why…why would she do that?"

"Because she loves God more than she loves me, which makes her able to love me completely. She has quickly become a godly woman and was willing to share me or lose me, if that's what God wanted."

Martha's eyes widened as she truly saw herself for the first time, and suddenly she began to weep. Isaac recognized the bitter sweetness of her tears of repentance.

"I've been so wicked!" She exclaimed.

"Yes, you have," Isaac said, surprising her before quickly adding, "We all have, but Jesus died on the cross for our sins. Martha, Jesus died for your sins."

That made her wail even louder.

"I've been so angry at Him for taking Joseph away. I didn't realize what He'd done for me. How can He ever forgive me for resenting Him for taking my Joseph away?"

"Jesus died for all of your sins, even that one. Father said that Jesus even prayed for forgiveness for those who crucified Him. Do you want to pray and ask for forgiveness?"

Martha nodded her head before bowing it and closing her eyes.

"Can we get on our knees?" She asked.

Isaac helped his sister kneel down and joined her on the ground.

She then began to pray, "Father, I've sinned so grievously against You. I've resented Your Son and haven't appreciated what He's done for me. Please forgive me and have mercy upon me. I want to love You above all, and yes, please keep Joseph safe and bring him back to me when it's the right time. *Amen.*"

Isaac whispered, *"Amen,"* and hugged his little sister. She would always be a little sister to him.

Josiah squeezed Deborah's hand as they listened to their daughter's prayer. Both had tears streaming down their faces. Without saying a word to alert their children, they turned and went back to the house. Now, all of their sheep were safe in the fold.

CHAPTER 22

He Lives!

1 Corinthians 15:6

After that, He was seen of above five hundred brethren at once.

The Feast of Weeks was fast approaching, and Josiah had not heard a word from Michael. Even the shepherd was getting a little worried. Martha's newfound faith sustained her, but she couldn't help but be concerned. Watching her older sister inspired her. Before her repentance, she'd hardly noticed the wonderful work of God's grace in Dinah. Her ability to rest in God's providence served as a comforting testimony to Martha as she awaited Joseph's return.

Miriam was waiting in anticipation for Michael. Her heart was thrilled when he told her that he would come back to her. Patiently, she watched for him, day after day.

It had been nearly forty days since the three men rode out of Bethlehem in search for the risen Jesus, when suddenly Martha heard the sound of horses approaching Ephraim's house. As soon as she opened the door and saw it was Joseph, she ran to him with tears streaming down her cheeks. This time her tears were those of joy. One look at his face quelled any fears she may have had about his affection for her. He immediately jumped down from Midnight's back and took her in his arms.

Miriam was more restrained as she emerged from the house, but her eyes sought out Michael. There was no doubt he was looking for her, and when he saw her his smile lit up his face. Their embrace was more discreet, but lingered.

"You came back to me," she whispered in his ear.

"I told you I would," he replied softly.

Josiah was next to come out of the house and immediately knew that Michael had seen Jesus. The countenance of his son was radiant and not only because Miriam was by his side.

"We've seen Jesus," he said to his father.

Samuel hurried inside to greet his father, who patiently waited in his bedroom.

"I've seen the Lord," Samuel said as he addressed his father for the first time in over a month.

Ephraim smiled contentedly, knowing now that he could finally go home in peace when the Lord decided to call him. Those were the words he was waiting to hear.

Martha gladly let go of Joseph so he could go with the other men into Ephraim's room. She was anxious to tell him what had happened to her, but that could wait for the proper time. Her heart was glad.

By that time Nathaniel and Zacharias had joined them, along with Isaac and Seth. After briefly greeting his son, the rabbi sat down in anticipation of what he was about to hear. He was eager to see what Jesus would do in fulfillment of the Feast of Weeks. All of the men were anxious to hear from the travelers.

"Tell us about it," Josiah said to Samuel, since he was the oldest witness.

"We saw Him on a mountain in Galilee," he declared, his face aglow with wonder. "Jesus has made several appearances to different groups and individuals. We learned that He first appeared to Mary Magdalene and then to some of the other women who approached the empty tomb early that first morning. He also appeared to Peter, and then to two disciples as they left the city on the Day of Resurrection. That first evening, while we were on our way to Galilee, He visited His disciples in Jerusalem, where they were hiding behind closed doors; and then they saw Him again a week later."

"What did you do in Galilee during that time?" Simon asked, having just entered the room.

"We rode around from place to place frequented by Jesus in Galilee before the crucifixion, but nobody had seen nor heard from Him. It was a long week for us. Finally, we were welcomed into the house of some family members of Andrew and Peter. We anxiously waited for them there and were confident that eventually they would come in obedience to Jesus. It was a joyful day when they arrived to tell us they'd seen the risen Lord."

Michael had remained strangely quiet, deferring to his older cousin to tell the news, until his younger brother prompted him.

"Michael, did you see the Lord?" Simon asked, not having heard his previous comment to their father.

"Yes," he said, his eyes widening.

Before he could say anything more, Ephraim spoke up, his voice trembling, "I want everyone to hear about this."

The old man struggled to lift the covers and tried to get out of his bed. For the first time Samuel noticed how frail his father had become since he'd left. He immediately moved to him to help him stand, but Ephraim's legs were too weak to hold him. Michael quickly joined him at Ephraim's side, and they almost had to carry him into the outer room.

"Father…" Samuel said in alarm, before being interrupted.

"Son, I've never felt better in my life," Ephraim declared, referring to his soul, if not his body.

The two men helped him get settled as the entire family gathered around the patriarch.

When Ephraim asked his son to continue, Samuel turned to Michael and said, "Michael, you tell them about when we saw Jesus."

Some of those who'd not been in Ephraim's room gasped out loud when Samuel mentioned seeing Jesus. Everyone was overjoyed by the news, and Miriam was proud of Michael as he stood and started to speak.

"We learned many wonderful things while in Galilee, especially from Peter and Andrew. Father, I can't wait for you to meet Peter. He reminds me of you."

Josiah had heard much about Andrew from both Sarah and Samuel, but was intrigued to meet his more outspoken brother.

"Often the disciples didn't know what to do with themselves in between the appearances of the Lord, and one day they decided to go up into the mountain, one Jesus had often used to teach them. I don't know where they all came from, but before we knew what was happening at least five hundred followers of Jesus had gathered there. Suddenly, I heard a murmur go through the crowd up ahead and then the noise got louder. 'It's Jesus!' Someone said. We happened to be near Peter and Andrew and when they hurried ahead of us we followed close behind them. Sure enough, it was Jesus, standing there in front of us."

"What did he say?" Simon asked unable to control himself.

"He didn't say anything at first," Michael replied.

"How did you know it was Him?" Little Naomi asked. "Did He look the same as He did on the steps of the Temple?"

"No, He didn't look the same, and for a moment I wondered if it was really Him."

"How did you know it was Him for sure?" Simon asked.

Tears came to Michael's eyes, as he looked around the room. He saw the faces of all of those he loved, his father and mother, his grandparents, Ephraim and Nathaniel, his brothers and sisters, and of course, Miriam. He began to weep, and Miriam moved quickly to comfort him.

Seeing his distress, Samuel said, "Do you need me to tell them?"

Michael shook his head and composed himself.

"No, I can do it," he replied.

Again, he paused to measure his words.

He…He lifted His hands…" that was all he could say before he burst into tears again.

This time Samuel didn't try to intervene. He knew his younger cousin needed to tell them what he saw.

"He lifted His hands and said, 'Peace to you.' Father, I saw His hands. I saw the scars in His hands. I saw where the nails went through His hands into the cross. He died there for me. He died for all of us. I knew Him by His scars."

Josiah couldn't keep from remembering those hands. He'd watched the bloody spectacle when the soldiers drove the nails through them. That vivid moment of revelation came to the shepherd, when he'd recognized Jesus' mother at the foot of the cross. That was when he remembered a time so long ago, when a tiny baby held his finger in his tender little hand. Then he'd looked to the cross and saw that same hand, torn and mangled. Now, his son had seen that hand, still bearing the scar of His suffering.

"But He's not dead anymore!" Josiah exclaimed.

"No, He's alive. I've seen Him!" A suddenly exuberant Michael cried out. "He still bears the scars that remind us of His death, but now He's alive. He lives!"

Everyone in the room responded intuitively, "He lives!"

"He lives!" Michael repeated.

"He lives!" The company rejoined.

"Yes, our Savior lives!" the young man declared.

"Death could not hold Him!" Ephraim cried, suddenly finding his voice, loud and strong. "He lives!"

A silence fell over those gathered as they contemplated the implications of what they'd heard.

"Did you talk to Him?" Naomi asked almost in a whisper.

"No, for as soon as He appeared, He was gone," her brother replied.

"What do you mean, 'He was gone?'" Simon asked.

"I don't have an answer. One moment He was standing before us, blessing us with the *shalom*, and the next moment He was gone. He had the same body, as witnessed by the scars, but it was different somehow. I can't explain it."

"He has a resurrection body," Ephraim declared, helping his young cousin. "We shouldn't be surprised that His raised body has different properties. In the resurrection our bodies will be changed as well. These bodies are corruptible, but in the resurrection we will be clothed with incorruption."

The weakness of Ephraim's aged flesh only accentuated his teaching.

"Remember, little children. Jesus was raised from the dead on the day of Firstfruits, because He is the firstfruits of those raised from the dead. He is the first, and at the end of this age, we will follow."

He lifted his blind eyes heavenward, yearning for the resurrection.

"Will you be able to see in the resurrection?" Naomi asked the old man.

A smile came to his face, "Yes, my dear. My eyes will see and my legs will hold me up. My weary bones will be strong in the resurrection; but remember, it's all because of Jesus and His resurrection."

Suddenly, everyone in the room began hugging each other, delighted with the good news they'd heard. It was true. Jesus had risen from the dead.

It was Josiah who got everyone's attention and asked them to be quiet.

"Samuel, what should we do?" He asked.

"We don't know what to do. Jesus instructed His eleven disciples to go back to Jerusalem to wait for Him there. We took this opportunity to come back home so we could tell you what we've learned."

"Are you going back to the disciples?" Martha asked out of concern, before she could stop herself.

She caught Joseph's eyes and was reassured by his smile.

"No, the disciples are gathered in the upper room of a house in Jerusalem, but we will stay here until we receive word from them. They know we're in Bethlehem."

"Will you be going to the feast with us?" Josiah asked, realizing it was less than two weeks away.

"I suppose we will," he replied.

"We'll all be going to the feast," Ephraim exclaimed.

Everyone looked at him, wondering if he would be able to make it physically. The trip for Passover had taken its toll on him.

"Josiah, I'll let you and the boys build that gurney for me this time," he said, settling the matter for good.

"Alright then, on the Feast of Weeks we will all be going to Jerusalem together." Josiah declared.

Everyone began to scatter as the meeting broke up. Joseph and Martha stepped outside to have a few precious moments alone, and Miriam took her place at Michael's side. Deborah watched all of this and marveled at how quickly her son and daughter had grown up. She couldn't have been happier about the mates God was giving them.

"This is right," Elizabeth whispered into her ear, nodding in the direction of Michael and Miriam, who were holding hands openly.

Deborah agreed and hugged her cousin, before looking over and watching Isaac tenderly caring for Haifa.

"Yes, this is right. The Lord does all things well," she replied.

Josiah and Samuel helped the ailing Ephraim back into his bedroom, and Nathaniel and Zacharias accompanied them at the old man's instruction.

Once they got him settled in the bed Samuel asked, "Father, are you sure you should try to make the trip to Jerusalem for the feast?"

"I'm certain, my son. That is, unless the Lord takes me home before the feast."

That was the last thing Samuel wanted to hear. He couldn't imagine life without his father, even though he'd been away from him for much of the previous year.

"Now, don't talk like that," he scolded.

Ephraim couldn't help but smile.

"At my age death would be a welcomed relief, but I do think that God will spare me to see what He has in store for us at the feast."

Remembering how Zacharias had taught them how Jesus fulfilled Passover, the Feast of Unleavened Bread and the Feast of Firstfruits, Ephraim asked him if he had any insight regarding the Feast of Weeks.

The rabbi had been meditating on the feast, but he had no real idea.

"I'm not sure," he said. "The feast is a celebration of the ending of the grain harvest, especially the wheat, and is also a time when God's people commemorate the giving of the Law at Sinai; but I have searched my mind and I cannot imagine what Jesus will do at the feast."

"Do you think this might be the time He will ascend Mount Zion as the risen king?" Nathaniel asked.

Zacharias thought about the question for a few moments before answering, "I don't think so. Like everyone else, I thought that was what Jesus was going to do on the first day of the Feast of Unleavened Bread, but we know that He was crucified that day instead. We shouldn't have been surprised when He was raised from the dead on the Feast of Firstfruits, but I don't have any idea what the significance of the Feast of Weeks will be. I just don't think it will be fulfilled in an earthly kingdom."

"Why not?" Samuel asked.

"If we've learned anything in recent weeks, it's that the salvation procured by Jesus is spiritual. He has delivered us from a deeper bondage – from bondage to sin. I just don't think He's interested in establishing an earthly rule at this time.

Michael had just entered the room and heard Zacharias' response. He'd been thinking about the feast as well and remembered a particular teaching he'd heard the rabbi give on the pilgrimage.

"Zacharias, I've been thinking about what must happen next and remembered a teaching you gave to us when we were at the Dead Sea. Do you recall that message?" He asked.

The rabbi's eyes widened with interest, "I do remember. It was Ezekiel's vision of the healing waters that flowed from the Temple into the Dead Sea bringing life where there was only death before."

"You told us that we should understand this as describing a Messianic blessing," Michael added.

"That's right," he replied, as Ephraim and Samuel in particular tuned their ears to listen.

"I believe that Messiah will cause the healing waters of the Spirit to flow in such a way to bring life to the nations," the rabbi declared.

Josiah remembered the teaching as well. It had given him hope. All of his life he'd prayed for God to open the blind eyes of the Kedarites. If Zacharias was right, then Messiah would begin that work. Of course, neither Josiah nor Zacharias had anticipated that the Messiah would be crucified when they got to Jerusalem.

"Maybe at the feast, Jesus is going to begin fulfilling Ezekiel's prophecy," Michael suggested.

All of them agreed with the rabbi's interpretation of the Ezekiel passage, but had no idea how it could be related to the feast. That night when they retired to their beds they still didn't know what Jesus was about to do. It was ten days until the feast. Surely, they would find out then.

CHAPTER 23

The Holy Spirit

Joel 2:28

*I will pour out My Spirit upon all flesh; and your sons
and your daughters shall prophesy, your old men shall
dream dreams, your young men shall see visions.*

Joseph and Martha lingered outside long after the others had gone to bed.
It had been so long since they'd seen each other; they just didn't want the
night to end. She had taken him to her secret place. It was no longer a
lonely place for her.

For much of the evening she sat enthralled as he went on and on about
his adventures in Galilee. He told her the story about seeing Jesus at least
three different times, but she never tired of hearing him. She especially
liked the stories he told about Peter and longed to meet the once rugged
fisherman, who was now a leader of Jesus' disciples.

Finally, Miriam slipped outside to remind Martha to come in. She
trusted her younger cousin's fidelity, but wanted them to avoid even the
appearance of impropriety.

She was careful as she approached them, and when Martha saw her
she said, "Just give us a few more minutes."

Miriam nodded her head and went to her secret place to spend a few
moments alone. As she approached the bench she was surprised to see
someone sitting there.

"I was waiting for you," Michael said with a smile.

In the privacy created by the darkness of the night, she hurried into
his arms. It was their first kiss.

"I couldn't stop thinking about you when I was gone," he whispered in her ear.

She nodded her head, unable to speak, and placed her head against his chest. She felt safe and loved with his arms around her.

"I better go in," Martha said to Joseph while looking into his eyes, before suddenly becoming overcome with emotion.

"What's wrong?" He asked as he held her close.

All night long, she'd been listening to him, admiring his faith and devotion to Jesus, but remembering the way she was before her repentance. That night, she realized that she was not the same person he had fallen in love with before he left.

A dreadful thought entered her mind, 'What if he doesn't love the real me?'

Martha cried for a few moments before she was able to compose herself enough to speak.

"I have to tell you something. I just hope you'll still love me after you hear what I have to say."

"Of course, I'll love you…" he replied in alarm, before she put her finger to his lips to hush him.

"I'm not the same person I was before you left for Galilee," she said.

He was confused and uttered, "What do you mean?"

She began to cry again before managing to say, "Oh Joseph, I don't think you really knew me before…"

"Of course, I knew you," he replied as she shook her head.

"You couldn't have known me, because I didn't even know myself," she said, confusing him even more.

"Let me explain," she finally said. "I always believed I loved God. It was what I was taught all my life by my parents. I learned the Scriptures. I prayed to Him, but when everything started to happen with Jesus, I became jealous."

Joseph tried to stop her, but she continued anyway, "No, you have to hear me out. After you left I prayed to God. I cried my heart out when I prayed, but I only asked for one thing. I selfishly begged God to bring you back to me."

"He did bring me back," he said, trying to reassure her.

"No, you don't understand. I didn't care about God or about Jesus. I began to resent Jesus because He was changing everything. I'd met you and fallen deeply in love with you. All I wanted was to marry you and to have your children."

"Martha, that's a good thing," he responded still trying to comfort her.

"No, it wasn't. I was being selfish and acting like a spoiled child. Joseph, I didn't deserve your love."

"It doesn't matter. I love you," he said soothingly.

"I know you do, and believe me, I'm grateful; but it still matters. It matters a great deal. One night, I was particularly troubled and Isaac saw me. He followed me to this very place, and like a caring big-brother should, he confronted me with my sin. He showed me that the things I wanted most in my life, while good, were not the best things. I don't think anyone else could have said those things to me."

"Why do you say that?" Joseph asked.

"Because he understood me in a way nobody else could. He was the same way I was before he left for Dumat al Jandal. He didn't want to make this pilgrimage to Israel to worship God. All he wanted to do was to get married to Miriam and start his own flock of sheep in Kedar."

"Miriam?" Joseph asked, suddenly aware that there must be things he didn't know.

"Yes, Isaac and Miriam were once in love; but when her brother was killed, Nathaniel wouldn't let them get married unless Isaac came with them to Israel. It's a long story, but in the end, he got angry and left. One night while you were gone, he told me something that touched my heart. He said that long before he left Father's tent in rebellion, he wanted the good things God gives us more than he wanted God. Joseph, I was just like that. I wanted you and our children. I wanted God to give me what I wanted, and didn't know that He wanted to give me Himself."

Joseph suddenly realized what she'd been going through. He hadn't known of her inner struggle; but looking back, he realized he should have.

She looked up into his eyes, wondering if he could still love her; when suddenly he smiled, got down on one knee, and said with great tenderness, "Martha, daughter of Josiah and Deborah of the Tribe Bin-Micah, would you marry me, the poor son of a rabbi from Elath?"

He had spoken of marriage to her before, announcing outside of the road to Mount Nebo that he intended to ask her father for her hand. He'd also told her that one day she would be his wife before he left for Galilee, but he'd never formally asked her to marry him.

She reached down and grabbed him, pulling him to his feet.

"Yes, yes, yes!!!" She began shouting before realizing she had to be quiet, lest she awaken those who were sleeping. "But you better ask Father first."

Michael and Miriam didn't mean to eavesdrop, but were happy they did. He squeezed her hand, and she knew that it was only a matter of time before he asked her the same question. She already knew the answer she would give him.

Joseph and Martha finally saw the other two, but neither of them was embarrassed. The two young men walked the women to Ephraim's house and started to enter with them, when Miriam stopped them both.

"Now that we are all officially courting, my mother and Deborah decided it was best for the two of you to sleep over at Michael's grandparent's house."

Both boys were surprised, but enjoyed the good night kisses they received. As soon as the girls closed the door to Ephraim's house, Michael slapped Joseph on the back.

"Congratulations, brother-in-law to be," he said.

"When are you going to ask Miriam?" Joseph retorted.

"Soon, my brother, soon," Michael replied, as the boys made their way to his grandfather's house.

Samuel just couldn't stay with them until the feast. He was so edgy, that after two days, Ephraim ordered him to go to Jerusalem to find the disciples. He was about to drive his father crazy pacing around the house. It didn't take long for him to pack his bags and head for the city, but not before he told Josiah that he would get word to them if anything new developed.

Neither Michael nor Joseph gave any indication of wanting to go with him. Both young men would go wherever God called them, but Jesus hadn't told them to go to Jerusalem. They were determined to continue to build their relationships with Miriam and Martha. The shepherd told the rest of the company that they would wait in Bethlehem until the Feast of

Weeks. The next few days were spent making preparations for all of them to make the journey to Jerusalem, including Ephraim on the gurney Josiah and the boys built for him.

Long before daylight on the Feast of Weeks they awoke and began the six mile journey to the city. Josiah hadn't been to the city since the Feast of Firstfruits. He simply couldn't bring himself to go up to the Temple for the morning or evening sacrifices after what they'd done to Jesus. However, the *Torah* compelled him to go up for the Feast of Weeks.

Other pilgrims were also in route along the road from Bethlehem to the holy city, but the crowds were not nearly as large as when they'd made the journey for Passover. Still, the streets of Jerusalem would be filled with people gathered for the feast.

Their pace was slowed because the boys had to carry Ephraim, but he wouldn't hear of staying in Bethlehem. Though Josiah feared for his health and safety, he knew how desperately the old sage wanted to experience the feast. Ephraim wanted to be there, just in case the risen Savior made an appearance.

The sun rose on the band as they made their way toward Jerusalem, and Michael hurried to the same spot where he'd spied the city for the first time on the Day of Presentation. The Temple still stood tall and impressive, but to the north remained a hill called *Golgotha*. None of them could ever forget what happened on the first day of the Feast of Unleavened Bread.

They entered the city just before the third hour and started following the other travelers toward the Temple, when suddenly they heard the sound of wind. At first, it was mixed with the noise of men and animals in the streets, but as it grew louder, everyone stopped to see what made the sound. Before long, it was like a gale; and some shrank from it in fear, but not the shepherd and those with him. He knew they were about to see the fulfillment of the Feast of Weeks with their own eyes.

He'd seen Jesus present Himself at the Temple on the Day of Presentation, and then watched as they crucified Him on the first day of the Feast of Unleavened Bread. He and his sons saw the empty tomb on the Feast of Firstfruits, and now, they were about to witness a visitation from God on the Feast of Weeks, or Pentecost, as it was also called.

The sound was coming from a house not far away, and suddenly through the windows it appeared as though the upper story was on fire.

There was fire, but the house did not burn. Josiah immediately thought of the burning bush where Moses met with God. That bush was burning but not consumed, and from it issued forth the voice of God.

"I Am That I Am!" God had declared to Moses.

The doors of the house opened and the inhabitants spilled out into the streets. Josiah immediately saw that Samuel was among them, and also the disciple he'd seen at the foot of the cross with Jesus' mother.

Those exiting the house were not in flight, but emerged with their hands lifted high as they praised God. Samuel saw his father and Josiah and immediately went to them. Though Ephraim recognized his son's voice, he couldn't understand a word he was saying; but Josiah could. He wasn't speaking in his native tongue of Aramaic, or even the Hebrew of the Scriptures or the Greek of commerce; he was speaking the distinct Kedarite dialect of Arabic.

In the tongue of Josiah's homeland, Samuel from Judea was declaring the mighty deeds of God.

"Speak clearly," Ephraim said to his son.

"He is!" Josiah retorted excitedly. "He's speaking of God's mighty acts in the language of my birth."

Ephraim was astonished and suddenly realized that something marvelous was taking place.

Josiah shouted to his cousin over the noise. "Ephraim, God's Word is being declared in all the languages of the world!"

"Praise be to God!" The old man exclaimed, and being full of the Scriptures declared, "Jesus has sent forth His Spirit and has undone Babel."

Josiah was perplexed until Zacharias reminded him of God's judgment on the nations at Babel.

"It was at the Tower of Babel that God divided the peoples by confounding their languages and cast them into darkness, deaf to His Word. Josiah, don't you see. Your prayers are being answered. The Word of God will once more be proclaimed to the nations, even to the Kedarites."

"Zacharias is wise," Ephraim declared. "Ezekiel's prophecy is about to be fulfilled by the Messiah. The dead waters of the Sea of Salt will be healed."

Not all of those observing the phenomenon had the same impression.

"These men are simply drunk!" One of the onlookers exclaimed.

By that time, those speaking in tongues began to fall silent and gathered around the disciples of Jesus. One of them stood, getting everyone's attention.

"That's Peter," Michael whispered to his father.

Josiah wasn't surprised. He looked just as the shepherd had imagined him; but it was his countenance that was striking. The shepherd had seen it before. It was the same zeal he'd seen on the face of the old man when he prophesied over the baby.

"Ye men of Judea, and all ye that dwell in Jerusalem," Peter began to preach. *"Be this known unto you, and hearken to my words: For these are not drunken as ye suppose, seeing it is but the third hour of the day. But this is that which was spoken by the prophet Joel; 'And it shall come to pass in the last days, saith God, I will pour out of My Spirit upon all flesh: and your sons and your daughters shall prophesy, and your young men shall see visions, and your old men shall dream dreams: And on My servants and on My handmaidens I will pour out in those days of My Spirit; and they shall prophesy: And I will shew wonders in the heaven above, and signs in the earth beneath; blood, and fire, and vapour of smoke: The sun shall be turned into darkness, and the moon into blood, before the great and notable day of the Lord come: And it shall come to pass, that whosoever shall call upon the name of the Lord shall be saved."*

Josiah looked first to Zacharias and Ephraim and then to Isaac and Michael. All of them had tears in their eyes. They knew the passage well and today saw it fulfilled before their eyes. Deborah drew near to him, and he put his arm around her as their younger children gathered close. It was a holy moment.

Joseph held Martha, and Michael embraced Miriam. In one accord they all listened as Peter, full of the Holy Spirit, preached the name of the Lord Jesus Christ, His death and resurrection.

The shepherd saw something remarkable happening as he continued to preach. The Holy Spirit was not only upon the hundred or so disciples who'd been in the upper room of the house, or upon Peter as he preached; but that same Spirit moved in the hearts of many who heard the message.

At one point Peter declared, *"Therefore let all the house of Israel know assuredly, that God made the same Jesus, whom ye have crucified, both Lord and Christ!"*

A murmur spread through the crowd as the Spirit did His work.

Spontaneously, someone cried out from the crowd, *"Men and brethren, what shall we do?"*

Peter looked straightway at the man and then let his eyes pass over the crowd before he declared, *"Repent, and be baptized every one of you in the name of Jesus Christ for the remission of sins, and ye shall receive the gift of the Holy Ghost. For the promise is unto you, and to your children, and to all that are afar off, even as many as the Lord our God shall call."*

He continued to preach for some time, and more and more of the people responded. When he concluded his sermon, he issued a call for all who wanted to be baptized. Josiah looked at his family and his closest friends. All of them were weeping for joy. Deborah smiled at him and nodded her head. The rest of them did the same, so the shepherd led his family to the front of the crowd to be baptized.

When Peter saw Michael, he smiled and nodded his head at him, and then looked at his father with recognition on his face. The disciple remembered how Michael had spoken of his father's piety and faith.

Water was brought to the apostles, and they began moving through the crowd baptizing all of those who had faith in Jesus. Peter made his way straightforward to Josiah.

"You're name is Josiah, and you are called the Shepherd of Kedar" he said to him.

Josiah simply nodded his head in humility. He didn't seek baptism because of his faithfulness, but because of God's grace through Jesus Christ. He knelt before the apostle, not in an act of worship of him, but out of reverence to God as Peter poured the water over his head.

"I baptize thee in the name of the Father, and of the Son, and of the Holy Ghost. *Amen.*"

He then moved to Deborah, and then Isaac and Haifa, as they lined up according to their ages, baptizing each and every one of them. Finally, he came to Naomi.

He paused before saying, "I saw you at the Temple with Jesus."

The little girl nodded her head.

"Jesus said of little ones like you, *'Of such is the Kingdom of Heaven.'* What is your name?"

"Naomi," the little girl replied.

"Naomi, daughter of Josiah, the Shepherd of Kedar, I baptize thee in the name of the Father, and of the Son, and of the Holy Ghost. *Amen*."

"*Amen*," the rest of the family responded.

By that time, Samuel brought Andrew over to join them and implored them to pray for his ailing father. Ephraim was still lying on the gurney, his body weakening, but his heart rejoicing. When the two apostles came to him to pray, he stopped them.

"Don't pray for God to raise me up, lest you rob me of my final pilgrimage to a city not made with the hands of men; and don't pray for my eyes to be opened, for I long to first look upon my Savior in heaven. Instead, please baptize me in Jesus' name."

Josiah watched in awe as Peter stooped over the patriarch of their family and poured the water upon his head.

When he stood up, Peter declared to all who could hear the sound of his voice, "This is true godliness – a seasoned saint, so near the portals of heaven, who still recognizes his need for God's grace in our Lord Jesus Christ."

Ephraim cried out from the gurney, "I am but a sinner saved by the blood of Jesus Christ. When God takes me home, that will be my only plea."

Peter bowed in honor of the old man before turning and following Andrew into the crowd. There were many more to be baptized.

CHAPTER 24

The Blessing of Love

Genesis 2:24

*Therefore shall a man leave his father and mother, and
shall cleave unto his wife: and they shall be one flesh.*

Josiah felt a tap on his shoulder and turned to look into the face of a friend. Omar had tears in his eyes, his head wet from the waters of baptism. The two men embraced in the street, truly brothers.

"You must have been circumcised," Josiah exclaimed.

"Yes, my brother, but more important than that, I've been baptized," Omar replied his face demonstrating his joy. "Remember my questions?"

Josiah nodded his head before replying, "Yes, we've found the answers haven't we."

"In Jesus!" Omar declared.

"He is the Lamb of God!" Josiah exclaimed.

"Yes, and He is both God and man," Omar replied.

At that moment Josiah didn't understand the full import of what his friend was saying.

Quickly, he introduced his former Idumean friend to Zacharias and Nathaniel, while Samuel and Miriam attended to Ephraim.

Before they parted ways, Omar whispered into Josiah's ear, "When you're ready to go back to Kedar stop by and see me. I have something for you."

He then told him where he'd settled, not far from the King's Highway in Edom. The two embraced, and Omar disappeared into the midst of the crowd.

When they left Bethlehem that morning it was their intent to return in the evening, but they knew things could change. Josiah gathered with the other men and they decided it would be better to stay in Jerusalem for a while. Ephraim's health was a concern. Even though the boys carried him from Bethlehem, the trip had taken its toll. He was simply too exhausted to return that evening, besides everything had changed that morning with the outpouring of the Holy Spirit. They needed to stay in touch with the disciples to see what they could learn.

Hannah and Joel were prepared for them to stay with them and had also made arrangements again with their neighbors for Nathaniel's family. A bond had grown between Nathaniel and his hosts, Asher and Mia, during the Passover feast, and they were glad for his family to stay as long as they needed. With Ephraim's weakening physical condition, they felt it best for him to stay at Hannah's house. She and Deborah quickly prepared quarters for him where he could get some rest.

After getting settled in, he seemed to be doing better and insisted that Samuel and Josiah go meet with the disciples. Michael and Joseph would have liked to have gone with them; but with so much happening that day, Samuel believed it would be best if only he and Josiah gathered with the brethren.

The boys found other ways to spend their time. Miriam had been Ephraim's primary caretaker for months and was determined to continue ministering to him. Michael joyfully volunteered to help her, and no one objected. It would give them quality time together serving someone they both loved and respected. Joseph decided it would be good to spend more time with Martha.

After supper, Josiah and Samuel headed to the house where the Holy Spirit came down from heaven that morning, and were warmly greeted, first by Andrew and then by Peter. Both Josiah and Peter had felt an immediate connection when he baptized him that morning. The apostle had grown fond of Michael during his stay in Galilee and loved hearing the exuberant young man talk of their life in Kedar. He was especially impressed with his knowledge of the Scriptures and knew it was because of his father's labors. He remembered a particular tale the young man had relayed to him and asked Josiah about it.

"Yes, that happened when I was ten years old," the shepherd replied.

"Would you tell me again what the old man prophesied?" Peter asked with great interest in light of everything that had happened.

Before Josiah could respond, Peter summoned a young man named John Mark and whispered something in his ear.

After the young man left, Peter turned his attention back to the shepherd.

"I remember his words like he spoke them yesterday. They've been etched in my mind by the Spirit since that day. The old man said, *'Lord, now lettest Thou Thy servant depart in peace, according to Thy word: For mine eyes have seen Thy salvation, which Thou hast prepared before the face of all people; a light to lighten the Gentiles, and the glory of Thy people Israel.'*"

Peter's eyes widened when he heard the words of the prophecy and said, "Jesus told us something very similar before He ascended back to the Father. He said, *'All power is given unto me in heaven and in earth. Go ye therefore, and teach all nations, baptizing them in the name of the Father, and of the Son, and of the Holy Ghost: teaching them to observe all things whatsoever I have commanded you: and, lo, I am with you always, even unto the end of the world.'*"

"Yes!" Josiah exclaimed. "Now is the time for the waters to be healed!"

Peter looked perplexed until he told him about Zacharias' sermon from Ezekiel.

"I'd like to meet this Zacharias," Peter declared.

"You met him today when you baptized him," Josiah replied.

He tried to recall those who were with Josiah earlier in the day, but there were so many to baptize he couldn't remember the face.

"There was a second part of the prophecy..." Josiah started to say when John Mark returned with a woman.

"Behold, this child is set for the fall and rising again of many in Israel; and for a sign which shall be spoken against; Yea, a sword shall pierce through thy own soul also, that the thoughts of many hearts may be revealed," the woman said softly before adding, "I tried to blot those words from Simeon's mouth out of my memory."

Josiah recognized her immediately. It was Mary, Jesus' mother. It was the first time he'd heard the name of the old man.

She looked at the shepherd with a twinkle in her eye, recalling a pleasant memory from long ago.

"You were that little boy," she said.

He nodded his head as she moved into his arms so he could hold her.

"I never forgot you," she whispered. "I felt so bad hurrying away from the Temple the way I did that day."

He smiled, "You don't need to apologize. We were all shocked by the old man's words."

"I just felt bad for you," she said. "You were just a little boy."

Then she looked carefully at him again.

"You were there..." she gasped, her words trailing off.

Again, he nodded his head, knowing what she was thinking.

"You caught me when I almost fell..."

Just at that moment John joined them.

"Let me thank you again for caring for her when she could have fallen and been hurt," he said as he recognized Josiah.

Peter quickly introduced them, and Mary said to John, "This young man and I go way back."

Josiah smiled when she called him a young man, but didn't say anything. Then he realized that Mary wasn't that much older than him – perhaps four or five years, yet what she'd endured had worked wisdom in her.

John had a confused look on his face, and Peter said, "Let's let these two spend some time together. I'll tell you what it's all about."

He nodded his head and the two of them headed across the room. There was so much to do after what had happened that day. How were they going to care for three thousand additional people, many of whom came to the feast from all over the world? The apostles were trying to figure it all out.

It felt good to Mary to have Josiah there with her. He was a connection to those early days. Joseph had died several years before, leaving her a widow, and now Jesus had ascended to heaven.

"John's doing a good job taking care of me," she said. "And now that James has seen his brother resurrected he will too."

Josiah nodded his head, remembering both the exchange he saw between Jesus and Mary at the cross, and the way John cared for her there. He had no idea who James was, but it didn't matter.

"That was a dreadful day," she said as a tear came to her eyes.

Even though she'd seen the risen Jesus and exulted in His victory, the images of His suffering on the cross continued to break her heart.

"The sword that pierced my soul was sharp…"

Josiah remembered her sorrow and in particular the vision of her holding His dead body at the foot of the cross while weeping. Even the victory of the resurrection couldn't remove the pain of watching Him suffer.

'And He did it for us,' the shepherd thought to himself.

Then Mary smiled, "But these are much happier days. Did you see Him after He arose?"

"No," Josiah replied, "But my son, Michael, did."

"Michael is your son?" She asked. "I should have known. Like father, like son. He's a precious young man."

Suddenly, the shepherd was a bit envious of the days his son had spent in Galilee. He'd heard many of his stories since he'd returned, but didn't know that he knew Mary so well.

After a while Peter came back; and he and Josiah took a walk outside the house, in part to get away from all the noise. They talked openly of many things, especially the Scriptures. Peter was amazed at the shepherd's grasp of the Word, and was anxious to meet Zacharias. The apostle rejoiced that God had prepared men who were not in Israel during Jesus' ministry. He realized they had a different perspective that could be helpful to the apostles as they prepared to carry out their commission from Jesus. Frankly, Peter didn't know where to begin.

When Peter finally met Zacharias he was delighted to learn that he was Joseph's father. The rabbi's grasp of the Scriptures even exceeded that of the apostles in some ways. Peter realized that they had been too close to Jesus to hear all that He'd been telling them.

Peter and Andrew made a habit of spending a few moments with Ephraim every day, no matter how busy they were with the large congregation God had given them. The old man would let them pray for him, but not for his healing. Though his heart was full of joy, his body continued to grow weaker by the day. Ephraim longed for heaven.

Miriam was distressed over his worsening condition. One day Ephraim could hear the tears in her voice. Michael silently brushed them away, not wanting to alarm him with her sadness.

"Daughter, don't weep for me," he said.

That was all she could take. She sat down beside his bed and put her head on his chest; letting her tears flow, weeping as the old man pushed her hair from her face. Michael saw the tender moment and felt helpless to comfort her.

"Michael, come here," he instructed.

"Miriam, take his hand."

She did as he told her.

"Do you see this man? He loves God, and he loves you. He will take care of you. You've got to let me go. I want to be with Jesus."

Miriam hugged Michael, realizing how selfish she was being. Ephraim was the tender grandfather she'd never known. Caring for him wasn't a chore, it was always a joy to her. In a sense, her relationship with him sustained her while she waited for Isaac to come. It gave her purpose, but now he was going away. Then she looked at Michael. She loved him with her whole heart and realized that her purpose would now be fulfilled by being his wife.

"Son," Ephraim said in the strongest voice he'd used in days.

"Yes Sir," Michael responded sheepishly.

"You best be talking to her father as soon as possible. I want to attend a wedding before I go home."

Michael turned red in the face and was for a moment glad that Ephraim was blind.

"Now, you two leave me so I can get some rest," he sighed as he pulled his blanket up to hide his little smile.

When Michael and Miriam walked out of the room, their mothers were standing there with knowing smiles on their faces. The two young people wondered if they might have overheard what Ephraim said. Michael grabbed Miriam's hand and nearly pulled her out of the door. Once they were alone, the ever talkative young man suddenly found himself tongue-tied.

Not knowing what to do, he grabbed her, pulled her to him, and gave her a big kiss.

The kiss ended, and she couldn't keep from laughing when he still appeared speechless.

"Do you have something you want to ask me?"

He stammered for a moment, before getting down on one knee as the two of them had seen Joseph do with Martha a few nights before.

"Miriam, would…would you marry me?" He finally blurted out.

Her smile betrayed her answer before she could express it, but he seemed to be frozen in place.

For a few moments she just looked at him, and then she pulled him up to his feet.

Putting her arms around him, she whispered in his ear, "Yes. I would be honored to be your wife."

Suddenly, he found his voice again in his excitement and just started talking about any and everything, about their future together, about the church, about Jesus. She let him go on and on until finally she'd had enough.

"Would you please hush and kiss me."

Another sheepish smile came to his face, but he immediately did as she asked. This time the kiss lingered, full of love and affection.

When the kiss ended, the young man had a smile on his face, until she said, "You know you need to speak to Father about this."

His heart began to race as he thought about talking to Nathaniel, but it shouldn't have. Elizabeth had already prepared her husband for this conversation.

Michael took Miriam's hand and led her back to the house. When they went inside, one of the first people he saw was her father. Needing reassurance, he looked for Joseph and saw him across the room with Martha.

"I want to talk to Joseph," he said to Miriam.

Martha could tell what he wanted when he asked to speak to Joseph, and the two girls were giggling before the boys made it outside.

He didn't beat around the bush and spoke to him as soon as they were out of earshot of the house, "I asked Miriam to marry me a few minutes ago."

"And what did she say?" Joseph asked, as if there was any doubt.

"She said yes, but that I had to ask her father. Have you spoken to Father about Martha yet?"

It was Joseph's time to look sheepish.

"I was hoping you would do it first," he said.

Both young men were frightened, but certainly in love.

"I'll tell you what. Let's get it over with now. We'll just march into the house and tell them we would like to talk to them," Michael said, his courage strengthened by the fact that Joseph was in the same predicament.

"Okay, let's do it," Joseph said, taking a step toward the house.

What began as a brisk pace slowed down considerably the closer they came to that ominous door.

Joseph grabbed Michael's arm, "What if your father says no?"

"He won't," Michael said with all confidence.

He only wished he was more confident of Nathaniel's answer. Somehow, they made it through the door and without even looking at the girls walked directly to Josiah and Nathaniel.

"Sir, could I have a word with you?" Michael asked Nathaniel.

The two men stopped their conversation, and Nathaniel just looked at the shepherd's son.

Josiah had a smile on his face until Joseph said, "Sir, I'd like to speak to you."

"To me?" He asked, pointing to himself, making it hard on the boy.

"Yes Sir," Joseph managed to say.

Both men shrugged and followed them out the door. Josiah and Joseph took a walk in one direction down the street, while Nathaniel and Michael headed up the other. An hour later both young men entered the house. The smiles on their faces told the story, and the girls rushed into their arms. Not realizing the spectacle they were causing, their celebration was interrupted by applause.

Then they heard a voice coming from Ephraim's room, "Josiah, you and Nathaniel, come in here."

Both men obeyed their mentor and closed the door behind them after they entered the room.

"My life is slipping away," the old man said. "I don't want you to dally with those young folks. I intend to see them married before I go to heaven."

Neither of them objected, and it was decided that a double wedding would take place in three days. That would give Deborah and Elizabeth the time they needed to make all the necessary arrangements. Josiah was hopeful that Peter would be kind enough to officiate. It would be the first wedding to take place in the new church.

CHAPTER 25

The Final Benediction

Psalm 134

Behold, bless ye the LORD, all ye servants of the LORD,
which by night stand in the house of the LORD. Lift up your
hands in the sanctuary, and bless the LORD. The LORD
that made heaven and earth bless thee out of Zion.

Peter was honored to be asked to officiate in the first wedding of the infant church in Jerusalem – and a double-wedding at that. The apostle took as his text one of the Messianic psalms. He made appropriate application of this wedding song to the unions before him but also demonstrated the true intent of the Holy Spirit – which was to describe the union of Christ with His Bride, the Church.

When he read the words, *"Thou art fairer than the children of men: grace is poured into Thy lips: therefore God hath blessed Thee forever,"* Naomi looked at her father, recalling when she sang those very words to Jesus in the Temple. Josiah saw his daughter's smile and remembered that moment. Even the little girl had known the words were written to Jesus.

Then when Peter turned his attention to the latter part of the psalm and read, *"The King's daughter is all glorious within: her clothing is of wrought gold. She shall be brought to the King in raiment of needlework,"* the shepherd realized those words extolled the glory of His Bride, the Church – the Church made beautiful through His redeeming act. He couldn't help but love not only the Messiah, but also His Bride. One look at Zacharias' face told the shepherd that the rabbi was taking it all in as well.

Michael was too nervous to listen carefully enough to hear what his father heard, because all he could think about was Miriam. She was truly beautiful both inside and out. He was a happy man, and when he looked at her he realized just how much God had blessed him.

Martha learned a wonderful truth as well. When she surrendered herself to love God first and foremost in her life, He gave her the very thing she'd desired most – Joseph. Only time would tell if the Lord would grant her deep desire for children, for lots of children. Whether He opened her womb or closed it, she was resigned to accept His will for her and to love and honor her husband as her duty to God.

Through this wedding the budding church learned an important lesson. Even though everything had changed with the coming of the Lord Jesus, life still goes on. In this life there will be marriage and giving in marriage. However, in the life to come the wedding between the Messiah and His Bride will transcend all human relationships.

Peter made this plain during his exposition when he reminded them of Jesus' words, spoken to the Sadducees, *"For in the resurrection they neither marry, nor are given in marriage, but are as the angels of God in heaven."*

Dinah was particularly touched by this teaching. Since Caleb's death she'd longed to be reunited with him in heaven. Now, she realized that their relationship would not be the same – it would be better, for they would share a complete devotion to Christ with all the other believers.

After the wedding, Peter wanted to speak with Josiah. The fisherman was as taken with the shepherd as the shepherd was with the fisherman.

"Josiah, why don't you and your family remain in Jerusalem? With our growing congregation we need all the help we can get," Peter said, almost pleading as they walked together through the streets of the city.

"I've never really considered leaving Kedar," Josiah replied, though he had to admit to himself it was tempting to stay because of everything that was happening.

The shepherd was amazed at how quickly he'd developed deep relationships on the pilgrimage. First, there was Zacharias. He would ever be Josiah's teacher, though the rabbi often thought he was the student of the shepherd instead; and now there was Peter. Perhaps the bond was so deep because each of them recognized they were pilgrims in this life. All three men felt their hearts knit together by God. Josiah's relationship with Nathaniel was much the same, but it had always been that way. Along with Ephraim and Samuel, there were many brethren that could tempt the shepherd to stay in Jerusalem, just for the fellowship.

He thought of the contrast between the first of the Songs of Ascents and the next to the last one. The first had often embodied the cry of anguish he felt in his heart, living among those who hated him and who hated his God; but the latter psalm is the cry of joy that comes to the heart when one has tasted the sweetness of the unity of the brethren. While in the holy land, Josiah had drunk deeply from the well of fellowship among the faithful, and was reluctant to return to the arid regions of Kedar. He wasn't thinking about the desert, but the hardened ground of the hearts of wicked men.

Deborah and Elizabeth had planned well to insure sufficient privacy for the newlywed couples on their wedding night, much to the embarrassment of Michael, Miriam and Joseph. Martha was so overjoyed about finally being Joseph's wife, nothing would have embarrassed her. She couldn't wait to be alone with him in their chambers.

Once everyone settled in for the night, Josiah found himself in that special place of refuge – lying next to his precious wife. Silently, he prayed it would become such a place for his son and daughter and their new spouses.

Deborah could always tell when he had something on his mind.

"What is it?" She asked softly as he held her.

"Peter asked me to stay in Jerusalem to help the apostles with all the people who are being saved."

She knew better than to offer her opinion as he contemplated things, but deep in her heart she longed to return to her home in Kedar.

"What did you say?" She asked.

"I didn't say anything," he replied, deep in thought. "It's very tempting to stay. I think Zacharias might remain in Jerusalem, and I've never met anyone like Peter."

Deborah smiled. She saw the connection between the fisherman and the shepherd. They were both raised as rugged men of the outdoors, yet God was calling them to a different vocation – to minister to Jesus' Bride. The two men had much in common that only a wife could fully see.

"I'd like to stay," the shepherd continued. "The Holy Spirit is moving powerfully, and I want to be a part of it. After Peter taught us about the Church from the Scriptures, I know I must love her and care for her."

He paused for a moment wondering what to say next.

"I love the sweetness of the fellowship we've found here, and I don't miss the loneliness of the desert. Yet, for as long as I can remember, I've been burdened for the Kedarites – that they would come to know the one true God. It seems to me that now is the time to speak to them."

Again, he hesitated, pondering, thinking first this and then that.

Finally in resignation he said, "We will stay at least as long as Ephraim needs us. God will lead us after that."

Deborah thought of the patriarch of the family. She loved him like she loved her own father, and knew he was weakening, even though he'd rallied to a degree. She also knew she would miss Elizabeth, her parents and her brother and sister if they returned to Kedar.

Knowing her husband had said all he was going to say, she put out the oil lamp and placed her head on his chest. Josiah fell asleep as his fingers gently played with her hair.

The next morning at the table, the two young couples had sheepish looks on their faces; but all four of them were beaming. Ephraim felt strong enough to sit at the table with them. It was a joyous occasion, but near the end of the meal the old man started to grow pale.

"Michael, you and Miriam help me to my room," he said, his voice little more than a whisper.

Both Josiah and Samuel jumped to their feet, but Ephraim instructed them to be seated. They obeyed him, but their concern showed on their faces.

"Help me get in the bed," he said to the young couple.

As soon as he was settled, he called them to sit near him. His voice was weak, but they were able to hear him.

"Come closer," he instructed.

Michael and Miriam leaned in very closely to him so he could reach out his arms and place his hands upon their heads.

"My time on the earth is coming to an end," he said, causing Miriam to sob.

"Remember, my daughter, don't weep for me."

He felt her nodding her head in submission to his instruction.

"Michael, your heart is tender toward the Lord," the patriarch declared in his blessing. "The Spirit of God will move mightily upon thee, and thou shalt be a preacher of this gospel. Many souls will be brought to God through thy ministry. And Miriam, the Lord has heard the cry of thy heart and made thee to be the help of this man of God. He shall open thy womb and grant to thee children, and God's covenant blessings shall fall upon them from one generation to the next."

Michael and Miriam humbly received the blessing, knowing that the power of God stood behind it.

"Now, go and send Joseph and Martha to me," he said.

Everyone in the large room outside of Ephraim's quarters wondered what was happening and were surprised to hear that he had summoned Joseph and Martha next. Deborah and Elizabeth went to Miriam to ask about him, but all she could do was shake her head. The two women knew his condition was grave, but also realized they must obey him.

When Joseph and Martha emerged from Ephraim's room, she was glowing with the news that God would grant her children from Joseph. Everyone realized that Ephraim's final blessings had prophetic power.

Isaac and Haifa had their turn with the patriarch and returned with humbled hearts, but content with the words they'd heard. After Isaac, Ephraim called for each of Josiah's remaining children beginning with Dinah and ending with Naomi in the order of their ages, to receive a blessing appropriate to them. As Josiah watched it unfold, he remembered in the Scriptures when Jacob blessed his sons in such a manner.

Expecting to be called after Naomi's turn, he was surprised when Ephraim began to call Nathaniel and his family one by one. There were so many to bless, the time passed by, and the noon meal was forgotten because of something far more important. Some said little as they emerged from his chambers, while others whispered the content of their blessing.

This gave opportunity for Josiah to think about what God might have in store for him. His heart was still torn between Peter's request of him and the lost souls of Kedar. Quietly, he hoped that God might give him counsel through Ephraim's blessing.

He called in Joel and Hannah, and then James and Esther. The patriarch even blessed Seth and Judith, even though they were of his generation. Still, Josiah and Deborah waited along with Samuel.

When he requested an audience with Zacharias and Zipporah it wasn't a conventional blessing, but an opportunity to say goodbye to a friend he respected above all other friends he'd ever known. Ephraim truly saw the rabbi as his equal, though Zacharias would never agree. The two men embraced, and the rabbi departed with a request from the patriarch – that he would watch over his flock.

Josiah assumed that he would be next, and that Ephraim's son, Samuel, would be the last; but was surprised when Samuel was called before him. He stayed with his father for a long time. There was much to discuss before he received his blessing. When he finally emerged from the room, tears were running down his face. He couldn't speak, but nodded at Josiah, indicating it was finally his turn. Deborah didn't know what to do, until Josiah led her through the door into Ephraim's presence.

The old man was very pale, but his face lit up when he heard his greeting.

"Come to me, my son," he exclaimed.

Josiah hurried to him and the two of them embraced upon Ephraim's bed.

"Where is your bride?" He asked, suddenly having more energy.

"My lord, I'm here," she said with all due respect and affection in her voice.

"Don't call me lord," he retorted, causing them to look at each other and smile.

"You are my daughter, not my servant," he said firmly as he placed his hand upon her head.

"Deborah, thou shalt be the mother of generations that will know the Lord. The Lord is faithful to His covenant promises. He has had mercy upon thee. Strengthen them and continue to be the help to thy husband thou hast been."

Deborah received her blessing with faith and stood, moving away so that Josiah could approach him. Suddenly, Ephraim sat up in the bed, looking heavenward, his face aglow with the Spirit. Josiah recognized his countenance. He'd seen it on a number of special occasions in his life – on the old man's face at the Temple when he was a boy, on the face of Zacharias as he preached after blowing the *shofar*, and on Peter's face when he preached at Pentecost.

"Come, my son, kneel before me. Deborah, hurry and gather the others. I have a word from the Lord and they all need to hear it.

She hurried out of the room, and quickly everyone crowded in, as many as could fit. Josiah's family all gathered around him.

"Michael and Miriam help me to stand," the patriarch declared.

Though they were concerned for his welfare they knew to obey him. Once he was standing he commanded the shepherd to kneel and placed both hands upon his head.

"Thus saith the Lord thy God," he began in a strong voice, indicating that these words even transcended a blessing. It was God speaking directly through the patriarch by prophetic word.

"My son, I have blessed thee all of thy days. Even thy enemies have called thee the Shepherd of Kedar because My hand hath rested upon thee and thy labors. I know the struggles of thy soul, the conflicting desires. I love that thou art willing to stay in this place in order to feed My lambs, but I have called others to fulfill that task. Thou shalt continue to be called the Shepherd of Kedar, but not because of sheep with wool, but because of My lost sheep, who are scattered among the descendants of Ishmael. I will put My Spirit upon thee to mightily preach My gospel to the heathen. Ye shall call them out of the darkness where they worship idols to bow before Me, the one true God, in the name of My only begotten Son, Jesus Christ. Arise and go without delay. Take thy family with thee. Arise before the dawn and return to the land where I have planted thee for a witness. Do not wait for the departure of My servant, Ephraim, nor to speak to the apostles. I will tell Peter of My plans for thee. Arise and go, My Spirit goes before thee, because thou hast believed My voice when I said to Abraham, *'And in thy seed shall all the nations of the earth be blessed; because thou hast obeyed My voice.'* I have called thee to be the Shepherd of Kedar. So let it be written. So let it be done."

Those gathered around were stunned by the proclamation, but none doubted that the word was from God. A reverent silence fell upon the assembly. Josiah and Deborah immediately began preparations for their departure aided by those they loved.

That night upon his bed, Josiah whispered to his beloved wife, "Today our pilgrimage to Jerusalem ended, but a new life begins tomorrow morning."

She snuggled close to her husband, the Shepherd of Kedar, confident that the Lord would be with them.

Early the next morning, he and his family emerged from the house of Joel and Hannah. Even Ephraim arose to say his goodbyes. It was bitter sweet for the shepherd because he knew he would not see the face of the patriarch of his family until they met again in heaven. After hugs, tears and prayers for safe travel, his family moved through the dark streets of Jerusalem. Their route took them past the Temple.

They paused to look one last time and saw the lights of those who served by night. The apostasy that had befallen the priesthood didn't matter to the shepherd any longer. Jesus was now the great High Priest. Besides, some of the priests had been baptized on the day of Pentecost. God had kept some of them for Himself, including Nahor, who'd assisted Josiah and his sons that first day at the Temple.

Suddenly, the shepherd lifted his hands toward the House of God and declared in the words of the concluding Song of Ascents:

"Behold, bless ye the LORD, all ye servants of the LORD, which by night stand in the house of the LORD. Lift up your hands in the sanctuary, and bless the LORD."

The Shepherd closed his eyes to listen in his heart for the benediction he longed to hear, before departing to go back to Kedar.

"The LORD that made heaven and earth bless thee out of Zion."

In his heart he'd received that final benediction when Ephraim, the oldest living patriarch of the once great tribe of Bin-Micah, had placed his hands upon his head. In the might of the Lord, the Shepherd of Kedar and his family began the long journey home.

EPILOGUE

The Shepherd's Sermon

Psalm 23:1

The Lord is my shepherd; I shall not want.

It was a cool spring night near the oasis in Kedar. Ten years had passed since the shepherd made his eventful pilgrimage with his family to Jerusalem. Gone was the visitor's tent that had served through the years to separate Jew from Gentile. In its place stood a large open tent where a sizeable congregation was gathered. All wayfarers were welcomed in Josiah's tent in the new age that had dawned with the coming of the Messiah.

He looked at the many faces before him, illumined by the oil lamps strategically placed around the tent. As always his eyes fell first to Deborah, his beloved wife and gracious hostess for the gathering. To him, she only became more beautiful with age.

Isaac was seated with Haifa, and their seventh child would be arriving within a few short weeks. God was gracious to the younger shepherd, giving him five sons already to help him work his flock. Little Micah had died a happy ram of old age, but one of his seed, of course named Micah, had assumed the role as his number one stud ram. He and Haifa pitched their tent in the pastures closer to Dumat al Jandal so they could be near her parents.

Miriam was as lovely as ever as she sat close to Michael. Thus far, they had five children, and had a secret to reveal to his parents after the service. They had another little one on the way. As prophesied by Ephraim, Michael became a shepherd of souls, rather than of sheep. The couple had settled in Dumat early on; and with the aid of Haifa's parents, he got an immediate hearing among their relatives. The Holy Spirit accompanied his powerful preaching and many were converted under his ministry. In God's goodness a congregation met faithfully in the once pagan city. Isaac served alongside of him as an elder in the church.

The shepherd was particularly thrilled to see his daughter, Martha, with her husband Joseph present in the congregation. They'd made the long journey from Elath, where Joseph served as the pastor of a growing church. Zacharias and Zipporah were in attendance as well, having come from Jerusalem, by way of Elath to visit. They enjoyed their six grandchildren as much as Josiah and Deborah did. Martha's face was beaming, until she looked over at one of her children who was whispering to his cousin a little too loudly. Josiah recognized the stern look on her face. He'd seen it many times on that of his wife, when their children were younger.

Then, there were the rest of the boys. Simon, Benjamin, Nathan and Jared were all young men in their early twenties, and each of them had been blessed with godly wives and children, though Jared and his wife only had an infant son thus far. Beside them sat the youngest boy, Judah, a handsome young man at nineteen. He had yet to marry, but was certainly keeping an eye on one of the young ladies sitting across the tent with a group of young people from Michael's church in Dumat.

Ruth sat beside her mother, and they looked more like sisters than mother and daughter. The similarity in their features and personalities was striking. She was not yet married, but had drawn the attention of a young man. That young man was Omar's nephew, and Josiah was overjoyed to have him and his uncle with them.

Naomi's face was beaming. It hadn't been that long ago, that Deborah had a conversation with her husband regarding their youngest and a certain young man from Dumat. Having just turned fifteen, the shepherd would have preferred she had stayed a little girl, but such is life that children grow up. The young man was Haifa's cousin and profoundly committed to the Lord. Michael had poured himself into him, teaching him the Scriptures, and had vouched for his character. It was hard for Josiah to let his baby go; but when he saw the way she looked at Rashad, he knew it was only a matter of time before he received a visit from the young man.

As the shepherd contemplated what had happened, he was staggered by how quickly things had changed. His children were married to Jews and Arabs, and it looked like Ruth would soon be engaged to an Idumean; but all of them were followers of Christ. God had truly fulfilled his promise to Abraham.

Then his eyes fell to Dinah, or what he could see of her. He had to smile. Her lap was full of nephews and nieces. They were sitting in front of her, and behind her, as well as crowding on either side of her. All of Josiah's grandchildren loved their Aunt Dinah. As much as she loved children, it saddened him to know that Asad's arrow had robbed her of her own; but when he looked again, she couldn't have been happier. She adored each and every one of them. God had given her multiple children.

Nathaniel, Elizabeth and their family had returned to Kedar from Bethlehem but only for a visit on this special occasion. He was determined to stay in the Holy Land, but with the dramatic changes ushered in by Jesus, had not hesitated to let Miriam return to Kedar with Michael.

Hannah, Deborah's sister, was present with her husband, Joel, and their soon to be ten year old son, Seth. They'd named him after his grandfather. Deborah's brother, James was seated with his wife, Esther. Samuel had come along with them as well, and seeing him reminded Josiah of his beloved patriarch, Ephraim, who was now with the Lord. He had passed from the Church Militant to the Church Triumphant the very night Josiah and his family left Jerusalem. Deborah still missed her parents who followed Ephraim to heaven a couple of years later.

In addition to Josiah's extended family, the numbers in the tent were increased by many visitors. Some were from the congregation in Dumat; and others were unbelievers who'd been brought by their friends to hear the gospel preached by the Shepherd of Kedar.

The occasion for the celebration was the ten year anniversary of the coming of the Lord Jesus Christ, His death and resurrection.

The shepherd stood up before the congregation, and a hush came over the crowd. He bowed his head to pray and those gathered did the same. In the silence, Josiah could hear his sheep out in the fields and silently gave thanks to God. He thought of Omar, and how he'd saved a hundred ewes and fifteen stud rams from the original flock as a gift for him to start rebuilding his flock. He'd tried to pay him for them that day in Edom, but his friend and brother wouldn't hear of it.

"Oh Lord, our God, bless Thy Word as it is read and preached. Open the blind eyes of unbelievers who are gathered in our midst to hear the

DeLacy A. Andrews, Jr.

gospel and encourage Thy people with Thy Word. I pray in the name of our Lord and Savior Jesus Christ, the one and only High Priest of God, who ceases not to make intercession for us before Thee. *Amen.*"

Then the shepherd began to preach:

Many of you call me the Shepherd of Kedar, but I've never been comfortable with that distinction. I look among you and see many others who tend their own flocks. You love your sheep as I love mine. However, I gladly accept for myself the designation of a sheep. It is precious to me that I am loved by my Shepherd, who is not only the true Shepherd of Kedar, but the Shepherd of the World.

One of my forefathers was a shepherd. No, I'm not speaking of Micah, though it is my delight to be his descendant. I'm speaking of David. You may think of David as the king, and he most certainly was king, but before he was a king, he was a shepherd; and all the while he reigned as king, he remained a shepherd to God's people. It was David who wrote the Shepherd's Song.

Listen to the wonderful words of this beloved psalm:

The LORD is my shepherd; I shall not want. He maketh me to lie down in green pastures: He leadeth me beside the still waters. He restoreth my soul: He leadeth me in the paths of righteousness for His name's sake. Yea, though I walk through the valley of the shadow of death, I will fear no evil: for Thou art with me; Thy rod and Thy staff they comfort me. Thou preparest a table before me in the presence of mine enemies: Thou anointest my head with oil; my cup runneth over. Surely goodness and mercy shall follow me all the days of my life: and I will dwell in the house of the LORD forever.

Have you ever heard more refreshing words in your life? Listen, in particular, you children listen. Can you hear the bleating of the sheep? They are content because we love them and care for them. Smell the air. Can you smell the clean waters from the oasis? Isn't it refreshing? Only a shepherd could have written this psalm.

But the psalm isn't about sheep is it? I'm not really a sheep; I'm a man, even though I told you that I gladly call myself a sheep. David knew, what I've grown to know; and I pray you will all

• 254 •

discover this wonderful truth, if you haven't yet. It's good to be a sheep when it is the Lord who is my shepherd.

Listen again to David's words, *"The LORD is my shepherd!"* The LORD – it is Jehovah who is my shepherd. That's God's covenant name. God has bound Himself to us in a covenant of grace, and He calls us His sheep. It is Jesus, God's Son, who said, "I am the good shepherd!" And now David declares, *"The LORD is my shepherd; I shall not want."*

Beloved, listen to what the king is saying to us. Because the Lord is my shepherd, I have everything I need. It is God who has abundantly blessed me, with my wife and family, with this tent, with the sheep bleating outside tonight in the pasture. But more importantly, it is God who has blessed me with salvation.

Ten years ago, God led me on a pilgrimage to Jerusalem, because there was something He wanted me to see. There were words He wanted me to hear. All my life, I knew the Lord loved me as a shepherd loves His sheep, but I didn't know the extent of His love.

It was while I was in Jerusalem that I learned a horrible truth about myself. I'd always known it. I just didn't know it like I should. I, the so-called Shepherd of Kedar, am a sinner before this God who declares Himself to be my Shepherd. He's loved me, but I rebelled against Him. Until I met His Son, the Lord Jesus Christ, whom I believe to be eternally His Son and God Himself who became man for us – until I met Jesus, I didn't know what righteousness is. I came face to face with Him on the steps of the Temple. He looked into my eyes. He saw me for who I am – a sinner; yet He didn't condemn me.

By what right do I declare, *"The Lord is my shepherd; I shall not want?"* How can I, a sinner, make such a presumptuous statement? You Gentiles among us, who worship idols, I do not declare the truths of this gospel to you as one who is righteous in himself. No, no, a thousand times no! I am no more deserving of the blessings of the Shepherd's Psalm than are you. Nevertheless, every precious promise I've read to you tonight from this psalm is mine.

"By what right are they yours?" You might ask.

Not by right, but by God's grace. Listen carefully, my beloved. All of you listen carefully.

None of us could claim the precious promises of the Shepherd's Psalm, if the event recorded in another of David's psalms hadn't occurred.

"What psalm, you may ask?"

Listen children, this is difficult for me because this psalm brings to memory things I never wanted to see, yet God led me to see them – despicable things, yet glorious things at the same time.

I'd sung this psalm all of my life, knew its words by heart; but on a particular day in Jerusalem ten years ago, I heard these words offered to God in abject terror.

What words?

"My God, My God, why hast Thou forsaken Me?"

I heard those words from Jesus' lips when He was hanging on the cross. At first, I thought He was quoting David, but then my eyes were opened to see something staggering. He wasn't quoting David when He was on the cross. Those words were His words not those He'd borrowed from someone else. I suddenly realized a glorious truth. Jesus wasn't quoting David from the cross, but David was quoting Jesus, when he wrote this psalm. God's Spirit came upon David and opened his eyes to see Jesus and Him crucified. The psalm describes in detail Jesus' inner groanings on the cross.

Later, it all became clear to me. The benefits that flow to me from the Shepherd's Psalm are mine because of Jesus' sufferings as depicted in the one just before it. He died, that I might live; and that's true for you, if you will believe in Him.

Every blessing of the Shepherd's Psalm is ours because of Jesus' sufferings. Look at them – each in turn.

How is it that I can sing, *"The LORD is my shepherd; I shall not want?"* It is because on the cross Jesus cried out, *"My God, My God, why hast Thou forsaken Me?"* He didn't deserve to be forsaken of God. If you could have only seen the look in His eyes when He made that cry. I saw Him. I saw Him with my own eyes and heard Him with my ears. Darkness had befallen the land for three hours, an ominous sign of God's judgment coming down upon His only Son in our stead. When the darkness lifted, I looked to see if He was still alive. I saw Him raise his head and look into the heavens. His eyes were searching for the Father He'd known from eternity, but God hid His face from Him. The cry was one of sheer agony. He was forsaken, that the Lord Himself might be our shepherd.

"He maketh me to lie down in green pastures: He leadeth me beside the still waters. He restoreth my soul." Every shepherd in here understands this blessing. We've led our own sheep to the good grasses, so they can feed, and to the still waters, so they can drink. We know the refreshment of good, clean water in the desert. In the Shepherd's Psalm it is God who feeds us and gives us drink, but not grass and water. He gives us His Word and we feed. He gives us His Spirit and we drink deeply.

By what right are we, who are sinners, spiritually nourished and refreshed by God?

Listen to what Jesus was thinking while on the cross. Hear His thoughts from David's words in the other psalm, *"I am poured out like water, and all My bones are out of joint: My heart is like wax; it is melted in the midst of My bowels. My strength is dried up like a potsherd; and My tongue cleaveth to My jaws; and Thou hast brought Me into the dust of death."*

Just before Jesus died, he looked up and said, *"I thirst."* Those inner groanings expressed in David's psalm escaped His lips with the simple words, *"I thirst."*

They took a hyssop branch that had a sponge tied to it, and dipped it in vinegar before placing it to His lips. I wondered why He accepted the drink. Earlier, He had refused a drink to numb the pain when it was offered. Then I realized that He wet His lips because He had something important to say. He needed to be heard.

I saw the look on His battered face when He spoke the words. He said, *"It is finished."*

Then He looked heavenward and prayed, *"Father, into Thy hands I commend My spirit."*

I saw Him. God the Son, now a man, bowed His head and died. Suddenly, I heard a rumbling in the earth and the ground began to shake. I wondered if God had given up on all of us, and if the earth was going to swallow me up; but the earth stopped quaking, and Jesus was dead. Beloved, He died on the cross in our place. All of us deserve the judgment of God because we have broken His commandments, but He has been merciful to us in His Son, the righteous one. He died in our place.

So I can say, *"He maketh me to lie down in green pastures: He leadeth me beside the still waters. He restoreth my soul,"* because Jesus said from the cross, *"I thirst,"* and in His heart He cried, *"My tongue cleaveth to My jaws; and Thou hast brought Me into the dust of death."*

"He leadeth me in the paths of righteousness for His name's sake."

How is it that I, a wicked man by birth, can now delight in God's law and walk in righteousness out of gratitude to Him? First, it is because God has declared me righteous because of Jesus' work on my behalf. I deserved to die, but He died in my place. He took the curse of the covenant in my stead. When I beheld Him hanging on the cross the contradiction was overwhelming. He was utterly innocent, even Pilate said so. I heard him with my own ears outside the *Praetorium*. Yet, He was crucified like a common criminal. An innocent man being cursed of God didn't make sense to me. Yet, now it does. It's my only hope.

There is no doubt that David saw by prophetic vision the crucifixion of Jesus when he penned the psalm that describes it.

Hear how detailed his description is, long before the Romans invented such an atrocious form of execution as crucifixion.

"For dogs have compassed Me: the assembly of the wicked have inclosed Me: they pierced My hands and My feet."

I watched them pound the nails in His hands before they lifted Him high on the cross, and then in His feet once they had Him suspended. David saw those wounds a thousand years before they were afflicted. I'll never forget when my son, Michael, first told us about seeing the risen Jesus. When we asked him how he knew it was truly Jesus, he became overwhelmed with emotion.

He recognized Jesus by His scars. Beloved, even in resurrection, He still bears the scars of His suffering on our behalf.

He was cursed, to remove the curse from us. He was cursed so that we could be blessed by God. God looks at us, sees His Son's righteousness and then declares us righteous. That is our justification.

But the blessing of the Shepherd's Psalm goes beyond our justification. It speaks of righteous paths, of how we now live our lives. Because of Jesus' work to remove our guilt by paying the price for our sin, the Holy Spirit works in us to make us holy. He is actually sanctifying us, making us more and more like Jesus. We are not perfect in this life, but God is perfecting us.

But, by what right are we justified and are being sanctified? Because Jesus said, *"They pierced My hands and My feet."*

"Yea, though I walk through the valley of the shadow of death, I will fear no evil: for Thou art with me; Thy rod and Thy staff they comfort me."

Beloved, in this life we face trying times. Even death looms at the door. I remember a time when my wife and children hid at the oasis, and my older sons and I hid among the sheep surrounding our tent in this very place because wicked men had conspired to kill us. God was with us and delivered our enemies into our hands that night. He is ever with us.

But, by what right do we have this comfort that He will never leave us nor forsake us? Because Jesus said, *"My God, My God, why hast Thou forsaken Me? Why art Thou so far from helping Me, and from the words of My roaring? O My God, I cry in the day time, but Thou hearest not; and in the night season, and am not silent."*

You can read those words right here in this scroll. David wrote them long ago, but Jesus uttered them from the cross. He was forsaken, so that we will never be forsaken.

You may say, "But one day we will *walk through the valley of the shadow of death*, and not walk out the other end. It is appointed to each of us to die."

Yes, that is true, but because of Jesus' death and resurrection, we need not even fear death itself. I watched them place His body in the tomb and returned to Bethlehem and to my family. I didn't know what God would do. On Sunday morning I arose early with my two oldest sons and went to the Temple for the Feast of Firstfruits. I took a sheaf of barley with me, a whole burnt offering and a grain offering, according to the commandments. That day we learned that the tomb was empty. My sons and I hurried to the place where they buried him and found the stone rolled away. Rumors began to circulate. The guards were paid to tell lies, but deep in our hearts we knew He'd been raised from the dead. Then in Galilee, Samuel, Joseph and Michael saw Him alive again. Talk to them, any of you who doubt the resurrection. They are eye witnesses, and they are here tonight. They saw the Lord. On the day of Firstfruits, Jesus was the firstfruits of those raised from the dead. Beloved, you need not even fear death itself. Jesus has robbed it of its victory. On the last day, we will all be raised.

"Thou preparest a table before me in the presence of mine enemies: Thou anointest my head with oil; my cup runneth over."

Beloved, even in the midst of tribulation we feast and celebrate, because of our great salvation. Note the abundant blessing of this portion of the psalm. *Thou anointest my head with oil; my cup runneth over.* Our cups run over, but never out. We feast even though the devil and the world would come against us. We are safe and secure in this tent.

But, by what right are we so abundantly blessed? Because Jesus said from the cross, *"But I am a worm, and no man; a reproach of men, and despised of the people."*

Jesus was treated by both God and men as no more than a worm. God crushed Him, that we not be crushed. And, Jesus did this for us willingly. I wondered why He didn't exercise His power and overcome His enemies. I agonized as I watched Him surrender to them, even unto death, but now I know why He did it. He did it for me. He did it for you, that we could say, *"The LORD is my shepherd; I shall not want."*

"Surely goodness and mercy shall follow me all the days of my life: and I will dwell in the house of the LORD forever."

In this life – goodness and mercy, and in the age to come we will dwell in God's house, forever and ever. Hear those words as they echo in the hills – forever and ever.

But, by what right do I have goodness and mercy in this life and eternal life in the age to come? Because Jesus said from the cross, *"My God, My God, why hast Thou forsaken Me?"*

Those who are within the sound of my voice, hear me! Do you own the marvelous blessings of the Shepherd's Song? Are they yours? Because of what Jesus has done, they can be yours.

The apostle Peter told me something Jesus once said to the multitudes, *"Come unto Me, all ye that labour and are heavy laden, and I will give you rest. Take My yoke upon you, and learn of Me; for I am meek and lowly in heart: and ye shall find rest unto your souls. For My yoke is easy, and My burden is light."*

He says this to all of you. Come to Him and He will *make you to lie down in green pastures.* He will *lead you beside the still waters.* He will *restore your soul.* Come to the True Shepherd of Kedar!

Afterword

Ascending Mount Zion, is book 2 of *The Shepherd of Kedar* in *The Godly Shepherd Chronicles*. If you have not had the opportunity to read book 1, it is entitled, *The Pilgrimage: The Shepherd of Kedar: Book 1* and can be purchased at Westbowpress.com.

Future books in *The Godly Shepherd Chronicles*:

The Exile: The Shepherd of Babylon – The story of Micah, Josiah's famous ancestor in Babylon.

The Wanderer: The Shepherd of the Wilderness – The story of Jared, the second son of Micah, who departed Babylon and settled in Kedar.

The Dreamer: The Shepherd of Judah – The story of Micah's grandson, Daniel, who returned to Jerusalem with the remnant to rebuild the Temple following the Babylonian Exile.

Scriptures Cited

Chapter 1
Joshua 4:20, Joshua 6:26, 1 Kings 16:34

Chapter 2
John 11:25-26, John 1:29, John 1:30-34, John 11:43, John 11:25-26, Luke 2:29-32, Luke 2:34-35, Luke 2:34

Chapter 3
Micah 5:2, Micah 5:2, Luke 2:10-12

Chapter 4
Genesis 29:30

Chapter 5
Psalm 87:3, Psalm 121, Jeremiah 31:15, Haggai 2:6-9, Psalm 87:3, Psalm 132:13-14, Psalm 122:3, Psalm 122:4, Psalm 126:4, Psalm 87:4-5

Chapter 6
Psalm 122:1, Psalm 132:8, Psalm 24:3-4, Leviticus 19:35-36, Psalm 134:1-2, Psalm134:3, Psalm 118:26

Chapter 7
Psalm 69:9, Zechariah 9:9, Psalm 118:26, Psalm 118:25-26, Mark 11:17, Psalm 69:9, Psalm 45:1, Psalm 45:2, Matthew 21:9, Mark 11:9-10, Matthew 21:16, Psalm 8:2, Mark 11:17

Chapter 8
Genesis 21:6, John 2:16, Genesis 21:6, Genesis 3:15, Luke 1:30-33, Luke 1:34, Luke 1:35, Isaiah 7:14

Chapter 9
Matthew 7:29, Matthew 21:25, Matthew 21:27, Matthew 21:31a, Matthew 21:31b, Psalm 1:1, Isaiah 5:20, Matthew 23:14, Matthew 23:27-28, Matthew 21:40, Matthew 21:42, Matthew 21:43-44, Psalm 22:1, Isaiah 53:4-6

Chapter 10
Psalm 2:12, Psalm 2:6-9, Psalm 2:1-3, Psalm 2:4-5, Psalm 2:6-9, Luke 2:34, Psalm 2:10-11, Psalm 2:12a, Psalm 2:12a

Chapter 11
Exodus 12:13, Psalm 133, John 5:6, John 5:7, John 5:8, John 6:9, John 6:35, John 6:54-56, Deuteronomy 6:4, Psalm 113:1, Psalm 113:2-9, Psalm 118:26, Psalm 118:27-29

Chapter 12
John 6:58, John 6:35, John 6:54-56, John 6:54-56, John 6:58, John 6:35, John 1:29

Chapter 13
Numbers 9:2, Deuteronomy 6:4, Psalm 104:15, Exodus 6:6-7, Exodus 12:39, Exodus 1:14, Psalm 113:1-3, Psalm 114, Psalm 133:1, Psalm 136:1, Psalm 136, Exodus 12:8

Chapter 14
Exodus 12:14, Psalm 120:7, Psalm 2:6, Psalm 2:7-9, John 6:35, John 6:54, Psalm 115:1, Psalm 118:25-26, Numbers 6:24-26

Chapter 15
Psalm 2:10-11, Psalm 2:10-11, Psalm 2:12

Chapter 16
John 19:26, Matthew 27:17, Matthew 27:21, Matthew 27:22, Luke 23:21, Matthew 27:22, Matthew 27:23, John 19:6, Psalm 118:26, Matthew 27:24,

Matthew 27:25, Luke 23:28-31, John 19:17, Luke 23:34, Luke 23:35, Mark 15:26, Luke 23:37, Luke 23:39, Luke 23:40-41, Luke 23:42, Luke 23:43, Luke 2:32, John 19:26, Luke 2:34-35, Luke 2:32

Chapter 17
Psalm 22:1, John 19:17, Mark 15:34, Mark 15:35-36, Psalm 22:1-2; 6-8, 16, John 19:28, Psalm 22:15, John 19:28, Psalm 22:15, John 19:28, John 19:30, Luke 23:46, Mark 15:39, Psalm 22:14; 16b, Psalm 22:8, Psalm 22:18

Chapter 18
Isaiah 52:7, John 19:30, Isaiah 53:7, John 1:29, Luke 23:34, Isaiah 52:7, John 19:26, Luke 2:34-35, Luke 2:29-32, John 1:29, Isaiah 53:4-5, Isaiah 53:6, Isaiah 53:11, Psalm 22:1, Psalm 22:22, Psalm 22:21, Genesis 3:15, Psalm 22:21, Psalm 22:22

Chapter 19
Isaiah 53:10, Deuteronomy 21:23, Psalm 22:1, Luke 23:43, Luke 23:46, Psalm 22:22, Isaiah 53:10, Isaiah 53:11, Isaiah 53:12, Isaiah 53:10

Chapter 20
Matthew 28:6, 1 Kings 19:14, I Kings 19:18, Luke 2:34, Matthew 28:6, John 20:17

Chapter 21
Isaiah 53:6, John 1:29, John 6:54, Luke 2:32, Exodus 20:3

Chapter 22
1 Corinthians 15:6

Chapter 23
Joel 2:28, Exodus 3:14, Acts 2:14-21, Acts 2:36, Acts 2:37, Acts 2:38-39, Matthew 19:14

Chapter 24
Genesis 2:24, Luke 2:29-32, Matthew 28:18-20, Luke 2:34-35

Chapter 25
Psalm 134, Psalm 45:2, Psalm 45:13-14, Matthew 22:30, Genesis 22:18, Psalm 134:1-2, Psalm 134:3

Epilogue
Psalm 23:1, Psalm 23, Psalm 23:1, Psalm 22:1, Psalm 23:2-3a, Psalm 22:14-15, John 19:28, John 19:30, Luke 23:46, Psalm 23:2-3b, John 19:28, Psalm 22:15b, Psalm 23:3b, Psalm 22:16, Psalm 22:16b, Psalm 23:4, Psalm 22:1-2, Psalm 23:4a, Psalm 23:5, Psalm 23:5b, Psalm 22:6, Psalm 23:1, Psalm 23:6, Psalm 22:1, Matthew 11:28-30, Psalm 23:2-3a

Glossary of Terms

Arabic Terms:

Khanjar – A curved dagger

Wadi – A dry river bed in the desert

Hebrew Terms:

Afikomen (Greek) – A piece of unleavened bread that serves as the dessert of the Passover meal.

Day of Presentation – The day paschal lambs were presented to the Temple to insure they were without spot or blemish. (Four days prior to Passover)

Feast of Unleavened Bread – A seven day feast immediately following Passover when only unleavened bread was to be eaten.

Feast of Weeks (Pentecost) – A feast beginning seven weeks after the Feast of Firstfruits. It was a celebration of the latter grain harvest and also the giving of the Torah.

Golgotha – The place of the skull; the location of the crucifixion of Jesus.

Hallel – Psalms 113 – 118; These psalms were sung during the sacrifice of the paschal lambs and also during the Seder Service.

Haroses – *A sweet jam eaten during the Passover meal, resembling in appearance the mortar the people made in Egypt while in bondage.*

Matzo – *Unleavened bread.*

Mikveh – *Ceremonial baths scattered around in the vicinity of the Temple for ceremonial washings.*

Moror – *Bitter herbs eaten during the Passover meal to remind the people of the bitterness of bondage in Egypt.*

Pesah (Paschal Lamb) – *the lamb (or kid goat) slain and eaten on Passover to commemorate God's deliverance of His people from Egypt.*

Passover – *Celebrated on the evening of Nisan 15, the Passover lamb was eaten to commemorate God's deliverance of His people from the plague upon the firstborn of Egypt on the night that God passed over the houses of the Jews who had applied the blood of the lamb to their doorposts.*

Reishit Katzir – *The Feast of Firstfruits; A wave offering of a sheaf of barley to celebrate the early grain harvest. The feast took place on the first day of the week following the Sabbath after the celebration of Passover. This was the day when Jesus was raised from the dead.*

Seder Service – *The liturgy of the worship service on Passover.*

Shofar – *A trumpet made from the horn of a ram.*

Songs of Ascents – *Psalms 120 – 134 all bear the title "A Song of Ascents." This title indicates that these psalms in particular were sung by God's people while on pilgrimage to Jerusalem, while ascending Mount Zion.*

Soreg – *a short balustrade before the wall that divided the Court of the Gentiles from the Court of the Women in the Temple. Engraved signs were posted along the Soreg warning the uncircumcised from entering upon the pain of death.*

Torah – *The Law of God.*